P9-CBN-367

THERE WAS AN OLD WOMAN

and

THE ORIGIN OF EVIL

By Ellery Queen

A SIGNET BOOK

NEW AMERICAN LIBRARY

TIMES MIRROR

PUBLISHER'S NOTE

These novels are works of fiction. Names, characters, places, and incidents are either the product of the author's imagination or are used fictitiously, and any resemblance to actual persons, living or dead, events, or locales is entirely coincidental.

Published by arrangement with Frederic Dannay and the late Manfred B. Lee. *There Was an Old Woman* and *The Origin of Evil* also appeared in paperback as separate volumes published by The New American Library.

 SIGNET TRADEMARK REG. U.S. PAT. OFF. AND FOREIGN COUNTRIES
REGISTERED TRADEMARK—MARCA REGISTRADA
HECHO EN CHICAGO, U.S.A.

SIGNET, SIGNET CLASSICS, MENTOR, PLUME, MERIDIAN AND NAL BOOKS *are published by The New American Library, Inc.,
1633 Broadway, New York, New York 10019*

First Printing (Double Ellery Queen Edition), July, 1980

1 2 3 4 5 6 7 8 9

PRINTED IN THE UNITED STATES OF AMERICA

THERE WAS
AN OLD WOMAN

Contents

Cast of Characters

PART ONE

1 . . . Who Lived in a Shoe

The pearl-gray planet of the supreme court building, which lies in Foley Square, is round in shape; whereby you may know that in New York County Justice is one with universal laws, following the conscience of Man like the earth the sun. Or so Ellery Queen reflected as he sat on the southern extremity of his spine in Trial Term Part VI, Mr. Justice Greevey not yet presiding, between Sergeant Thomas Velie of Homicide and Inspector Queen, waiting to testify in a case which is another story.

"How long, O Lord?" yawned Ellery.

"If you're referring to that Gilbert and Sullivan pipsqueak, Greevey," snapped his father, "Greevey's probably just scratching his navel and crawling out of his ermine bed. Velie, go see what's holding up the works."

Sergeant Velie opened one aggrieved eye, nodded ponderously, and lumbered off in quest of enlightenment. When he lumbered back, the Sergeant looked black. "The Clerk says," growled Sergeant Velie, "that Mr. Justice Greevey he called up and says he's got an earache, so he'll be delayed two hours gettin' down here while he gets—the Clerk says 'irritated,' which I *am*, but it don't make sense to me."

"Irritation," frowned Mr. Queen, "or to call it by its purer name 'irrigation'—irrigation, Sergeant, is the process by which one reclaims a dry, dusty, and dead terrain . . . a description, I understand, which fits Mr. Justice Greevey like a decalcomania."

The Sergeant looked puzzled, but Inspector Queen muttered through his ragged mustache: "Two hours! *I'd* like to irrigate him. Let's go out in the hall for a smoke." And the old gentleman marched out of Room 331, followed by Sergeant Velie and—meekly—Ellery Queen; and so barged into the fantastic hull of the Potts case.

For a little way down the corridor, before the door of

9

Room 335, Trial Term Part VII, they came upon Charley Paxton, pacing. Mr. Queen like the governor of Messina's niece, had a good eye and could see a church by daylight; so he noted this and that about the tall young man, mechanically, and concluded [*a*] he was an attorney (brief case); [*b*] his name was Charles Hunter Paxton (stern gilt lettering on same); [*c*] Counselor Paxton was waiting for a client and the client was late (frequent glances at wrist watch); [*d*] he was unhappy (general droop). And the great man, having run over Charles Hunter Paxton with the vacuum cleaner of his glance, made to pass on, satisfied.

But his father halted, twinkling.

INSPECTOR: Again, Charley? What is it this time?

MR. PAXTON: *Lèse-majesté,* Inspector.

INSPECTOR: Where'd it happen?

MR. PAXTON: Club Bongo.

SERGEANT VELIE *(shaking the marble halls with his laughter):* Imagine Thurlow in that clip joint!

MR. PAXTON: And he got clipped—make no mistake about that, my friends. Clipped on the buttonola.

INSPECTOR: Assault and battery, huh?

MR. PAXTON *(bitterly):* Not at all, Inspector. We mustn't break our record! No, the same old suit for slander. Young Conklin Cliffstatter—of the East Shore Cliffstatters. Jute and shoddy.

SERGEANT: Stinking, I bet.

MR. PAXTON: Well, Sergeant, just potted enough to tell Thurlow a few homely truths about the name of Potts. *(Hollow laugh.)* There I go myself—"potted," "Potts." I swear that's all Conk Cliffstatter did—make a pun on the name of Potts. Called 'em "crack-Potts."

ELLERY QUEEN *(his silver eyes gleaming with hunger):* Dad?

So Inspector Queen and Charley-Paxton-my-son-Ellery-Queen, and the two young men shook hands, and that was how Ellery became embroiled—it was more than an involvement—in the wonderful case of the Old Woman Who Lived in a Shoe.

A court officer plunged his bald head into the cool of the corridor from the swelter of Room 335, Trial Term Part VII.

"Hey, Counselor, Mr. Justice Cornfield says Potts or no Potts he ain't waitin' much longer for your cra—your client. What gives, in God's good name?"

"Can't he wait another five minutes, for goodness' sake?" Charley Paxton cried, exasperated. "They must have been held up—Here they are! Officer, tell Cornfield we'll be right in!" And Counselor Paxton raced toward the elevators, which had just discharged an astonishing cargo.

"There she is," said the Inspector to his son, as one who points out a clash of planets. "Take a good look, Ellery. The Old Woman doesn't make many public appearances."

"With the getup," chorted Sergeant Velie, "she could snag a job in the movies like that."

Some women grow old with grace, others with bitterness, and still others simply grow old; but neither the concept of growth nor the devolution of old age seemed relevant to Cornelia Potts. She was a small creature with a plump stomach and tiny fine-boned feet which whisked her about. Her face, like a tangerine, was almost entirely lacking in detail; one was surprised to find embedded in it two eyes, which were as black and hard as coal chips. Those eyes, by some perverse chemistry of her ego, were unwinkingly malevolent. If they were capable of changing expression at all, it was into malicious rage.

If not for the eyes, seeing Cornelia Potts in the black taffeta skirts she affected, the boned black lace choker, the prim black bonnet, one would have thought of her as a "Sweet old character," a sort of sexless little kobold who vaguely resembled the Jubilee pictures of Queen Victoria. But the eyes quite forbade such sentimentalization; they were dangerous and evil eyes, and they made imaginative people—like Ellery—think of poltergeists, and elementals, and suchlike creatures of the unmentionable worlds.

Mrs. Cornelia Potts did not step sedately, as befitted a dame of seventy years, from the elevator—she darted from it, like a midge from a hot stream, followed by a widening wake of assorted characters, most of whom were delighted ladies and gentlemen of the press, and at least one of whom—palpably *not* a journalist—was almost as extraordinary as she.

"And who," demanded the astonished Mr. Queen, "is that?"

"Thurlow," grinned Inspector Queen. "The little guy Charley Paxton was talking about. Cornelia's eldest son."

"Cornelia's eldest *wack*," Sergeant Velie, the purist, said.

"He resents," winked the Inspector.

"Everything," said the Sergeant, waving a flipper.

"Always taking—what do you educated birds call it?— umbrage," said the Inspector.

"Resents? Umbrage?" Ellery frowned.

"Aw, read the right papers," guffawed the Sergeant. "Ain't he *cute?*"

With a thrill of surprise Ellery saw that, if you were so ill-advised as to strip the black taffeta from old Mrs. Potts and reclothe her in weary gray tweeds, you would have Thurlow, her son. . . . No, there was a difference. Thurlow radiated an inferior grade of energy. In a race with his mother, he would always lose. And, in fact, he was losing the present race; for he toddled hurriedly along in the Old Woman's wake, clutching his derby to his little belly, and trying without success to overtake her. He was panting, perspiring, and in a pet.

A lean glum man in a morning coat, carrying a medical satchel, stumbled after mother and son with a sick smile which seemed to say: "I am not trotting, I am walking. This is not reality, it is a bad dream. Gentlemen of the press, be merciful. One has to make a living."

"I know *him*," growled Ellery. "Dr. Waggoner Innis, the Pasteur of Park Avenue."

"She treats Innis like some people treat dogs," said Sergeant Velie, smacking his lips.

"The way he's trotting after her, he looks like one," said the Inspector.

"But why a doctor?" protested Ellery. "She looks as healthy as a troll."

"I always understood it was her heart."

"What heart?" sneered the Sergeant. "She ain't got no heart."

The cortege swept by and through the door of Room 335. Young Paxton, who had tried to intercept Mrs. Potts and received a blasting "Traffic!" for his pains, lingered only long enough to mutter: "If you want to see the show, gentlemen, you're welcome"; then he dashed after his clients.

So the Queens and Sergeant Velie, blessing Mr. Justice Greevey's earache, went in to see the show.

Mr. Justice Cornfield, a large jurist with the eyes of an apprehensive doe, took one look from the eminence of his bench at the tardy Old Woman, damp Thurlow Potts, blushing Dr. Waggoner Innis, and their exulting press and immediately exhibited a ferocious vindictiveness. He screamed at the Clerk, and there were whisperings and scurryings, and lo! the calendar was readjusted, and the case of *Potts v. Cliffstatter* found itself removed one degree in Time, so that *Giacomo v. Jive Jottings, Inc.*, which had been scheduled to follow it, now found itself with priority.

Ellery beckoned Charley Paxton, who was hovering about Mrs. Cornelia Potts; and the lawyer scooted over thankfully.

"Come on outside. This'll take hours."

They shouldered their way out into the corridor again.

"Your client," began Mr. Queen, "fascinates me."

"The Old Woman?" Charley made a face. "Have a cigaret? It's Thurlow, not Mrs. Potts, who's the plaintiff in this action."

"Oh. From the way he was tumbling after his mother, I gathered—"

"Thurlow's been tumbling after Mama for forty-seven years."

"Why the elegant Dr. Waggoner Innis?"

"Cornelia has a bad heart condition."

"Nonsense. From the way she skitters about—"

"That's just it. Nobody can tell the old hellion *anything*. It keeps Dr. Innis in a constant state of jitters. So he always accompanies the Old Woman when she leaves the Shoe."

"Beg pardon?"

Charley regarded him with suspicion. "Do you mean to say, Queen, you don't know about the *Shoe?*"

"I'm a very ignorant man." said Ellery abjectly. "Should I?"

"But I thought everybody in America knew! Cornelia Potts' fortune was made in the shoe business. *The Potts Shoe.*"

Ellery started *"Potts Shoes Are America's Shoes— $3.99 Everywhere?"*

"*That's* the Potts."

"No!" Ellery turned to stare at the closed door of Room 335. The Potts Shoe was not an enterprise, or even an institution; it was a whole civilization. There were Potts Shoe Stores in every cranny of the land. Little children wore Potts Shoes; and their mothers, and their fathers, and their sisters and their brothers and their uncles and their aunts; and what was more depressing, their grandparents had worn Potts Shoes before them. To don a Potts Shoe was to display the honor badge of lower-income America; and since this class was the largest class, the Potts fortune was not merely terrestrial—it was galactic.

"But your curious reference," said the great man eagerly, turning back to the lawyer, "to 'when she leaves the Shoe.' Has a cult grown up about the Pottses, with its own esoteric terminology?"

Charley grinned. "It all started when some cartoonist on a pro-Labor paper was told by his editor to squirt some India ink in the general direction of Cornelia. Don't you remember that strike in the Potts' plant?" Ellery nodded; it was beginning to come back to him. "Well, this genius of the drawing board drew a big mansion—supposed to represent the Potts Palace on Riverside Drive—only he shaped it like an old-fashioned high-top shoe; and he drew Cornelia Potts like the old harridan in the *Mother Goose* illustration, with her six children tumbling out of the 'shoe', and he captioned it: 'There Was an Old Woman Who Lived in a Shoe, She Had So Many Children She Couldn't Pay Her Workers a Living Wage,' or something like that. Anyway, the name's stuck; she's been 'the Old Woman' ever since."

"And you're this female foot potentate's attorney?"

"Yes, but most of my activity is devoted to Thurlow, bless his sensitive little heart. You saw Thurlow? That tubby little troglodyte with the narrow shoulders?"

Ellery nodded. "Built incredibly like a baby kangaroo."

"Well, Thurlow Potts is the world's most insultable man."

"And the money to do something about it," mourned Mr. Queen. "Very sad. Does he ever win one of these suits?"

"Win!" Paxton swabbed his face angrily. "It's driven me to sobriety. This is *the thirty-seventh suit for libel or slander* he's made me bring into court! And every darned one of the first thirty-six has been thrown out."

"How about this one—the Club Bongo inbroglio?"

"Cornfield'll throw it out without a hearing. Mark my words."

"Why does Mrs. Potts put up with this childishness?"

"Because in her own way the Old Woman's got an even crazier pride in the family name than Thurlow."

"But if the suits are all silly, why do you permit them to come to court, Charley?"

Charley flushed. "Thurlow insists, and the Old Woman backs him up. . . . I know I've been accused of milking them, Queen." His jaw shot forward. "I've earned every damn cent I've ever collected being their attorney, and don't you think I haven't!"

"I'm sure you have—"

"I've had nightmares about them! In my dreams they have long noses and fat little bottoms and they spit at me all night! But if *I* didn't do it, they'd find a thousand lawyers who'd break their necks to get the business. And wouldn't be so blamed scrupulous, either! Beg your pardon. My nerves—"

Sergeant Velie stuck his head out of Room 335. "Charley! The judge settled that hot-trumpet case, and the Old Woman's bellowin' for you."

"May she crack a cylinder," muttered Counselor Paxton; and he marched back into Trial Term Part VII with the posture of one who looks forward only to the kiss of Madame Guillotine.

"Tell me, Dad," said Ellery when he had fought his way back with Sergeant Velie to the Inspector's side. "How did Charley Paxton, who seems otherwise normal, get mixed up with the Pottses?"

"Charley sort of inherited 'em," chuckled Inspector Queen. "His pappy was Sidney Paxton, the tax and estate lawyer—fine fella, Sid—many a bottle of beer we cracked together." Sergeant Velie nodded nostalgically. "Sid sent Charley to law school, and Charley got out of Harvard Law with honors. Began to practice criminal law—everybody said he had a flair for it—but his old man died, and Charley had to chuck a brilliant career and step in and take over Sid's civil practice. By that time the Potts account was so big Sid had had to drop all his other clients. Now Charley spends his life trying to keep out of the nut house."

Thurlow Potts could scarcely contain himself at the front of the room. He squirmed in his seat like a fat boy at the circus, the two gray tufts behind his ears standing up nervously. He exuded a moist and giggly fierceness, as if he were enjoying to the full his indignation.

"That little man," thought Ellery, "is fitten fodder for a psychiatrist." And he watched even more intently.

Ensued a brilliant but confusing battle of bitternesses. It was evident from the opening sortie that Mr. Justice Cornfield meant to see justice done—to Mr. Conklin Cliffstatter, who sat bored among his attorneys and seemed not to care a tittle whether justice were done or not. In fact, Ellery suspected Mr. Cliffstatter suckled only one ambition—to go home and sleep it off.

"But Your Honor—" protested Charley Paxton.

"Don't Your Honor me, Counselor!" thundered Mr.

Justice Cornfield. "I'm not saying it's your fault—heaven knows lawyers have to live—but you ought to know better than to pull this stunt in my court for—how many times does this make?"

"Your Honor, my client has been grossly slandered—"

"My Honor my eye! Your client is a public nuisance who clutters up the calendars of our courts! I don't mind his wasting *his* money—or rather his mother's—but I do mind his wasting the taxpayers'!"

"Your Honor has heard the testimony of the witness—" said Counselor Paxton desperately.

"And I'm satisfied there was no slander. Case dismissed!" snapped Mr. Justice Cornfield. He grinned evilly at the Old Woman.

To Charley Paxton's visible horror, Thurlow Potts bounced to his feet. "Your Honor!" Thurlow squeaked imperiously.

"Sit down, Thurlow," gasped Charley. "Or rather let's get out of here—"

"Just—one—moment, Counselor," said Mr. Justice Cornfield softly. "Mr. Potts, you wish to address the Court?"

"I certainly do!"

"Then by all means address it."

"I came to this court for justice!" cried Thurlow, brandishing his arms as if they were broadswords. "And what do I get? *Insults.* Where are the rights of Man? What's happened to our Constitution? Don't we live in the last refuge of personal liberty? Surely a responsible citizen has the right of protection by law against the slanders of *drunken, irresponsible persons?*"

"Yes?" said Mr. Justice Cornfield. "You were saying—"

"But what do I find in this court?" screeched Thurlow. "Protection? No! Are my rights defended by this court? No! Is my name cleared of the crude insinuations of this defendant? No! It is a valuable name, Your Honor, an honorable name, and this person's slander has reduced its value by considerable sums—!"

"I'll reduce it still more, Mr. Potts," said the judge with enjoyment, "if you don't stop this outrageous exhibition."

"Your Honor," Charley Paxton jumped forward. "May I apologize for the hasty and ill-considered remarks of my client—"

"*Stop!*" And the Old Woman arose, terrible in wrath.

Even the judge quailed momentarily.

"Your *Dishonor,*" said Cornelia Potts, "—I can't address you as Your Honor, because you haven't any—Your Dishonor, I've sat in many courtrooms and I've listened to many judges, but never in my long life have I had the misfortune to witness such *monkey's* antics, in such a court of Baal, presided over by such a wicked old *goat*. My son came here to seek the protection of the court in defense of *our good name*—instead he is insulted and ridiculed and our good name further held up to *public scorn*. . . ."

"Are you quite finished, Madam?" choked Mr. Justice Cornfield.

"No! How much do I owe you for contempt?"

"Case dismissed! Case dismissed!" bellowed the judge; and he leaped from his leather chair, girding his robe about him like a young girl discovered *en déshabille*, and fled to chambers.

"This is surely a bad dream," said Ellery Queen exultantly. "What happens next?"

The Queens and Sergeant Velie joined the departing Potts parade. Bravely it swept into the corridor, Queen Victoria in the van flourishing her bulky bumbershoot like a cudgel at the assorted bondsmen, newspaper folks, divorce litigants, attorneys, attendants, rubbernecks, and tagtails who had joined the courtroom exodus. The Old Woman, and then steaming little Thurlow, and red-faced Dr. Innis, and Charles Hunter Paxton, and Sergeant Velie, and the Queens *père et fils*. Bravely it swept onto the balcony under the rotunda, and into the elevators, and downstairs to the lobby.

"Uh, uh. Trouble," said Sergeant Velie alertly.

"How she hates cameramen," remarked Inspector Queen.

"Wait—no!" shouted Ellery. "Charley! Somebody! Stop her. For goodness' sake!"

The photographers had lain in ambush. And she was upon them.

The guns of Cornelia Potts's black eyes sent out streams of tracer bullets. She snarled, grasped her umbrella handle convulsively, and rushed to the attack. The umbrella rose and fell. One camera flew through the air to be caught willy-nilly by a surprised man in a derby. Another fell and tumbled down the steps leaving a trail of lens fragments.

"Break it up, break it up," said Sergeant Velie.

"That's just what she's doing," panted a cameraman. "Joe, did you get anything?"

"A bust in the nose," groaned Joe, regarding his encar-

mined handkerchief with horror. He roared at the old
lady: "You old crackpottia, you smashed my camera!"

"Here's the money to pay for it," panted Cornelia
Potts, hurling two hundred-dollar bills at him; and she
darted into her limousine and slammed the door shut
behind her, almost decapitating her pride and heir, Thurlow, who was—as ever—just a step too late.

"I *won't* have public spectacles!" she cried through her
tonneau window. The limousine jerked away, slamming
the old lady against her physician, who had craftily sought
the protection of the car before her, and leaving Thurlow,
puffing and blowing, on the field of glory where, after a
momentary panic at this being left alone to the
weapons of the enemy, he drew himself up to his full five
foot and grimly girded his not inconsiderable loins.

"Happens this way every time," said Inspector Queen
from the top of the courthouse steps.

"If she's smashed one camera, she's smashed a hundred," said Sergeant Velie, shaking his head.

"But why," wondered Ellery, "do the cameramen keep
trying? Or do they make a profit on each transaction? I
noticed two rather impressive-looking greenbacks being
flung at the victim down there."

"Profit is right," grinned his father. "Take a look. That
fella who had his camera broken. Does he look in the
dumps?"

Ellery frowned.

"Now," instructed his father, "look up there."

Ellery sighted along the Inspector's arm to a window
high in the face of the courthouse. There, various powerful camera eyes glittered in the sun, behind them human
eyes intent on Thurlow Potts and Charley Paxton on the
sidewalk before the courthouse.

"Yes, sir," said Sergeant Velie with respect, "when
you're dealing with the Old Woman you just naturally got
to be on your toes."

"They caught it all from that window," exclaimed Ellery softly. "I'll bet that smashed camera was a dummy
and Joe a rascally, conniving stooge!"

"My son," said the Inspector dryly, "you've got the
makings of a detective. Come on, let's go back upstairs
and see if Mr. Justice Greevey's over his irrigation."

"Now listen, boys," Charley Paxton was shouting on the
sidewalk. "It's been a tough morning. What d'ye say? Mr.
Potts hasn't one word for publication—You better not

have," Charley said through his teeth three feet from Thurlow's pink ear, "or I walk out, Thurlow—I swear I walk out!"

Someone applauded.

"You let me alone," cried Thurlow. "I've got *plenty* to say for publication, Charles Paxton! I'm through with you, anyway. I'm through with *all* lawyers. Yes, and judges and courts, too!"

"Thurlow, I warn you—" Charley began.

"Oh, go fish! There's no justice left in this world—not a crumb. Not a particle!"

"Yes, little man?" came a voice.

"No Justice, Says Indignant Citizen."

"Through with all laywers, judges, and courts, he vows."

"What a break for all lawyers, judges, and courts."

"What you gonna do, Pottso—protect your honor with *stiletti?*"

"You gonna start packing six-shooters, Thurlow-boy?"

"Thurlow Potts, Terror of the Plains, Goes on Warpath, Armed to the Upper Plates."

"Stop!" screamed Thurlow Potts in an awful voice; and, curiously, they did. He was shaking in a paroxysm of rage, his small feet dancing on the sidewalk, his pudgy face convulsed. Then he choked: "From now on I take justice in my own hands."

"Huh?"

"Say, the little guy actually means it."

"Go on, he's hopped to the eyeballs."

"Wait a minute. Nuts or no nuts, he can't be left running around loose. Not with *those* intentions, brother."

One of the reporters said, soberly: "Just what do you mean—you'll take justice in your own hands, Mr. Potts?"

"Thurlow," muttered Charley Paxton, "haven't you raved your quota? Let me get you out of here—"

"Charles, take your hand off my arm. What do I mean, gentlemen?" said Thurlow quietly. "I'll tell you what I mean. I mean that I'm going to buy myself a gun, and the next person who insults me or the honorable name I bear won't live long enough to hide behind the skirts of your corrupt courts!"

"Hey," said a reporter. "Somebody better tip off Conk Cliffstatter."

"This puffball's just airy enough to do it."

"Ah, he's blowing."

"Oh, yeah? Well, maybe he'll blow bullets."

Thurlow launched himself at the crowd like a little ram, butting with his arms. It parted, almost respectfully; and he shot through in triumph. "He'll get a bullet in his guts, that's what he'll get!" howled the Terror of the Plains. And he was gone in a flurry of agitated little arms and legs.

Charley Paxton groaned and hurried back up the steps of the courthouse.

He found Ellery Queen, Inspector Queen, and Sergeant Velie emerging from Room 331. The Inspector was holding forth with considerable bitterness on the subject of Mr. Justice Greevey's semicircular canals, for it appeared that the justice had decided to remain at home sulking in an atmosphere of oil of wintergreen rather than venture out into the earacheless world; consequently the case which had fetched the Queens to court was put off for another day.

"Well, Charley? What's happening down there?"

"Thurlow threatened to buy a gun!" panted the lawyer. "He says he's through with courts—the next man who insults him gets paid back in lead!"

"That nut-ball?" scoffed the Sergeant.

Inspector Queen laughed. "Forget it, Charley. Thurlow Potts hasn't the sand of a charlotte russe."

"I don't know, Dad," murmured Ellery. "The man's not balanced properly. One of his gimbals out of socket, or something. He might mean it, at that."

"Oh, he means it," said Charley Paxton sourly. "He means it *now*, at any rate. Ordinarily I wouldn't pay any attention to his ravings, but he's been getting worse lately and I'm afraid one of these days he'll cross the line. This might be the day."

"Cross what line?" asked Sergeant Velie, puzzled.

"The Mason-Dixon line, featherweight," sighed the Inspector. "What line do you think? Now listen, Charley, you're taking Thurlow too seriously—"

"Just the same, don't you think we ought to take precautions?"

"Sure. Watch him. If he starts chewing his blanket, call Bellevue."

"To buy a gun," Ellery pointed out, "he'll have to get a license from the police department."

"Yes," said Charley eagerly. "How about that, Inspector Queen?"

"How about what?" growled the old gentleman in a disgusted tone. "Suppose we refuse him a license—then what? Then he goes out and buys himself a rod without a license. Then you've got not only a nut on your hands, but a nut who's nursing a grudge against the police department, too. Might kill a cop. . . . And don't tell me he can't *buy* a gun without a license, because he can, and I'm the baby who knows it."

"Dad's right," said Ellery. "The practical course is not to try to prevent Thurlow from laying hands on a weapon, but to prevent him from using it. And in his case I rather think guile, not force, is what's required."

"In other words," said the Sergeant succinctly, "yoomer the slug."

"I don't know," said the lawyer with despair. "I'm going bats myself just trying to keep up with these cormorants. Inspector, can't you do *anything?*"

"But Charley, what d'ye expect me to do? We can't follow him around day and night. In fact, until he pulls something our hands are tied—"

"Could we put him away?" asked Velie.

"You mean on grounds of insanity?"

"Whoa," said Charley Paxton. "There's plenty wrong with the Pottses, but not to that extent. The old girl has drag, anyway, and she'd fight to her last penny, and win, too."

"Then why don't you get somebody to wet-nurse the old nicky-poo?" demanded Inspector Queen.

"Just what I was thinking," said the young man cunningly. "Uh—Mr. Queen . . . would *you*—?"

"But definitely," replied Mr. Queen with such promptness that his father stared at him. "Dad, you're going back to Headquarters?"

The Inspector nodded.

"In that case, Charley, you come on up to my apartment," said Ellery with a grin, "and answer some questions."

2 . . . She Had So Many Children

Ellery mixed Counselor Paxton a scotch and soda.

"Spare me nothing, Charley. I want to know the Pottses as I have never known anybody or anything before. Don't proceed to the middle until you've arrived at the end of the beginning, and then repeat the process until you reach the beginning of the end. I'll try to have something constructive to say about it from that point on."

"Yes, *sir*," said Charley, setting down his glass. And, as one who is saturated with his subject, the young lawyer began to pour forth facts about the Pottses, old and young, male and female—squirting them in all directions like an overloaded garden hose relieving itself of intolerable pressure.

Cornelia Potts had not always been the Old Woman. Once she had actually been a child in a small town in Massachusetts. She was a ragged Ann, driven from childhood by a powerful purpose. It was to be rich and to live upon the Hill. It was to be rich and to live upon this Hill and any hill that was higher than its neighbor. It was to be rich and to multiply.

Cornelia became rich and she multiplied. She became rich almost wholly through her own efforts; to multiply, unhappily, it was necessary to enlist the aid of a husband, God having so ordered the creation. But the least Cornelia could do was improve upon the holy ordinance. This she did by taking, not one, but two husbands; and thus she multiplied mightily, achieving six children—three by her first husband, and three by her second—before that other thing happened which God has also ordained.

("The second husband," said Charley Paxton, "is still around, poor sap. I'll get to *him* in due courses.")

Husband the First was trapped by Cornelia in 1892, when she was twenty and possessed the dubious allure of a wild-flower growing dusty by the roadside. His name was Bacchus, Bacchus Potts. Bacchus Potts was that classic paradox, a Prometheus bound—in this case, to a cobbler's bench, for he was the town shoemaker, a man of whom all the girls in the village were gigglingly afraid, for by night he wandered in the woods and sang rowdy songs under the moon while his feet danced a dance of impotent wanderlust.

It has been said of the Old Woman (said Charley) that if she had married the village veterinary, she would have turned him into a Pasteur; if she had married the illegitimate son of an illegitimate son of an obscure sprig of the royal tree, she would have lived to be queen. As it was, she married a cobbler; and so, in time, she made him the leading shoe manufacturer of the world.

If Bacchus Potts dreamed defeated dreams over his bench, it was surely not of larger benches; but larger benches he found himself possessor of, covering acres and employing thousands. And it happened so quickly that he, the dreamer, could not grasp its dreamlike magic; or perhaps he wished not to. For as Cornelia invested his life's savings in a small factory; as it fed, and bulged, and by process of fission became two, and the two became four . . . Bacchus could only sit helplessly by, resenting the miracle and its maker.

Every so often he would vanish. When he returned, without money, dirty, and purged, he crept meekly back to Cornelia with the guilty look of a repentant tomcat.

After some years, no one paid any attention to Bacchus' goings or comings—not his employees, not his children, certainly not his wife, who was too busy with building a dynasty.

In 1902, ten years after their marriage, when Cornelia was a plump and settling thirty, and the Pottses owned not only factories but retail stores over all the land, Bacchus Potts one day dreamed his greatest dream. He disappeared for good. When months passed and he did not return, and the authorities failed to turn up any trace of him, Cornelia shrugged him off and became truly Queen of Egypt land. After all, there was a great deal of work involved in building a pyramid, and she had three growing children to care for between crackings of the overseer's whip. If she missed Bacchus, it was not for any reason discernible in daylight.

Then came the seven fat years, at the expiration of which the queen exhorted the lawmakers; and the law, that stern Pharaoh, being satisfied, Bacchus Potts was pronounced no longer a living man but a dead one, and his wife no longer a wife but a widow, able to take to herself without contumely another husband.

That she was ready and willing as well became evident at once.

In 1909, at the age of thirty-seven, Mrs. Potts married another shy man, Stephen Brent, to whom even at the altar she flatly refused to give up her name. Why she should have felt a loyalty to that first fey spouse upon whom she had founded her fortune remained as much a mystery as everything else about her relationship with him; or perhaps there was no loyalty to Bacchus Potts, or sentiment either, but only to his name, which was a different thing altogether, since the name meant the Potts Shoe, $3.99 Everywhere.

Cornelia Potts not only refused to give up her name,

she also insisted as a condition of their marriage that Stephen Brent give up his. Brent being the kind of man to whom argument is an evil thing, to be shunned like pestilence, feebly agreed; and so Stephen Brent became Stephen Potts, according to legal process, and the Potts dynasty rolled on.

It should be remembered (Charley Paxton reminded Ellery) that in December of 1902 Cornelia had moved her three fatherless children to New York City and built a house for them—the Potts "Palace," that fabulous square block of granite and sward on Riverside Drive, facing the gentle Hudson and the smoky greenery of the Jersey shore. So Cornelia had met Steve Brent in New York.

"It's a wonder to me," growled the young attorney, "that Steve tore himself away from Major Gotch long enough to be alone with the old girl and ask her to marry him—if he did ask her."

Stephen Brent had come to New York from the southern seas, or the Malay Peninsula, or some such romantic place, and with him, barnacle-like, had come Gotch—two vagabonds, of the same cloth, united by the secret joy of idleness and tenacious in their union. They were not bad men; they were simply weak men; and men of weakness seemed to be Cornelia's weakness.

Perhaps this was why, of the two wanderers, she had chosen Steve Brent to be her prince consort, and not Major Gotch; for Major Gotch evinced a certain minor firmness of fiber, not exactly a strength but a lesser weakness, which happily his friend did not possess. It was this trait of his character which enabled him to stand up to Cornelia Potts and demand sanctuary with his Pythias. "Marry Steve—yes, ma'am. But Steve, he'll die without me, ma'am. He's just a damn' lonesome man, ma'am," Major Gotch had said to Cornelia. "Seeing that you're so well-fixed, seems to me it won't ruffle your feathers none if I sort of come along with Steve."

"Can you garden?" snapped Cornelia.

"Now don't get me wrong," said Major Gotch, smiling. "I ain't asking for a job, ma'am. Work and me don't mix. I'll just come and set. I got a bullet in my right leg makes standin' something fierce."

For the first time in her life Cornelia gave in to a man. Or perhaps she had a sense of humor. She accepted the condition, and Major Gotch moved right along in and settled down to share his friend's incredible fortune and make himself, as he liked to say, thoroughly useless.

"Was Cornelia in love with Stephen?" asked Ellery.

"In love?" Charley jeered. "Say, it was just animal magnetism on Cornelia's part—I'm told Steve had 'pretty eyes,' though they're washed-out now—and a nice business deal for old Steve. And it's worked out not too badly. Cornelia has a husband who's given her three additional children, and Steve's lolled about the rich pasture after a youth of scratching for fodder. Fact is, he and that old scoundrel Major Gotch spend all their time together on the estate, playing endless games of checkers. Nobody pays any attention to them."

"The three children of the Old Woman's first marriage— the offspring of Cornelia and the 'teched' and vanished Bacchus Potts—are crazy," Charley continued.

"Did you say 'crazy'?" Ellery looked startled.

"You heard me." Charley reached for the decanter.

"But Thurlow—"

"All right, take Thurlow," argued young Mr. Paxton. "Would you call him sane? A man who spends his life trying to hit back at people for imaginary insults to his name? What's the difference between that and a mania for swatting imaginary flies from your nose?"

"But his mother—"

"It's a question of degree, Ellery. Cornelia's passion for the honor of the Potts name is kept within bounds, and she doesn't hit out unless she has a vulnerable target. But Thurlow spends his life hitting out, and most of the time nothing's there but a puzzled look on somebody's face."

"Insanity is a word neurologists don't like, Charley," complained Ellery Queen. "At best, standards of normality are variable, depending on the age and mores. In the Age of Chivalry, for example, Thurlow's obsession with his family honor would have been considered a high and virtuous sign of his sanity."

"You're quibbling. But if you want proof, take Louella, the second child of the Cornelia-Bacchus union.... I'll waive Thurlow's hypersensitivity about the name of Potts; I'll accept his impractical extravagant nature, his childish innocence on the subject of business values or the value of money—as the signs of merely an unhappy, maladjusted, but essentially sane man."

"But Louella! You can't argue about Louella. She's forty-four, never married, of course—"

"What's wrong with Louella?"

"Louella believes herself to be a great inventor."

Mr. Queen looked pained.

"Nobody pays much attention to Louella, either," growled Charley. "Nobody except the Old Woman. Louella's got her own 'laboratory' at the house and seems quite happy. There's an old closet in the Potts zoo where the Old Woman throws Louella's 'inventions.' One day I happened to catch the old lady sitting on the floor outside the closet, crying. I admit," said Charley, shaking his head, "for a few weak seconds I felt sorry for the old she-pirate."

"Don't stop now," said Ellery. "What about the third child of the first marriage?"

"Horatio?" The lawyer shivered. "Horatio's forty-one. In many ways Horatio's the queerest of the trio. I don't know why, because he's not at all the horrible object you might think. And yet ... I never see him without getting duck bumps."

"What's the matter with Horatio?"

"Maybe nothing," said Charley darkly. "Maybe everything. I just don't know. You'll have to come and talk to him in his self-made setting to believe he really exists."

Ellery smiled broadly. "You're very clever. You've already learned that my type of mind simply can't resist a mystery."

Paxton looked sheepish. "Well ... I want your help."

Ellery stared at him hard. "Charley, what *is* your interest in this extraordinary family?" The lawyer was silent. "It can't be merely professional integrity. There are some jobs that aren't worth any amount of compensation, and from what I've seen and heard already, being legal adviser to the Pottses is one of them. You've got an ax to grind, my friend, and since it doesn't seem to be made of gold ... what *is* it made of?"

"Red hair and dimples," said Charley defiantly.

"Ah," said Mr. Queen.

"Sheila's the youngest of the three children who resulted from the marriage of Cornelia and Steve. *They're* rational human beings, thank God! Robert and Mac are twins—a sweet pair—they're thirty." Charley flushed. "I'm going to marry Sheila."

"Congratulations. How old is the young lady?"

"Twenty-four. Can't imagine how Sheila and the twins got born into that howling family! The Old Woman still runs the Potts Shoe business, but Bob and Mac really run it, with the help of an old-timer who's been with Cornelia for I don't know how many years. Nice old Yank named

Underhill. Underhill superintends production at the plants; Robert's vice-president in charge of sales, Mac's vice-president in charge of advertising and promotion—"

"What about Thurlow?"

"Oh, Thurlow's vice-president, too. But I've never found out what he's vice-president of: I don't think he has, either. Sort of roving nuisance. And, speaking of nuisances, how are we going to prevent Thurlow from doing something silly?"

Ellery lit a cigaret and puffed thoughtfully. "Assuming that Thurlow meant what he said when he threatened to get a revolver, have you any idea where he'd go to buy one?" he asked.

"Cornwall & Ritchey, on Madison Avenue. He has a charge there—keeps lugging home sports equipment he never uses. It's the logical place."

Mr. Paxton was handed the telephone. "Call Cornwall & Ritchey and make discreet inquiries."

Mr. Paxton called that purple house of commerce and made discreet inquiries. When he set the telephone down, he was purple, too. "He meant it!" cried Charley. "Know what the wack's done? He must have hotfooted it down there right from the Supreme Court Building!"

"He's bought a gun?"

"*A* gun? He's bought *fourteen!*"

"What!"

"I spoke to the clerk who waited on him. Fourteen assorted pistols, revolvers, automatics," groaned Paxton. "Said he was starting a collection of 'modern hand weapons.' Of course, they know Thurlow well down there. But see how cunning he's becoming? Knew he had to give an extraordinary excuse for purchasing that number of guns. Collection! What are we going to do?"

"Then he must have had a license," reflected Ellery.

"Seems he came magnificently prepared. He's planned this for a month—that's obvious now. Must have got his wind up in that last libel suit he lost—the one before Cliffstatter. He *does* have a license, a special license he snagged by pull somewhere. We've got to have that license revoked!"

"Yes, we could do that," agreed Ellery, "but my father was right this morning—if Thurlow's denied the legal right to own a gun, he'll get one somewhere illegally."

"But fourteen! With fourteen guns to play with, he's a menace to the public safety. A few imaginary insults, and Thurlow's likely to start a one-man purge!"

Ellery frowned. "I can't believe yet that it's a serious threat, Charley. Although obviously he's got to be watched."

"Then you'll take over?"

"Oh, yes."

"White man!" Charley wrung Ellery's hand. "What can I do to help?"

"Can you insinuate me into the Potts Palace today without getting everybody's wind up?"

"Well, I'm expected tonight—I've got some legal matters to go over with the Old Woman. I could wangle you for dinner. Would tonight be too late, do you think?"

"Hardly. If Thurlow's the man you say he is, he'll be spending the afternoon fondling his fourteen instruments of death and weaving all sorts of darkly satisfactory dreams. Dinner would be splendid."

"Swell!" Charley jumped up. "I'll pick you up at six."

3 . . . *She Didn't Know What to Do*

"We're going to call for somebody," announced counselor Paxton as he drove Ellery Queen downtown that evening. "I particularly wanted you to meet this person before—well, before."

"Aha," said Ellery, deducting like mad, but to himself.

Charley Paxton parked his roadster before an apartment building in the West Seventies. He spoke to the doorman, and the doorman rang someone on the house phone. Charley paced up and down the lobby, smoking a cigaret nervously.

Sheila Potts appeared in a swirl of summery clothes and laughter, a small slim miss with nice red hair. It seemed to Ellery that she was that peculiar product of American society, a girl of inoffensive insolence. She would insist on the rightness of things and cheerfully do wrong to make them right; she would be impatient with men who beat their breasts, and furious with the authors of their misery. (Ellery suspected that Mr. Paxton beat his breast upon occasion for the sheer glum pleasure of calling attention to himself.) And she was delicious and fresh as a mint bed by a woodsy brook. Then what, wondered Ellery as he took Sheila's gloved hand and heard her explanation of having been visiting—"Don't dare laugh, Mr. Queen!"— a sick friend, was wrong? Why that secret sadness in her eyes?

He learned the answer as they drove west to the Drive, the three of them crowded into the front seat of the roadster.

"My mother's against our marriage," said Sheila simply. "You'd have to know Mother to know just how horrible that can be, Mr. Queen."

"What's her reason?"

"She won't give one," complained Charley.

"I think I know her reason," said Sheila so quietly Ellery almost missed the bitterness. "It's my sister Louella."

"The inventor?"

"Yes. Mother makes no bones about her sympathies, Mr. Queen. She's always been kinder to the children of her first marriage than to Bob and Mac and me. Maybe it's because she never did love my father, and by being cold to us she's getting back at *him*, or something. Whatever it is, I do know that Mother loves poor Louella passionately and *loathes* me." Sheila sucked in her lower lip, as if to hide it.

"It's a fact, Ellery," growled Paxton. "You'd think it was Sheila's fault that Louella's a skinny old zombie, swooping around her smelly chem lab with an inhuman light in her eye."

"It's very simple, Mr. Queen. Rather than see me married while Louella stays an old maid, Mother's perfectly willing to sacrifice my happiness. She's quite a monster about it."

Ellery Queen, who knew odd things, thought he saw wherein the monster dwelt. The children of the Old Woman's union with Bacchus Potts were off normal. On these, the weaklings, the misfits, the helpless ones, Cornelia Potts expended the passion of her maternity. To the offspring of her marriage with Stephen Potts, *né* Brent, therefore, she could give only her acid anger. The twin boys and Sheila were what she had always wanted fussy little Thurlow, spinster-inventor Louella, and the still-unglimpsed Horatio to be. This much was clear. But there was that which was not.

"Why do you two stand for it?" Ellery asked.

Before Charley could answer, Sheila said quickly: "Mother threatens to disinherit me if I marry Charley."

"I see," said Ellery, not liking Sheila's reply at all.

She read the disapproval in his tone. "It's not of myself

I'm thinking! It's Charley. You don't know what he's gone through. I don't care a double darn whether I get any of Mother's money or not."

"Well, I don't either," snapped Charley, flushing. "Don't give Ellery the impression—The hours I've spent arguing with you, sweetie-pie!"

"But darling—"

"Ellery, she's as stubborn as her mother. She gets an idea in her head, you can't dislodge it with an ax."

"Peace," smiled Ellery. "This is all new to me, remember. Is this it? If you two were to marry against your mother's wishes, Sheila, she'd not only cut you off but she'd fire Charley, too?" Sheila nodded grimly. "And then, Charley, you'd be out of a job. Didn't I understand that your whole practice consists in taking care of the Potts account?"

"Yes," said Charley unhappily. "Between Thurlow's endless lawsuits and the legitimate legal work of an umpteen-million-dollar shoe business, I keep a large staff busy. There's no doubt Sheila's mother would take all her legal work elsewhere if we defied her. I'd be left pretty much out on a limb. I'd have to start building a practice from scratch. But I'd do it in a shot to get Sheila. Only—she won't."

"No, I won't," said Sheila. "I won't ruin your life, Charley. Or mine for that matter." Her lips flattened, and Charley looked miserable. "You'll hate me for this, Mr. Queen. My mother's an old woman, a sick old woman. Dr. Innis can't help that awful heart of hers, and she won't obey him, or take care of herself, and we can't make her. . . . Mother will die very soon. Mr. Queen. In weeks. Maybe days. Dr. Innis says so. How can I feel anything but relief at the prospect?" And Sheila's eyes, so blue and young, filled with tears.

Ellery saw again that life is not all caramel candy and rose petals, and that the great and hardy souls of this earth are women, not men.

"Sometimes," said Sheila, sniffing, "I think men don't know what love really is." She smiled at Charley and ruffled his hair. "You're a jerk," she said.

The roadster nosed along in traffic, and for some time none of them spoke.

"When Mother dies, Charley and I—and my dad, and the twins—we'll all be free. We've lived in a jail all our lives—a sort of bedlam. You'll see what I mean tonight. . . . We'll be free, and we'll change our names back to Brent, and we'll become folks again, not animals in a zoo. Thurlow's furious about the name of Brent—he hates it."

"Does your mother know all this, Sheila?" frowned Ellery.

"I imagine she suspects." Sheila seized her young man's arm. "Charley, stop here and let me out."

"What for?" demanded Charley suspiciously.

"Let me out, you droogler! There's no point in making Mother madder than she is already. I'll cab home from here, while you drive Mr. Queen into the grounds—then Mother can only *suspect* I've been seeing you on the side!"

"What in the name of the seven thousand miracles," demanded Ellery as he got out of his host's roadster, "is that?"

The mansion lay far back from the tall Moorish gates and iron-spiked walls which embraced the precious Potts property. The building faced Riverside Drive and the Hudson River beyond; between gates and house lay an impressive circle of grass and trees, girded as by a stone belt with the driveway which arched from the gates to the mansion and back to the gates again. Ellery was pointing an accusing finger at the center of this circle of greenery. For among the prim city trees stood a remarkable object— a piece of bronze statuary as tall as two acrobats and as wide as an elephant. It stood upon a pedestal and twinkled and leered in the setting sun. It was the statue of an Oxford shoe. A shoe with trailing laces in bronze.

Above it traced elegantly in neon tubing were the words:—

THE POTTS SHOE
$3.99 EVERYWHERE

4 . . . She Gave Them Some Broth without Any Bread

"It's a little early for dinner," said Charley, his robust voice echoing in the foyer. "Do you want to absorb the atmosphere first, or what? I'm your man."

Ellery blinked at the scene. This was surely the most

wonderful house in New York. It had no style; or rather, it partook of many styles, borrowing rather heavily from the Moorish, with Gothic subdominant. It was large, large; and its furnishings were heavy, heavy. There was a wealth of alfresco work on the walls, and sullen, unbeautiful hangings. Knights of Byzantium stood beside doorways stiffly on guard against threats as empty as themselves. A gilded staircase spiraled from the foyer into the heaven of this ponderous dream.

"Let me take the atmosphere in bits, please," said Ellery. He half-expected Afghan hounds to come loping out of hidden lairs, bits of rush clinging to their hides, and Quasimodos in nut-brown sacking and tonsured pates to serve his shuddering pleasure. But the only servant he had seen, an oozy prig of a man in butler's livery, had been conventional enough. "In fact, Charley, if you could give me a glimpse of the various Pottses before dinner in their native habitat I should be ever so much obliged."

"I can't imagine anyone wanting to meet them except through necessity, but I suppose that's what distinguishes you from all other men. This way, Professor. Let's see which Potts we can scare up first."

At the top of the staircase stood a landing, most specious and hushed, and long halls leading away. Charley turned a corner, and there yawned the entrance to what looked like a narrow tower. "That's just what it is," nodded Charley. "Up wi' ye!"

They mounted a steep coil of steps. "I didn't notice this campanile from outside. Why, Charley?"

"It's a peculiarity of construction. The tower faces an inner court and can't be seen from the street."

"And it leads where?"

"To Louella's lair . . . Here."

Charley knocked on a door with a grille in it backed by thick glass. A female face goggled through the glass, eyed Mr. Paxton with suspicion, withdrew. Bolts clanked. Ellery felt a sensible prickling along his spine when the door screeched open.

Louella Potts was not merely thin—a more desiccated figure he had not seen outside the Morgue. And she was utterly uncared-for. Her gray-dappled coarse brown hair was knotted at her scrawny neck and was all wisps and ends over her eyes. The eyes, like the eyes of the mother, fascinated him. But these, while brilliant, were full of pain, and between them the flesh was set in a permanent puzzle of inquiry. Louella Potts wore a laboratory smock

which fitted her like a shroud, and shapeless *huaraches*.
No stockings, Ellery noted. He also noted varicose veins,
and looked away.

The laboratory was circular—a clutter of tables, retorts,
goose-necked flasks, Bunsen burners, messy bottle-filled
shelves, taps, benches, electrical apparatus. What it was all
for Ellery had no idea; but it looked impressive in a cine-
matic sort of way.

"Queen?" she shrilled in a voice as tall and thin as
herself. "Queen." The frown deepened until it resembled
an old knife wound. "You aren't connected with the
Mulqueen General Laboratories, are you?"

"No, Miss Potts," said Ellery tensely.

"You see, they've been after my invention. Just thieves,
of course. I have to be careful—I do hope you'll understand. Will you excuse me now? I have a tremendously
important experiment to conclude before dinner."

"Reminds you of the Mad Scientist in *The Crimson
Clue*, doesn't she?" Charley shuddered as they made their
way down the tower stairs.

"What's she inventing?"

"A new plastic to be used in the manufacture of shoes,"
replied Charley Paxton dryly. "According to Louella, this
material she's dreaming up will last forever. People will be
able to buy one pair of shoes and use them for life."

"But that would ruin the Potts Shoe Company!"

"Of course. But what else would you expect a Potts to
spend her time inventing? Come on—I'll introduce you to
Horatio."

They were in the foyer again. Charley led the way
towards a panel of tall French doors set in a rear wall.

"House is built in a U," he explained. "Within the U are
a patio and an inner court, and more grounds, and Horatio's dream house and so on. I've had architects here
who've gone screaming into the night ... Ooops. There
are Steve and the Major."

"Sheila's father and the companion of his Polynesian
youth?"

They were two crimson-cheeked elderly men, seemingly
quite sane. They were seated in a small library directly off
the rear of the foyer, a checkerboard between them. The
rear wall of the library was a continuation of the French
doors, looking out upon a flagged, roofed terrace which
apparently ran the width of the house.

As the two young men paused at the foyer doorway,

one of the players—a slight, meek-eyed man with a straggly gray mustache—looked up and spied them. "Charley, my boy," he said with a smile. "Glad to s-see you. Come in, come in. Major, I've got you b-beaten anyway, so s-stop pretending you'll w-wiggle out."

His companion, a whale of a man with a whale's stare, snorted and turned his heavy, pocked face towards the doorway. "Go away," he said testily. "I'll whip this snapper if it takes all night."

"And it will," said Stephen Brent Potts in a rush. Then he looked frightened and said: "Of course we'll p-play it out, Major."

Paxton introduced Ellery, the four men chatted for a moment, and then he and Ellery left the two old fellows to resume their game.

"Goes on by day and by night," laughed Charley. "Friendly enemies. Gotch is a queer one—domineering, swears all over the place, and swipes liquor. Otherwise honest—it pays! Steve lets Gotch walk all over him. And everybody else, for that matter."

They left through the French doors in the foyer and crossed the wide terrace, stepping out upon a pleasant lawn, geometrically landscaped, with a path that serpentined to a small building lying within the arms of the surrounding garden walls like a candy box.

"Horatio's cottage," announced Charley.

"Cottage?" gulped Ellery. "You mean—someone actually lives in it? It's not a mirage?"

"Positively not a mirage."

"Then I know who designed it." Ellery's step quickened. "Walt Disney!"

It was a fairy-tale house. It had crooked little turrets and a front door like a golden harp and windows that possessed no symmetry at all. Most of it was painted pink, with peppermint-striped shutters. One turret looked like an inverted beet—a turquoise beet. The curl of smoke coming out of the little chimney was green. Without shame Ellery rubbed his eyes. But when he looked again the smoke was still green.

"You're not seeing things," sighed Charley. "Horatio puts a chemical from his chem set on the fire to color the smoke."

"But *why?*"

"He says green smoke is more fun."

"The Land of Oz," said Ellery in a delighted voice. "Let's go in, for pity's sake. I *must* meet that man!"

Charley played on the harp and it swung inward to reveal a very large, very fat man with exuberant red hair which stood up all over his head, as if excited, and enormous eyes behind narrow gold spectacles. He reminded Ellery of somebody; Ellery tried desperately to think of whom. Then he remembered. It was Santa Claus. Horatio Potts looked like Santa Claus without a beard.

"Charley!" roared Horatio. He wrung the lawyer's hand, almost swinging the young man off his feet. "And this gentleman?"

"Ellery Queen—Horatio Potts."

Ellery had his hand cracked in a fury of welcome. The man possessed a giant's strength, which he used without offense, innocently.

"Come in, come in!"

The interior was exuberant, too. Ellery wondered, as he glanced about, what was wrong with it. Then he saw that nothing was wrong with it. It was a perfect playroom for a child, a boy, of ten. It was crowded with large toys and small—with games, and boxes of candy, and construction sets, and unfinished kites, with puppies and kittens and at least one small, stupid-looking rabbit which was nibbling at the leg of a desk on which were piled children's books and scattered manuscript sheets covered in a large, hearty hand with inky words. A goosequill pen lay near by. It was the jolliest and most imaginatively equipped child's room Ellery had ever seen. But where was the child?

Charley whispered in Ellery's ear: "Ask him to explain his philosophy of life to you."

Ellery did so.

"Glad to," boomed Horatio. "Now you're a man, Mr. Queen. You have worries, responsibilities, you lead a heavy, grown-up sort of life. Don't you?"

"Well . . . yes," stammered Ellery.

"But it's so simple!" beamed Horatio. "Here sit down—throw those marbles on the floor. The happiest part of a man's life is his boyhood, and I don't care if he was brought up in Gallipolis, Ohio, or Hester Street, New York." Ellery wiggled his brows. "All right, now take *me*. If I had to make shoes in a factory, or tell other men to make 'em, or write advertising, or dig ditches, or do any of the tiresome things men have to do to be men—why, I'd be like you, Mr. Queen, or like Charley Paxton here, who always goes around with a worried look." Charley grinned feebly. "But I don't have to. So I fly kites, I run miniature trains, I build twelve-foot bridges and airplane models, I read Superman and Hairbreadth Harry, detective stories, fairy tales, children's verses ... I even write 'em." Horatio seized a couple of highly colored books from his desk. "*The Little Old Dog of Dogwood Street*, by Horatio Potts. *The Purple Threat*, by Horatio Potts. Here are a dozen more boys' stories, all by me."

"Horatio," said Charley reverently, "publishes 'em himself, too."

"Right now I'm writing my major opus, Mr. Queen," roared Horatio happily. "A new modern version of *Mother Goose*. It's going to be my monument, mark my words."

"Even has his meals served there," said Charley as they strolled back to the main house. "Well, Ellery, what do you think of Horatio Potts?"

"He's either the loonist loon of them all," growled Mr. Queen, "or he's the only sane man alive on the planet!"

Dinner was served in a Hollywood motion-picture set by extras—or so it seemed to Ellery, who sat down to the most remarkable meal of his life. The dining-room ceiling was a forest of rafters, and one had to crane to count them. Everything was on the same Brobdingnagian scale— a logical outgrowth, no doubt, of the giant that was Pottsism. Nothing less than a California redwood could have provided the one-piece immensity of the table. The linen and silver were heavier than Ellery had ever hefted, the crockery was grander, and the stemware more intricate. The *credenza* groaned. If the Old Woman was hen of a batty brood, at least she did not make them scratch for their grub. This was the board of plenty.

The twins, Robert and Maclyn, had not appeared for dinner. They had telephoned their mother that they were held up "at the office."

Cornelia Potts was a not ungracious hostess. The old lady wanted to know all about "Mr. Queen," and Mr. Queen found himself talking when he had come to listen. If he was to gauge the temper and the sanity of Thurlow Potts, he could not distract himself with himself. So he was annoyed, deliberately. The Old Woman stared at him with the imperial surprise of a woman who has lived seventy years on her own terms. Finally she rejected him, turning to her children. Ellery grinned with relief.

Sheila ate brightly, too brightly. Her eyes were crystal with humiliation. Ellery knew it was for him, for being witness to her shame. For Cornelia ignored her, as if

Sheila were some despised poor relation instead of the daughter of her flesh. Cornelia devoted herself almost wholly to Louella, who bothered not at all to respond to her mother's blandishments. The skinny old maid looked sullen; she ate wolfishly, in silence.

Had it not been for Stephen Potts and his friend Major Gotch, the dinner would have been intolerable. But the two cronies chattered away, apparently pleased at having a new ear to pour their reminiscences into, and Ellery had some difficulty extricating himself from Papuan paradises, Javanese jungles, and "the good old days" in the South Seas.

Thurlow had come to the table bearing two books. He set them down beside his service plate, and once in a while glanced at them or touched them with a glowering pleasure. From where Charley Paxton sat he could read the titles on their spines; Ellery could not.

"What are those books, Charley?" he mumbled.

Charley squinted. *"The History of Dueling—"*

"History of dueling!"

"The other is *A Manual of Firearms.*"

Mr. Queen choked over his melon.

During the soup course—an excellent chicken consommé—Ellery looked about and looked about and finally said in an undertone to Charley: "I notice there's no bread on the table. Why is that?"

"The Old Woman," Charley whispered back. "She's on a strict diet—Innis has forbidden her to eat bread in any form—so she won't have it in the house. Why are you looking so funny?"

Thurlow was explaining to his mother with passion the code of duello, and Major Gotch interrupted to recall some esoteric Oriental facts on the broader subject; so Mr. Queen had an opportunity to lean over to his friend and chant, softly:—

"There was an *old woman* who lived in a *shoe,*
She had *so many children* she didn't know what to *do,*
She gave them both *broth without any bread . . ."*

Charley gaped. "What are you talking about?"

"I was struck by certain resemblances," muttered Ellery. "The Horatio influence, no doubt." And he finished his broth in a thoughtful way.

Suddenly Louella's cricket-voice cut across the flow of table talk. "Mother!"

"Yes, Louella?" It was embarrassing to see the eagerness in the old lady's face as her elder daughter addressed her.

"I need some more money for my plastic experiments."

"Spend your allowance already?" The corners of the Old Woman's mouth sank, settled.

Louella looked sullen again. "I can't help it. It's not going just right. I'll get it this time sure. I need a couple of thousand more, Mother."

"No, Louella. I told you last time—"

To Ellery's horror the forty-four-year-old spinster began to weep into the puddle in her consommé cup, weep and snuffle and breathe without restraint. "You're mean! I hate you! Some day I'll have millions—why can't you give me some of my own money now? But no—you're making me wait till you die. And meanwhile I can't finish my greatest invention!"

"Louella!"

"I don't care! I'm sick of asking you, asking you—"

"Louella dear," said Sheila in a strained voice. "We have guests—"

"Be quiet, Sheila," said the Old Woman softly. Ellery saw Sheila's fingers tighten about her spoon.

"Are you going to give me my own money or aren't you?" Louella shrieked at her mother.

"Louella, leave the table."

"I won't!"

"Louella, leave the table this instant and go to bed!"

"But I'm hungry, Mother," Louella whined.

"You've been acting like an infant. For that you can't have your supper. Go this instant, Louella."

"You're a horrible old woman!" screamed Louella, stamping her foot; and, bouncing up from the table, she stormed from the dining room, weeping again.

Mr. Queen, who had not known whether to rise for the woman or remain seated for the child, compromised by assuming a half-risen, half-seated posture; from which undignified position he murmured, but to himself:—

"And whipped them all soundly and put them to bed. . . ."

After which, finding himself suspended he lowered himself into his chair. "I wonder," he wondered to himself, "how much of this a sane mind could take."

As if in answer, Sheila ran from the dining room,

choking back sobs; and Charley Paxton, looking grim, excused himself after a moment and followed her. Steve Potts rose; his lips were burbling.

"Stephen, finish your dinner," said his wife quietly.

Sheila's father sank back in his chair.

Charley returned with a mumble of apology. The Old Woman threw him a sharp black look. He sat down beside Ellery and said in a strangled undertone: "Sheila sends her apologies. "Ellery, I've got to get her out of this lunatic asylum!"

"Whispering Charles?" Cornelia Potts eyed him. The young man flushed. "Where is Sheila?"

"She has a headache," muttered Charley.

"I see."

There was silence.

5 . . . There Was a Little Man and He Had a Little Gun

From the moment Robert and Maclyn Potts entered the dining room to be introduced to the guest and seat themselves at table, a breath of sanity blew. They were remarkably identical twins, as alike in feature as two carbon copies. They dressed alike, they combed their curly blond hair alike, they were of a height and a thickness, and their voices had the same pleasant, boyish timbre.

Charley, who introduced them, was obviously at a loss; he made a mistake in their identities at once, which one of them corrected patiently. They tackled their broth and chicken with energy, talking at a great rate. It seemed that both were angry with their eldest brother, Thurlow, for having interfered in the conduct of the business for the hundredth time.

"We wouldn't mind so much, Mother—" began one, through a mouthful of fried chicken.

"Yes, Robert?" said the Old Woman grimly. She, at least, could distinguish between them.

"If Thurlow'd restrict his meddling to unimportant things," continued the other. *Ergo*, he was Mac.

"But he doesn't!" growled Robert, dropping his fork.

"Robert, eat your dinner."

"All *right*, Mother."

"But Mother, he's gone and—"

"One moment *please*," said Thurlow icily. "And what is it I'm supposed to have done this time, Maclyn?"

"Climb off it, Thurl," grumbled Mac. "All right, you're a vice-president of the Potts Shoe Company—"

"You pretend you're running a God-knows-how-many-million-dollar firm," exploded Robert, "and that's okay as long as you pretend—"

"But why in hell don't you stick to wasting the family's money on those silly lawsuits of yours—"

"Instead of canceling our newspaper-advertising plans for the Middle West, you feeble-minded nitwit?"

"Robert, don't speak to your eldest brother that way!" cried their mother.

"How you protect your white-haired boy, Mother," grinned Robert. "Although there isn't much of it left.... You know Thurlow would ruin the business if—"

"Just—one—moment, *if* you please," said Thurlow. His fat nostrils were quivering. "I've got as much to say about running the company as you two have—Mother said so! Didn't you, Mother?"

"I won't have this disgraceful argument at the dinner table, boys."

"He said I'd ruin the business!" cried Thurlow.

"Well, wouldn't you?" asked Bob Potts with disgust.

"Bob, cut it out," said his twin in a low voice.

"Cut nothing out, Mac!" said Robert. "We always have to sit by and watch old fuddy-pants pull expensive boners, then we've got to clean up his mess. Well, I'm damned good and tired of it!"

"Robert, I warn you—!" shouted Thurlow.

"Warn my foot. You're a nice fat little bag of wind, Brother Thurlow," said Bob Potts angrily, "a fake, a phony, and a blubbering jerk, and if you don't keep your idiotic nose out of the business—"

Thurlow grew very pale, but also a look came into his eyes of cunning. He snatched his napkin, jumped up, ran over to where Robert was watching him with a puzzled expression, and then whipped the napkin over his younger brother's face with an elegance—and a force—that caused Bob's mouth to open.

"What the devil—"

"You've insulted Thurlow Potts for the last time," choked the chubby little man. "Brother or no brother, I demand satisfaction. Wait here—I'll give you your choice of weapons!" And, triumphantly Thurlow stalked out of the dining room.

Surely, thought Ellery Queen, this is where I wake up and stretch.

But there was the doorway through which Thurlow Potts had passed, here was the long board with its congress of amazed faces.

"Well, I'll be a monkey's uncle," said Mac, looking blank. "Thurlow's gone clean off his chump at last! Pop—did you hear that?"

Steve Potts rose indecisively. "Maybe if I g-go speak to Thurlow, Mac—"

Mac laughed. "He's stark, raving mad!"

Bob was feeling his cheek. "Why don't you face the facts, Mother? How can you sit by and let Thurlow have anything to do with the business? If Mac and I didn't countermand every stupid order he gives, he'd run us into bankruptcy in a year."

"You baited him, Robert. Deliberately!"

"Oh, come, Mother—"

Suddenly the air was windy with recriminations. The only member of the household who seemed to enjoy it was Major Gotch, who sat back puffing a pipe and following the play of words like a spectator at a tennis match.

"That book, Ellery," exclaimed Charley Paxton under cover of the argument. "Reads *The History of Dueling* and challenges Robert to a duel!"

"He can't be serious," muttered Ellery. "Can't be."

Thurlow popped in, his eyes shining. Ellery rose like a released balloon. Thurlow was brandishing two pistols.

"It's all right, Mr. Queen," said Thurlow gently. "Sit down, please."

Mr. Queen sat down. "What interesting-looking little guns," he said. "May I look at them, Mr. Potts?"

"Some other time," murmured Thurlow. "From now on, we must do everything according to the code."

"The code?" Ellery blinked. "Which code is that, Mr. Potts?"

"The code of duello, of course. Honor before everything, Mr. Queen!" And Thurlow advanced upon his brother, who sat transfixed. "Robert, take one of these. The choice is yours."

Bob's hand came up in a mechanical motion; it fell grasping a shiny nickel weapon which Ellery recognized as a Smith & Wesson, "S. & W. .38/32," a .38-caliber revolver. It was not a large weapon, being scarcely more than half a foot long, yet it hung like a submachine gun from Robert's paralyzed hand. Mac sat by his twin with an identical expression of stupefaction.

Thurlow glanced down at the weapon remaining—a Colt "Pocket Model" automatic pistol of .25 caliber, a flat and miniature gun which looked like a toy beside the small revolver in Robert's hand, for it was only 4½ inches long. Thurlow with a flourish put the little automatic into his pocket. "Mr. Queen, you're the only outsider here. I ask you to act as my second."

"Your—" began Ellery, finding the word stick to his gums.

But Charley Paxton whispered frantically to him: "Ellery, for Pete's sake! Humor him!"

Mr. Queen nodded wordlessly.

Thurlow bowed, a not inconsiderable feat; but the action had a certain dignity. "Robert, I'll meet you at dawn in front of the Shoe."

"The Shoe," said Bob stupidly.

Ellery caught a clairvoyant glimpse of the two brothers in the coming dawn approaching from opposite directions that ugly bronze on the front lawn, and he almost laughed. But then he glanced at Thurlow again, and refrained.

"Thurlow, for the love of Mike—" began Mac.

"Keep out of this, Maclyn," said Thurlow sternly, and Mac glanced quickly at his mother. But the Old Woman simply sat, a porcelain. "Robert, each one of these weapons has one bullet in it. You understand?"

Bob could only nod.

"I warn you, I'll shoot to kill. But if you miss me, or just wound me, I'll consider my honor satisfied. It says so in the book."

It says so in the book, Ellery repeated to himself, dazed.

"Dawn at the Shoe, Robert." A huge contempt came into Thurlow's penny-whistle voice. "If you don't show up, I'll kill you on sight." And Thurlow left the dining room a second time, prancing, like a ballet dancer.

Sheila came running into a thickly inhabited silence. "I just saw Thurl go up to his bedroom with a little gun in his hand—" She stopped, spying the glittering nickel in Bob's hand.

The Old Woman simply sat.

Charley got up, sat down, got up again. "It's nothing,

Sheila. A—joke of Thurlow's. About a duel at dawn at the Shoe on the front lawn, or some such nonsense—"

"A duel!" Sheila stared at her brother.

"I still think it's some weird gag of Thurl's," Bob said with a shaky smile, "although God knows he's never been famous for a sense of humor—"

"But why are you all *sitting* here?" cried Sheila. "Call a doctor, a psychiatrist! Call Bellevue!"

"Not while I live," said the Old Woman.

Her husband's face waxed and waned, purple and white. "Not while you live!" he spat at her. Then he ran from the room, as if ashamed . . . as he had been running, Ellery suddenly knew, for over thirty years.

"You're grown men, aren't you?" The old lady's mouth was wry.

"Mother," said Mac. "You can stop this craziness. You know you can. All you have to do is say a word to Thurlow. He's scared to death of you . . ." She was silent. "You *won't?*"

The Old Woman banged on the table. "You're old enough to fight your own battles."

"If precious li'l Thurl wants a duel, precious li'l Thurl gets it, hey?" Mac laughed angrily.

But his mother was on her way to the door.

Sheila stopped her with a choked cry. "You never interfere except when it suits you—and this time it doesn't suit you, Mother! You don't care anything about the twins and me—you never have. Your darling Thurlow—that poor, useless lunatic! You'd let him have his way if he wanted to kill the three of us . . . the three of us!"

The Old Woman did not even glance at her younger daughter. She eyed Ellery instead. "Good night, Mr. Queen. I don't know what Charles Paxton's purpose was in bringing you here tonight, but now that you've seen my family, I hope you'll be discreet enough to hold your tongue. I want no interference from strangers!"

"Of course, Mrs. Potts."

She nodded and swept out.

"What do you think, Ellery?" Charley's tone was brittle, ready to crack. "It's a bluff, isn't it?"

The twins stared at Ellery, and Paxton, and Sheila . . . but not Major Gotch, who, Ellery suddenly realized, was no longer among those present. The canny old goat had managed to slip out some time during the farce.

"No, Charley," said Mr. Queen soberly, "I don't think this is a bluff. I think Thurlow Potts is in earnest. Of course, he's touched; but that won't keep Bob Potts out of the way of a bullet tomorrow morning. Let's put our heads together, the five of us."

6 . . . Ellery Betrays the Code of Duello

"The steps we can take," said Ellery without excitement, "are legion, but they have a common drawback—they involve the use of force. Thurlow can be arrested on some picturesque charge—there may be an old statute on the law books which forbids the practice of dueling, for example. Or he might be charged with threatening homicide. And so on. But he'd be out on bail—if I read your mother correctly—before he was fairly in the clink, and moreover he'd be smarting under a fresh 'injustice.' Or we could ship him off to Bellevue for observation. But I doubt if there are sufficient grounds either to keep him there or put him away in a mental hospital . . . No; can't be force."

"Bob could duck out of town," suggested Mac.

"Are you kidding?" growled his twin.

"Besides, Thurlow would only follow him," said Sheila.

"How about humoring him?" Charley scowled.

Ellery looked interested. "What do you mean exactly?"

"Why not go through with the duel, but pull its teeth?"

"Charley . . . that's it!" cried Sheila.

"Fake it?" frowned Bob.

"But how, Charley?" asked Mac.

"Thurlow said he'd be satisfied if each man fired a single shot, didn't he? In fact, he said each gun was loaded with just one bullet. All right. *Let* each man fire one cartridge apiece tomorrow morning, but see that those cartridges are *blank*."

"The legal mind," moaned Ellery. "These simple solutions! Charley, you're a genius. My hand, sir."

They shook hands solemnly.

"I knew I'd fallen in love with a Blue Plate special," laughed Sheila. She kissed Charley and then put her arms about her twin brothers.

"What d'ye think, Bob?" asked Mac anxiously.

The intended victim grinned. "To tell the truth, Mac, I was frightened blue. Yes, if we substitute blank cartridges for the real ones in the two guns, old Nutsy'll never know the difference."

Sheila was to decoy Thurlow into the library at the rear of the house, on the ground floor, and keep him there while the men did the dirty work.

"The real dirty work's *my* assignment," said Sheila darkly. And she sallied forth to find Thurlow.

Mac volunteered to stand guard at the outpost. Ellery and Charley, it was agreed, must do the actual deed. Bob was to stay out of everything.

Within ten minutes Mac was back with a report, his blue eyes glittering. He had seen Thurlow and Sheila come down from upstairs, chatting earnestly. They had gone into the library. Sheila had shut the door, winking at the hidden twin that all, so far at any rate, went well.

Ellery stood musing. "Bob—can you shoot a revolver?"

"If you show me the place where the blame thing goes off."

"Ouch," said Mr. Queen. "Can Thurlow?"

"He can shoot," said Mac shortly.

"Oh, my. In that case, this mustn't fail. Charley, where's The Purple Avenger's lair?"

The twins sped upstairs to their room. Charley Paxton and Ellery followed, and Charley led the great man to one of the numerous doors studding the upper hall.

"Thurlow's?"

Charley nodded, looking around uneasily.

Ellery listened for a moment. Then, boldly, he went in. He stood in a tall and pleasant sitting room, profuse with fresh flowers and easy-chairs and books, and furnished with surprising good taste. Aside from a rather sexless quality, the room was cloistered and fragrant peace for anyone.

"I see what you meant by Thurlow's potentialities, Charley," remarked Ellery "Did he fix this up himself?"

"All by his little self, Ellery—"

"The man has dignity. I wonder what he reads." He ran his eye along the bookshelves. "Mm, yes. A little heavy on Paine, Butler, and Lincoln—ah, of course! Voltaire. No light reading at all, of course . . ."

"Ellery, for heaven's sake." Charley glanced anxiously at the door.

"It gives the man a perspective," mused Ellery, and he moved on to Thurlow Potts's bedroom. This was a wee, chaste, almost monastic chamber. A high white bed, a highboy, a chair, a lamp. Ellery could see the little man clambering with agility into his bed, clad—no doubt this was an injustice—in a flannel nightshirt, and clutching a volume of *The Rights of Man* to his thick little bosom.

"There it is," said Charley, who had his mind on his work.

The Colt automatic lay on top of the highboy. Ellery picked it up negligently. "Doesn't look very formidable, does it?"

"Has it got one cartridge in it, as Thurlow said?"

Ellery investigated. "But of course it would. He's an honest man. Let us away, Charles." He slipped the Colt into his jacket and they left Thurlow's apartment, Charley acting furtive and relieved at once.

"Where the devil do we get blank cartridges this time of night?" he asked in the hall. "All the stores are closed by now."

"Peace, peace," said Ellery. "Charley, go downstairs to the library and join Sheila in keeping Mr. Thurlow Potts occupied. I don't want him back in his bedroom till I'm ready for him."

"What are *you* going to do?"

"I," quoth Mr. Queen, "shall journey posthaste to my daddy's office at Police Headquarters. Don't stir from the library till I get back."

When Charley had left him, Ellery ambled to the door through which he had seen Bob and Mac Potts disappear, knocked gently, was admitted, gave his personal reassurances that everything was going off as planned—and requisitioned Robert's Smith & Wesson.

"But why?" Bob asked.

"Playing it safe," grinned Ellery, from the hall. "I'll put a blank in this one, too."

"But I don't like it, Ellery," grumbled Inspector Queen at Headquarters, when his son had told him and Sergeant Velie the story of Thurlow Potts's great adventure.

"It ain't decent," said Sergeant Velie. "Fightin' a duel in the year of our Lord!"

Ellery agreed it was neither decent nor to be condoned; but what, he asked reasonably, was a sounder solution of the problem?

"I don't know. I just don't like it," said the Inspector irritably, jamming a blank cartridge into the magazine of the Colt. He tossed it aside and slipped a center-fire blank into the top chamber of the Smith & Wesson.

"That den of dopes've been in every screwball scrape

you can imagine," complained the Sergeant, "but this one takes the hand-embroidered bearskin. Fightin' a duel in the year of our Lord!"

"With the sting removed from Thurlow's stingers," argued Ellery, "it makes a good story, Sergeant."

"Only story *I* want to hear," grunted his father, handing Ellery the two weapons, "is that this fool business is over and done with."

"But Dad, there's no danger of anything going wrong when both guns are loaded with blanks."

"Guns are guns," said Sergeant Velie, who was the Sage of Center Street.

"And blanks are blanks, Sergeant."

"Stop chattering! Velie, you and I are going to watch Thurlow Potts's duel at dawn tomorrow from behind that big Shoe on the front lawn," snapped Inspector Queen. "And may God have mercy on all our souls if anything goes haywire!"

Ellery slipped back into the Potts mansion under an impertinent moon; but he made sure only the moon's eye saw him. Mr. Queen had a way with front doors.

The foyer was empty. He stole towards the rear, listened for voices at the study door, nodded, and made his way in noiseless leaps up the staircase.

Several minutes later he knocked on the twins' door. It opened immediately.

"Well?" asked the Potts twins in one voice. They were nervous: cigaret butts littered the trays, and a bottle of Scotch had been, if not precisely killed, then at least criminally assaulted.

"The deed is done," announced Mr. Queen, "the Colt and its blank are back on Thurlow's highboy, and here's your Smith & Wesson, Bob."

"You're sure the damned thing won't kill anybody?"

"Quite sure, Bob."

Robert placed it gingerly on the night table between his bed and Mac's.

"Then nothing can go wrong tomorrow morning?" growled Mac.

"Oh, come. You're acting like a couple of children. Of course nothing can go wrong!"

Ellery left the twins and cheerily went downstairs to the library. To his surprise, he found Thurlow in a mood more mellow than melancholy.

"Hi," said Thurlow, describing a parabola with his left hand. His right was clasped about a frosty glass. "My second, ladies 'n' gentlemen. Can't have a duel without a second. Come in, Misser Queen. We were just discussing the possibility of continuing our conversation in more con-congenial surroundings. Know what I mean?" And Thurlow leered cherubically.

"I know exactly what you mean, Mr. Potts," smiled Ellery. Perhaps Thurlow in his cups might prove a saner man than Thurlow sober. He nodded slightly to Sheila and Paxton, who looked exhausted. "A hot spot, eh, kid?"

"Hot spot 'tis," beamed Thurlow. "Tha's my second, ladies 'n' gentlemen. Won'erful character." And Thurlow linked his arms in Ellery's, marching him out of the library to the tune of a rueful psalm which went: "Eat, drink, an' be merry, for tomorrow I'll be glad when you're dead, you rascal youuuuu . . ."

Thurlow insisted on Club Bongo. All their arguments could not dissuade him. Ellery could only hope fervently that Mr. Conklin Cliffstatter, of the East Shore jute and shoddy Cliffstatters, was getting drunk elsewhere this night. In the cab on their way downtown, Thurlow fell innocently asleep on Ellery's shoulder.

"This seems kind of silly," giggled Charley Paxton.

"It is not, Charley!" whispered Sheila. "Maybe we can get him into such a good mood he'll call the duel off."

"Hush. Uneasy lies the head." And indeed at that moment Thurlow awoke with a whoop and took up his dolorous psalm.

Mr. Queen, Miss Potts, her eldest brother, and Mr. Paxton spent the night at Club Bongo, keeping its death watch with the curious characters who seemed to find its prancing maidens and tense comedians the most hilarious of companions.

Fortunately, Mr. Cliffstatter was not among them.

Mr. Queen was his suavest and most persuasive; he inserted little melodies of reasonableness into the chit-chat; he suggested frequent libations at the flowing bowl.

But all his efforts, and Sheila's, and Charley's, availed nothing. At a certain point, diabolically, Thurlow stopped imbibing; and to all suggestions that he call off the duel and make a peace with Bob, he would smile sadly, say, "Punctilio is involved my good frien's," and applaud the *première danseuse* enthusiastically.

7 . . . Pistols at Dawn

They got back to the Potts grounds on the drive at a quarter of six. The dawn was dripping and jellyfish-gray, not cheerful. The thing was beyond reason, but there it was. A duel was to be fought in this clammy dawn, with pistols, on a sward, and with trees as sentinels.

The three were exhausted; but not baggy-pantsed, tweed-coated Thurlow. He egged them on in his high-pitched voice, made higher than ordinary by a sort of ecstasy. Sheila and Charley and Ellery could scarcely keep step with him.

They went directly from the sidewalk before the front gates across the grass to the obscene bronze bulk of the Shoe, above which the neon inscription, THE POTTS SHOE, $3.99 EVERYWHERE, still glowed faintly against the early morning sky.

Thurlow glanced up at the silent windows of his mother's mansion beyond the Shoe. "Mr. Queen," he said formally, "you will find my pistol on the highboy in my bedroom."

Ellery hesitated; then he bowed and hurried off to the house. In every story Ellery had ever read about a duel, the seconds bowed.

As he rounded the Shoe, the Inspector's voice came to him in a low and wondering snarl. "He's going through with it, Velie!"

"They'll never believe this downtown," whispered the Sergeant with hoarse awe. "Never, Inspector."

The two men nodded tensely to Ellery as he strode by, and he nodded back. It wasn't so bad, he thought, as he vaulted up the front steps. In fact, it was rather fun. He realized how gay life had been for those old boys of the romantic age, and felt almost thankful to Providence for having brought Thurlow Potts into the world a century or two late.

He realized, too, that part of his enjoyment derived from a certain giddiness of the brain, which in turn came from having tried to set Thurlow a Scotch example all night. Things were a little hazy as he tiptoed into the house, having used his magic on the lock of the front door.

49

Where was everybody? Wonderful household! Two brothers are to duel to the death, and of their blood none cares sufficiently to let off snoring and be miserable. Or perhaps the Old Woman was awake, peering through the curtains of her bedroom window at the scene in miniature to be enacted on the grass before her Moloch. What could she be thinking, that extraordinary mother? And where was Steve Brent Potts? Probably drunk in his bed.

Ellery stopped very suddenly halfway up the main staircase leading from the foyer to the bedroom floor. The house was silent, with that eeriest of silences which pervades a house at dawn, the silence of gray light.

Not a sound. Not even a shadow. But—something?

It seemed to be on the bedroom floor, and it seemed to pass the door of Thurlow Potts's apartment. Was it . . . *someone coming out of those two rooms?*

Ellery sped up the remaining steps and stopped catlike on the landing to survey the hall, both ways. No one. And the silence again.

Man? Woman? Imagination? He listened very hard.

But that deep, deep silence.

He went into Thurlow's apartment, shut the door behind him, and began to search for more palpable clues. He spared neither time, eyesight, nor his clothes. But crawl and peer and pry as he might, he could detect no least sign that anyone had been there since he himself had left the premises the night before on his last visit. The tiny Colt lay exactly where he had placed it with his own hand after his trip to Police Headquarters for the blank cartridges—on Thurlow's highboy.

Ellery seized Thurlow's automatic and left the apartment.

Robert and Maclyn Potts appeared promptly at six. They marched from the house shoulder to shoulder, appeared not to notice Inspector Queen and Sergeant Velie in the shadows at the base of the Shoe's pedestal, rounded the Shoe, and stopped.

The two parties stared solemnly at each other.

Then Thurlow bowed to his brothers.

Bob hesitated, glanced at Ellery, then bowed back. Behind Thurlow, Charley grinned and clasped his hands above his head. Bob's left eyelid drooped ever so little in reply.

But Mac's expression was serious. "Look here, Thurl," he said, "hasn't this fool farce gone far enough? Let's shake hands all around and—"

Thurlow glared disapprovingly at his adversary's twin. "You will please inform the gentleman's second," he said to Ellery, "that conversation with the principals is not considered good form, Mr. Queen."

"I so inform him," replied Mr. Queen frigidly. "Now what do I do, Mr. Potts?"

"I should be obliged if you would act as Master of Ceremonies as well as my second. It's a little irregular, but then I'm sure we can take a few liberties with the code."

"Oh, of course," said Ellery hastily. Improvise, Brother Queen, improvise. Must be some sense in the code of duello somewhere, or was. "Mr. Thurlow Potts, your weapon," said Ellery in a grave voice. He handed the Colt, walnut stock forward, to his man.

Mr. Thurlow Potts dropped the automatic into the right pocket of his coat. Then he turned and walked off a few paces, to stand there stiffly, a man alone with his Maker. Or so his back said.

"I believe," continued Ellery, turning to Maclyn Potts, "that as your principal's second you should be addressed. The Master of Ceremonies should ask somebody if the duelists won't call the whole thing off. What say?"

Before Mac could reply, Thurlow's voice came, annoyed. "No, no, Mr. Queen. As the offended party, the option is mine." It didn't sound right to Mr. Queen; more like a business conference. "And I insist: Honor satisfied."

"But isn't there something in the code," the Master of Ceremonies asked respectfully, "about the duel being called off if the offender apologizes, Mr. Potts?"

"I'll apologize. I'll do any blasted thing," snapped Bob, "to get off this damp grass."

"No, *no!*" screamed Thurlow. "I won't have it that way. Honor satisfied, Mr. Queen, honor satisfied!"

"Very well, honor satisfied," replied Mr. Queen hastily. "I think, then, that the principals should stand back to back. Right here, gentlemen. Mac, is your man ready?"

Mac nodded disgustedly, and Robert took from his pocket the Smith & Wesson Ellery had returned to him the night before. Robert and Thurlow now approached each other, Thurlow producing from his pocket the Colt Ellery had just handed him and gripping it nervously. Thurlow was pale.

"Back to back, gentlemen."

The brothers executed the *volte-face*.

"I shall count to ten. With each number of the count," continued Ellery with stern relish, "you gentlemen will walk one pace forward. At the end of the count you will be twenty paces from each other, facing in opposite directions. Is that clear?"

Thurlow Potts said in a strained voice: "Yes." Robert Potts yawned.

"At the end of the count, I shall say 'Turn!' You will then turn and face each other, raise your weapons, and take aim. I will thereupon count to three, and at three you each fire just one shot. Understand?"

Sheila giggled.

"Very well, then. Start pacing off. One. Two. Three ..." Ellery counted solemnly. When he said "Ten," the two men obediently stopped pacing. "Turn!" They turned.

Thurlow's chubby face gleamed wet in the gray light. But his mouth was set in a stubborn line, and he scowled fiercely at his brother. He raised his Colt shoulder high, aiming it. Robert shrugged and aimed too.

"One," said Ellery. This is all wrong, he thought testily. I should have read up on it. Maybe when Thurlow finds out how I've messed up his duel, he'll insist on a retake.

"Two." And what were the Inspector and Velie thinking behind that horrible statue? He'd never hear the end of this. He spied the two men's heads peeping cautiously from behind the pedestal.

"Three!"

There was one cracking report. Smoke drifted from the muzzle of Thurlow's little weapon.

Ellery became aware of a leaden silence, and of a curious look on Thurlow Potts's face. He whirled. Behind him Sheila gurgled, and Charley Paxton said: "What the—" and Maclyn Potts stared at the grass. And Inspector Queen and Sergeant Velie were racing around the pedestal, waving their arms frantically.

For Robert Potts lay on the grass, on his face, the undischarged Smith & Wesson still in his hand.

"Bob, Bob, get off the grass," Mac kept saying. "Stop clowning. Get the hell up off the grass. You'll catch cold—"

Somebody—it was Charley—took Mac's arm and steered him, still prattling, off to one side.

"Well?" asked the Inspector in an unreal voice.

Ellery rose, mechanically brushing at grass stains on his trouser knees which would not come off. "The man's dead."

Sheila Potts ran blindly for the house. She made a wide,

horrified detour around Thurlow, who was still standing there, gun in hand, looking at them all with a bewildered expression.

"Smack in the pump," breathed Sergeant Velie, pointing. Ellery had turned Bob Potts over: there was a dark spot on his clothing, from which an uneven bloodstain had spread, like the solar corona.

Thurlow threw down his automatic as if it burned his hand. He walked off unsteadily.

"Hey—!" began Sergeant Velie, taking a step toward him. But then the Sergeant stopped and scratched his head.

"But—how?" howled the Inspector, finding his normal voice. "Ellery, I thought you said—"

"You'll find the blank cartridge you yourself placed in Robert's Smith & Wesson still in the chamber," Ellery said in a stiff tone. "He never even fired. There *was* a corresponding blank in Thurlow's Colt too—when I deposited it on Thurlow's highboy last night after my trip to Headquarters. But someone—*someone in this house*, Dad—substituted a *real* bullet for the blank you'd put in Thurlow's gun last night!"

"Murder," said the Inspector. He was white.

"Yes," mumbled Ellery. "Murder to which we were all eyewitnesses—yet none of us lifted a finger to stop it . . . in fact, we aided and abetted it. *We saw the man who fired the shot, but we don't know who the murderer is!*"

PART TWO

8 . . . The Paramount Question of Opportunity

A premeditated murder is not unlike a child. First it must be conceived, second gestated; only then can it be born. These three steps in the fruition of the homicide are usually unwitnessed; when this occurs, there is a Mystery, and the function of the Detective is to go back along its blood line, for only in this way can be established the paternity of the crime—which is to say, solve the mystery.

Ellery Queen had never before been privileged to attend the delivery, as it were; and the fact that, having attended it, he knew as little about its parentage as if he had not neither irritated nor angered him, for if a murder had to be committed and could not be averted, then Ellery preferred it to be a mystery at the beginning, just so that he could dig into it and trace it backward and explain it to himself at the end.

He stood by himself, deep in thought, in the lightening morning under one of the Old Woman's pedigreed blue spruces, watching his father and Sergeant Velie go to work. He stood by, musing, as Hesse, and Flint, and Piggott, and Johnson, and others of the Inspector's staff arrived, as radio patrol cars gathered on the Drive outside the high wall, as the police photographer came, the fingerprint men, and Dr. Samuel Prouty, Assistant Medical Examiner of New York County—petulant at having had to leave spouse, progeny, and couch so early of a summer morning. As of old, Doc Prouty and Inspector Queen set about snarling at each other over Robert Potts's sprawled corpse, like two fierce old dogs over a bone. As always Sergeant Velie, the Great Dane, chuckled and growled between them. Eventually the body was lifted to an improvised stretcher, under the fussy superintendence of Doc Prouty; a moment later Dr. Waggoner Innis's big sedan roared up under police motorcycle escort, and the doctor's long legs carried him in almost eager strides after the cortege, to

54

confer with the assistant Medical Examiner over the technical details of the homicide. The whole party disappeared into the house, leaving Inspector Queen and his son, alone, at the pedestal of the bronze Shoe.

The air was chill, and the Inspector shivered a little. "Well?" he said.

"Well," said Ellery.

"We'd better talk fast," said the Inspector after a pause. "The newspapers will be here soon, and we'd better figure out what to say to them. At the moment, my mind's a blank."

Ellery frowned over his cigaret.

"A duel," the Inspector continued with bitterness. "I let myself be talked into a duel! And this happens. What'll I say to the boss? What'll I say to anybody?"

Ellery sighed and flipped his butt into the damp grass. The sun was struggling to wipe the clouds from its eye; the feeble glance that escaped flung the ugly shadow of the Shoe toward the Hudson. "Why," complained Mr. Ellery Queen, "does the sun invariably stay hidden when you want it, and come out when it doesn't matter any more?"

"What are you talking about?"

"Well, I mean," smiled Ellery, "that if the light had been better we might have been able to see something."

"Oh. But what, Ellery? The dirty work was done during the night."

"Yes. But—a glance, a change of expression. You never know. Little things are so important. And the light was dismal and gray, and details likewise." And the great man sank into silence again.

The Inspector shook his head impatiently. "Light or no light, the point is: Who could have substituted a live bullet for the blank I put in Thurlow's automatic at Headquarters last night?"

"Opportunity," murmured Ellery. "Dat ol' debil. Yes. In a moment, Dad. But tell me—you've examined the shell?"

"Of course."

"Anything unusual about it?"

"Nope. The cartridge used was ordinary Peters 'rustless.' M.C. type of bullet for a .25 automatic, 2-inch barrel. Ballistics penetration of three inches, figured on the usual seven-eighths pine board. Exactly the ammunition that was in the automatic when you handed it to me at Headquarters."

"Really?"

"Don't get excited," scowled the Inspector. "That ammunition can be bought any place."

"I know, but it's also the ammunition Thurlow used, Dad. Have you checked with Thurlow's supply? He must have got some at Cornwall & Ritchey's when he bought the guns yesterday."

"I told Velie to root around."

And indeed at this moment Sergeant Velie swung out of the house and came rocking across the lawn to the Shoe. "What kind of buggery is this, anyway?" he exploded. "Here's a guy dead, murdered, and most of his folks don't even seem to care. What am I saying? Care? They're not even payin' attention!"

"You'll find them a rather unorthodox family, Sergeant," said Ellery dryly. "Have you checked back on Thurlow's ammunition?"

"I ain't had a chance yet to look at it myself, but Little Napoleon says he bought a lot of ammunition yesterday, and the box of .25 automatic cartridges has got some missing out of it, he says. A handful. Says *he'd* only took out one last night—the one he put into the Colt automatic. Can't understand what all the fuss is about, he says. 'It was a duel, wasn't it?' he grouses to me. 'All right, so my brother got laid out,' he says. 'So what's the cops here for?' he says. 'It's all legal and aboveboard!' " And the Sergeant shook his head and stamped back to the mansion.

"The big point is, Thurlow's already checked back on his ammunition supply," murmured Ellery. "Then he doesn't know about the blanks, does he, Dad?"

"Not yet."

"Worried. All legal and aboveboard, but—worrisome, too, Dad. I think you'd better locate Mr. Thurlow's armory and appropriate it with dispatch. The stuff's a menace."

"It's a cinch he's cached it somewhere cute, like the squirrel he is," growled the Inspector, "and nobody but he knows where. The boys are keeping an eye on Mr. Thurlow, so it'll hold for a few minutes. What about this opportunity business, Ellery? Let's go over the ground to make sure. Just what did you do last night after you left Headquarters with the Colt and S. & W.?"

"I returned to the house here immediately, slipped back into Thurlow's bedroom, replaced the blank-loaded Colt automatic on the highboy exactly where I'd found it

earlier in the evening, then I went to the twins' room and
gave Bob Potts the blank-loaded Smith & Wesson."

"Anybody spot you entering or leaving Thurlow's
room?"

"I can't swear, but I'm convinced no one did."

"The twins knew about it, though, didn't they?"

"Naturally."

"Who else?"

"Charley Paxton and Sheila Potts. All the others had
left by the time we discussed the plan to substitute blanks
for the live cartridges in the two guns."

"All right," grunted his father, "you left the Colt right
where you found it, in Thurlow's bedroom, you gave
Robert his doctored revolver, and then what?"

"I left the twins in their room and went downstairs to
the library. Charley and Sheila still had Thurlow cornered
down there, as I had instructed. Thurlow was in a gay
mood—Sheila'd fed him some drinks in an effort to
restore his sanity. He insisted on our all going out on a
tear, which we did, just as we were—the four of us. We
left the house in a group, from the library, cabbed
downtown, and spent the entire night at Club Bongo, on
East 55th Street. We didn't get back to the Palace—"

"The what?"

"Forgive me. I'm only using the family's own terminology. We got back here about a quarter of six this morning."

"Was Thurlow, Paxton, or Sheila in a position to get to
that Colt automatic in Thurlow's room at any time during
the night, after you left it there?"

"That's what makes this part of it so beautiful," declared Ellery. "No, those three were with me, within sight
and touch, from the moment I stepped into the library
until we got out of the cab at dawn this morning."

"How about when you got back? What happened?"

"I left Thurlow, Charley, and Sheila on the lawn, right
over there, as you saw. Thurlow'd sent me into the house
to fetch his gun. I went up and—" He stopped.

"What's the matter?" asked his father quickly.

"I just remembered," muttered Ellery. "It seemed to me
as I went up that spiral staircase to the landing that I . . .
not exactly *heard*, but *felt* someone or something moving
in the hall outside the bedrooms."

"Yes?" said the Inspector sharply. "What? Who?"

"I don't know. I even had the feeling it came from
around the area of Thurlow's door. But that may have

been an excited imagination. I was *thinking* of Thurlow's apartment."

"Well, was it or wasn't it, son? For the love of Peter's pants! *Did* somebody come out of Thurlow's rooms around six A.M.?"

"I can't say yes, and I can't say no."

"Very helpful," groaned the Inspector. "You got the gun and came right back down here to the lawn? No stops?"

"Exactly. And handed the gun to Thurlow. He dropped it in the right-hand outside pocket of his tweed jacket the moment I handed it to him." The Inspector nodded; he had observed the same action. "He didn't touch it again until he was ordered to during the duel. I had my eyes on him every second. Nor did anyone approach near enough to him to have done any funny work."

"Right. I was watching him, too. Then the only possible time the blank could have been removed and the live cartridge substituted in the Colt was during the night—between the time you left it on Thurlow's highboy last night and the time he sent you up there at six this morning to get it for the duel. But where does that take us? Nowhere!" The Inspector waved his spindly arms. "Anybody in this rummy's nightmare could have sneaked into Thurlow's room during those ten hours or so and made the switch of bullets!"

"Not anybody," said Ellery.

"What? What's that?"

"Not anybody. Anybody," said Ellery patiently, "minus three."

"Talk so that my simple mind can understand, Mr. Queen," said the Inspector testily.

"Well, Thurlow couldn't have sneaked into his bedroom during those hours," murmured Mr. Queen. "Nor Charley Paxton. Nor Sheila Potts. Couldn't possibly. Those three are eliminated beyond the least shadow of the least doubt."

"Well, of course. I meant one of the others."

"Yes," mused Ellery, "here's a case in which we can actually delimit and define the suspects. The rest of the Potts menagerie were in the house during the period of opportunity, and so any one of them could have made the switch from blank to lethal bullet. Aside from the servants, there are: the Old Woman herself, her husband Steve, that old parasite Major Gotch, Louella the 'scientist,' Mac the twin, and Horatio."

"That's the son you told me sleeps in some kind of—what did you call it, Ellery?"

"Fairy-tale cottage. Yes," replied the great man crossly. "Yes, the Philosopher of Escapism could have done it, too, even though he sleeps in his dream cottage. Horatio could have slipped into the main house through the inner court, patio, and French doors, and slipped out again via the same route, without necessarily being seen."

"Six likely suspects," mumbled the Inspector. "Not so bad. Let's see how they stand on motive. As far as the old hell-cat's concerned . . ."

Ellery yawned. "Not now, Dad. I'm not Superman—I need sleep occasionally, and last night was heigh-de-ho. Ditto Sheila and Charley. Let us all sleep it off."

"Well, you ring me here from home when you wake up."

"When I wake up," announced his son, "I shall be practically at my father's elbow."

"Now what's *that* mean?"

"I'm requisitioning a bed in the Potts Palladium. And if you don't think," added the Inspector's pride and joy, "that I'll investigate it microscopically before I climb in to make sure it isn't the bed of Procrustes . . ."

"Who's that?"

"A Greek robber who occasionally whittled his victims down to size," said Ellery with another yawn.

"You won't need his bed to do that," said the Inspector grimly. "I have a hunch this case'll do it for you, my son."

"Making any bets?" Ellery drifted off toward the house.

9 . . . The Narrow Escape of Sergeant Velie

Ellery fell asleep like a cat and awoke like a man. As his senses unfolded he became conscious of unnatural quiet and unnatural noise. The house, which should have been filled with the sounds of people, was not; the front lawn, which had been empty, was filled with the sounds of people.

He leaped from his borrowed bed and ran to one of the windows overlooking the front lawn. The sun was high now, in a hot blue sky, and it glared down upon a swarm of men. They surrounded the Shoe, near the base of which the Inspector stood at bay. There was a great deal of shouting.

Ellery threw on his clothes and raced downstairs. "Dad! What's the trouble?" he cried, on the run.

But the Inspector was too busy to reply.

Then Ellery saw that this was not a mob, but a group of reporters and newspaper photographers engaged—if a trifle zealously—in the underpaid exercise of their duty.

"Ah, here's the Master Mind!"

"Maybe *he's* got a tongue."

"What's the lowdown, Hawkshaw?"

"Your old man's all of a sudden got a stiff upper lip."

"Say, there's nothing lenient about the lower one, either!"

"Loosen up, you guys. What are you holding so tight?"

"What gives here at six A.M.?"

Ellery shook his head good-humoredly, pushing his way through the crowd.

The Inspector seized him. "Ellery, tell these doubting Thomases the truth, will you? They won't believe *me*. Tell 'em the truth so I can be rid of 'em and get back to work—God help me!"

"Gentlemen, it's a fact," said Ellery Queen. The murmurs ceased.

"It's a fact," a reporter said at last, in a hushed voice.

"A real, live, fourteen-carat *duel?*"

"Right here, under the oxford?"

"Pistols at twenty paces and that kind of stuff?"

"Hey, if they wore velvet pants I'll go out of my mind!"

"Nah, Thurlow had on that lousy old tweed suit of his—"

"And poor Bob Potts wore a beige gabardine—wasn't that what Inspector Queen said?"

"Nuts. I'd rather it was velvet pants."

"But, my God—"

"Listen, Jack, not even the readers of *your* rag'll believe this popeyed peep show!"

"What do I give a damn whether they believe it or not? I'm paid to report what happened."

"Me, I'm talking this over with the boss."

"Hold it, men—here comes the Old Woman."

She appeared from the front door and marched towards the marble steps, flanked on one side by Dr. Innis and on the other by Sergeant Thomas Velie. Each escort, in his own fashion, was pleading with her.

The reporters and cameramen deserted the Queens

shamelessly. In a twinkling they had raced across the lawn and set up shop at the foot of the steps.

"Bloomin' heroes," said Ellery. He was squinting at the Old Woman, disturbed.

There was no sign of grief on that face; only rage. The jet snake's eyes had not wept; they had kept the shape and color of their reptilian nature. "Get off my property!" she screamed.

Cameras were raised high; men fired questions at her.

If these intrepid explorers of the news had the wit, thought Ellery, they would shrink and flee before an old woman who accepted her young son's bloody murder without emotion and grew hysterical over a transitory trespass on the scene of his death. Such a woman was capable of anything.

"It's the first peep out of her today," remarked the Inspector. "We'd better get on over there. She may blow her top any minute."

The Queens hurried toward the house. But before they could reach the steps, Cornelia Potts blew, and blew in an unexpected manner.

One moment she was standing there like an angry pouter pigeon, glaring down at her tormentors; the next her claws had flashed into a recess in the overlapping folds of her taffeta skirt and emerged with a revolver. It was absurd, but there it was: an old lady, seventy years old, pointing a revolver at a group of men.

Somebody said: "Hey," indignantly; then they grew very quiet.

It was a long-barreled revolver alive with blue fires in the sun. All eyes were on it.

Dr. Innis took a quick backward step. On the Old Woman's other side, Sergeant Velie looked dazed. Ellery had seen the Sergeant disarm five thugs all by himself without excitement laying them out in a neat and silent row; but the spectacle and the problem of a septuagenarian who resembled Queen Victoria brandishing a heavy revolver evidently frustrated him.

"One of Thurlow's mess of guns," the Inspector said bitterly, eyes intent on the talon that was crooked about the trigger. "So she knew where Thurlow'd hid 'em after all. I swear, anyone who mixes with these crazy drooglers gets addled—even me."

"Someone ought to stop her," said Ellery nervously.

"Care to volunteer your services?" And since there was no answer, his father lit a stogie and began to puff on it without relish. "Mrs. Potts," he called, "put that naughty thing down and—"

"Stand where you are!" said the Old Woman grimly to the Inspector; at which he looked surprised, for he had exhibited no least intention of moving from the spot. She turned back to the fascinated group below her. "I told you men to get off my property." She waved the revolver shakily.

One witless enthusiast raised his camera for a furtive shot of Cornelia Potts Draws Bead on Press. There was a shot, but it came towards the camera, not from it. It was a bad shot, merely nicking one edge of the lens and ricocheting off to bury itself in the grass; but it had the magical property of causing a group of grown men to disappear from the foot of the steps and reintegrate behind the solid bronze of the Shoe some yards away.

"She's loco," said the Sergeant hoarsely to Dr. Innis.

"Get out!" shrieked Cornelia Potts to the men cowering behind the Shoe. "This is my family's business and I won't have it all over the dirty newspapers. Out!"

"Piggott, Hesse," said the Inspector wearily. "Where in time are you men? Escort the boys from the grounds."

Several heads peered from behind several trees, and it was seen that they were the heads of several large persons —what was more shameful, of detectives attached to Inspector Queen's staff.

"Well, go on," said the Inspector. "All she can do is kill you. That's what you're paid for, isn't it? Get these brave men out of here!"

The detectives emerged, blushing. Whereupon Mr. Queen enjoyed the spectacle of numerous male figures scampering helter-skelter toward the front gates, their flank covered, as it were, by plain-clothes men who were running as energetically as they. Within seconds only the three at the top of the steps and the two a short way off on the grass were left to watch the fires burn blue on the barrel of the faintly smoking revolver.

"That's the way it is," said the Old Woman with satisfaction. "Now what are *you* men waiting for?" The barrel waggled again.

"Madam," said the Inspector, taking a step.

"Stop, Inspector Queen."

Inspector Queen stopped.

"I'll say this now, and not again. I don't *want* you. I don't *want* an investigation. I don't *want* police. I don't want *any* outside interference. I'll handle my son's death in my own way, and if you don't think I mean it—"

Ellery said respectfully: "Mrs. Potts."

She gave him a sharp glance. *"You've* been hanging around to no good, young man. What d'ye want?"

"Do you quite realize your position?"

"My position is what I make it!"

"I'm afraid not," said Ellery sadly. "Your position is what your impulsive son Thurlow has made it. Or rather whoever was using Thurlow as a witless fool to commit a revolting crime. You can't get out of your position, Mrs. Potts, with revolvers, or threats, or loud tones of voice. Your position, Mrs. Potts, if you'll reflect for a moment, dictates that you hand that revolver to Sergeant Velie, go into your house, and leave the rest to those whose business it is to catch murderers."

Sergeant Velie, thus obliquely brought into the conversation, gave a nervous start and cleared his throat.

"Don't move," said Cornelia Potts sharply; and the Sergeant gave a feeble laugh and said: "Who, me, Mrs. Potts? I was just shiftin' to the other foot."

She backed up, grasping the revolver more firmly. "Did you hear what I said? Get out, Innis—you too!"

"Now, Mrs. Potts," began the physician, pallidly. "Mr. Queen is quite right, you know. Besides, all this excitement is bad for your heart, very bad. I shan't be responsible—"

"Oh, fiddlesticks," she snapped. "My heart's my own. I'm sick of you, Dr. Waggoner Innis, and what I've been thinking of to let you mess around me I can't imagine."

Dr. Innis drew himself up. "For the last time, you men— are you going to leave, or do I have to shoot one of you to convince you I mean what I say?"

Inspector Queen said: "Velie, take that gun away from her."

"Dad—" began Ellery.

"Yes, sir," said Sergeant Velie.

Several things happened at once. Dr. Innis stepped aside with extraordinary agility to get out of the way of Sergeant Velie, who was advancing cautiously towards the old lady; and of the old lady, who had twisted about to train her revolver on the advancing Sergeant. At the same moment Ellery darted from his station on the grass and hurled himself at the steps. Simultaneously the front door opened and eyes clustered, staring, while on the grass Inspector Queen took two kangaroo steps to the left, pulling from his pocket as he did so his large and ponderous fountain pen, and let fly.

Ellery, pen, and Cornelia Potts met at the identical instant that the revolver cracked. The fountain pen struck her hand, joggling it; Ellery struck her legs, upsetting them; and the bullet struck Sergeant Velie's hat, causing it to dart from his head like a bird.

The revolver clanked to the porch.

Sergeant Velie pounced on it, mumbling incredulously: "She took a shot at me. She took a shot at me! Blame near got me in the head. In the head!" He gaped at Cornelia Potts as he rose, clutching the gun.

Ellery got up and brushed himself off. "Forgive me," he said to the furious old lady, who was struggling between Inspector Queen and Dr. Innis.

"I'll have the law on you!" she screamed.

"Let me get you inside, Mrs. Potts," murmured Dr. Innis, twisting her arm. "Quiet you down—your heart—"

"The law on you . . ."

Inspector Queen smote his forehead. *"She'll* have the law on *us!"* he roared. "Flint, Piggott, Johnson! Get this maniac into her house—come out of hiding there, you yellow-bellied traitors! She'll have the law on us, will she? *Velie!"*

"Huh?" Sergeant Velie was now staring at his hat, which stared back at him with its new eye.

"Those fourteen shooting irons Thurlow bought," the old gentleman snarled. "We've got three of 'em now—the two he used in the duel this morning, and this one his mother swiped. Round up those other eleven, understand me, or don't come back to Center Street. Every last one of 'em!"

"Yes, sir," mumbled Sergeant Velie. He shambled into the house after Dr. Innis and the fighting Old Woman, still shaking his head as one who will never understand.

10 . . . The Mark of Cain

The wake is quite all for the living, and no man eats more heartily than the butcher.

Ellery suddenly found himself craving sustenance. He was rested by his nap, Robert Potts lay irrevocably downtown on Dr. Prouty's autopsy table, and Mr. Queen was hungry, hungry. He beat a path to the dining room, one eye out for a servant; but the first living soul he met was Detective Flint, hurrying through the foyer toward the front door.

"Where's the Inspector, Mr. Queen?"

"Outside. What's wrong now, Flint?"

"Wrong!" Detective Flint mopped his face. "Inspector says 'Flint, keep an eye on this Horatio Potts,' he says. 'The one that lives in that pink popcorn shack in the court,' he says. 'I don't cotton to that billygoat,' he says, 'and a guy who'll play marbles at his age'd slip a live cartridge into his brother's rod just out of clean, boyish fun,' he says. 'Probably like to hear 'em pop good and loud,' he says—"

"Spare me," said Mr. Queen. "I'm a starving man. What's the matter?"

"So I watch Horatio," said Detective Flint. "I watch and I watch till my eyes are fallin' out of my head, and what do I see?" Flint paused to mop his face again.

"Well, well?"

"His brother's layin' downstairs dead, see? Young guy, everything to live for—dead. Murder. House full of cops. Hot hell let loose. Does Horatio get scared?" demanded Detective Flint. "Does he go around bitin' his nails? Does he dive into bed and pull the covers over his yap? Does he cry? Does he make with the hysterics? Does he yell he's gonna get revenge on whoever the bloody murderin' killer was who—"

Ellery moved off.

"Wait!" Flint hurried after him. "I'm gettin' to it, Mr. Queen."

"And so is starvation to me," said Mr. Queen gently.

"But you don't get it. What does Big Brother Horatio—cripes, what a name!—do? He sits himself down at his desk in that Valentine's box he built himself back there in the garden and he says to me—friendly, see? 'Sir,' he says 'sir, this gives me a honey of an idea for a new kiddy book,' he says. 'There is somethin' uny—uny—' "

"Versal," said Ellery, perking up.

"That's it—'unyversal in the manly code of punk-something or other—' I didn't get the word, but it sounded like Spick talk—'and anyway,' he says, 'it's always a good theme for a child's work,' he says, 'so I'm gonna sit me down with your permission, sir, of course,' he says, 'and I'm gonna make some notes on a swashbucklin' Stevensonian romance for boys of the early teen age,' he says, 'based on two brothers who fight a dool to the death,' he says, and I'm a shyster lawyer if that big slob don't pick up one of them chicken feathers he writes with and start in writin' away like his life depends on it. Then he stops writin' and looks at me. 'Seventeenth century, of course,' he says. And he writes again. And again he stops and looks at me. 'You'll find apples and preserved ginger and cookies in the cupboard, Mr. Flint,' he says to me." Detective Flint looked around cunningly. "Do you s'pose the wack did it to get material for a book?" he whispered. "That's what I gotta tell Inspector Queen. It's a theory, Mr. Queen, you can't break down!"

"You'll find the oldest living iconoclast out front," sighed Mr. Queen; and he hastened on.

Sheila and Charley Paxton were seated in the dining room pecking at a salad luncheon.

"No, don't go," said Sheila quickly.

"I wasn't intending to." Ellery came in. "Not with food so near."

"Oh, dear. Cuttins!" The long-shanked butler materialized, trembling. "Cuttins," said Sheila in a deadly voice, "can't decide whether to quit our service or stay, Mr. Queen. Suppose you tell him what the situation is."

"The situation," said Mr. Queen, impaling Cuttins on his glance, "is that this house and everyone in it are under surveillance of the police, Cuttins, and since you can't very well skip out without a police alarm being broadcast in your honor, you'd be well advised to get me something to eat instantly."

"Very good, sir," muttered Cuttins; and he oozed rapidly out.

"I'm still punchy," said Sheila vaguely. "I can't seem to get it through my thick head that Bob's dead. *Dead*. Not of pneumonia. Not hit by an automobile. Killed by a bullet from Thurlow's gun in a *duel*. Such a s-silly way to die!" Sheila bent suddenly over her plate. She did not look at Charley Paxton, who sat stricken.

"Something's happened between you two," said Ellery keenly, glancing from one to the other.

"Sheila's called off our engagement," murmured Charley.

"Well," said Ellery cheerfully, "don't treat it like some major convulsion of nature, Charley. A girl has a right to change her mind. And you're not the handsomest specimen roving the New York jungle."

"It isn't that," said Sheila quickly. "I still—" She bit her lip.

"It isn't?" Ellery stole a slice of bread from Charley's bread-and-butter plate. "Then what is it, Sheila?"

Sheila did not answer.

"This is no time to split up," cried Charley. "I'll never understand women! Here's a girl up to her neck in trouble. You'd think she'd want my arms around her. Instead, she pushed me away just now! Won't let me kiss her, won't let me share her unhappiness—"

"Every fact has a number of alternative explanations," murmured Mr. Queen. "Maybe you had garlic for lunch yesterday, Charley."

Sheila smiled despite herself. Then she said in despair: "There's nothing else for me to do, I tell you."

"Just because poor Bob was murdered," Charley said bitterly. "I suppose if my father had died on the gallows rather than home in bed, you'd run out on *me*, wouldn't you?"

"Cough up, sweetheart," said Mr. Queen gently.

"All right, I will!" Sheila's dimples dug hard. "Charley, I've always told you that the main reason I was holding off our marriage was because Mother would cut me off without a cent if we went through with it, and that that wouldn't be fair to you. Well, I wasn't being honest. As if I cared two cents whether Mother left me anything or not! I'd be happy with you if I had to live in a one-room shack."

"It isn't that?" The young lawyer was bewildered. "But then what possible reason, darling—?"

"Charley, *look* at us. Thurlow. Louella. Horatio—"

"Wait a minute—"

"You can't get away from the horrid truth just by ignoring it. They're insane, every one of them." Sheila's voice soared. "How do I know I haven't got the same streak in me? How do I *know?*"

"But Sheila dearest, they're not your full brothers and sisters—they're half-brothers, Louella's a half-sister."

We have the same mother."

"But you know perfectly well that Thurlow, Louella, and Horatio inherited their—whatever they inherited—not from your mother but from their father, whose blood isn't in *you* at all. And there's certainly nothing wrong with Steve—"

"How do I know that?" asked Sheila stridently. "Look at my mother. Is she like other people?"

"There's nothing wrong with the Old Woman but plain, ordinary cussedness. Sheila, you're dramatizing. This childish fear of insanity—"

"I won't marry you or anybody else until I know, Charley," said Sheila fiercely. "And now with a murderer in the family—" She jumped up and fled.

"No, Charley," said Ellery quickly, as with the look of a wounded deer the lawyer started after her. "Abide with me."

"But I can't let her go like this!"

"Yes, you can. Let Sheila alone for a while."

"But it's such nonsense! There's nothing wrong with Sheila. There's never been anything wrong with the Brents—Steve, Sheila, Bob, Mac—"

"You ought to be able to understand Sheila's fears, Charley. She's in a highly nervous state. Even if she weren't a naturally high-strung girl, living here would have made her a neurotic."

"Well, then, solve this damned case so I can take Sheila out of this asylum and pound some sense into her!"

"I'll do my best, Charley." Ellery looked thoughtfully over his chicken salad, which, now that the first pangs of his hunger had been assuaged, he realized with annoyance he had always detested.

When Inspector Queen and Sergeant Velie bustled into the dining room, Ellery was low in his chair, smoking like a sooty flue, and Charlie was tormenting his nails.

"Shhh," whispered Charley. "He's thinking."

"He is, is he?" snapped the Inspector. "Then let him think about this. Velie—set 'em down."

There was a crash. Ellery looked up with a start. Sergeant Velie had dumped an armful of revolvers and automatics on the dining-room table.

"Well, well. Thurlow's arsenal, eh?"

"Me, I found it," pouted Velie. "Don't I ever get credit for nothin'?"

"A regular Pagliacci," snarled Inspector Queen. "The fact is, son, here's the kit and caboodle of 'em, and there's two missing."

"Not fourteen?" Ellery looked distressed. In some things he had the soul of a bookkeeper; a mislaid fact irked him —two drove him mad.

"Count them yourself."

Ellery did so. There were twelve. Among them he found Thurlow's .25 Colt automatic, Robert's stubby S. & W. .38/32, and the long-barreled revolver with which

Cornelia Potts had almost assassinated Sergeant Velie—a Harrington & Richardson .22-caliber "Trapper Model."

"What's Thurlow got to say?" demanded Charley.

"Can you make sense out of a pecan?" asked the Sergeant. "Thurlow says he had fourteen, and that's what the sportin'-goods store says he bought. Also, Thurlow says nobody but himself knew where he hid the guns. So I says: 'Then how come two are missin'? What did they do—pick themselves up and take a walk?' So he looks at me like *I'm* nuts!"

"Where *did* he have them cached, Sergeant?" asked Ellery.

"In a false closet in his bedroom along with some boxes of ammunition he'd bought."

"Oh, there," said Charley Paxton disgustedly. "Then of course everybody knew. Thurlow's been 'hiding' things in that false closet since the house was built. In fact, he had the closet installed. The whole household knows about it."

"It's a cinch the Old Woman got his Harrington & Richardson there," said Inspector Queen, sitting down and dipping into the salad bowl for a shred of chicken. "So why not Louella, or Horatio, or anybody else? Fact is, two guns are missing, and I won't sleep till they're found. Guns loose in *this* hatchery!"

Ellery studied the armory on the table. Then he produced pad and pencil and began to write.

"Inventory," he announced at last. "Here's what we now have." His memorandum listed the twelve weapons:—

1. Colt Pocket Model automatic } *murder weapon*
   Caliber: .25

2. Smith & Wesson .38/32 revolver } *Robert's weapon*
   Caliber: .38

3. Harrington & Richardson Trapper } *Cornelia's weapon*
   Caliber: .22

4. Iver Johnson safety hammerless automatic
   Caliber: .32 Special

5. Schmeisser safety Pocket Model automatic
   Caliber: .25 Automatic

6. Stevens "Off-Hand" single-shot Target
   Caliber: .22 Long Rifle

7. I. J. Champion Target single action
   Caliber: .22

8. Stoeger Luger (Refinished)
   Caliber: 7:65 mm.

9. New Model Mauser (10-shot Magazine)
   Caliber: 7:63 mm.
10. High Standard hammerless automatic Short
    Caliber: .22
11. Browning 1912
    Caliber: 9 mm.
12. Ortgies
    Caliber: 6.35 mm.

"So what?" demanded the Inspector.

"So very little," retorted his son, "except that each one of the guns is of different manufacture. Ought to make the check-back easier. Sergeant, phone Cornwall & Ritchey and get an exact list of the fourteen guns Thurlow purchased."

"Piggott's on that angle."

"Good. Make sure you locate those two missing toys of Thurlow's."

"And while we're playing detective," put in the Inspector dryly, "we might start thinking about who had a motive to want Bob Potts six feet south. We already know who had your blasted whatchamacallit—opportunity."

"I can't imagine who'd want Bob out of the way," muttered Charley. "Except Thurlow, because Robert was always picking on him. But we know Thurlow couldn't have done it."

"Cockeyedest case I ever saw," grumbled the Sergeant. "Guy who fires the shot *can't* be the killer. Say, this chicken salad ain't bad."

"Point is," frowned Inspector Queen, "somebody wanted Robert Potts dead, so somebody had a reason. Maybe if we find the reason we'll find the somebody, too. Any ideas, Ellery?"

Ellery shrugged. "Charley, you're attorney to the family. What are the terms of Cornelia Potts's will?"

Charley looked nervous. "Now wait a minute, Ellery. The Old Woman's very much alive, and the terms of a living testator's will are confidential between attorney and client—"

"Oh, that mullarkey," said the Inspector disgustedly.

"Come on Ellery, we've got to talk to the old gal direct."

"Better take along a bullet-proof vest!" Sergeant Velie shouted after them through the mouthful of chicken salad.

11 . . . "Infer the Motive from the Deed"

"But only for a few minutes, Inspector Queen." Dr. Waggoner Innis was pinch-pale, but he had recovered his stance, as it were; and here, in Cornelia Potts's sitting room, he was very much the tall and splendid Physician-in-Ordinary.

"How is she?" inquired Ellery Queen.

"Nerves more settled, but heart's fluttering badly and pulse could be improved. You've got to co-operate with me, gentlemen—"

"One side, Doctor," said the Inspector; and they entered the Old Woman's bedchamber.

It was a square Victorian room crowded with those gilded phantasms of love which in a more elegant day passed by the name of "art." Everything swirled precisely in a cold paralysis of "form," and everything was expensive and hideous. There were antimacassars on the overstuffed petit-point chairs, and no faintest clue to the fact that a man shared this room with its aged mistress.

The bed was a piece for future archeologists. Its corners were curved, the foot forming a narrower oval than the head. There was no footboard, and the headboard was a single curved piece which extended, unbroken, although in diminishing height, along the sides. Ellery wondered what was wrong with the whole production aside from its more obvious grotesquerie. And then he saw. There were no front legs; the foot of the bed rested on the floor. And since the head stood high, supported on a single thick, tapering block of wood, the sides showed a downward slant, while the spring and mattress had been artfully manufactured to maintain a level. It was all so unbelievable that for a moment Ellery had no eyes for its occupant, but only for her couch.

Suddenly he recognized it for what it was. The bed was formed like a woman's oxford shoe.

The Old Woman lay in it, a lace cap set on her white hair, the silk comforter resting on her plump little stomach. She was propped up on several fat pink pillows; a portable typewriter lay on her thighs; her claws were slowly seeking out keys and upon discovery striking them

71

impatiently. She paid no attention to the four men. Her black eyes were intent on the paper in her machine.

"I told you, Mrs. Potts—" began Dr. Innis peevishly, raising his careful eyes ceilingward—and hastily lowering them, since they had encountered there the painful spectacle of two plaster cupids embracing.

"Shut up, Innis."

They waited for her to complete her inexplicable labors.

She did so with a final peck, ripping the sheet of white paper from the typewriter; quickly she glanced over it, made a snapping movement of her jaws, like an old bitch after flies, then reached for a thick soft-leaded pencil on the bed. She scribbled her signature, picked up a number of similar typewritten white sheets near the portable, signed those; and only then looked up. "What are you men doing in my bedroom?"

"There are certain questions, Mrs. Potts—" began Inspector Queen.

"All right. I suppose I can't be rid of you any other way. But you'll have to wait. Charles!"

"Yes, Mrs. Potts."

"These memos I've just typed. Attend to them at once."

Charley took the sheaf of signed papers she thrust into his hands and glanced through them dutifully. At the last one his eyes widened. "You want me to *sell* your Potts Shoe Company stock—*all* of it?"

"Isn't that what my memorandum says?" snapped the Old Woman. "Isn't it?"

"Yes, Mrs. Potts, but—"

"Since when must I account to you, Charles? You're paid to follow orders. Follow 'em."

"But I don't get it, Mrs. Potts," protested Charley. "You'll lose control!"

"Will I." Her lip curled. "My son Robert was active head of the company. His murder and the scandal, which I tried so hard just now to avoid—" her voice hardened— "will send Potts stock down. If I can't avoid the scandal, at least I can make use of it. Selling my stock will send the price down still further. It opened at 84 this morning. When it hits 72, buy it all back." Charley looked dazed. "Why are you standing here?" shrilled the old lady. "Did you hear what I said? Go and phone my brokers!"

Charley nodded, curtly. As he passed Ellery he muttered: "What price Mama, Mr. Q? Takes advantage of her son's murder to make a few million boleros!" And the young lawyer stamped out.

Dr. Innis bent over the Old Woman with his stethoscope, shook his head, took her pulse, shook his head, removed her typewriter, shook his head, and finally retired to the window to look out over the front lawn, still shaking his head.

"Ready for me now, Madam?" asked the Inspector courteously.

"Yes. Don't dawdle."

"Don't—!" The inspector's hard eyes glittered. "My dear Mrs. Potts," he exclaimed softly, "do you know that I could have you put in jail this minute on a charge of attempting homicide on an officer of the law?"

"Oh, yes," nodded the Old Woman. "But you haven't."

"I haven't! Mrs. Potts, I warn you—"

"Fiddlesticks," she snarled. "I'm much more use to you in my own house. Don't think you're doing me favors, Inspector Queen. I know your kind. You're all nosey, meddling, publicity-seeking grafters. You're in this case for what you can get out of it."

"Mrs. Potts!"

"Stuff. How much d'ye want to pronounce my son's death an accident?"

Mr. Queen coughed behind his hand, watching his father with enjoyment.

But the Inspector only smiled. "You'd play a swell game of poker, Mrs. Potts. You say and do a lot of contradictory things, all to cover up the one thing you're afraid of—that I'll call your bluff. Let's understand each other. I'm going to do my best to find out who murdered your son Robert. I know that's what you want, too, only you're full of cussedness, and you want to do it your own way. But I hold all the cards, and you know that, too. Now you can cooperate or not, as you see fit. But you won't stop me from finding out what I want to know."

The Old Woman glared at him. He glared back. Finally, she wriggled down under her silk comforter like a young girl, sullenly. "Talk or get out. What d'ye want to know?"

"What," said the Inspector instantly, with no trace of triumph, "are the terms of your will?"

Ellery caught the flash from her shoe-buttony eyes, the snick of her jaws. "Oh, that. I don't mind telling you that, if you promise not to give it to the papers."

"That's a promise."

"You, young man? You're his son, aren't you?"

Ellery glanced at her. She glanced away to Dr. Innis. The physician's back was like a wall.

"My will sets forth three provisions," she stated in a flat, cold tone. "First: On my death, my estate is to be divided among my surviving children, share and share alike."

"Yes?" prompted Inspector Queen.

"Second: My husband, Stephen Potts, gets no share at all, neither principal nor income. Cut off. Without a penny." Her jaws snicked again. "I've supported him and Gotch for thirty-three years. That's plenty."

"Go on, Mrs. Potts."

"Third: I am President of the Board of Directors of the Potts Shoe Company. On my death, a new President will have to be elected by the Board. That Board will consist of all my surviving children, and I specifically demand that Simon Underhill, manager of the factories, have one vote, too. I don't know whether this last will hold up in law," she added with the oddest trace of humor, "but I don't imagine anyone involved will take it that far. My word's been law in life, and I guess it'll be law in death. That's all, gentlemen. Get out."

"Extraordinary woman," murmured Ellery as they left Cornelia Potts's apartment.

"This isn't a case for a cop," sighed his father. "It needs the world's ace psychiatrist."

Charley Paxton came running upstairs from the foyer, and the three men paused in the upper hall. "Is Innis with her?" panted Charley.

"Yes. Does he get much of a fee, Charley?" the Inspector asked curiously.

"An annual retainer. A whopper. And he earns it."

The Inspector grunted. "She told us about her will."

"Dad went to work on her," chuckled Ellery. "By the way, Charley, where does she keep that will?"

"With her other important papers in her bedroom."

"Was that typewriting exhibition a few minutes ago something new, Charley?"

"Hell, no. We once had a difference of opinion about one of her innumerable verbal 'instructions.' She claimed she'd told me one thing, and I darned well knew she'd told me another. We had quite a row over it, and I insisted that from then on I wanted written, signed instructions. Only time she and I've agreed on anything. Since then she types out her memos on that portable, and always signs them with one of those soft pencils."

The Inspector brushed this aside. "She told us she'd cut her husband, this Stephen Brent Potts, off without a cent. Is that legal, Charley? I always thought a husband in this state came in for one third of a wife's estate, with two thirds going to the surviving children."

"That's true nowadays," nodded the attorney. "But it's been true only since August 31, 1930. Before that date, a husband could legally be cut out of any share in his wife's estate. And the Old Woman's will antedates August 31, 1930, so it's quite legal."

"Why," asked Ellery pointedly, "is Sheila's father being cut off?"

Charley Paxton sighed. "You don't understand that old she-devil, Ellery. Even though Cornelia Potts married Steve Brent, he never was and never will be a genuine Potts to her except in name."

"A convenience, huh?" asked the Inspector dryly.

"Just about. The children are part of *her,* so they're Pottses. But not Steve. You think Thurlow's got an exaggerated respect for the Potts name? Where do you suppose he got it from? The Old Woman. She's drummed it into him."

"How much is the old witch worth?"

Charley grimaced. "It's hard to say, Inspector. But on a rough guess, after inheritance taxes and so on are deducted, I'd say she'll leave a net estate of around thirty million dollars."

Mr. Queen gurgled.

"But that means," gasped the Inspector, "that when Bob Potts was alive, the Old Woman's six kids would have inherited five million *apiece?"*

"An obscene arithmetic," groaned his son. "Five million dollars left to a woman like Louella!"

"Don't forget Horatio," said Charley. "And for that matter, Thurlow. Thurlow can buy a mess of guns for five million dollars."

"And with Robert out of the way," mused the Inspector, "there's only five to split the loot, so that makes it about *six* million apiece. Robert's murder was worth a million bucks cold to each of the Potts heirs!" He rubbed his hands. "Let's see what we've got. Our active suspects are Cornelia, hubby Steve, Major Gotch, Louella, Horatio, and Mac . . ."

Ellery nodded. "The only ones who had opportunity to switch bullets."

"All right, Cornelia first." The Inspector grinned. "Lord knows I never thought I'd be serious about thinking a mother'd kill her own son, but anything's possible in this family."

Charley shook his head. "It's true she hated Robert—she's always hated the three children of her marriage to Steve—but murder . . ."

"I'm not impressed, either," said Ellery with a frown.

"Unless she's loco in the coco," said the Inspector.

"I think she's sane, Dad. Eccentric, but sane."

"Well, theoretically she's got a hate motive. Now how does Stephen, the husband, stack up?"

"I can't see that Steve would have any motive at all," protested Charley. "Since he's cut out of the will—"

"By the way," interrupted Ellery, "does the whole family know the terms of Cornelia's will?"

Charley nodded. "She's made no bones about it. I'm sure they do. Anyway, with Steve not getting a cent, he'd have nothing to gain financially by cutting down the number of heirs. So I can't see a motive for him."

"Let's not overlook the fact, too," Ellery pointed out, "that Stephen Brent Potts is a perfectly sane man, and perfectly sane men don't murder their sons in cold blood."

"Steve loved Bob, I think, even more than he loves Mac and Sheila. I can't see Steve for a moment."

"How about the old panhandler, Gotch?" demanded the Inspector.

"Nothing to gain financially by Bob's death."

"Unless," said Ellery thoughtfully, "he's in the pay of one of the others."

The Inspector looked startled. "You're kidding."

Ellery smiled. "By the way, I've had a fantastic notion about Gotch. It gives the man a possible motive."

"What's that?" asked both men quickly.

"I'd rather not be explicit now. I've got quite accustomed myself to the timbre of this case—the operatic timbre. I can only conjecture absurdly without intellectual conviction. But Dad, I'd like to see a report on Gotch's background."

"I'll send a couple of cables . . . Now Louella." The Inspector stroked his chin. "Didn't you say you heard her rant about the money she needs for her laboratory 'experiments,' and how Mama turned her down?"

"Seems to me an excellent motive for killing her mother," retorted Ellery, "not Bob. But I grant that Louella gains by Bob's death."

"Then there's Horatio, the Boy Who Never Grew Up—"

"Aaa, Horatio has no interest in money," grunted Charley. "And I don't think he's said ten words to Bob in a year. He gains, but I can't see Horatio as the one behind this."

Ellery said nothing.

"And the twin brother, Maclyn?" asked the Inspector.

Charley stared. "Mac? Kill Bob? That's ridiculous."

"He had opportunity," argued the Inspector.

"But what motive, Inspector?"

"Strangely enough," said Ellery slowly, "Mac had a sounder theoretical motive to seek Bob's death than any other."

"How do you figure that out?" said Charley belligerently.

"Don't get sore, Charley," grinned Mr. Queen. "These are speculations only. Both twins were active vice-presidents of the Potts Shoe Company, weren't they?" Charley nodded. "When the Old Woman dies—an event that, according to Dr. Innis, is imminent—who'd be most likely to take full charge of the business? The twins, of course, who seem to have been the only practical business-men of the family." Ellery shrugged. "I toss it out for what it's worth. The death of his twin brother gives Mac a clear field when his mother yields the reluctant ghost."

"You mean," said Charley incredulously, "Mac might have been jealous enough of Bob to murder him so he could become head of the company?"

"Now that," the Inspector snapped, "is a motive that appeals to me."

Ellery opened his mouth to say something, but at this moment Sergeant Velie came plowing up the stairs, so he refrained.

"I give up," said the Sergeant in disgust. "I and the boys've turned this joint upside down and we can't find those two missing pieces of artillery. We even been in the Old Woman's rooms. She gave us hail Columbia, but we stuck it out. *I* dunno where they are."

"Did you check with Cornwall & Ritchey about what kind of guns those two missing ones were?" asked the Inspector.

Velie looked about cautiously; but the upper hall was deserted. "Get this. The thirteenth rod was a Colt Pocket Model Automatic—*a .25 caliber*—"

"But that's precisely the type of weapon Thurlow used in the duel this morning," Ellery said sharply.

"And the fourteenth was an S. & W. .38/32 with a two-inch barrel—a .38 caliber," Velie nodded.

"Like the one Bob Potts carried!" The Inspector stiffened.

"Yes, sir," said the Sergeant, shaking his head lugubriously, "it's a funny thing, but the two guns missin' are exact duplicates of the two guns used in the duel this mornin'!"

12 . . . *The Importance of Being Dead*

Mac was a puzzle. For the most part he shut himself up in the room he and Robert had shared since their birth, staring at nothing. He was not dazed; he was not grim; he was simply empty, as if the vital fluid in him had drained off. At such times as he quit his room, he wandered about the house with a restless air, as if he were looking for something. Sheila spent hours with him, talking, holding his cold hand. He would only shake his head; "Go to the old man, Sheila. He needs you. I don't."

"But Mac honey—"

"You don't understand, sis."

"No, I don't! You're fretting yourself into a nervous breakdown—"

"I'm not fretting myself into anything." Mac would pat her burnished hair. "Go on to Pop, Sheila. Let me alone."

Once Sheila, herself confused and conflicted, sprang to her feet with the cry: "Don't you realize what's happened? Of all the people, Mac I thought *you*—your own twin . . ."

Mac raised his blue eyes. When Sheila glimpsed the fires raging there, she burst into tears and fled.

It was true: her father needed her more than her brother. Steve Potts crept about the house more timidly than ever, stuttering apologies, getting into everyone's way, and through it all with head cocked, as if he were listening for a distant voice. Sheila walked him in the garden, supervised his feeding, read the *National Geographic* to him, dialed radio programs for him, tucked him into bed. He had taken to sleeping in one of the spare rooms on the top floor; without explanation he had refused any longer to share Cornelia Potts's regal bedchamber.

Major Gotch made overtures in a clumsy way. But for once the little man found no comfort in his bulky friend. He would shake his head at sight of the worn checkerboard, squeeze his lips, squeeze and blink and, wiping his nose with an oversized handkerchief, putter off. Major Gotch spent more and more time alone in the downstairs study, raiding the cigar humidor and the liquor cabinet and brooding over the vacant board.

Then Robert Potts's body was released by the Medical Examiner's office, and it was buried in the earth of Manhattan, which is an odd story in itself, and after that neither his brother Maclyn nor his father Stephen listened for anything, since there is no finality more final than interment, not even death itself.

After that they listened for livelier voices—especially Mac.

Dr. Samuel Prouty, the peppery Assistant Medical Examiner, had known a unique intimacy with thousands of dead men. "A stiff is a stiff," he would say as he sat on the abdomen of a corpse to brace himself for a *rigor mortis* tussle, or struck a match on the sole of a mortified foot. Nevertheless, Doc Prouty showed up in a new derby at Robert Potts's funeral.

Inspector Queen was flabbergasted. "What are *you* doing here, Doc?"

"I thought you was only too glad to get rid of 'em," exclaimed Sergeant Velie, who wore a hunted look these days. "How come you're startin' to follow 'em around?"

"It's a funny thing," said Doc Prouty bashfully. "I don't usually go soft on a cadaver. But this boy's sort of taken my fancy. Nice-looking youngster, and didn't fight me one bit—"

Ellery was startled. "Didn't *fight* you, Doc?"

"Well, sure. Any undertaker'll tell you. Some corpses fight right back, and some co-operate. Most of 'em you can't get to do a blame thing you want. But this Potts boy—he co-operated every inch of the way. I suppose you might say I took a shine to him." Dr. Prouty blushed for the first time within memory of the oldest pensioner. "Least I could do was see him decently buried."

Sergeant Velie backed away, muttering.

As an afterthought, Dr. Prouty said that the autopsy had revealed nothing they did not already know about the cause of Robert Potts's death.

The other interesting element was the burial ground

itself. There was a statute on the New York books which forbids interment of the dead within the confines of Manhattan. A few old city churchyards, however, predating the statute, may still inter fresh dead under certain tiresome restrictions. Usually these interments are restricted to "first families" who have owned plots from time beyond memory.

St. Praxed's had such a yard—that sunken, cramped little cloister off Riverside Drive, a few blocks north of the Potts mansion, where scattered yellow teeth of old graves still protrude from the gums of the earth, and the rest are crypts invisible. How Cornelia Potts muscled into St. Praxed's must ever remain a mystery. It was said that a branch of her New England family had burial rights there, and that she inherited them. Whatever mumbo jumbo the Old Woman performed, the fact was she had legal papers to prove her rights, and so her son Robert Potts was buried there.

Police reserves attended.

Charles Hunter Paxton was beginning to thin out. Mr. Ellery Queen was in an excellent position to observe the progressive attenuation, for the young man had taken to seeking refuge in the Queen apartment, which he roamed like the vanishing buffalo.

"If she'd only listen to reason, Ellery."

"Well, she won't, so be a man and have another drink."

"Why not?"

"Isn't your practice suffering these days, Charley?"

"What practice? Thurlow has no suits to be pressed, and I'm not speaking sartorially. My staff is taking care of the routine Potts work. Wrestling with tax and state problems. The hell with them. I want Sheila."

"Have another drink."

"Don't mind if I do."

The two men filled the Queen apartment with smoke, Scotch bouquet, and endless chatter about the Robert Potts murder. It was maddening how few facts led anywhere. Robert was dead. Someone had stolen into his brother Thurlow's unoccupied room during the eve of the duel and had slipped a live cartridge into Thurlow's Colt .25, removing the blank. Probably the cartridge had been filched from one of the ammunition boxes from Thurlow's bedroom cache; even this was uncertain; for laboratory tests had failed to educe an unarguable conclusion. What had happened to the replaced blank cartridge was any man's guess.

"Anything," said Charley. "Down the toilet drain, or flung into the Hudson."

Ellery looked sour. "Has it occurred to you, Charley, to ask how it came about that somebody made a substitution of bullets at all?"

"Huh?"

"Well, as far as the household knew, that Colt automatic in Thurlow's bedroom the night before the duel was *already* loaded with a live cartridge. *We* know it wasn't, because I'd taken the gun downtown secretly and had Dad slip a blank into it in place of the live ammunition. *We* know that; *how did the murderer know it?* Know it he certainly did, for he subsequently stole into that room, removed the blank Dad had slipped into the magazine, and put a live shell in its place. Any ideas?"

"I can't imagine. Unless you and Sheila and the twins and I were overheard by someone when we discussed the plan in the dining room."

"An eavesdropper?" Ellery shrugged. "Let's drive over to the Potts place, Charley—my head's useless today, and Dad may have turned up something. I haven't heard from him all day."

They found Sheila and her father at the Shoe on the front lawn, old Steve slumped against the pedestal in an attitude of dejection, while Sheila talked fiercely to him. When she spied Ellery and Charley Paxton, she stopped talking. Her father hurriedly swiped at his red eyes.

"Well," smiled Mr. Queen. "Out for an airing?"

"H-hello," stuttered Steve Potts. "Anything n-new?"

"I'm afraid not, Mr. Potts."

The old man's eyes flickered for an instant. "Don't c-call me that, please. My name is Brent." His lips tightened. "Never should have let C-Cornelia talk me into changing it."

"Hello," said Sheila stiffly. Charley glared at her with the hunger of advanced malnutrition. "If you'll excuse my father and me now—"

"Certainly," said Ellery. "By the way, is *my* father in the house?"

"He left a few minutes ago to go back to Police Headquarters."

"Sheila?" said Charley hoarsely.

"No, Charley. Go way."

"Sheila, you're acting like a ch-child," said Steve Potts

fretfully. "Charley, I've been t-trying to get Sheila to forget this s-silliness about not marrying you—"

"Thanks, Mr. Pot—Mr. Brent! Sheila, hear that? Even you own father—"

"Let's not discuss it," said Sheila.

"Sheila, I love you! Let me marry you and take you out of here!"

"I'm staying with Daddy."

"I w-won't have it!" said old Steve excitedly. "I won't have you w-wasting your young life on me, Sheila. You marry Charley and get out of this house."

"No, Daddy."

Ellery sat down on the grass and plucked a blade, examining it studiously.

"No. You and Mac and I have to stick together now— we *have* to. I won't ruin Charley's life by mixing him up in our troubles. I've made my mind up." Sheila whirled on Charley. "I wish Mother'd discharge you, get another lawyer, or something!"

"Sheila, you're not going to get rid of me this way," said young Paxton in a bitter tone. "I know you love me. That's all I give a hoot about. I'll stick around, I'll hound you, I'll climb ladders to your window, I'll send you love letters by carrier pigeon . . . I won't give up, darling."

Sheila threw her arms around him, sobbing. "I do love you, Charley—I do, I do!"

Charles, the Unhappy, was so surprised he lost his opportunity to kiss her.

Sheila put her hands on his chest and pushed, and ran to her father and took his arm and almost dragged him off to the house.

Charley gaped.

Ellery rose from the grass, flinging the dissected blade away. "Don't try to understand it, Charley. Now let's scout around and see if we can't come up with something."

13 . . . Thurlow Potts, Terror of the Plains

Something caught their eye, and they paused in the downstairs study doorway. There was the familiar game table in the center of the study, flanked by the two inevitable chairs; on the table lay the checkerboard; a fierce game was in progress. Major Gotch sat crouched in one of the chairs, his broad black chin on a fist, studying the board with aggressive eyes. The other chair, however, was unoccupied.

Suddenly the old pirate moved a red checker toward the center of the board. He sat back and smacked his thigh, exulting. But then he jumped from his chair, dodged round the table, and sat down in the opposite chair to fall into the same dark brown study over the board. He shook his head angrily, moved a black checker, jumped up, rounded the table again, sat down in the original chair, and with every indication of triumph jumped three black checkers, his red coming to rest with a bang on the black king row. The Major leaned back and folded his thick arms across his chest majestically.

At this point Mr. Queen coughed.

Gotch's arms dropped as he looked around, his ruddy cheeks turning very dark. "Now, I don't like that," he roared. "That's spying. That's a sneaky Maori trick, that is. I mind mine, Mister—mind yours!"

"Sorry," said Ellery humbly. "Come in, Charley—we may as well have a chat with Major Gotch."

"Oh, is that you, Charley?" growled Major Gotch, mollified. "Eyes ain't so good any more. That's different. That's a technical difference, that is."

"Mr. Queen," explained Charley mystified, "is helping to find out who killed Bob, Major."

"Oh, that. Thurlow killed him." The Major spat through one of the French doors onto the terrace, contemptuously.

"Thurlow merely pressed the trigger," sighed Ellery. "There was supposed to be a blank in that Colt, Major Gotch. But there wasn't. Someone substituted a live cartridge during the night."

Major Gotch scraped his jaws. "Well, now," he said. "Wondered what all the boilin' and bubblin' was. But Thurlow thinks he killed Bobby fair and square in that shenanigan."

"I'm afraid Thurlow's still a bit confused," said Ellery sadly. "Major, did you kill Bob?"

"Me? Hell, no." Gotch spat again, calmly. "Too old, Mister. Did my killin' forty, forty-five year ago, round and about." He chuckled suddenly. "We did plenty of it, Steve and me, in our day."

"Steve?" Paxton looked skeptical.

"Well, Steve never had too much pepper for killin', I'll admit that. Sort of took after me, though. Looked up to me like a big brother. Many a time I saved his life from a brownskin's knife. Never could stomach knives, Steve. Too much blood made him sick. Hankered after guns, though."

"Uh ... where did all this manslaughter take place, Major?" asked Ellery courteously.

"Nicaragua. Solomons. Java. One hitch down in Oorgawy."

"Soldiers of fortune, eh?"

The Major shrugged. "Seems to me I told you already."

"Didn't you two gentlemen spend most of your early days in the South Seas and Malaysia?"

"Oh, sure. We were all over. Raised plenty of hell, Steve and me. I remember once in Batavia—"

"Yes, yes," said Ellery hurriedly. "By the way, Major, where were you the other evening? The night before the duel?"

"Bed. Sleepin'. Charley, how about a game of checkers?"

Charley muttered something discouraging.

"And Major." Ellery lit a cigaret scrupulously. "Have you ever been married?"

The old man's jaw dropped. "Me? Hitched? Jipers, no."

"Any idea who might have murdered Robert Potts?"

"Same question that old albatross was askin' me. Nope, not a notion. I'm a man minds his own business, *Tuan*. Live an' let live, that's how I figger it. Sure you won't play a game o' checkers, Charley?"

Charley knocked on the tower door. Louella's bony face appeared behind the glass-protected grille and grinned at them. She unlocked her laboratory door quickly and welcomed them into her den of retorts with a frenetic eagerness that raised lumps on Ellery's scalp. "Come in! So glad you've come to visit me. The most wonderful thing's happened! See—here—" She kept chattering as she bustled them over to her workbench and exhibited a large porcelain pan heaped with some viscid stuff of a greengray, dead color, like sea slime. It had a peculiarly pervasive and unavoidable stench.

"What is it, Miss Potts?"

"My plastic." Louella lowered her voice, looking about. "I think I'm very near my goal. Mr. Mulqueen—I really do. Of course, I put you on your honor not to mention this to *anyone*—even the police. I don't trust police, you know. They're all in the pay of the corporations, and armed with authority as they are, they can come in here and steal my plastic and I wouldn't be able to do a *thing* about it. I know your father is that little man, the Inspector, but Charley's assured me you have no connection with the police department, and—"

Ellery comforted her. "But, Miss Potts, I understood that you needed more funds to carry on your work. I heard your mother refuse you the other evening—"

Louella's dry face twisted with rage. "She'll feel sorry!" she spat. "Oh, that's always the way—the great unselfish ones of science have to accomplish their miracles despite *every* hardship and obstacle! Well, Mother's avarice won't stop *me*. Some day she'll regret it—some day when the name of Louella Potts . . ."

So Louella's tortured strivings in her smelly laboratory were run by the same dark generator that moved Cornelia Potts, and Thurlow Potts, and even Horatio Potts, to glorification and defense of the Name. The Name . . . Mr. Queen could wish it were lovelier.

He asked Louella several offhand questions, calculated not to alarm her. No, she had been in her laboratory, working on her plastic, the night before the duel. Yes, all night. Yes, alone.

"I *like* to be alone, Mr. Mulqueen," she said, her bony face glowing. And, as if her own statement had brought in its train a whole retinue of old black moods, she lost her enthusiasm, her eagerness palled, her face grew sullen, and she said: "I've wasted enough time. Please. If there's nothing else—I have my Work to do."

"Of course, Miss Potts." Ellery moved toward the door; Charley was already there, nibbling his fingernails. "Oh, incidentally," said Ellery lightly, turning around, "do you keep any guns up here? We're trying to round up all the guns in the house, Miss Potts, after that terrible accident to your brother Robert—"

"I hate guns," said Louella, shivering.

"No bullets, either?"

"Certainly not." Her eyes wandered to the dingy mess in the porcelain pan. "Oh, *guns*," she said suddenly. "Yes, they've been inquiring about that. That large man—Sergeant Something-or-other—he forced his way in here and turned my laboratory upside down. I had to hide my plastic under my gown . . ." Her voice became vague.

They fled, depressed.

Dr. Innis was just striding out of Cornelia Potts's apartment when the two men came down from Louella's tower.

"Oh, Doctor. How's Mrs. Potts?"

"Not good, not good, Mr. Queen," said Innis fretfully. "Marked cardiac deterioration. We're doing what we can, which isn't much. I just administered a hypo."

"Maybe we ought to have a consultant in, Dr. Innis," suggested Charley.

Dr. Innis stared as if Charley had struck him. "Of course," he said icily. "If you wish it. But Mr. Thurlow Potts has every confidence in me. I suggest you discuss it with him, and—"

"Oh, come down, Doc," said Charley irritably. "I know you're doing what you can. I just don't want anyone saying we haven't gone through the motions. How about a nurse?"

Dr. Innis was slightly appeased. "You know how she is about nurses. Goes into tantrums. I really feel it would be bad to cross her in that. That old woman in the house—"

"Bridget?"

"Yes, yes. She's adequate." Dr. Innis shook his head. "These heart conditions, Mr. Paxton—we know so little about the heart, there's so little we can do. She's an old lady, and she's driven herself hard. Now this excitement of the past few days has dangerously weakened her, and I'm very much afraid her heart won't hold out much longer."

"Too bad," said Ellery thoughtfully.

Dr. Innis glanced at him in amazement, as if it had never occurred to him that anyone could rue the possible passing of Cornelia Potts. "Yes, certainly," the physician said. "Now if you gentlemen will excuse me—I must phone the pharmacy for some more digitalis." He hurried off with his elegant strides.

They made their way downstairs through the foyer to the French doors leading to the terrace and court. Ellery barely glanced into the study as they passed. He knew that Major Gotch was still hopping from chair to chair, playing checkers with himself.

"Horatio?" sighed Charley Paxton.

"None other."

"You won't get any more out of him than you got out of Louella. Ellery, we're wasting our time."

"I'm beginning to think so. Dad's been all through this, anyway, and he said he'd got exactly nowhere." They paused in the doorway, looking out across the gardens to the multi-colored cottage. "I must have been born under a very subtle curse. I live in hope always that some rationale can be applied to even the most haphazard human set-up. This time I think I'm licked . . . *Voici* Horatio."

The burly figure of Horatio Potts appeared from behind the little house, carrying a long ladder, his red bristles a halo in the sun. He wore filthy ducks tied about his joggled paunch with a piece of frayed rope, and tattered sandals on his broad feet. Perspiration stained his blouse darkly.

"What the devil's he *doing?*"

"Watch."

Horatio padded to the nearest tree, a patriarchal sycamore, and set the ladder against the trunk. Then he began to climb, the ladder protesting clearly all the way across the garden. He disappeared among some lower branches, his fat calves struggling upward, disembodied.

The two men waited, wondering.

Suddenly the legs began to dangle; Horatio appeared again, blowing in triumph. One hand firmly clasped the crosspiece of a kite. Carefully the fat man descended from the tree; then he ran out into the open, busily tying the broken end of the kite cord to a large ball of twine from one of his bulging pockets. In a few moments he had his kite whole again, and Messrs. Queen and Paxton stood some yards away, in a doorway, enjoying the spectacle of an elephantine red-haired man racing with whoops through the gardens to let the wind catch a Mickey Mouse kite and lift it bravely into the air above Riverside Drive, New York City, the United States of America, Planet Earth.

"But I thought you wanted—" began Charley, as Ellery turned back into the house.

"No," growled Ellery. "It wouldn't do any good. Leave Horatio alone with his kites and his picaresque books and his gingerbread house. He's too immersed in the fairy tale he's living to be of any terrestrial use in the investigation of such a grown-up everyday business of murder."

"Strangest case I've ever seen," complained Ellery as they strolled back to the foyer. "Usually you get *somewhere* in questioning the people in an investigation. If they don't tell the truth, at least they tell lies, which are often more revealing than truths. But in this Potts fantasy—nothing! They don't even know what you're talking about. Their answers sound like Esperanto. First time in my life I've felt completely disheartened in such an early stage."

"Now you know why I want to get Sheila out of here," said Charley quietly.

"I certainly do." Ellery stopped short. "Now what's *that?*"

They were at the foot of the spiral staircase. Somewhere beyond the upper landing raged a bedlam of thumpings, yells and cracking furniture. There was nothing playful in these sounds. If murder was not being committed upstairs, it was at the very least assault and battery with murderous intent.

Ellery took the staircase in rejuvenated bounds: violence was an act, and acts are measurable; something had broken out into the open at last. . . . A little way down the foyer, Major Gotch thrust a startled head out of the study. Seeing the two young men speed upstairs, and hearing the noise, the Major thundered out, tightening his belt.

Ellery followed his ears; they led him to Maclyn Potts's room.

Mac and his eldest brother were rolling over and over on the bedroom floor, bumping into the twin beds, in the débris of the overturned and splintered night table and its lamp. Mac's shirt was torn and there were four angry parallel gouges on his right cheek all bleeding. Thurlow's cheeks were gory, already turning purple in splotches. Both were screaming curses as they wrestled; and each was quite simply trying to kill the other with his bare hands. Mac, being younger, hard, and quicker, was closer to his objective. Thurlow looked forlorn.

Ellery plucked the younger man from the floor and held him fast; Charley pounced on Thurlow. Thurlow's little eyes were shooting jets of hate across the disordered bedroom through swollen blackening lids.

"You killed my brother!" shouted Mac, struggling in Ellery's arms. "You killed him in cold blood and I'll make you pay for it, Thurlow, if I have to go to the Chair!"

Thurlow deliberately rolled over, avoiding Charley Paxton's frantic clutch, and scrambled to his feet. He began to paw his baggy tweeds with blind, bleeding strokes.

Sheila and her father ran in, brushing Major Gotch aside. The Major had chosen to remain a spectator.

"Mac, what's happening?" Her eyes widened. "Did he—" Then Sheila sprang at Thurlow, and he cringed. "Did you try to kill my brother Mac, too?" she shrieked. *"Did* you?"

"Mac, y-your face," stammered his father. "It's all b-bloody!"

"His damned womanish fingernails," panted Mac. "He doesn't even fight like a man, Pop." He pushed Ellery away. "I'm all right, thanks."

Thurlow uttered a peculiar sound. Where his face was not puffed and stained, it was deadly white. His fat cheeks sucked in and out nervously; he kept trying not to lick his cracked lips. There was intense pain on his face. Slowly Thurlow took a handkerchief from his hip pocket, slowly unfolded it, grasped it by one corner and walked over to his brother. He flicked the handkerchief across Mac's wounded cheek.

As in a dream, they heard his voice.

"You've insulted me for the last time, Maclyn. I'll kill you just the way I killed Robert. This can only be wiped out in blood. Meet me at the Shoe tomorrow at dawn. I'll get two more guns—they've taken all of mine. Mr. Queen, will you do me the honor of acting for me once again?"

And, before they could recover from their astonishment, Thurlow was gone.

"I'll meet you!" Mac was roaring. "Bring your guns, Thurlow! Bring 'em, you murdering coward!"

They were holding him down forcibly—Ellery, Charley, Major Gotch. Steve Potts had dropped into a chair, to look at his writhing son without hope.

"You don't know what you're saying, Mac. Stop it, now. Daddy, do something. Charley . . . Mr. Queen, you can't let this happen again. Oh God," Sheila sobbed, "I'm going mad myself . . ."

Her terror brought Mac to his senses. He ceased struggling, shook off their arms. Then he twisted to lie prone on his bed, face in his hands.

Ellery and Charley half-carried Sheila into the hall. "That maniac—he'll kill my Mac," she wept. "The way he killed Bobby. You've got to stop Thurlow Mr. Queen. Arrest him—something!"

"Stop your hysterics, Sheila. Nothing's going to happen. There won't be another duel. I promise you."

When Charley had led Sheila off, still crying, Ellery stood for a moment outside Mac's room. Steve Potts was trying to soothe his son in an ineffectual murmur. Major Gotch's brassy voice was raised in a reminiscence half biography and half advice, and concerned a Borneo incident in which the artful use of knee and knife had saved his younger, more valuable life.

From Mac silence.

Ellery ran his hand desperately through his hair and hurried downstairs to telephone to his father.

14 . . . Mac Solves the Mystery

The old woman suffered a heart attack that evening. For a few moments Ellery suspected malingering. But when Dr. Innis, hastily summoned, took over, and Ellery permitted himself an oral expression of his cynicism, without a word the physician handed him the stethoscope. What Ellery heard through those sensitive microphones banished all suspicions and gave him a respect for Dr. Innis he had not had before. If the Pasteur of Park Avenue had kept this wheezing, stopping, skipping, racing organ from ceasing to function altogether, then he was a very good man indeed.

Cornelia Potts lay gasping high on pillows. Her lips were cyanosed and her eyes, deeply socketed, in agony. With each breath she flung herself upward, as if to engulf the elusive air with her whole body.

Dr. Innis busied himself with hypodermics under Ellery's eye. After a few minutes, seeing the Old Woman's struggles for breath subside a little, he left on tiptoe. Outside the Old Woman's door he found Detective Flint.

"Old Woman kick the bucket?" Flint inquired with a hopeful inflection. When Ellery shook his head, Flint shook his. "Got a message for you from the Sarge. He's tailing Thurlow."

"Thurlow's left the house?" Ellery said quickly.

"A couple of minutes ago. Sergeant Velie's hangin' on to his tail like a tick, though."

"I suppose Thurlow's in quest of two more revolvers," mused Ellery. "Let me know when he gets back, will you, Flint?" He went into Mac's room. Major Gotch had vanished for some hole of his own in the vast building, but Stephen Potts was hovering over his son's bed, and Sheila and Charley Paxton.

"I don't know what you're all hanging around me for," Mac was saying listlessly as Ellery came in. The twin of dead Robert lay on his back, staring at the ceiling. "I'm fine. Don't treat me as if I were a baby. I'm all right, I tell you. Pop, go to bed. Let me alone. I want to sleep."

"Mac, you're planning to do something foolish." Sheila held tightly to her brother's hand.

"He wants a duel, he'll get a duel."

Old Steve made washing ~~motions with his gnarled hands.~~

Ellery said: "Did you people know that Mrs. Potts has had a heart attack?"

It was cruel, but informative. Perhaps not so cruel, considering the startled hope that sprang into those faces, and the slow turn of Mac's head.

Sheila and her father ran out.

It took Charley and Ellery until past midnight to get Mac Potts to sleep. By the time they left his room and shut the door softly, Cornelia Potts not far along the hall was also in a deep sleep. They met Sheila and her father coming wearily out of the Old Woman's apartment with Dr. Innis.

"Condition's improved," said the doctor briefly. "I think she'll pull through this one. Amazing woman. But I'll stay here for another hour or so, anyway." He waved and returned to his patient.

Ellery sent Sheila and Stephen Potts to bed. They were both exhausted. Charley, who looked in hardly better case, commandeered a spare room, recommended that Ellery do the same, and trudged off after Sheila.

Mr. Queen was left alone in the upper hall. He spent much time there, smoking cigarets and pacing before the silent row of doors.

At 1:10 A.M. Thurlow Potts came home. Ellery heard him tottering upstairs. He dodged into the entrance to the turret staircase; Thurlow passed him, lurching. The elder Potts was toting a badly wrapped package. He meandered down the hall and finally wandered into his own rooms.

A moment later Sergeant Velie came upstairs, softly.

"Guns, Sergeant?"

"Yeah. Scared up some old bedbug in a hockshop down on West Street who sold 'em to him." Velie kept his eye on Thurlow's door. "Two big babies. I couldn't go in and find out what they were or I would a lost *my* bedbug. They looked heavy enough to sink a sub."

"Why so late?"

"He stopped into a row of gin mills on his way back. Got tanked to the eyeballs. For a little guy he sure can lap it up." The Sergeant chuckled. "Mr. Thurlow Potts ain't doin' any dueling tonight. I can tell you that. This is one that gets slept off, brother, unless he's been kiddin' me."

"Good work, Velie. Wait till he falls asleep. Then go in there and take that package away from him."

"Yes, sir."

Ten minutes later Sergeant Velie slipped out of Thurlow's apartment with the poorly tied package in his arms.

"Beddy-by," grinned the Sergeant. "Flopped on his flop with his clothes on, and he's snorin' away like a water buffalo. What do I do now?"

"Give me the package for one thing," replied Ellery, "and for another get some sleep. Tomorrow I think, will be a large fat day."

Velie yawned and went downstairs. Ellery saw him stretch out in a plush chair in the foyer, tip his hat over his eyes, fold his hands on his hard stomach; heard him settle back with voluptuous sighs.

Ellery opened the package. It contained two colossal revolvers, single-action Colt .45's, the weapon that played so important a role in the winning of the West. "Six-shooters, by thunder!" He hefted one of the formidable guns and wondered how Thurlow had ever expected to handle it: its shape and the size of its grip were adapted for big brawny hands, not the pudgy little white hands of the Thurlow Pottses of this world. Both guns were loaded.

Ellery retied the package, placing it at his feet, and curled up on the top step of the spiral staircase.

At 2:30 Dr. Innis emerged from the Old Woman's apartment, yawning. "She'll sleep through the night now, Mr. Queen. This last hypo injection would put an elephant to sleep. 'Night."

"Good night, Doctor."

"I'll be back first thing in the morning. She's in no danger." Dr. Innis trudged downstairs and disappeared.

Ellery rose, clutching Thurlow's newest arsenal, and made a noiseless tour of the floor. When he had satisfied himself that everyone was asleep, or at least in his room, he hunted up an empty bedroom on the top floor, flung himself on the bed with his arms about Thurlow's package, and fell instantly asleep.

At six o'clock sharp, in the red-gold of a charming dawn, Thurlow Potts dashed out of the Potts Palace and raced down the steps to the Shoe. He stopped short. A delegation awaited him.

Inspector Queen, Sergeant Velie, Sheila and her father, Charles Hunter Paxton, a half-dozen plainclothes men, and Ellery Queen.

"My guns!" Thurlow saw the package in Ellery's hands, beaming with relief. "I was *so* alarmed," he said, wiping his forehead with a silk handkerchief. "But I might have known as my second you'd take care of everything, Mr. Queen."

Mr. Queen did not reply.

"Is everything ready for the duel, gentlemen?"

Inspector Queen spat out the end of his first cheroot of the day. "There's going to be no duel, Mr. Potts. Understand that? I'll repeat it for your benefit. There's going to be no duel. Your dueling days are over. And if you want to argue about it, there are plenty of judges available. Now how about it? Will you settle this fight with your brother sensibly or do I swear out a warrant for your arrest?"

Thurlow blinked.

"Ellery, get this boy Mac down here. You said last night over the phone he'd threatened to kill Thurlow. Get him down here and we'll settle this foolishness once and for all."

Ellery nodded and went back into the house. It was quiet; no servants stirred as yet; Dr. Innis had arrived fifteen minutes before and gone into Cornelia Potts's room with the same heavy tread which had carried him out of the house a few hours earlier.

Ellery went to Mac's door. It was a silent door.

"Mac?"

There was no answer. He opened the door.

Mac was lying on his back in bed, covered to the chin, a very peaceful young man. His eyes were open.

But Mr. Queen's eyes were open, too—wide. He ran over to the bed and pulled back the cover.

Some time during the night Maclyn Potts had solved the mystery of his brother's death. For his brother's murderer had visited him here, and he had looked with those staring eyes upon that creature, and that creature had left behind a hard reflection of his nature—a bullet in Mac's heart.

Ellery stood still, his heart pounding. He felt himself growing enraged. And then a coldness settled down on him. His eyes narrowed. The pillow on which Mac's head rested showed powder burns and one bullet hole.

There were some strange marks on Mac's face—long thin blue marks. As if the second twin had been whipped.

On the empty bed of departed Robert there stood a bowl of gold-spotted liquid. Ellery sniffed it, touched its bland surface with a cautious finger tip. It was cold chicken broth.

He looked around. The door through which he had just come ... A little behind it lay a crop, a crop such as horsemen use to whip their mounts. And, near it, a small revolver with a familiar look.

PART THREE

15 . . . And Whipped Them All Soundly and Put Them to Bed

Dr. Samuel Prouty, Assistant Medical Examiner of New York County, squinted past his fuming cigar at the body of Maclyn Potts and said through his stained teeth: "I've seen a lot of monkey business but the Potts madness passeth understanding. I can't even bellyache any more. It's too fascinating."

"Spare me your fascinations, Prouty," snarled Inspector Queen, glaring at Mac's corpse with bitterness.

"Those marks on his face," said Dr. Prouty thoughtfully. "Very provocative. I tell you, boys, Freud's at the bottom of this."

"Who?" asked Sergeant Velie.

"Perhaps," remarked Ellery Queen, "perhaps Sigmund's dark land is, Prouty; but I do believe we can touch on nearer shores, if you're referring to the welts on poor Mac's face."

"What d'ye mean, Ellery?" frowned Doc Prouty.

"Not very much, Doc."

The Potts mansion was quiet. The mud had been roiled and beaten; now it settled into new patterns. Mac's body lay on his bed, as Ellery had found it. Nothing had been disturbed except the weapon, which had been taken downtown for ballistics examination.

The photographer, the fingerprint crew, had come and gone. These had been dutiful motions, for the sake of the record. The photographs preserved forever the visual memory of the scene; the fingerprints had no significance except to satisfy the undiscriminating appetite of routine and regulation. They told a story Inspector Queen already knew. Those who were known to have visited deceased's room since its last cleaning by the housemaids had left the marks of their hand there; of those who were not known to have visited the room, there was no fingerprint evi-

95

dence. But this could have been because the murderer of Maclyn Potts wore a protective covering on the hands.

Ellery was inclined to this theory. "The fact that no prints at all have been found on the pistol, on the riding crop, or on the bowl of broth indicates gloves, or a very careful wiping off of prints afterwards." In any event, the fingerprints that were present and those that were not had no clue or evidential value.

"When was the boy murdered, Doc?" asked the Inspector.

"Between three and four A.M."

"Middle of the night, huh?" said the Sergeant, who had a passion for simplification.

"The shot was fired through the pillow." Ellery pointed to the powder burns and the bullet hole.

"That's why no one heard it," his father nodded.

"Probably," reflected Ellery, "when the killer stole in here at three or four A.M. Mac's head had either slipped off the pillow in his sleep or was resting on one corner of it, so that his murderer easily slipped it from under his head. Certainly Mac didn't wake up until a second or two before the shot was fired, otherwise there'd be signs of a tussle, and there aren't."

"Maybe the picking up of the pillow was what woke him," suggested Velie.

Ellery nodded. "Quite possibly. But he had no time to do more than stare at the face bent over him. The next moment he was dead."

Dr. Prouty shivered the least bit. "The things people do."

Inspector Queen had no mind for moralizing; upon him lay the pressure. "Then after the shot was fired, this killer stuck the pillow back under Mac's head——"

"Neat soul," murmured Mr. Queen. "Yes, the things people do . . ."

"And took that riding crop and smacked the boy over the face with it? Is that the way it happened, Doc?"

"Yes," said Prouty, gazing at the thin blue welts, "the whipping was administered shortly after death, not before. I'd say within seconds. Yes, he dropped the gun and picked up the crop and whacked away. I'd say he whacked away even before he replaced the pillow, Dick."

Inspector Queen shook his head. "It's beyond me."

"But not beyond Mr. Queen," boomed the Sergeant. "This is the kind of stuff you specialize in, ain't it, Mr. Queen?"

Mr. Queen did not react to this obvious sarcasm.

"And another thing," grumbled the Inspector. "That bowl of soup. For Mike's sake, did this crazy killer bring up a midnight snack with him?"

"How d'ye know he brought it up for himself?" argued the Sergeant. "Maybe he was bringin' it up to this young guy. In case Mac woke up and said, 'What the hell are you doin' in my bedroom at four o'clock in the morning, you so-an-so?' Then he could show the bowl of soup and say: 'I figgered you might want some soup before the duel. Chicken broth is swell just before duels,' he could say. Get his confidence, see? Then—whammo! And he's killed another chicken." The Sergeant flushed in the silence. "Anyway," he said doggedly, "that's the way *I* look at it."

"When I said 'midnight snack,' Velie," said the Inspector, softly savage, "I was just trying to express in my crude way the fact that this is a wacky kill, Velie—madness—lunacy. Ellery, what are some more synonyms? Velie, dry up!"

"Okay, okay."

"The strange part of the Sergeant's theory," murmured Ellery, "is not its wrongness, but its rightness."

His father stared, and Velie looked amazed.

"Oh, it's not right," Ellery hastened to add. "It's all wrong, in fact. But it's on the right track. I mean it's a reasonable theory—it attempts to put a reasonable construction on an absurdity. And that's definitely correct, Dad."

"You're getting deluded, too, Ellery," said Doc Prouty.

"Not at all. This bowl of chicken broth was brought up here by the killer—incidentally, it *was* the killer, because the soup wasn't here when I left Mac asleep in bed last night—and, what's more, the killer brought the soup up for a completely logical reason."

"To eat it?" sneered the Inspector. "Or to have Maclyn Potts eat it?"

"No, it wasn't brought here to be eaten, Dad."

"Then why?"

"For the same reason the crop was brought ... *and used*. By the way, whose riding crop is it, Dad? Have you identified it yet?"

"It belonged to Mac himself," replied the Inspector with a sort of frustrated satisfaction, as if to say: And see what you can make out of that little pearl of information!

"And the soup and bowl?"

"From the kitchen. That Mrs. Whatsis, the cook, says she always keeps chicken broth handy in the refrigerator. The Old Woman has to have it."

"So this killer," said Sergeant Velie, undaunted, "this killer, before he comes up to the future scene of his foul crime, this killer goes downstairs to the kitchen, takes a bowl, fills it up with cold soup from the icebox, and pussyfoots it upstairs here. There's even a splash or two on the staircase, where the soup slopped over as he carried it up. Cold soup," he said thoughtfully. "I've heard of jellied soup," he said, "and hot soup, but just plain cold soup . . ."

"Don't fret yourself into a breakdown over it, Velie," yipped Inspector Queen. "Just check back with downtown and see if they've done a ballistics yet on that rod. Ellery, come on."

Dr. Prouty left, reluctantly, saying to Mr. Queen that this was one case he wished he could follow through *ex officio*, you lucky dog, you. The body was to be picked up and carted down to the Morgue for routine autopsy, but nothing more could be expected in the way of discoveries: the mouth had shown no trace of soup, or poison, death resulted from one .38-caliber bullet in the heart, and so it was all dirty work from here on in, and he didn't even think he'd attend the funeral. (*Exit* Dr. Prouty.)

Inspector Queen and his son made a grand tour of the mansion before retiring for further conversations.

These were dreary rounds. Sheila lay on a chaise longue in her boudoir without tears, staring at her ceiling. (Mr. Queen was uneasily reminded of her brother, who lay in a similar attitude a few doors down the hall, not breathing.) Charley Paxton kept chafing Sheila's hands, his swollen eyes fixed fearfully on her expressionless face. It was Stephen Brent Potts's voice which emerged, almost without stuttering, in loving reassurance.

"There's no sense in giving in, Sheila lambie," he was saying as the Queens stole in. "Mac's dead. All right, he's dead. M-murdered. What are we supposed to do—commit suicide? Curl up and d-die? Sheila, we'll fight back. We're not alone, baby. The p-police are our friends. Charley's on our sis-side . . . Aren't you, Charley?" Old Steve dug Charley sharply in the ribs.

"I love you, darling," was all Charley could say as he chafed Sheila's cold hands.

"Don't lie there that way, Sheila," old Steve said desperately. "Do you want a doctor?"

"No." Sheila's voice was faint.

"If you don't snap out of this, I'll call one. I'll call two. I'll make your life miserable. Sheila honey, don't go under. Talk to me!"

"Never would have believed it of the old duck," muttered the Inspector as he and Ellery left, unobserved. "Of all these people, he's the one with guts. Where's that sucker Gotch?"

"Taking a nap in his room, Velie told me." Ellery seemed pained by the memory of that white, frozen face.

"Taking a nap!"

"Steve sent him to bed. It seems," growled Mr. Queen, "that the worm has turned and, coincidentally with the illness of his mate and the murder of his second son, has developed hair on his chest. I like that little man."

"Like—dislike!" raved his father. "Who cares how wonderful they are? I want to see this case solved and get the kit and caboodle of 'em out of my hair! What did he send Gotch to bed for?" he asked suspiciously.

"Gotchie-boy has been 'worrying' about him too much, it appears. Hasn't had his proper rest. Stephen Brent Potts version."

"Gotchie-boy has been hitting the bottle too much, that's what Gotchie-boy's been doing," rasped the Inspector. "If this ain't all a smoke screen. I don't get that old pirate at all."

"It's very simple, Dad—he found snug harbor, and he's dug in like a barnacle. By the way, have you had a report on the Major yet?"

"Not yet."

They hunted Louella in her ivory tower, they took wing and visited Horatio in his house in the clouds, they returned to the Palace and looked in on Thurlow. Louella was still creating sea slime in her porcelain pans. Horatio was still wielding a quill on the greater *Mother Goose*— wielding it even more zestfully. And Thurlow was sleeping like a just man who has offered to do the honorable thing and been absolved by forces beyond a chevalier's control. An aroma of alcohol hovered over his pillow, like angel's wings.

Nothing had changed except that, as Horatio Potts put it, looking up from his versifying, "one person less lives in the house."

The Inspector crossed lances with Dr. Innis upstairs in Cornelia Potts's sitting room. The Inspector was determined to speak with mother of deceased; Dr. Innis was equally determined that the Inspector should not speak to mother of deceased.

"Unless," said Dr. Innis stiffly, "you promise you won't mention this latest development, Inspector."

"Promise your jaundiced liver," said the Inspector. "What would I want to speak to her about if not this 'latest development,' as you put it so delicately?"

"Then I'm sorry. She's a very sick woman. The shock of another murder—another son's death—would undoubtedly kill her on the spot."

"I doubt it, Doctor," said the Inspector grumpily; but he gave up the joust and took Ellery down to the study. "Sit down, son," sighed the old gentleman. "You generally have a cockeyed slant on cockeyed cases. How about squinting at this one? I'm groggy."

"I'm a little crocked myself," admitted Ellery with a wry smile.

"Sure, but what are you thinking?"

"Of Bob. Of Mac. Of life and death and how ineffectual people really are. Of Sheila . . . What are *you* thinking?"

"I don't know what to think. In the past this family of drizzle-birds, while they've been mixed up in plenty of trouble, have always wound up in the civil courts. Little stuff, inflated big. But now murder! And two in a row . . . I'm thinking something's been smoking under the surface for a long time. I'm thinking the fire's broken through. And I'm thinking: Is it out, or isn't it?"

"You think there may be further attempts?"

The Inspector nodded. "It might be just the beginning of a plot to wipe out the lot of them. Not that that wouldn't be a good thing," he added dourly. "Except that I wish they'd started on the nuts rather than those two nice young fellas."

"Yes," said Ellery grimly.

"Is that all you're going to say—'yes?' Then there's this crazy lashing of Mac Potts's dead face. That looks to me like pure hate—psychopathic. The chicken broth certainly indicates an unbalanced mind, in spite of that fancy speechifying you made upstairs to Velie."

"But the whipping and the leaving of a bowl of chicken broth are easy, Dad," said Ellery patiently. "As I said, they were both introduced into the murder's stew for identical reasons."

"Flog a corpse—leave soup around." The Inspector shook his head. "You'll have to show me, son."

"Certainly." And Ellery paused a moment. Then he did

the most absurd thing. He began to chant, with an expression of utter gravity, a nursery rhyme:—

"There was an old woman who lived in a shoe,
She had so many children she didn't know what to do.
She gave them some broth without any bread,
And whipped them all soundly, and put them to bed."

And Mr. Queen clasped his hands behind his head and gazed steadily at his father.

His father's eyes were like new quarters.

"The Old Woman," continued Ellery quietly. "She lives in a Shoe—or rather a house that the Shoe built. And there's even a nice, literal Shoe on the front lawn. She has so many children . . . yes, indeed. Six! That she doesn't know what to do with them I should think is evident to anyone; all her eccentricity and cruelty are masks for her frustration and helplessness."

"She gave them some *broth*," muttered the Inspector. "That chicken broth in Mac's room!"

"Without any bread," his son added dryly. "Don't overlook that precious coincidence. Or perhaps you're not aware that on Dr. Innis's orders Mrs. Potts may not eat bread, and consequently she serves none at her table."

"And *whipped* them all soundly—!"

"Yes, or at any rate whipped Mac. And the bed motif? Mac was killed in bed. You see?"

The Inspector jumped up, fire-red. "No, blast it, I don't see! Nobody could make me believe—"

"But you do believe, Dad," sighed Ellery. "You're terribly impressed. A number of people crazy, and now apparently a series of crimes following a Mother Goose pattern. Well, of course. Would crazy people commit rational crimes? No, no. Crazy people would commit crazy crimes. Mother Goose crimes . . . Don't you see that you're *supposed* to believe in the lunacy of these two crimes? Don't you see that a *sly brain is creating an atmosphere of madness,* or rather utilizing the one that exists, *in order to cloak the reality?* And what could madness cloak but sanity?"

The Inspector drew a grateful breath. "Well, well. And I'd have fallen for it, too. Of course, son. This is the work of a sane one, not a crazy one."

"Not necessarily."

The Inspector's jaw dropped.

Ellery smiled. "We just don't know. I was merely expounding an attractive theory. As far as logic is concerned, this might well be the work of a madman."

"I wish you'd make up your mind," said his father irritably.

Ellery shrugged. "You've got to have more than theories to bring to the District Attorney."

"Let's get on with it, let's get on with it!"

"All right, we'll proceed on the rational theory. What comes to mind immediately?"

The Inspector said promptly: "We're supposed to pin this on Horatio Potts. *He's writing a modern 'Mother Goose.'* "

Ellery laughed. "You saw that, you old fox."

"Plain as the nose on your face. If this is the work of a sane mind, then Horatio is being framed for the murders of his two half-brothers."

"Yes, indeed."

"Horatio being framed . . . why, the man hardly knows what's going on!"

"Don't be too sure of that," said Ellery, knitting his brows. "Horatio's a good deal of a *poseur*. He knows lots more than he lets on.

"*Now* what d'ye mean?"

"Just speculating, Dad. The man's not a fool. Horatio has an unorthodox slant on life and a great cowardice where adult problems are concerned, but he's aware of the score at all times. Believe me."

"You're no help at all," grumbled the Inspector. "All right, score or no score, Horatio's supposed to take the rap; we're to think he's behind all this. That means he isn't."

"Not necessarily," said Ellery.

"*Will* you stick to one point of view?" howled the Inspector, now maddened beyond reason. His face was very red indeed. "Look," he began again, desperately. "Certain things we *know*—"

"You wouldn't be referring," asked Ellery, "to the arithmetic involved?"

"Yes, the arithmetic involved! When all six children were alive, each one stood to come into five millions at the death of the Old Woman. Then Robert Potts was knocked off, leaving five. Now Mac's gone, leaving four. Four into thirty millions makes seven and a half million apiece—*so the murder of the twins means over two and a half million bucks extra* to each of the four surviving children!"

"I can't get excited over a mere two and a half million," moaned Mr. Queen. "I doubt if anyone could, where five millions are guaranteed. Oh, well, I'm probably wrong. It's your fault for having brought into the world the son of a poor man, Dad."

Providentially, Sergeant Velie came in.

Velie tramped in to ease his two hundred and twenty-five pounds into Major Gotch's favorite chair. He was yawning.

"Well?" snapped the Inspector, turning the wind of his fury on this more vulnerable vessel.

The Sergeant looked pained. "What did I do now? Don't follow orders, get bawled out. Follow orders—"

"What order are you following now?"

"The ballistics check-up."

"Well, what do you think this is, the gentlemen's lounge at the Grand Street Turkish Baths? Report!"

"Yes, sir." Velie rose with a noticeable lack of fatigue. "The Lieutenant says the gun found on the floor upstairs is the gun with which Maclyn Potts was homicidally and with murderous intent shot to death—"

"That," said the Inspector, spreading his hands to Ellery, "is news, is it not? The gun is the gun. We're certainly progressing! What else?"

"That's all," said the Sergeant sullenly. "What did you expect, Inspector—the Lieut should come up with the name of the killer?"

"Just what kind of gun was it, Sergeant?" interposed Ellery. "I didn't get a good look at it."

"It's a Smith & Wesson .38/32 revolver, 2-inch barrel, takes an S. & W. .38 cartridge—"

Mr. Queen gave voice to a strangled exclamation.

His father stared. "What's the matter? Sick?"

Ellery sprang to his feet. "Sick! Don't you recall the fourteen guns Thurlow bought at Cornwall & Ritchey's? Don't you remember that you've accounted for only twelve? Don't you remember that two guns are missing, that the missing guns are exact duplicates of the two used in the Bob-Thurlow duel—don't you remember that, according to the store's check list, *one of those two missing guns is a Smith & Wesson .38/32 with a 2-inch barrel?* And now you tell me the gun which shot Mac Potts to death last night is a Smith & Wesson .38/32 with a 2-inch barrel!"

After a long time the Inspector choked: "Velie, phone the Lieutenant at H.Q. and get the serial number of the

gun in Maclyn Potts's murder. Then phone Cornwall &
Ritchey and get the serial number of the missing Smith &
Wesson. Right away, please."

Dazed by this politeness, Sergeant Velie staggered out.
Five minutes later he returned with the information that
the Smith & Wesson which had taken Mac's life was the
same Smith & Wesson that appeared on the check list as
unaccounted for.

One of the two missing revolvers had been found.

"Clearer and foggier," moaned Inspector Queen. "Now
we know why the killer of Robert hid two of the fourteen
guns Thurlow bought—to use one of 'em, the S. & W., for
a second murder."

"The murder of Mac," put in Velie, the simplifier.

"That's certainly the look of it," Ellery mumbled. "But
why did he steal and hide *two* guns?"

Sergeant Velie's face fell. "You mean we ain't
through?"

"Of course we 'ain't' through!" snarled his superior.
"Two guns missing, one of 'em turns up in a murder, so
what would the killer be doing with the other if he isn't
planning still another killing?"

"A third murder," Ellery muttered. "Everything points
to it. Not only the missing guns . . ." He shook his head.

"Then we got to find that last gun—the colt .25 automatic that didn't turn up," said the Sergeant with a groan,
"or go fishin' for dreams."

"Not that finding the missing Colt would necessarily
stop a third murder," Ellery pointed out. "We have no
Achilles here, and there are more ways of killing than by
an arrow. But finding the missing Colt might uncover a
clue to the person who secreted it. By all means search for
it. And at once."

"But where?" whined the Sergeant. "My gosh, we've
turned this coocoo's nest upside down, and not only the
house but the grounds, too. It's a pipe to hide a little bitty
thing like that vest-pocket Colt in a square block of house
and grounds! It would take twelve squads twenty-four
weeks—"

The Inspector said: "Find that gun Velie."

16 . . . And Then There Were None

But Sergeant Velie did not find that gun. Nor Sergeant Velie, nor Detectives Flint, Piggott, Hesse, Johnson, and company, searching at all hours, in odd places, under irritated or indifferent or astonished noses.

There were days of this fruitless exploration in the Potts mansion and on the Potts grounds, and while some interesting exhibits were turned up—a Spanish leather chest, for instance, buried behind Horatio's cottage and filled with broad and crooked coins which Mr. Queen delightedly pronounced to be pieces of eight, at the disinterment of which Horatio went into a tantrum and howled that it had taken him years to gather an authentic Spanish "treasure" and a week of dark nights with an iron lantern and a cutlass between his jaws to bury it, and he wasn't going to stand by and see a lot of cursed policemen spoil his fun—the duplicate Colt Pocket Model .25 automatic remained in the limbo of lost things. The cursed policemen tramped off on aching feet, leaving Horatio to reinter his pirate's chest angrily.

Inspector Queen staged a mild tantrum himself, but for other reasons.

Then Mac was buried in the family plot at St. Praxed's churchyard. A section four blocks square was roped off for the ceremony, traffic was re-routed, and police cordons exercised their muscles.

Somehow Cornelia Potts, recovering from her heart attack in the big house, learned of her son's death.

The first inkling that the Old Woman knew came on the morning of her son's funeral. She sat up in bed and called for her maid, a woman almost as old as she, Bridget Conniveley by name, whom Dr. Innis detested. Od Bridget, who was a bent and sibilant crone, threw over the yoke of the Old Woman's authority and telephoned Dr. Innis. Innis came rushing over, pale and stammering. It was impossible. He could not be responsible. She must be sensible. She could no nothing more for Maclyn. He forbade her to leave her bed.

To all this the Old Woman said nothing. She calmly crept out of bed and flayed Bridget with her tongue. Bridget scurried, cowering, to draw her mistress's bath.

When the Inspector heard about it from the detective on guard outside the Old Woman's apartment, his face glowed with a dark joy. "Mustn't talk to her, huh?" he said to Dr. Innis. And he strode by into the Presence.

It was a short, bitter interview. The Old Woman spoke scarcely at all. What she did say was acrid and precise. No, nobody had told her. She just "knew." And she was going to Maclyn's funeral; the State Militia could not stop her. Get out and let an old woman dress, you fool.

The Inspector got out. "It's a cinch little Thurlow spilled the beans to Mama," he grunted. "What a bunch!"

Cornelia Potts was assisted from her Palace by Dr. Innis and Bridget Conniveley, wrapped in shawls, only the buttery tip of her nose showing. Her expression was one of gloomy interest. She shed no tears, nor would she gaze upon her son's face before the mortician's assistant closed the coffin.

At St. Praxed's Ellery kept watching her with amazement. That aged heart, to whose stuttering and whimpering he had laid his own ear, seemed unmoved by the second death of a son within a week. She was built of granite, and sulphuric acid coursed through her veins ... She did not glance at Sheila, or at Stephen her husband, or at Major Gotch, who looked pinched and confused this morning. She did not seem surprised that her other children were not present.

Back at the house, Bridget undressed her and she crawled into bed. She closed her eyes and asked Dr. Innis for "a little something to put me to sleep."

And she fell asleep and slept restlessly, moaning.

"Well," demanded the Inspector when it was all over, "where do we go from here?"

"I wish I knew, Dad."

"You're stumped?"

His son shrugged. "I can't believe this case is insoluble. There's sense in it somewhere. Our job is to spot it."

The Inspector threw up his hands. "If *you* can't see any light, I certainly can't, Ellery. All we can do is keep a close watch on these people and follow up the few clues we have. Let's go home."

A few days after Mac's funeral, Ellery Queen had two breakfast callers.

He was startled by the change in Sheila Potts. Her face seemed half its normal size, the skin gray; her blue eyes were darker and deeper blue and more liquid, their sockets underscored as by a paintbrush. She was in black, a pitiable figure of distress.

Charley Paxton looked thin and ill, too. And his eyes shared with Sheila's that burden of anxiety which Mr. Queen had come to associate with the troubled ones of this world who find themselves caught in a tangle from which there is no escape.

The Inspector had been about to leave for his office, but when he saw the haggard faces of the two young people he phoned Police Headquarters to say he would be delayed and became mine host cunningly. "How's your mother this morning?" he asked Sheila, with an elaborate expression of concern.

"Mother?" said Sheila vaguely. "About the same."

Charley braced himself "Now you'll see it's all stuff, darling," he said in a cheery voice. "Tell Ellery and the Inspector about it."

"It isn't stuff, Charley, and you know it," Sheila said tiredly. "Sometimes you make me sick. I know I've done an awful lot of weeping and squalling, but I'm not a child—I can add. This adds up to more, and you know it. You see," she said, turning to the Queens before Charley could reply. "I've been thinking, Mr. Queen—"

"Ellery," said Ellery.

"Ellery. I've been thinking, and I've seen—well, a dreadful design in what's been happening."

"Have you? And what design is that?"

Sheila shut her eyes. "At first I was shocked. I couldn't think at all. Murder is so ... newspapery. It doesn't happen to *you*. You read about it in a paper, or in a detective story, and it makes you wriggle with disgust, or sympathy. But it doesn't *mean* anything."

"That's quite true."

"Then—it happens to you. There are police in your house. Somebody you love is dead. Somebody you've been with all your life is ... a fiend of some sort. You look at the faces around you, the familiar faces, even the ones you dislike ... and you die yourself. Inside. A thousand times. It doesn't seem possible. But there it is.

"And there *you* are. . . . When Bob died I couldn't believe anything. I was all mixed up; none of it seemed real. I just went through the motions. Then Mac ..." She put her hands quickly to her face.

Charley reached out to touch her, but Ellery shook his head and Charley turned away to stare blindly out the Queens' window at the quiet street below.

Inspector Queen kept his hard eyes on the weeping girl.

After a while Sheila groped in her bag and took out a handkerchief. "I'm sorry," she sniffed. "All I seem to do these days is imitate a fountain." She blew her little nose with energy and put her handkerchief away, sitting back and even smiling a little.

"Go ahead, Miss Potts," said Inspector Queen. "This personal stuff is interesting."

She looked guilty. "I don't know why I wandered that way . . . What I began to say was—I've been thinking since Mac died. There have been two murders in the house. And who's been murdered? Robert. Mac. My twin brothers." Her blue eyes flashed. "Not one of Mother's first husband's three children—oh, no! Not one of the *crazy* ones. Only the Brents are dying. Only the Brents— *the sane ones*."

Charley cleared his throat.

"Let me finish, Charley. It's as clear as anything. We Brents are being killed off, one by one. First Robert, then Mac . . . *then either my father or me*. Charley, it's true and you know it! One of us is next on the list, and if Daddy gets it, I'll be the only Brent left, and I'll get it."

"But why?" shouted Charley, out of control. "It doesn't make sense, Sheila!"

"What's the difference why? Money, hate, just plain insanity . . . *I* don't know why, but I know it's true, as truly as I'm sitting here this minute. And what's more, *you* know it, too, Charley! Maybe Mr. Queen and the Inspector don't know it, but you know it—"

"Miss Potts—" began the Inspector.

"Please call me Brent. I don't want ever to be called by that horrible name again."

"Of course, Miss Brent."

Ellery and his father exchanged glances. Sheila was right. It was what they themselves feared, a third murder. With even more reason: the missing automatic.

The Inspector went to one of the front windows. After a moment, he said: "Miss Brent, would you mind coming here?"

Sheila wearily crossed the room to stand beside him in the sun.

"Look down there," said the Inspector. "No, across the street. The service entrance of that apartment house. What do you see, Miss Brent?"

"A big man smoking a cigaret."

"Now look on this side, a few yards up, towards Amsterdam Avenue. What do you see?"

"A car," said Sheila, puzzled. "With two men in it."

The Inspector smiled. "The man in that areaway, and the two men in that car, Miss Brent, are detectives assigned to follow you wherever you go. You're never out of their sight. When you're in your mother's house, other detectives have their eye on you every possible moment. The same is true of your father. No one can get near you two, Miss Brent, unless the men on duty feel sure you're running no risk."

Sheila flushed. "Don't think I'm ungrateful, Inspector. I didn't know that, and it does make me feel better. And I'm happy for Daddy's sake. But—you know perfectly well if I were surrounded by a cordon twenty-four hours a day—if you put the whole police department to guarding us—sooner or later we'd be caught. A shot through a window, a hand aiming around a door—"

"Not at all," said the Inspector crossly. "I can promise you *that* won't happen!"

"Of course it won't, dear," said Charley. "Be sensible, now—let me take you out somewhere. We can have lunch at the Ritz and go to the Music Hall or some place—get your mind off things—"

Sheila shook her head, smiling faintly. "Thank you, darling. It's sweet of you." And then there was a silence.

"Sheila." She turned to Ellery very quickly. His eyes were admiring, and a little color came into her face. "You have something specific in mind—a most excellent mind, by the way," he said dryly. "What is it?"

Sheila said in a grim tone: "Have them put into an institution."

"Sheila!" Charley was appalled. "Your own mother?"

"She hates me, Charley. And she's got a sick brain. If mother had tuberculosis, I'd send her to Arizona, wouldn't I?"

"But—to put her away . . ." said Charley feebly.

"Don't make me sound like a monster!" Sheila cried. "But none of you knows my mother as I do. She'd cheerfully kill me if she thought it would help some 'plans' of hers. Her brain's twisted, I tell you! I won't feel safe until Mother and Thurlow and Horatio and Louella are behind bars somewhere! Now call me anything you like," and Sheila sat down and wept again.

"We've already considered that plan," said Ellery gently. She looked up, startled. "Oh, yes. We haven't overlooked any bets, Sheila. But Charley will tell you there'd be no legal grounds whatever for committing your mother to an institution. Thurlow, Louella, Horatio? It would be very difficult, as there's no doubt whatever that your mother would fight any such move with every penny of the considerable fortune she possesses. It would take a long time, with no certainty of success—they're borderline cases, I should say, if they're mentally deficient in any medical sense at all.

"Meanwhile, they could be doing ... damage. No, we abandoned the idea of trying to commit anyone in the Potts family to a mental hospital. Later, perhaps, when this case is settled. Now it would be futile and even dangerous, as it might force someone's hand."

"Then there's the possibility of throwing the lot of them in jail," said Inspector Queen quietly. "We've considered that, too. We could hold them as material witnesses, maybe. Or on some other charge. Whatever the charge, I can tell you—and Charley as a lawyer will bear me out—that we couldn't hold them indefinitely. Your mother's money and pull would get them out eventually, and you'd be back where you started. We need more evidence before we can take that step, Miss Brent."

"It doesn't leave me very much except to order the latest shroud, does it?" said Sheila with a white smile.

"Sheila, please! Stop talking like that!" cried Charley.

"Meanwhile," continued the Inspector, "everything's being done that can be. Every member of your household is under a twenty-four hour guard. We're doing all we can to dig into the background of this case, in the hope that we'll find some clue to the truth. Yes, there's always the danger of a slip. But then," added the Inspector in a peculiar tone, "you could slip on a banana peel this afternoon, Miss Brent, and break your neck."

"Now hold on, Inspector," said Charley angrily. "Can't you see she's scared blue? I know you're doing all you can, but—"

"Shut up, Charley," said the Inspector.

Ellery glanced at his father quickly. This had not been on the agendum. Charley was shocked.

"How about Charley's taking Sheila away somewhere?" asked Ellery innocently. "Out of range of any possible danger, Dad?"

The Inspector's cheeks darkened to a crimson gray. "I think not," he snapped. "No. Not out of the state, Ellery."

Ellery drew his horns in very quickly indeed. So that was it!

"I wouldn't go, anyway," said Sheila listlessly. "I won't leave Dad. I didn't tell you that my father doesn't think he ought to leave. He says he's an old man and he won't start running away at his age. He wants me to go, but of course I can't. Not without him. It's all rather hopeless, isn't it?"

"No," smiled Ellery. "There's one person who can put a stop to all this."

"Huh?" The Inspector looked incredulous. "Who?"

"Cornelia Potts."

"The Old Woman?" Charley shook his head.

"But Mr. Queen——" began Sheila.

"Ellery," said Ellery. "You see, Sheila, your mother is the lord and the law in Potts Palace. At least to the three children of her first marriage. I have the ridiculous feeling suddenly that if she could be persuaded to issue an ultimatum——"

"You saw how hard she tried to stop the duel between Bob and Thurlow," said Sheila bitterly. "I tell you she wants us Brents dead. She's been happy about it in her own perverted way. She went to poor Mac's funeral to gloat! You're wasting your time, Ellery."

"I don't know," muttered Charley. "I'm not defending your mother, darling, but that's a bit hard on her, it seems to me. I think Ellery's right. She could put a stop to all this, and it's up to us to make her do it."

"It's an idea," said the Inspector unexpectedly. But it was evident he was thinking of other fish to fry. "As long as Sheila's mother is alive, she rules that roost. They'd quit on her say-so. . . . Yes. It's worth a try."

17 . . . *How the Old Woman Got Home*

They met Dr. Innis in the driveway. The physician had just driven up for his daily visit to the Old Woman.

They all went in together.

The Inspector kept a sharp eye out for his men. What he saw seemed to satisfy him. He grunted and stumped on upstairs, keeping his counsel.

Sheila kept saying: "I tell you it's hopeless," in a tone appropriate to the utterance.

At the top of the spiral staircase, Ellery said to Dr.

Innis: "By the way, Doctor, Mrs. Potts seems to have come through this last heart attack and the death of Mac very well indeed. What would you say is the prognosis now?"

Dr. Innis shrugged. "You can't make over a heart like hers, Mr. Queen. We don't know very much about stamina, and the will to live. But that woman's alive this moment, I'm convinced, only because she wants to be. No other reason. In fact, there's every reason to believe her heart should have given out years ago."

"We may talk to her freely? There's one question I'm anxious to ask her, Doctor, that I should have asked long ago. And then we have a rather grim job."

The physician shrugged again. "I'm through trying to make people around here do what they ought to do. Every medical sign indicates that absolute rest and freedom from excitement are called for. I can only ask that you take as little time with her as possible."

"Fair enough."

"She'll live forever," said Sheila wildly. "She'll be alive when we're all dead."

Dr. Innis glanced at Sheila oddly as they went to the door of Cornelia Potts's apartment. He began to say something, but then Inspector Queen knocked softly, so he refrained. When there was no answer the Inspector opened the door and they went into the sitting room, and Dr. Innis opened the door to the bedroom.

"Mrs. Potts," said Dr. Innis.

The Old Woman lay in her incredible bed, rather high on two fat pillows, as usual, with her eyes open and her mouth open and the lace cap a trifle askew on her head.

Sheila screamed and ran, and Charley, crying out, ran after her.

"It's the good Lord's gospel," wept old Bridget. "She rings for me not an hour and a half gone, and she says I'm not to come blunderin' in, may she rest in peace, because seein' as how she wants to be alone, poor soul— alone with the good Lord and His heavenly saints, as it turns out, but how was a miserable sinner like me to know that? That's all I know, sir, so help me God.... Dead— the Old Woman dead! It's like the end of the world, it is."

Inspector Queen said harshly: "Don't monkey with that body, Doctor."

"I'm not monkeying," shrilled Dr. Innis. "You asked me to examine her, and I am. This woman was my patient, and she died while under my care, and it's my right to examine her, anyway! I have to sign the death certificate—"

"Gentlemen, gentlemen," said Ellery in a weary voice. "Did Cornelia Potts die in the conventional manner, Dr. Innis, or was she assisted into the hereafter? That's what I want to know."

"Death from natural causes, Mr. Queen. Heart gave out, that's all. She's been dead about one hour."

"Normal death." The Inspector gnawed his mustache, eyeing that silent, pudgy corpse as if he expected it at any moment to gush blood.

"Excitement and the strain of the past week have been too much for her. I warned you this was coming." Dr. Innis picked up his hat, bowed frigidly, and left.

"Just the same, *Dr.* Innis," said the Inspector under his breath, "old Doc Prouty's going to check your findings, and Jehovah help you if you're covering something up! Ellery, what are you doing?"

"It might be called," grunted Ellery, " 'looking over the scene of the crime,' except that there seems to have been no crime, so let's call it simply finding out what the hell Cornelia Potts had been writing when the Dark Angel paid her his long-overdue visit."

"Writing?" The Inspector came over swiftly.

Ellery indicated the portable typewriter on its stand, beside the bed. Its case was on the floor, as if the machine had been used and death had come before the cover could be replaced. On the night table stood a large box of varisized notepapers and envelopes, its hinged lid thrown back.

"So what?" frowned the Inspector.

Ellery pointed to the dead woman's right hand. It was almost buried in the bedclothes, and the Inspector smoothed them a little to see better. What he saw made his brows huddle together over his eyes.

In Cornelia Potts's right hand lay a large sealed envelope, undoubtedly one of the envelopes from the box by her bed.

The Inspector snatched the envelope from the stiff hand and held it up to the light. The face bore the typewritten words: LAST WILL AND TESTAMENT. Beneath this was the scrawled signature, in the broad strokes of the soft-leaded pencils the Old Woman affected: *Cornelia Potts*.

"I've got Sheila quiet," said Charley Paxton distractedly, running. "What is it? Murder, Ellery?"

"Dr. Innis pronounces it a natural death."

"I won't believe it till Doc Prouty tells me so," said Inspector Queen absently. "Charley, here's what we just found in Cornelia's hand. I thought you said she *had* a will."

"Yes." Charley took the proffered envelope with a frown. "Don't tell me she's made a *new* will!"

"I hardly think so," said Ellery. "Tell me, Charley. Did she have possession of the original of her will?"

"Oh, yes."

"Where did she usually keep it, do you know?"

"In the night-table drawer. Right by her bed."

Ellery looked into the drawer. It was empty.

"Was it in an envelope, or loose?"

"Not in an envelope the last time I saw it."

"Well, this is a fresh one, and the typing and signature look fresh, too, so I'd say she felt herself going, took the old will from the drawer, pulled over the portable, typed an envelope, scrawled her signature, and sealed the will in the envelope just before she died."

"I wonder why," mused the Inspector.

Ellery raised his brows.

The Inspector raised his shoulders. "Well, we'll find out when the will's opened after the funeral." He handed Charley Paxton the sealed envelope for safekeeping, and they left the Old Woman alone in her bed.

And so Cornelia Potts was dead, and that was the end of the world, as old Bridget Conniveley had sobbed, for a number of servants, many of whom had never known another mistress; it was the end of a dynasty for certain others whose memories were yellow-tinged; and for those who had been closest to the stiffly dead it was ... as nothing.

This was the remarkable thing about the Old Woman's death. It seemed to concern none of her children—not those she loved, nor Sheila whom she hated. Sheila after that first scream had felt a weight slip from her heart. She was ashamed, and frightened—and relieved.

Sheila remained in her quarters, resting and alone. Outside her door Detective Flint smoked a five-cent panatela and read a racing form.

As for the bereaved husband, he called quietly to his crony, Major Gotch, and the two men went into Steve Brent's room with two virgin fifths of Scotch and two whiskey glasses and shut themselves firmly in. An hour later they were singing Tahitian beach songs at the tops of their voices, uproariously.

18 . . . Who'll Be Chief Mourner? "I!" Said the Dove

Dr. Prouty said that this was getting to be a personal affair and perhaps he had better resign from the Medical Examiner's office and become private mortician to the Pottses. "I'm getting to know 'em intimately," said Doc Prouty to Ellery, on the morning when he handed Inspector Queen his official post-mortem finding *in re* Cornelia Potts, deceased. "Now take the Old Woman. A fighter. She gave me a battle all the way. Not like those two fine sons of hers, Bob and Mac. She was a hell-raiser, all right. Could hardly do a thing with her."

Ellery, who was at breakfast, closed his eyes and murmured: "But the report, Prouty."

"Aaaa, she died of natural causes," said the Inspector before Prouty could reply. "At least that's what his old poop's report says."

"What are you so grumpy about, you cantankerous fuddy-duddy?" demanded Doc Prouty. "Haven't you had enough murders at that address? Are you disappointed?"

"Well, if she had to die," grumbled Inspector Queen, "I wish she'd done it in such a way as to leave some clue to this screwy business. Natural death! Go on, get back to your boneyard."

Dr. Prouty snarled and went out, muttering something about O base ingratitude thou are a viper's fang.

Now you must believe a wonderful thing, you who have read of the Pottses and their Shoe and their duels and their laboratories and their boys who never grew up and the improbable house they all lived in.

You must believe that this woman, this Old Woman, who had once inexplicably been a child and a girl and who married a dark character named Bacchus Potts and was thereafter bewitched by his name, who had founded a dynasty and built a pyramid and lived on its apex like a queen, who had spawned three dark children and lived to defend them with her considerable cunning against their own dark natures and so defend herself against the pricks of conscience—you must believe that this Cornelia Potts, who had lived only for those three, who had built and been ruthless only for those three, who had lied and scratched and spent her substance upon those three, who had cuffed them and nurtured them and kept them out of public institutions—you must believe that she went to her grave in St. Praxed's churchyard unattended by any of them, to lie by her sons whom she did not love and whose violent death meant no more to her than the violation of her sacred precincts—if indeed that much.

Mr. Ellery Queen took the astonishing census before and during the last rites. Mr. Queen was not interested in the details of the Old Woman's interment. She was dead of natural causes; *requiescat in pace*. But the three troglodytes of her womb—ah, Confusion!

Check them off, Mr. Queen:— *Louella* . . . The mother was an old pink goddess whose claws held the lever of life. She punished, she denied, she ruled. Yes, she endeavored to love. But what is love to Louella? A mating of guinea pigs (a most interesting experiment which Louella can watch tirelessly, and does). Love is an impediment: a wall, a wood of black and tangled depths standing between Louella and the temple, where the stuff of life may be played with in ritual worship. Good riddance, love.

Louella remains faithful to the sexless god of knowledge. In its fane there is no room for sentiment. Like all eunuchs, it is stern, and cruel, and above mankind . . . Louella could have seen the cortege making its way up Riverside Drive to St. Praxed's from her tower window, but Ellery doubted if she even bothered to straighten up from her packing cases.

For in the three days between her mother's death and funeral, Louella, the scientist, truly went mad of her science. Went mad with the relaxation of those biting claws of motherhood. Now there was no old pink goddess to say her nay, or even yea. Now there was a many-armed telephone, and the riches of all the laboratory supply houses of the world within its genie's reach.

Equipment poured in: an electric oven, retorts, racks of brilliant new test tubes, motors, a refrigerator, chemicals in blue, and brick, and yellow, and silver, and magenta— lovely colors, lovely colors . . . Louella was unpacking crates, clambering over boxes, in her tower all that day when her mother was borne up the Drive to eternity.

Horatio . . . Horatio fascinates Ellery Queen. Horatio is

a phenomenon to Ellery, a mythological figure. Ellery was unceasingly astonished to see Horatio caper about the Potts estate in the quivering flesh. It was like seeing Silenus on Times Square grinning down from the moving news sign on the Times Building. It was like having Vulcan change your tire at Ye Olde Garage.

Horatio and Death have no *simpatico*. Horatio is above Death. Horatio is Youth, when Death is inconceivable, even the death of the old.

Informed by Ellery and Charley Paxton of his mother's death, Horatio scarcely turned a hair. "Come, come, gentlemen. Death is an illusion. My mother is still in that house, in her bed, being crotchety about something." Horatio tossed a bean-bag frog into the air and caught it clumsily in its descent. "Always being crotchety about something, Mother," he boomed. "Good scout at heart, though."

"For heaven's sake, Horatio," cried Charley, "will you try to realize that she *isn't* in the house any more? That she's lying on a slab in the Morgue and that she'll be buried six feet deep in a couple of days?"

Horatio chuckled indulgently. "My dear Charley. Death is an illusion. We're all dead, and we're all living. We die when we grow up, we live when we're children. You're dead right now, only you haven't sense enough to lie down and be shoveled under. Same with you, sir," said Horatio, winking at Ellery. "Lie down, sir, and be shoveled under!"

"Aren't you even going to the funeral?" choked Charley.

"Gosh, no," said Horatio. "I've got a swell new kite to fly. It's simply super!" And he seized a large red apple and ran munching out into the gardens, joyously.

When the cortege passed, Horatio saw it. He must have seen it, for he was perched on the outer wall disentangling the cord of his swell new kite from the branches of an overhanging maple. He must have seen it, because instantly he turned his meaty back and jumped off the wall, abandoning his kite. He capered off towards his sugarloaf house, whistling *Little Boy Blue Come Blow Your Horn* bravely. Horatio didn't believe in Death, you see.

Thurlow ... Thurlow, the Terror of the Plains, is a bold bad man this day. His not to display unmanly grief before the vulgar. His to mourn in the solitude of his apartment, hugging a bottle of cognac to his plump bosom. This is the way of men who are masculine. The mother is dead—God rest her, gentlemen. But let the son alone; he mourns.

Ellery suspected other Thurlovian thoughts, in the light of subsequent events. Ellery suspected that among Thurlow's thoughts ran one like a Wagnerian leitmotif: The Queen is dead; long live the King. Ellery suspected royalist thoughts because it was evident shortly after the funeral that Thurlow had planned—during his manly, solitary session with the cognac—to seize his mother's ermine and seat himself upon her throne instanter.

No, Thurlow the Killer did not attend his mother's funeral. He had too many affairs of state to think through.

So, Old Woman, this is your final bitterness, that the children you loved turned their backs on you, and the child you hated came to weep at your grave.

Sheila wept without explanation, with Charley Paxton supporting her on one side and Stephen Brent on the other. Sheila wept, and Stephen Brent did not. He followed the coffin with his eyes into the grave, whiskey-reddened eyes without expression.

Major Gotch wore an old jacket of Horatio's, the only member of the household with a commensurate girth. The Major sneezed frequently and carried himself with great dignity. He seemed to regret the Old Woman's passing in a bibulous sort of way. As the earth clumped on the coffin, he was actually seen to shed a tear, at which he swiped surreptitiously with the back of Horatio's sleeve. But then a reporter was so unwise as to ask the Major what he was Major of, and where he had been honored with his Majority. Whereupon Major Gotch did an unmilitary thing: he kicked the press. There were some moments of confusion.

Another was there, a stranger both to Ellery Queen and to his father. He was an elderly gentleman with a pointed Yankee face and mild, observing eyes, dressed plainly but correctly, whom Sheila addressed as "Mr. Underhill." Mr. Underhill had the hands of a workman. Charley Paxton presented him to the Queens as the man who managed the Potts factories.

"Knew Cornelia when she was a young woman, Inspector," Mr. Underhill said, shaking his head. "She was always one to stand on her own two feet. I'm not saying she didn't have faults, but she always treated me fine, and I'm darned sorry to see her go." And he blew his nose exaggeratedly in the way men do at funerals.

No photographers allowed. No windy eulogy. Just a

funeral with a handful of curious passers-by and, beyond, the police cordon.

"So that's how the Old Woman got home," mumbled Mr. Queen as the last shovelful of earth was patted into place by the gravedigger's spade.

"How's that?" The Inspector was absently searching the faces of those beyond the cordon.

"Nothing. Nothing, Dad."

"Thought you said something. Well, that's over." The Inspector pulled his jacket more tightly about him. "Let's go back to the house and listen to the reading of the will." He sighed. "Who knows? There may be something there."

19 . . . The Queen Wills It

Thurlow came downstairs grasping the bottle of cognac by the neck like a scepter. "In the library?" he squeaked, stepping high. "Yes, in the library. Very nice. Nice and proper." He paused gallantly to permit Sheila to precede him into the study. "I trust everything went off nicely at the funeral, my dear?" asked Thurlow.

Sheila swept by him with a noble loathing. Thurlow clucked, narrowed his eyes into a leer, and then, gravely, stepping higher, he crossed the threshold and waded into the study.

"Aren't the others c-coming?" asked Steve Brent.

"I've sent for them twice," replied Charles Hunter Paxton.

"What good would it do?" cried Sheila. Then she looked down and took a seat, flushing a little.

"Send for them again," suggested Inspector Queen.

Cuttins was summoned. Yes, he had delivered Mr. Paxton's message in person to Miss Louella and Mr. Horatio.

"Deliver it again," said Charley irritably. "We're not going to wait forever. Five minutes, Cuttins."

The butler bowed and drifted off.

No one spoke as they waited.

It was late afternoon and the westering sun was being coy above the Palisades. It sliced its blades into the library through the French doors, cutting the gilt of book titles, flicking Sheila's hair, stabbing at the dregs of gold in Thurlow's bottle. Ellery, looking about, thought he had never beheld Nature in such an undiplomatic mood. There should be no sharp sparkle in this place; it should be all browns and glooms and dullnesses.

He turned his attention to Thurlow. Thurlow's eyes were still narrowed in that absurd leer. I am master here, he seemed to say. Beware my wrath, for it is terrible. The Queen is dead—long live the King, and you'd better be good subjects! Read, read the will, slave; your master waits.

And Thurlow beamed upon them all: upon Sheila; upon Steve Brent, a haggard man ill at ease and out of place; upon quiet, watching Mr. Underhill; upon Major Gotch, who also sat uneasily, but in a corner, as if he felt himself tied to this house and these people only by the slenderest of Minoan threads; upon harassed Charley Paxton, who stood behind the small kneehole desk in one of the angles of the library, which he had used frequently to transact the Old Woman's business, and tapped a nervous tattoo upon the sealed envelope Inspector Queen had entrusted to his care; upon the Queens, who stood together near the door, forgotten, watching everything.

And no one spoke, and the mahogany grandfather clock which Cornelia Potts had hauled from her first "regular" house up north pick-picked away at the silence, patiently.

Cuttins reappeared in the doorway. "Miss Louella cannot be disturbed for anything," he announced to the opposite wall. "I am to say that she is engaged in a very important experiment. Mr. Horatio regrets that he cannot attend; I am to say that he is composing a verse and may lose his inspiration."

Sheila shuddered.

"All right, Cuttins. Close the door," said Charley.

Cuttins backed away; the Inspector made sure the door was shut. Charley picked up the sealed envelope.

"Just a moment," said Inspector Queen. He advanced to the desk and turned to face Thurlow. "Mr. Potts, you understand why I'm here?"

Thurlow blinked, looking uncertain. Then he beamed. "As a friend, of course. A friend in our sad troubles."

"No, Mr. Potts. As the officer in charge of the investigation of two murders which occurred in this house. I admit they're posers, and that we know very little about them, not even the motive ... for sure. That's why I'm interested in your mother's will. Do you grasp that?"

Thurlow shrank a little. "Why do you tell me these

things?" he asked in frightened tones. The King had run to cover.

"You're head of the family now, Mr. Potts, the eldest." Thurlow swelled again. "I want you to be sure everything's aboveboard. This envelope—" the Inspector took it from Charley— "was found in your mother's dead hand upstairs. The flap was pasted down tight, as you see it. We have not opened the envelope. It says it's Cornelia Potts's will, and it has her signature on it, but we've no way of knowing until it's opened for the first time, here in this room, whether it's her old will, which was made out many years ago, or a new will which she typed and signed just before she died.

"The odds are it's the old will, because we can find no one in the house who witnessed her signature the other day, as would have had to be done if your mother had made a new will. But new or old, this is her will, and I want you to be satisfied that nobody's putting one over on you or anybody else who might be mentioned in it. All clear, Mr. Potts?"

"Of course, of course," said Thurlow grandly, waving his bottle. "Very kind of you, I'm sure."

The Inspector grunted, tossing the envelope onto the desk. "Make sure you don't forget it, Mr. Potts," he said mildly. "Because there are a lot of witnesses in this room who won't." And he returned to Ellery's side and made a sign to Charley Paxton. Charley picked up the envelope again and ripped off an edge. He shook the envelope out. A blue-backed document fell to the desk.

"It's the old will, Inspector," said Charley, seizing it. "Here's the date and the notary's seal. You were right— she just put it into this envelope to get it ready for us ... What's this?"

A smaller envelope, bearing a few typewritten lines, had fallen out of the folds of Cornelia Potts's will. Charley read the legend on the envelope aloud:—

To be opened after the reading of my will and the election of a new President of the Potts Shoe Company.

He turned the smaller envelope over; it was sealed. Charley stared inquiringly at the Queens.

Father and son came forward eagerly and examined the small envelope.

"Same typewriter."

"Yes, Dad. Also the same make of envelope as the

larger one. There were both sizes in that box of stationery on her night table upstairs."

"So that's why she typed out a large envelope before she died."

"Yes. She wrote something on the portable, enclosed it in this smaller envelope, then enclosed envelope and the will from her night table in this large envelope." Ellery looked up at his friend. "Charley, you'd better get on with the formal reading. The sooner we can open this small envelope officially the sooner we'll find out what I feel in my bones is a vital clue in the case."

Charley Paxton read the will rapidly aloud. There was nothing important in it that the Queens had not heard from the Old Woman's own lips the day the Inspector had demanded she tell him the terms of her will.

There were, as she had said, three main provisions:—Upon her death her estate, after all legal debts, taxes, and expenses of the funeral had been paid, was to be divided "among my surviving children" share and share alike. Stephen, "my husband by my second marriage," was to get no share whatever, "either in real or personal property." The election of a new President of the Board of Directors of the Potts Shoe Company was to be held immediately upon her death, or as soon after the funeral as possible.

The Board, as currently constituted, comprised the Potts family (except for Stephen Brent Potts). The new Board was to be the same, plus Simon Bradford Underhill, surperintendent of the factories, who was, like the others, to have one vote.

"While the enforcement of this provision is not strictly speaking within my powers as testatrix" (Charley Paxton read), "I nevertheless enjoin my children to obey it. Underhill knows the business better than any of them."

There were certain minor provisions:—The Potts property on Riverside Drive was to remain the joint property of "my designated heirs." "All of my clothing is to be burned." "My Bible, my dental plates, my wedding rings" were bequeathed to "my daughter Louella."

That was all. No bequests to charity, no bequests to old Bridget or the other servants, no endowments to universities or gifts to churches. No specific mention of her daughter Sheila or of her sons Robert and Maclyn. Or of Major Gotch.

Thurlow Potts listened with an indulgent expression, his eyes nearly closed and his head nodding benevolently with every sentence, as if to say: "Quite so. Quite so."

"Dental plates," muttered the Inspector.

Charley finished reading and began to put the will down. But then he looked startled and picked it up again. "There's a . . . codicil at the bottom of this last sheet, under the signatures of testatrix and witnesses," he exclaimed. "Something typed in and typesigned 'Cornelia Potts' . . ." He scanned it quickly, his eyes widening.

"What is it?" demanded Ellery Queen. "Here, let me see that, Charley."

"I'll read it to you," said Charley grimly. That forbidding tone sat Thurlow upright in his chair and brought the others half out of theirs.

"It says: 'Hold the Board of Directors meeting right after the reading of the will. As soon as a new President of the Potts Shoe Company is elected, open the enclosed sealed envelope—'"

"But we know that," said Ellery with a trace of impatience. "That's practically the same thing she typewrote on the small envelope itself."

"Wait. This message attached to the will isn't finished." Charley was tense. "It goes on to say: *'The statement inside the small envelope will tell the authorities who killed my sons Robert and Maclyn.'*"

20 . . . The Old Woman's Tale

Inspector Queen bounded across the room. "Give me that envelope!" He snatched it and held it fast, glaring about as if he expected someone to try to take it away from him.

"She knew," said Sheila in a wondering voice.

"She knew?" cried her father.

Major Gotch rubbed his jaw agitatedly.

Thurlow grasped the arms of his chair.

At the door Mr. Queen had not stirred.

"Hold that blasted Board meeting right now!" the Inspector yapped. "Can't do a thing without that Board meeting. Come on, get it over with. I want to open this envelope!" He chuckled and peered at the envelope. "She knew," he chortled. "The old harridan knew all along, bless her." Then he growled to Charley: "Did you hear what I said? Get it over with!"

Charley stammered something ridiculously like "Y-yes,

sir," and then he shook his head. "I've got nothing to do with the Board, Inspector. No power and no authority."

"Well, who has? Speak up!"

"I should imagine if anyone has to take charge, it's Thurlow. Cornelia was President—she's dead. Bob and Mac were Vice-presidents—and they're dead. Thurlow's the only officer left."

Thurlow rose, frightened.

"All right, Mr. Potts," said the Inspector testily. "Don't just stand there. Call your Board to order and start nominating, or whatever it is you're supposed to do."

Thurlow drew himself up. "I know my duties. Charles— I'll sit at that desk, *if* you please."

Charley shrugged and went over to sit with Sheila, who took his hand in hers but did not look at him.

Thurlow edged behind the desk, picked up a paper-weight, and rapped with it.

"The meeting will come to order," he said, and harrumphed. "As we all know, my dear mother has passed on, and—"

"Kindly omit flowers," said Inspector Queen.

Thurlow flushed. "You make this difficult, Inspector Queen, most difficult. Things must be done decorously, decorously. Now the first question is the question of—" Thurlow paused, then continued in an acid, querulous tone, "Simon Bradford Underhill. He has not been a member of this Board—"

"Least I can do, Thurlow." The speaker was Underhill, and he was smiling very sadly. "Cornelia's request, you know."

Thurlow frowned. "Yes. Yes, Underhill, I know." He cleared his throat again. "Wouldn't dream of having it otherwise." He sat down suddenly in the chair behind the desk; it might almost be said that he fell down. He looked longingly at the bottle of cognac, which he had left behind him in the other chair. Then he harrumphed a few more times and said sternly: "I believe we have a quorum. I will accept nominations for the Presidency of the Board of Directors of the Potts Shoe Company." And now Thurlow did an extraordinary thing: he rose, circled the desk, faced the unoccupied chair, said: "I nominate myself," nodded defiantly, then went round the desk again and reseated himself. "Any other nominations?"

Sheila sprang to her feet, her dimples plunging deep. "This is the last straw! Everybody here knows you haven't the ability to manage a peanut stand, let alone a business that earns millions every year!"

"What's that? What's that?" said Thurlow excitedly.

"You'd ruin the company in a year, Thurlow. My brothers Bob and Mac *ran* this business, and you've never had a single constructive thing to do with it! All you ever did was make ridiculous mistakes. And you've got the nerve to nominate yourself President!"

"Now Sh-Sheila," stuttered her father. "Don't upset yourself, d-dear . . ."

"Dad, you know yourself that if the twins were alive, one of them would have become the new head of the firm to take Mother's place. You *know* it!"

Thurlow found his voice. "Sheila, if you weren't a female—"

"I know, you'd challenge me to a duel," said Sheila bitterly. "Well, your dueling days are over, Mr. Potts. And you're not going to ruin the company. I'd nominate Daddy if he were a member of the Board—"

"Stephen?" Thurlow gazed with astonishment at his stepfather, as if he had never contemplated the possibility of such a watery character's usurping his prerogatives.

"But since I can't I nominate Mr. Underhill," cried Sheila. "Mr. Underhill, please. At least you know the business, you know how to make shoes, you're the oldest employe, you own stock in the company—"

Thurlow now turned his astonishment upon the lean old Yankee.

But Underhill shook his head. "I'm very grateful, Sheila. But I can't accept the nomination. I'm an outsider. You know how set your mother was about keeping the firm in the family—"

Thurlow nodded vigorously. "That's right. Underhill's got no business sticking his nose in at all. I won't let him be President. I'll discharge him first—"

Color stained the old man's cheeks. "Now that makes me mad, Thurlow. That makes me real mad. Sheila, I've changed my mind. I'll accept that nomination, by Godfrey!"

The Inspector stamped. "My envelope!" he cried. "For Joe's sake, get this musical comedy over with!"

Thurlow looked desperate. Suddenly he shouted: "Wait!" and scuttled out of the library.

The delay caused by Thurlow's disappearance almost reduced the Inspector to tears. He kept looking at the sealed envelope piteously, looking at his watch, sending

Sergeant Velie "to see what that oakum-headed fool Thurlow's up to," and occasionally berating Ellery in a bitter undertone for standing there and doing nothing.

"Play it out, Dad," was all Ellery would reply.

Eventually Thurlow returned, and the meeting was resumed. Thurlow looked smug. Something bulged in his breast pocket which Sergeant Velie, who had followed him, whispered to the Inspector was "papers, some kind of papers. He's been racin' all over the joint wavin' papers."

"Meeting will come to order again," said Thurlow briskly. "Any other nominations? No? Then we will proceed to a vote by the showing of hands. The nominees are Simon Bradford Underhill and Thurlow Potts. All those in favor of Mr. Underhill who have a legal vote on this Board please signify by raising your hands."

Two hands went up—Sheila's, and Underhill's.

Two votes for Mr. Underhill." Thurlow smacked his lips. "Now. I have here," and he brought out of his pocket two envelopes, unsealed, "the absentee votes of the other members of this Board, Louella Potts and Horatio Potts. I have their votes by proxy."

Sheila paled.

"Louella Potts." Thurlow drew from one of the envelopes a signed statement. "Votes for Thurlow Potts." He threw down Louella's paper with a disdainful gesture and took up the second envelope. "Horatio Potts. Votes for Thurlow Potts." And Thurlow Potts held up one pudgy hand triumphantly. "Tally—two votes for Underhill, three for Thurlow Potts. Thurlow Potts is elected President of the Board of Directors of the Potts Shoe Company by a plurality of one."

Thurlow rapped on the desk. "The meeting is adjourned."

"No," said Sheila in a voice full of hate. "No!"

Charley gripped her shoulder.

"Finished?" Inspector Queen strode forward. "In that case, we'll get down to business. Ellery, open this smaller envelope!"

Ellery wielded a letter knife on Cornelia Potts's envelope, slowly. This letter was going to do something final to the Potts murder case: it would name the murderer. Why this should annoy him Mr. Queen did not quite know, except the patently outlandish reason that the naming of murderers had always been a Queen specialty.

They had forgotten the small envelope in their absorption with the Board election. Now they watched him unfold a single long typewritten sheet, and scan it, and there was no sound of anything but the pick-picking of the grandfather clock.

"Well?" cried the Inspector.

Ellery replied in a quite flat voice: "This is the letter Cornelia Potts wrote. It is dated the afternoon of her death, the time specified being 3.35 P.M. The message goes:—

I, Cornelia Potts, being of sound mind and in full possession of my faculties, and knowing that I am shortly to die of my heart ailment, and in prayer that I may be forgiven in Heaven for what I have done, make this statement:

I ask not the world to judge me, for what I have done will be condemned by the world as if it were a fixed jury and I know that its judgment will be prejudiced.

Only a mother knows what motherhood is, how the mother loves the weak and hates the strong.

I have always loved my children Thurlow, Louella, and Horatio. Their weaknesses cannot be laid to them. They are what they are because of their father, my first husband. This I came to know shortly after he disappeared; and I have never forgiven him for it. May he rot. I took his name and made something of it; it is more than he ever did for me or mine.

My first children have always needed me, and I have always been their strength and their defender. The children of my second marriage have never needed me. I hated the twins for their independence and their strength; I hate Sheila for hers. Their very existence has been a daily reminder to me of the folly and tragedy of my first marriage, to Bacchus Potts. I have hated them since their childhood for their health, for their laughter, for their cleverness, for their sanity.

I, Cornelia Potts, killed my twin sons Robert and Maclyn.

It was I who substituted the bullet for the blank cartridge the police had put into Thurlow's weapon. It was I who took the Harrington & Richardson revolver from Thurlow's hiding place with which I held up the newspaper people and made them leave my estate. Later it was I who stole one of Thurlow's other guns and hid it from the police and went with it into my son Maclyn's bedroom in the middle of the night and shot him with it—yes, and whipped him.

I will be called a monster. Perhaps. Let the world cast stones at me—I shall be dead.

I confess these crimes of my own free will, and let this be an end to them. I will answer for them before my Creator.

"The letter," continued Ellery Queen in the same even voice, "is signed in the usual soft-pencil scrawl, 'Cornelia Potts.' Dad," he said, "let's have a look at the Old Woman's other two written signatures—the one on the big envelope and the one on the will."

It was still in the room.

Ellery looked up. "The signature on this confession," he announced, "is the authentic handwriting of Cornelia Potts."

Sheila threw back her head and laughed and laughed.

"I'm glad," she gasped. "I'm glad! Glad she was the one. Glad she's dead. Now I'm free. Daddy's free. We're safe. There won't be any more murders. There won't be any more murders. There won't be any . . ."

Charley Paxton caught her as she crumpled.

The Inspector very carefully pocketed Cornelia Potts's will, her confession, and the two envelopes.

"For the record," he grunted. The Inspector looked tired, but relaxed. He glanced about the empty study, the overturned chair in which Sheila had been sitting, the desk, the books twinkling their titles in the playful sun. "That's that, Ellery. Case of Potts and Potts *kaput*, killed off like a case of Irish whiskey at a wake." He sighed. "A nasty business from beginning to end, and I'm glad to be rid of it."

"If you are rid of it," said Ellery fretfully.

The Inspector stiffened. "If? Did you say 'if,' son?"

"Yes, Dad."

"Don't go highfalutin on me, for cripe's sake," groaned the Inspector. "Aren't you ever satisfied?"

"Not when there's a ragtag end."

"Talk English!"

Ellery lit a cigarette. He blew smoke at the ceiling without relish, swinging his leg idly against the desk on which he was perched. "One thing bothers me, Dad. I wish it didn't but it does." He frowned. "I don't think I'll ever be able to sweep it out of my skull."

"What's that?" asked his father, almost with fear.

"There's still a gun missing."

PART FOUR

21 . . . The Uneasiness of Heads

Now was the winter of their discontent, and that was strange, for the Potts case was solved. Wasn't there a confession? Hadn't the newspapers leaped upon it with venal joy? Weren't old cuts of Landru lifted from morgues the length and breadth of the land? Didn't the tabloids begin to serialize still again that old standby of circulation joggers, *Famous Murders of Fact and Fiction?* Was not Herod evoked, and Lady Macbeth?

One tabloid printed a cartoon of the Old Woman, smoking gun in hand, sons writhing at her feet, with the witty inscription: "He that spareth his *rod* hateth his son. (PROVERBS, XIII, 24.)" A more dignified journalist résumé began with the quotation: "Innocent babes writhed on thy stubborn spear . . . P. B. SHELLEY, *Queen Mab*, VI)."

But Ellery Queen thought the Order of the Bloodstained Footprint should have been awarded to the wag who resurrected the old labor-capital cartoon of the Old Woman in the Shoe, with her six children tumbling out, across two of whom however he now painted large black X's, and composed to explain it the following quatrain:—

There was an Old Woman who lived in a Shoe,
She had so many children she didn't know what to do,
She started to slaughter them, one child by one,
Only Death overtook her before she was done.

Work was begun in the studio of a Coney Island waxworks museum on a tableau, showing Maclyn Potts lying agonized in a bed weltering in thick red stuff, while the chubby figure of his mother, clad in voluminous black garments and wearing a black shawl and bonnet tied under the chin, gloated over the corpse like some demonized little Queen Victoria.

Several eggs, coming over the wall from Riverside

Drive, splashed against the Shoe the afternoon the newspapers announced the discovery of the Old Woman's confession.

A stone broke Thurlow Potts's bedroom window, sending him into a white-lipped oration on the Preservation of
Law and Order; a charge of criminal mischief went begging
only because of Thurlow's failure to identify the miscreant.

Various detectives of Inspector Queen's staff went home
for the first time in days to visit with their children.
Sergeant Velie's wife prepared a mustard bath for his
large feet and tucked him into bed full of aspirin and
love.

Only in the apartment of the Queens were there signs
that all was not well. Usually at the conclusion of a case
Inspector Queen made jokes and ordered two-inch steaks
which he devoured with the gusto of one who has labored
well and merits appropriate reward. Now he scarcely ate
at all, glowering when spoken to, was grumpy with Ellery,
and fell back into the routine of his office without enjoyment.

As for Ellery Queen, it could not be said that his spirits
soared above sea level. There was no taste in anything,
matter or music. He went back to a detective novel he
had been composing when the case of the Old Woman and
her six children had thrown it into eclipse; but the shadow
was still there, hanging heavily over the puppets of his
imagination and making the words seem just words. He
went over the Potts case in his mind endlessly; he fell
asleep to the scudding of far-fetched theories.

But the days came and went, the house on Riverside
Drive gradually became just a house, the newspapers
turned to fresh sensations, and it began to appear that the
Potts case had already passed into criminal history, to be
no more than a footnote or a paragraph in some morbid
reference book of the future.

One morning, three weeks after the disclosures in Cornelia Potts's confession had officially closed the dossier on
the case, Inspector Queen was about to leave for Police
Headquarters—he had already grunted "Toodle-oo" to his
son, who was still at breakfast—when suddenly he turned
back from the door and said: "By the way, Ellery, I got a
cable yesterday afternoon from the Dutch East Indies."

"Dutch East Indies?" Ellery absently looked up from his
eggs.

"Batavia. The prefect or commissioner of police there,

or whatever they call him. You know, in reply to my cable about Major Gotch."

"Oh," said Ellery. He set down his spoon.

"The cable says Gotch has no record down there. I thought you'd like to know . . . just to clear up a point."

"No record? You mean they haven't anything on him?"

"Not a thing. Never even heard of the old windbag."

The Inspector sucked his mustache. "Doesn't mean much. All I could give them was the name and description of a man forty years older than he'd been if he'd ever been there, and what's in a name? Or else Gotch is just a liar—a lot of these old-timers are—even though he swore he'd raised Cain in the Dutch East Indies in his time."

Ellery lit a cigaret, frowning over the match. "Thanks."

The Inspector hesitated. Then he came back and sat down, tipping his hat over his eyes as if in shame. "The Potts case is a closed book and all that, son, but I've been meaning to ask you—"

"What, Dad?"

"When we were talking over motives, you said you'd figured out that this old Major had a possible motive, too. Not that it's of any importance now—"

"I also said, I believe, that it was impossibly fantastic."

"Never mind knocking yourself out," snapped his father. "What did you have in mind?"

Ellery shrugged. "Remember the day we went over to the Potts house to ask the Old Woman to use her authority to stop the killings, and found her lying dead in bed?"

"Yes?" The Inspector licked his lips.

"Remember on the way upstairs I said to Dr. Innis that there was one question I'd been meaning to ask Mrs. Potts?"

"I sure do. What was the question?"

"I was going to ask her," said Ellery deliberately, "whether she'd ever seen her first husband again."

Inspector Queen gaped. "Her *first* husband? You mean this Bacchus Potts?"

"Who else?"

"But he's dead."

"Dead in law, Dad. That's quite another thing from being dead in fact. It struck me at one point in the case that Bacchus Potts might be very much alive still."

"Hunh." The Inspector was silent. Then he said: "That hadn't occurred to me. But you haven't answered my question. What did you have in mind when you said Major Gotch had a possible motive, too?"

"But I have answered your question, Dad."

"You . . . mean . . . Bacchus . . . Potts . . . Major Gotch—" The Inspector began to laugh, and soon he was wiping away the merry tears. "I'm glad the case *is* over," he choked. Another week and you'd have been measured for a restraining sheet yourself!"

"Amuse yourself," murmured his son, unruffled. "I told you it was fantastic. But on the other hand, why not? Gotch *might* be Potts the First."

"And I might be Richard the Second," chuckled his father.

"Fascinating speculation at the time, as I recall it," murmured Ellery. "Cornelia Potts has her husband declared dead after he's been absent seven years. She marries Steve Brent. He has a companion, 'Major Gotch.' Many years have passed since she last saw hubby number one, and the tropics change physiognomies wonderfully. Suddenly Cornelia discovers that Major Gotch is none other than Bacchus Potts! Makes her a bigamist or does it? Anyway, it's embarrassing. Situation."

"Rave on."

"And the worst of it is, 'Major Gotch' has found himself a comfortable nest. Sees no point in waving farewell. Pals with the new husband, and all that. New husband defends him. Cornelia's trapped . . . That theory appealed to me, Dad, wild as it was. Charley Paxton, in telling me the story of the Old Woman's life, had been vague—as well he might be!—about Cornelia's reason for permitting Gotch to live in her household. Mightn't that have been the reason? A hold Gotch had on her? That she wasn't legally married to Brent and therefore her children—her reputation—her business—?"

"Hold it," said the Inspector testily. "I'm an idiot for listening to this fairy tale, but suppose Gotch *is* Potts the First. What motive for murdering the twins would that give him?"

"The two husbands, inseparable companions," said Ellery dreamily, "living in the same house, playing endless checker tournaments with each other . . . What? Oh, his possible motive. Well, Dad, we agreed at the time that the Potts clan may have been going through a process of liquidation, one member at a time. And who were liquidated? Sheila Brent spotted it immediately. Only the sane ones were dying. The Brents."

"So?"

"So suppose the first Potts *had* come back in the person

of 'Major Gotch'? Mightn't he come to hate his successor, the second Potts—no matter how fast their friendship had been in the atolls of the South Seas?"

"Aaaa," said the Inspector.

"Mightn't he come to hate the three additional children Cornelia and Steve Brent brought into the world? Mightn't he resent the shares of Sheila, Bob, and Mac in what would seem to him *his* millions? Mightn't he reason, too, that their very existence jeopardized the security of his own children, the Three Goons—Thurlow, Louella, and Horatio? And because of all this, mightn't Bacchus Potts' 'Gotch' brood and plan and finally go over the deep end and begin to eliminate those not of his blood?—one by one?—Robert, Maclyn, then Sheila, and finally Steve Brent himself? Don't forget, Dad, if Gotch is Potts, he's insane. Potts's three children are proof enough of *that*."

The Inspector shook his head. "I'm glad the Old Woman's confession spared you the embarrassment of having to spout *that* theory!"

"The Old Woman's confession . . ." echoed Ellery in a queer tone.

"What's the matter with the Old Woman's confession?" The Inspector sat up straight.

"Your tone—"

"Did I say anything was the matter with it?"

"It's my gout, Father," smiled Mr. Queen. "My gout? I must remember to take the waters."

The Inspector threw a cushion at him. "And I must remember to send that will and confession back to Paxton. We've got photostatic copies for the files, but the pay-off is that Thurlow—Thurlow!—wants the confession for 'the family records'! . . . Oh, son." The Inspector stuck his head back through the doorway, grinning. "I promise not to tell a soul about that Gotch-is-Potts theory of yours."

Ellery threw the cushion back.

For Ellery Queen the path of literature this morning was paved merely with good intentions. He scowled at his typewriter for almost an hour without pecking a word. When he finally did begin to write, he found the usual digital difficulties insuperable. He had developed a mysterious habit of shifting the position of his hands one key to the left, so that when he thought he had written the sentence: "There were bloody stripes on Lecky's right elbow," he found that it actually read—more interestingly but less comprehensibly—"Rgwew qwew vkiist areuowa ib

Kwzjt&a eufgr wkviq" This he felt would place an unfair burden upon his readers; so he ripped the sheet out and essayed a new start. But this time he decided that there was no special point to putting bloody stripes on Lecky's right elbow, so there he was, back at the beginning. Curse all typewriters and his clumsiness with them!

Really ought to have a stenographer, he brooded. Take all this distracting mechanical work off his hands. A stenographer with honey-colored hair . . . no, red hair. Small. Perky. But sensible. Not the kind that chewed gum; no. A small warm package of goodies. Of course, purely for stenographic purposes. No reason why a writer's stenographer shouldn't also be inoffensive to the eye, was there? In fact, downright pleasant to look at? Like Sheila Brent, for instance. Sheila Brent . . .

Ellery was seated before his reproachful machine a half hour later, hands clasped behind his head and a self-pitying smile on his face, when the doorbell rang. He started guiltily when he saw who his caller was. "Charley!"

"Hullo," said Charley Paxton glumly. He scaled his hat across the room and dropped into the Inspector's sacred armchair. "Have you got a Scotch and soda? I'm pooped."

"Of course," said Ellery keenly. As he busied himself being host, he watched Charley out of the corner of his eyes. Mr. Paxton was looking poorly. "What's the matter? Strain of normal living proving too much for you, Charley?"

Charley grinned feebly. "It's a fact there hasn't been a murder in almost a month. Tedious!"

"Here's your drink. Why haven't I seen you since confessional?"

"Conf— Oh. *That* day." Charley scowled into his glass. "Hands full. Keeping the mobs of salesmen away from the Potts Palladium, as you call it. Handling a thousand legal details of the estate."

"Is it as large as you estimated?"

"Larger."

"I suppose a niggardly million or so?"

"Some pittance like that."

"How's Sheila?"

Charley did not answer for a moment. Then he raised his hollow eyes. "That's one of the reasons I came here today."

"Nothing wrong with Sheila, I hope?" Ellery said quickly.

"Wrong? No." Charley began to patrol the Queen living room.

"Oh. Things aren't going so well between you and Sheila—is that it?"

"That's putting it mildly."

"And I thought," murmured Mr. Queen, "that you'd come to invite me to the wedding."

"Wedding!" said Charley bitterly. "I'm further from the altar now than I ever was. Every time I say: 'When are we going to take the jump?' Sheila starts to cry and say she's the daughter of a two-times killer, and she won't saddle me with a murderess for a mother-in-law, even if she *is* dead, and a lot of similar hooey. I can't even get her to move out of that damned house. Won't leave old Steve, and Steve says he's too decrepit to start bumming again. . . . It's hopeless, Ellery."

"I can't understand that girl," mused Ellery.

"It's the same old madhouse, only worse, now that the Old Woman's not there to crack down. Louella's filling it with useless, expensive apparatus—I swear she'll blow that place up some night!—buying on credit, and of course she's getting all she wants now that the Old Woman's dead and the trades-people know what a lulu of a fortune Louella's coming into.

"Thurlow's lording it over them all—cock of the roost, Thurlow is. Sits at the head of the table and makes with the lofty cracks to Steve and Major Gotch, and is otherwise a complete pain in the—"

"As I was saying," said Ellery, "Sheila baffles me. Her attitude strikes me as inconsistent with my conception of the whole woman. Charley, there's something wrong somewhere, and it's up to you to find out what."

"Of course there's something wrong. She won't marry me!"

"Not that, Charley. Something else . . . Wish I knew . . . Might make . . ." Mr. Queen stopped guillotining his sentences in order to think. Then he said crisply: "As for you, my dear Gascon, my advice is to stick to it. Sheila's worth fighting for. Matter of fact," he sighed, "I'm inclined to be envious."

Charley looked startled.

Ellery smiled sadly. "It won't come to a duel at dawn, I promise you. You're her man, Charley. But just the same—"

Charley began to laugh. "And I come here to ask your advice. John Alden stuff!" His grin faded. "Say, I'm sorry as hell, Ellery. Although as far as I can see, anybody's got a better chance with Sheila than I have."

"She loves you. All you have to do is be patient and understanding, now that the case is closed—"

Charley stopped pacing. "Ellery," he said.

"What?"

"That's another reason I came to see you today."

"What's another reason you came to see me today?"

Charley lowered his voice. "I don't think the case *is* closed."

Ellery Queen said "Ah," and turned around like a dog seeking a place to settle. Instead, he freshened Charley Paxton's drink and mixed one for himself. "Sit down, Brother Paxton, and tell Papa all about it."

"I've been thinking—"

"That's always salutary."

"Two things still bother me. So much I can't sleep—"

"Yes?" Ellery did not mention his own insomnia of the past three weeks.

"Remember the Old Woman's confession?"

"I think so," said Ellery dryly.

"Well, one statement the Old Woman made in it strikes me as pretty peculiar," said Charley slowly.

"Which statement is that?"

"The one about the guns. She wrote she was the one who swiped the Harrington & Richardson revolver from Thurlow with which she held up the reporters the day of the first murder—the gun she almost killed Sergeant Velie with—"

"Yes, yes."

"Then she said: 'Later it was I who stole one of Thurlow's other guns and hid it from the police and went with it into my son Maclyn's bedroom in the middle of the night and shot him with it."

"Yes?"

" '*One* of Thurlow's other guns'!" exclaimed Charley. "But Ellery, *there were two guns missing.*"

"Indeed," said Ellery, as if he had never thought of that. "What do you make of it, Charley?"

"But don't you see?" cried the young lawyer. "What happened to that second gun, the one that's still missing? Where is it? Who has it? If it's still in the house, isn't Sheila in danger?"

"How's that?"

"Thurlow, Louella, Horatio! Suppose one of those poppy-eaters takes it into his head to continue the Old Woman's massacre on the Brent part of the family? Anything is possible with those three, Ellery. They hate Sheila and Steve as much as the Old Woman—maybe more. What do you think?"

"I've concocted more fantastic theories myself," murmured Mr. Queen. "Go on talking, Charley. I've been pining to discuss the case for three weeks now, but I haven't dared for fear I'd be disowned."

"I've been bursting, too! I can't get these thoughts out of my mind. I've had another—theory, suspicion, whatever you choose to call it. This one's driving me wild."

Ellery looked comforted. "Talk."

"The Old Woman knew she was going to die, Ellery. She said so in her confession, didn't she?"

"She did."

"Suppose she thought one of her precious darlings had killed the twins! She knew she was dying, *so what did she have to lose by taking the blame on herself?*"

"You mean—"

"I mean," said Charley tensely, "that maybe the Old Woman's confession was a phony, Ellery. I mean that maybe she was covering up for one of her crazy gang—*that there's still an active killer in that house.*"

Ellery swigged deeply. When he set his glass down, he said: "My dear fraternal sleuth, that was the first thought I had when we opened the envelope and read the Old Woman's confession."

"Then you agree it's possible?"

"Of course it's possible," said Ellery slowly. "It's even probable. I just can't see Cornelia Potts killing those two boys. But—" He shrugged. "My doubts and yours, Charley, won't stand up against that confession bearing Cornelia Potts's signature. . . . By George!" he said.

"What's the matter?"

Ellery jumped up. "Listen to this, Charley! The Old Woman was dead an hour or so at the time we found her body. Suppose someone had gone into her bedroom during that hour she lay there dead? The door wasn't locked. And anyone could have typed out that confession right there—on the portable which was standing conveniently by the bed!"

"You think someone, the real killer, *forged* that confession, Ellery?" gasped Charley. "I hadn't thought of that!" But then he shook his head.

"I didn't say I think so. I said it's possible," said Ellery irritably. "Possible, possible! That's all I do in this blasted case—call things 'possible'! What are you shaking your head for?"

"The Old Woman's signature, Ellery," said Charley in a depressed tone. "You compared it yourself with the other signatures—the one at the end of the will, the one on the large envelope. And you pronounced the signature genuine."

"There's the rub, I admit," muttered Ellery. "On the other hand, it was only a quick examination. It might be an extremely clever forgery that only the most minute study will disclose. The traps one's sense of infallibility sets! Stop feeling sorry for yourself, Mr. Queen, and start punching!"

"We've got to go over the signatures again?"

"What else?" Ellery clapped Charley on the shoulder. Then he fell into a study. "Charley. Remember when we visited the Old Woman early in the case to question her about the terms of her will? At that time, I recall, she handed you a slough of memorandums. I saw her sign them myself with the same soft pencil she apparently used always. What happened to those memos?"

"They're at the house, in that kneehole desk in the downstairs study."

"Well, those memos bear her authentic signature; that I'll swear to. Come on."

"To the house?"

"Yes. But first we'll stop at Headquarters and pick up the original of the confession, Charley. Maybe *one* theory in this puzzle will come out right side up!"

22 . . . *Mene, Mene, Tekel, Upharsin*

They found no one about but the servants, as usual. So they made directly for the library, and Ellery shut the door, rubbing his palms together, and said: "To work. Those signed memos, please."

Charley began rummaging through the drawers of the kneehole desk. "Got the shakes," he muttered. "If it's only . . . Here they are. What do we do now?"

Ellery did not reply at once. He riffled the sheaf of memorandums with an air of satisfaction. "Employ the services of a rather large ally," he said. "Nice sunny day, isn't it?"

"What?"

"Silence, brother, and reap 'the harvest of a quiet eye,' as Wordsworth recommends."

"Seems to me you're in an awfully good humor," grumbled Charley Paxton.

"Forgive me. This is like a breath of forest air to a man who's been shut up in a dungeon for three weeks. It's hope, Charley, that's what it is."

"Hope of what? More danger for Sheila?"

"Hope of the truth," cried Ellery. He went to the nearest window. The sun, that "large ally," made the window brilliant; by contrast, the study was in gloom.

"Perfect." Ellery took the topmost memorandum of the sheaf and held it flat against the pane with his left hand. The sunshine made the white paper translucent.

"The confession, Charley. Wasn't Dad curious!"

Ellery placed the confession over the memorandum on the windowpane, shifting it about until its signature lay superimposed upon the signature of the memorandum, visible through it. Then he studied the result. "No."

The signatures were obviously written by the same hand, but minor variations in the formation and length of certain letters caused a slight blurry effect when the two signatures were compared, one upon the other.

Ellery handed the memorandum to the lawyer. "Another memo, Charley."

Charley was puzzled. "I don't understand what you're doing."

"No," said Ellery again. "Not this one, either. *And* the next, Mr. Paxton."

When he had exhausted the pile of memorandums, he said to Charley in an assured voice: "Would you mind handing me again that memo which instructed you to sell all the Potts Shoe Company stock and buy back at 72?"

"But you've examined it!"

"Nevertheless."

Charley located it in the heap and handed it to him. Ellery once more placed it over the confession against the window.

"Look here, Charley. What do you see?"

"You mean the signatures?"

"Yes."

Charley looked. And then he said in an astonished voice: "*No blurriness!*"

"Exactly." Ellery took the papers down. "In other words, the Cornelia Potts signature on this stock-selling memorandum and the Cornelia Potts signature on the confession *match perfectly*. There are no slightest variations in the formation and size of characters. Line for line, curve for curve, the two signatures are exact duplicates. Twins, like Bob and Mac. Even the dot over the *i* is in the identical spot."

"And the signature on the stock-selling memo is the *only* memo signature that does match exactly?" asked Charley hoarsely.

"That's why I went through the entire batch—to make sure. Yes, it's the only one."

"I think I see where all this leads . . ."

"But it's so clear! No one ever writes his name in precisely the same way twice—that's a scientific fact. There are invariably minor differences in the same person's signature, and there would be if you had a million samples to compare. Charley, we've established a new fact in the Potts case!"

"One of these two signatures is a forgery."

"Yes."

"But which one?"

"Come Charley. The Old Woman signed this stock-selling memo in our presence. Therefore the memo signature must be genuine. Therefore the signature on the confession is the forgery."

"Somebody got hold of this memo, typed out that phony confession, and then traced the signature of the memo off on the bottom of the confession?"

"Only way it could have produced an identical signature; yes, Charley. The stock memo's been in the desk in this study since the day the Old Woman typed out all these instructions—"

"Yes," mumbled Charley. "After I made the various phone calls necessary that day, I put the memos in this desk, as usual. . . ."

"So anyone in the house could have found them and used this one to trace off its signature. It was probably done just the way I've illustrated—by slapping the stock memo against the sunny windowpane, placing the typed confession over the memo, and then tracing the memo signature onto the confession by utilizing the sunlight-created translucence of both sheets."

"And the house is full of those soft pencils the Old Woman used—"

"And it would have been child's play to slip into the Old Woman's bedroom and use her portable typewriter for the typing of the 'confession' and that note at the bottom of the will. The whole operation was undoubtedly done between the time the Old Woman died alone in her bed and the time we all came back to the house—you, Sheila, Dad, and I—and found her body with the large sealed envelope in her hand. There was about an hour for the criminal to work in—and a few minutes would have been ample."

Ellery went to the telephone.

"What are you going to do?"

"Bring joy to my father's heart." He dialed Police Headquarters.

"What?" repeated the Inspector feebly.

Ellery said it again.

"You mean," said the old gentleman after another pause, "you mean . . . it's open again?"

"What else can it mean, Dad? The confession signature is now patently a tracing job, so Cornelia Potts never wrote the confession. Therefore she didn't confess to the murders at all. Therefore we still don't know who killed the Potts twins. Yes, I'm afraid the case *is* open again."

"I might have known," muttered the Inspector. "All right, Velie and I will be up there right away."

When Ellery turned from the telephone, there was Sheila, her back against the door. Charley was licking his lips.

"I heard you tell your father," said Sheila.

"Sheila—!"

"Just a minute, Charley." Ellery advanced across the study with outstretched hands. Hers were cold, but steady. "I think you know, Sheila, that I'll—"

"I'm all right, thanks." She was tightly controlled. She slipped her hands from his, and clenched them. "I'm past being shocked or surprised or sent into hysterics by anything, Ellery."

"You sensed this all along."

"Yes. Instinct, I guess." Sheila even laughed. She turned to Charley Paxton, her face softening. "That's why I refused to leave the house, darling. Don't you see now?"

"No, I don't see," muttered Charley. "I don't see anything any more!"

"Poooor Charley."

Ellery was quite suffused in admiration.

Sheila kissed her troubled swain. "You don't understand so many things, lambie-pie. I've been a coward long enough. Nobody can make me afraid any more." Her chin tilted. "Somebody's out for my blood, is he? Well, I won't run away. I'll see this through to the bitter end."

23 . . . The Fruit of the Tree

Now the house of Potts bore palls once more, shadows that shrank in stealth from them, like cats.

It became intolerable. They walked out onto the terrace overlooking the inner court to be rid of it. Here there was some graciousness in the flagged floor, the Moorish columns, the ivies and flowers and the view of grass and tall trees. The sun was friendly. They sat down in warm-bottomed steel chairs to wait for Inspector Queen and Sergeant Velie. Sheila sat close to Charley; their hands clasped, and after a moment her head dropped, defeated, to his shoulder.

It was interesting, Ellery thought, how from the terrace one could view all the good and all the evil in this manmade scene. Directly before him, at the end of a path bordered not unpleasantly with geraniums and cockleshells, stood Horatio's Ozzian house, a distortion of a dream, but with the piquancy of all sugar-coated fantasy. Surrounded as it was by civilized lawn and serene and healthy trees, it could not offend; in certain moods, Ellery agreed as he tried not to look at Sheila and Charley, it might even charm.

The tower of Louella was another thing. It cast its squat shadow over the gracious garden, its false turret crenelated as if against a besieging army, a flag (which Ellery noticed for the first time) whipping sullenly above the mock battlements. He watched the fluttering pennant curiously, unable to make out its design. Then the breeze straightened it for a moment, and he saw it whole. It bore a picture of a woman's oxford, and across it the words, simply: THE POTTS SHOE.

"It isn't even the grotesquerie," Ellery thought to himself impatiently. "It's the downright bad taste. This flag, the bronze Shoe on the front lawn."

He turned to glower at it, for its gigantic toe box was

visible from where he sat, the rest cut off by the angle of the house. THE PO he read, backwards. In neon tubing!

Ellery wondered how Cornelia Potts had neglected in her will to leave instructions for her tombstone. Perhaps, he thought uncharitably, the Old Woman had foreseen the reluctance of St. Praxed's to permit erection of a Vermont marble lady's oxford, tombstone size, within its hoary yard.

Stephen Brent and Major Gotch were raptly playing checkers under a large green table umbrella to one side of the court lawn. They had not even noticed in their absorption the appearance of Sheila, Charley Paxton, and Ellery. Birds sang ancient melodies, and Ellery closed his eyes and dozed.

"Sleeping!"

Ellery awoke with a jerk. His father stood over him, in the scowling mood of frustration. Behind him bulked Sergeant Velie, belligerent. Sheila and Charley were on their feet. On the lawn, where old Steve and the Major had been bent over their checkerboard, stood merely an umbrella table and two iron chairs.

"Are we boring you, Mr. Queen?" asked the Inspector.

Ellery jumped up. "Sorry, Dad. It was so peaceful here—"

"Peaceful!" The Inspector was red of face, and Sergeant Velie perspired freely; it was evident the two men had rushed uptown from Center Street. "I can think of other words. Blasted case busted wide-open again!"

"Now I suppose I got to start lookin' for the missing rod all over again," growled Sergeant Velie in his basso profundo. "I was only tellin' the wife last night how the whole thing seemed like a bad dream—"

"Yes, yes, the gun, Sergeant," said Ellery absently.

Velie's anvil jaw swelled. "I searched this house, I dug up practically this whole square block—I tell you, Maestro, if you want to find that gun, go look for it yourself!"

"Stop it, Velie." Inspector Queen sat down with a groan. "Who's got that confession and stock memo? Hand 'em over."

The Inspector superimposed the signatures, as Ellery had done, and held them up to the sun for a squint. "No doubt about it. They're identical." He jammed both papers into his pocket. "I'll keep these. They're evidence now."

"Evidence against who?" grumbled Sergeant Velie, making up in scorn what he lacked in grammar.

At this moment Horatio Potts, in character, chose to enter the scene. That is to say, he appeared from the other side of his improbable dwelling, bearing the now familiar ladder. He waddled to a tall sycamore tree between his cottage and the umbrella table, set the ladder against the bole, and began to climb.

"Now what in the name of thunder is *he* doing?" asked Inspector Queen.

"It's his kite again," said Sheila grimly.

"Kite?" Ellery blinked. "Still at it, eh?"

"While you were napping here, he came out of his shack and began to fly one of 'em," explained Charley. "It got snarled in that big tree, so I suppose he's going after it."

The ladder was shaking under Horatio's weight.

"That Horatio's going to take a mighty tumble one of these days," said Charley critically. "If only he'd act his age—"

"Stop!" shouted Ellery Queen. They were thunderstruck. Ellery had cried out in a sort of terror, and now he was streaking across the lawn towards the sycamore with all the power of his long legs. "Stop, Horatio!" he shouted.

Horatio kept climbing.

The Inspector began to run after his son; Sergeant Velie began to run after the Inspector with a mine-not-to-reason-why expression; and so Sheila and Charley ran, too.

"Ellery, what the devil are you yelling 'Stop!' for?" cried the Inspector. "He's only—climbing—a—tree!"

"Mother Goose!" Ellery roared back over his shoulder, not slackening his pace for an instant.

"What?" screamed the Inspector.

"Suppose the ladder's been tampered with? Horatio's big—and fat—he'd fall—'Humpty Dumpty—had a great—fall . . .'"

The Inspector gurgled and dug his tiny heels into the turf for traction. Ellery continued to shout at Horatio, and Horatio continued to ignore him. By the time the great man had reached the base of the sycamore, Horatio was almost invisible among the branches overhead. Ellery could hear him puffing and wheezing as he struggled to free the half-torn kite that was impaled above him. "Be careful, Mr. Potts!" Ellery yelled up.

"Ellery, are you coocoo?" panted the Inspector, coming up. Velie, Sheila, Charley were a few steps behind him.

They were all frightened; but when they saw Horatio in motion in the tree, the ladder intact, and nothing amiss save the excitement on the Queen countenance, their concern changed to bewilderment.

"Mr. Potts, be careful!" Ellery roared again, craning.

"What's that?" Horatio's jovial face peeped redly down from between two leafy branches. "Oh, hullo there, nice people," beamed Horatio. "Darned kite got stuck. I'll be right down."

"Watch your step on the way down," implored Ellery. "Test each rung with one foot before you put your whole weight on it!"

"Oh, nonsense," said Horatio a little crossly. "As if I'd never climbed a ladder." And, the kite in one paw, he brought his right foot crashing down on one of the uppermost rungs.

"The fool will break his neck," said Ellery angrily. "I don't know why I even bother."

"What *are* you babbling about?" demanded his father.

"Hey, he stopped," said Sergeant Velie. "What's the matter up there, Horatio?" the Sergeant called up. "Gettin' cold feet? A great big boy like you!"

Horatio had paused in his descent to reach far over and thrust his fat hand into the foliage of a lower branch. The ladder rocked precariously, and Ellery and Velie in panic grabbed to steady it.

"Bird's nest," said Horatio, straightening. "Lots of fun, birds' nests." The kite in one hand, a starling's nest in the other, he continued his descent, pressing against the ladder's sides with his enormous forearms. "Just noticed it on that branch," he said, reaching the ground. "Nothing I like better than a good old bird's nest, gentlemen. Sets me up for the whole day."

"Beast," said Sheila; and she turned away from the nest clutched in his paw.

"Now, sir," said Horatio, beaming at Ellery, "you were saying something about being careful? Careful about what?"

Ellery had taken the ladder down and, with the Inspector and Velie, was examining it rung by rung. As he looked over the last rung, his face grew very red indeed.

"I don't see anything wrong," said the Sergeant.

"Well." Ellery laughed and tossed the ladder aside.

"Mother Goose—Humpty Dumpty," snarled his father. "This case has got you, son. Better go home and call a doctor."

"What's the matter Horatio?" asked Charley.

Sheila turned quickly.

Horatio stood there, a large enigma, one hand plunged into the starling's nest.

"What is it, Mr. Potts?" demanded Ellery.

"Of all things!" guffawed Horatio, recovering. "Imagine finding *this* in a starling's nest." And he withdrew his great paw. On his palm lay a small, snub-nosed automatic pistol a little patchy with bird slime. It was a Colt .25.

"But that's the gun Bob Potts was plugged with," said Sergeant Velie, staring.

"Don't be a *schtunk* all your life, Velie!" cried Inspector Queen, grabbing for the automatic. "The murder gun's in the Bureau files—they all are!"

"Then this," said Ellery in a low voice, "this is the duplicate Colt .25—the missing weapon."

Later, when the lawn was empty, Ellery took his father by the arm and steered him to the umbrella table. "Sit down, Dad. I've got to think this out."

"Think what out?" demanded the old gentleman, nevertheless seating himself. He glanced at the Colt; it was loaded with a single cartridge. "So we've found the missing gun. Whoever's been pulling these jobs hid the Colt in that nest—blast that Velie for not looking in the trees!—and I suppose had the duplicate S. & W. .38/32 hidden up there, too, in preparation for the Maclyn Potts kill. But so what? The way things stand now—"

"Please, Dad."

The Inspector sat back. Ellery sat back, too, to stare with eyes that at first saw, and later did not see, the automatic in the Inspector's lap. And after a long time he smiled, and stretched, and said: "Oh, yes. That's it."

"Oh, yes, what's it?" asked his father petulantly.

"Would you do something right away, Dad? Spread the word through the house that the finding of the last gun in that bird's nest this afternoon has solved the case."

"Solved the case!" The Inspector rose and the automatic fell to the grass. Mechanically he stooped to retrieve it. "Solved the case?" he repeated faintly.

"Make sure they all understand clearly that *I know who murdered Cornelia's twin sons*."

"You mean . . . you really do know? On the level, son?" The Inspector licked his lips.

But Ellery shook his head cryptically. "I mean I want everyone to think I do."

24 . . . Queen Was in the Parlor

The time: evening. The scene: the downstairs study. As Curtain rises, we see the study in artful dim light, creating full-bodied shadows on the walls of books. Most of the furniture lies within the aura of the gloom. Only in right foreground near the French doors is there illumination, and it is evident that this concentration of light has been deliberately effected. It emanates from a standing lamp which throws its rays chiefly upon a straight-backed, uncomfortable chair which stands before a leather-topped occasional table. The boundary of brightness just touches an object lying upon the table—a .25 Colt automatic spotted with bird slime and lying half out of a raped starling's nest.

Ellery Queen leans against the lintel of one of the open French doors immediately outside the illuminated area, a little behind and to one side of the table. All the doors are open, for it is a warm evening (but we may suspect, knowing the chicanery potential of the Queen mind, that the barometer is not the sole, or even the principal reason). Ellery faces the straight-backed chair beyond the table; he also faces the door from the foyer, off left.

The terrace, which lies behind him, is in darkness. Offstage, from beyond the terrace, we hear the vibrant songs of crickets.

In the shadows of the study, well out of the light's orbit, sit Sheila Brent and Charles Hunter Paxton, still, expectant, and baffled spectators.

Ellery looks around in a last survey of his set, nods with a self-satisfied air, and then speaks.

ELLERY (*sharply*): Flint! (*Detective Flint pokes his head into the study from the foyer doorway.*)

FLINT: Yes, sir, Mr. Queen?

ELLERY: Thurlow Potts, please. (*Detective Flint withdraws. Thurlow Potts enters. The foyer door swings shut behind him; he looks back over his shoulder nervously. Then he advances into the scene, pausing uncertainly just outside the circle of lamplight. In this position the chair and the table with the gun and the bird's nest on it are between him and Ellery. Ellery regards him coldly.*)

THURLOW: Well? That detective said— (*He stops. Ellery*

147

*has suddenly left his position at the French window and,
without speaking, comes downstage and around the table
to turn and pause so that he faces Thurlow, forcing him
to follow him with his eyes.)*

ELLERY *(sternly)*: Thurlow Potts!

THURLOW: Yes, Mr. Queen? Yes, sir?

ELLERY: You know what's happened?

THURLOW: You mean my mother?

ELLERY: I mean your mother's confession!

THURLOW: No. I mean yes. I mean I can't understand
it. Well, that's not quite true. I don't know quite how to
say it, Mr. Queen—

ELLERY: Stop pirouetting, Mr. Potts! Do you or don't
you?

THURLOW *(sullenly)*: I know that man—your father—
told us Mother's confession was forged. That the case is
opened again. It's very confusing. In the first place, I shot
Robert to death in the duel—

ELLERY: Come, come, Mr. Potts, we've been all
through your Dunasian career and you know perfectly
well we substituted a blank cartridge for your lethal one
to keep you from doing a very silly thing, and that
someone managed to slip into your bedroom the night
before the duel and put a live cartridge back into the
automatic so that when you fired, Bob would die—as he
did, Mr. Potts, as he did.

THURLOW: *(touching his forehead)*: It's all very confusing.

ELLERY *(grimly)*: Is it, Mr. Potts?

THURLOW: Your tone, sir!

ELLERY: Why do you avoid looking at this table, Mr.
Potts?

THURLOW: I beg your pardon?

ELLERY: This table, Mr. Potts—t-a-b-l-e. This handsome little piece just beyond the end of your nose, Mr.
Potts. Why haven't you looked at it?

THURLOW: I don't know what you mean, and what's
more, Mr. Queen, I won't stand here and be insulted—

ELLERY *(suddenly)*: Sit down, Mr. Potts.

THURLOW: Uh?

ELLERY *(in a soft tone)*: Sit down. *(Thurlow hesitates,
then slowly seats himself in the uncomfortable chair beside
the table, knees together and pudgy hands in his lap. He
blinks in the strong light of the lamp, wriggling. He still
has not glanced at the weapon or the bird's nest.)* Mr.
Potts!

THURLOW (*sullenly*): Well? Well?

ELLERY: Look at the gun, please. (*Thurlow licks his lips. Slowly he turns to stare at the table. He starts perceptibly.*) You recognize it?

THURLOW: No! I mean it looks just like the gun I used in my duel with Robert. . . .

ELLERY: It *is* just like the gun you used in your duel with Robert, Mr. Potts. But it isn't the same gun. It's a duplicate, the duplicate you bought from Cornwall & Ritchey, Remember?

THURLOW (*nervously*): Yes. Yes, I seem to recall there were two Colt .25's among the fourteen I purchased—

ELLERY: Indeed. (*He steps forward suddenly, and Thurlow makes an instinctive backward movement. Ellery picks up the automatic from its nest, removes the magazine, bending over to let the light catch the cartridge inside. Thurlow follows his movements, fascinated. Suddenly Ellery rams the magazine back into place and tosses the automatic into the nest.*) Do you know where we found this missing loaded gun of yours today, Mr. Potts?

THURLOW: In—in the sycamore tree? Yes, I've heard about that, Mr. Quueen.

ELLERY: Why did you put it there?

THURLOW (*gasping*): I never did! I haven't seen this weapon since the day I bought it with the other thirteen!

ELLERY (*with a cynical smile*): Really, Mr. Potts? (*Then sharply.*) That's all! You may go.

(*Thurlow blinks, hesitates, rises, openly surprised and upset by this peremptory dismissal. Then, without a backward glance, he hurries from the scene.*)

ELLERY: Flint! Louella Potts.

And now it became evident that Mr. Queen's scene with Thurlow Potts was a deliberate design for the scenes that followed. For when Louella Potts swept in, a violently self-assured Louella, quite altered from that sullen and sour spinster who had been under her mother's thumb, Ellery's script adapted itself to the unpredictable dialogue of this second character smoothly and with scarcely an emendation.

Again Ellery put the preliminary questions, again they led to the gun on the table, again he picked it up, fiddled with its magazine, displayed its cartridge, replaced the magazine, tossed the automatic back on the table, and asked the last question. "Why did you hide this loaded gun of Thurlow's in the starling's nest, Miss Potts?"

Louella sprang from the straight-backed chair, her

saffron features convulsed. "Is it for this childish nonsense I've been dragged away from my important experiments? I never saw this weapon before, I didn't put it in the nest, I know nothing about it, and I'll ask you, Mr. Queen, to stop interfering with the progress of science!" And Louella strode out, all bones and indignation.

But Mr. Queen only smiled to Sheila and Charley Paxton and summoned Horatio Potts.

Horatio was immense in more ways than one. For purposes of this scene he had become a completely reasonable man. If the truth were known, the sudden sanity of his answers and a certain unexpected acuteness of insight into the trend of Mr. Queen's questions rather took the spotlight away from that great man and focused it brilliantly upon his victim.

"Very interesting, sir," said Horatio indulgently at one point. "I never did believe my mother murdered the twins. Too gory, you know. Madame Tussaud stuff. No, indeed. That confession, though. Very clever. Don't you think so, Mr. Queen?"

Mr. Queen thought so.

"And now you know who did it all," said Horatio at another point. "At least that's what I heard."

Ellery pretended to be angry at the "leak."

"I wish you'd enlighten me," continued the fat man, chuckling. "Sounds like good material for a book."

"You don't know of course."

"I?" Horatio was astonished.

"Come, Mr. Potts. You hid this loaded automatic in the starling's nest, didn't you?" And again Ellery went through the business of opening the gun, displaying its cartridge, and closing it again.

"I hid it in the nest?" repeated Horatio. "But why?"

Ellery said nothing.

"As a matter of fact," continued Horatio reflectively, "the very idea's silly. If I hid Thurlow's gun in the tree and wanted it to stay hidden, would I have found it under your nose this afternoon, Mr. Queen? No, no, sir, you're on the wrong track."

Ellery could only wave Horatio Potts feebly out and call for Stephen Brent.

With Sheila's father the script resumed its character. The old man was nervous, and while Ellery was gentle with him Brent's nervousness was not allayed.

He denied with bewilderment having known anything about the gun in the tree, and left in a trot.

His stuttering had been pronounced.

Sheila began to examine Ellery with an ominous grimness. Charley had to restrain her from jumping up and running after her father.

With Major Gotch Ellery was severe. The old pirate showed his teeth at once. "I've taken a lot of berserker nonsense in this house, Mister," he roared, "but you've no call to speak to me this way. I don't know a cursed thing, and that's a fact you can't deny!"

"I thought you were well-known in the Dutch East Indies," said Ellery, departing from the script.

Gotch snorted. "One of its notorious characters, Mister. Bloomin' myth. Left my mark, I did."

"They never heard of you, Major."

He looked aghast. "Why, the muckin' liars!"

"Ever use another name, Major?"

The man sat still. Then he said: "No."

Ellery, lightly: "We can find out, you know."

"Find and be damned to you!"

"Don't have to, as it turns out. This is the last round-up, Major. Our friend the killer hasn't much grace left. Why'd you put the gun in the bird's nest?"

"You're barmy," said the Major, shaking his head; and he left as Ellery opened the automatic for the fifth time and played with the cartridge.

"Well, Mr. Queen?" asked Detective Flint from the foyer doorway. "Where do we go from here?"

"*You* exit quietly, Flint."

Flint shut the foyer door with a huffy bang.

Sheila jumped out of the shadows at once. "I don't see why you had to drag my father into this," she said tartly. "Treating him like the others—!"

"Smoke screen, Sheila."

"Yes?" she said suspiciously.

"I had to go through the motions of treating all the suspects equally."

Sheila did not seem convinced. "But why?"

"I can't imagine what you're driving at, Ellery," said Charley gloomily, "but whatever it is, you haven't learned a darned thing as far as *I* can see."

"Grilling Daddy!" said Sheila.

"It's all part of a plan, part of a plan," said Ellery cheerfully. "It hasn't quite worked out yet—"

"Shhh," whispered Sheila. "Someone . . ."

"On the terrace . . ." Charley whispered.

Ellery waved them back into the gloom imperiously. He

himself darted out of range of the light, flattening against a wall. There was no sound but the beating of the grandfather clock. Then they heard a quick cautious step from the terrace darkness. In his shadow, Ellery crouched on the balls of his feet.

Inspector Queen stepped into the study through one of the French doors.

Ellery shook his head, chuckling. "Dad, Dad."

The Inspector peered about the dimly lit room, trying to locate the source of his son's voice, moving uncertainly.

"Ellery, you fox!" cried Charley, jumping forward. "Darned if I don't get the point!"

"But Ellery, if that's it," cried Sheila, running forward too, "you *mustn't*. It's dangerous!"

"What is this?" demanded Inspector Queen, blinking at them. "Mustn't do what, Ellery?"

"Nothing, nothing, Dad." Ellery came out of his shadow quickly. "Out of the light, Dad. We're waiting."

"Waiting for what? All right, I spread the word and stayed out of sight, but I'm not going to wait all night—"

Ellery pulled his father into the shadows.

"I don't like it," grumbled the Inspector. "What's going on here? Why were you so tense when I came in? So quiet?" And then he spied the Colt automatic in the nest on the table.

Ellery nodded.

"So that's it," said the Inspector slowly. "That's why you wanted the kit and caboodle of 'em to think you knew who the killer was. It's a trap."

"Of course," said Sheila breathlessly. "He's just interviewed everybody, asking a lot of useless questions—"

"Just so he could show them this gun on the table," said Charley, "right near the terrace!"

"Ellery you can't do it," said the Inspector with finality. "It's too dangerous."

"Nonsense," said the great man.

"Suppose one of them sneaked onto the terrace. You mightn't hear him. You certainly couldn't see him." The Inspector went to the table. "All he'd have to do would be stick his hand in here from the terrace, grab the gun, and fire at you point-blank."

"It's loaded, too, Inspector!" said Sheila. "Ellery, your father's right."

"Of course it's loaded," said Charley frowning. "He went to an awful lot of trouble to show 'em it's loaded."

"You wouldn't have a chance, Ellery," said the Inspector. "You've set a trap, all right—they all think you know who did it and here's a loaded gun within easy reach—you've set a trap, but if you think I'm going to let you use yourself as live bait—"

"I've taken a few precautions," said Ellery lightly. "Come over here, the three of you."

The Inspector followed Ellery into the heavier shadows, away from the windows. "What precautions?"

Charley and Sheila backed off from the windows, joining them. "You'd better get out of here, Sheila—"

"Just a minute, Charley," snapped the Inspector. "*What* precautions, Ellery?"

Ellery grinned. "Velie's posted outside on the terrace behind one of those Moorish pillars. He'll nab whoever comes in before—"

"Velie?" The Inspector stared. "*I* just came in from the terrace and Velie didn't see or hear *me*. It's dark as a coal passer's glove out there—he couldn't have known it was me—so why didn't he nab me before I stepped through the French door?"

Ellery stared back at his father. "Something's gone wrong," he muttered. "Velie's in trouble. Come on!" He took two strides toward the open French door behind the occasional table, the others following. But then he stopped. On the very edge of the circle of lamplight.

A slender thing had darted in from the black terrace, a snake. But it was not a snake; it was a human arm. Even this was the impression of an instant, for it all occurred so quickly that they could only halt, Ellery included, and glare, powerless to move, unable to comprehend its nature or its purpose.

The hand was gloved, a gloved blur. It snatched the .25 automatic from the bird's nest on the table, brought it to a level in an amazingly fluid extension of its original movement, and for the fragment of a second poised the snub nose of the weapon on a direct line with Ellery's heart.

In that instant several things happened. Sheila screamed, clutching Charley. Ellery's hand came up from his side, defensively. With a snarl the Inspector dived head-first at Ellery's legs.

But one thing happened before any of the other three got fairly started ... The gloved finger squeezed the trigger of the Colt and smoke and flame enveloped it. Ellery toppled to the floor.

25 . . . The Light That Succeeded

The arm, the hand, the weapon disappeared. Only the smoke remained, hovering over the table, a little cloud. It began to drift lazily toward the lamp.

Inspector Queen, on the floor, rolled over swiftly and grasped Ellery by his jacket lapels. "Ellery. Son."

He shook Ellery.

Sheila whispered: "Is he . . . ? Charley!" She hid her face in Paxton's coat.

"Inspector—" Charley paid no attention. "Ellery," he said, and tugged.

Ellery groaned, opening his eyes.

"Ellery!" The Inspector's voice lifted with incredulity. "Are you all right, son?"

"All right?" Ellery struggled to sit up. He shook his head. "What hit me? I remember an arm—a shot—"

"The Inspector dived for your legs," said Sheila, dropping to her knees beside him. "Don't move now—lie back! Charley, take a look. Help me get his jacket off—"

"Sit still now, you blinking hero," growled Charley. "Setting traps!"

"Please," said the Inspector. They sat back on their haunches. Ellery was still shaking his head. "Where does it hurt, son? I don't see any blood—"

"Doesn't hurt anywhere," said Ellery testily.

"Out of his head," Sheila whispered. "Do you think . . . possibly . . . internal injuries?"

"Let's get him over to that easy-chair," said Charley in a low voice.

The Inspector nodded, bent over again. "Now look, son. Don't you try to do a thing. We're going to pick you up and carry you over to that chair. It can't be your back, because you sat up by yourself, so I think it's safe enough to try—"

"Sheila," whispered Charley, "call a doctor."

Ellery looked around suddenly, as if for the first time conscious of what was going on about him. "What is this?" he snarled. "Why are you fussing over me? Get after that murdering maniac!" And he sprang to his feet.

The Inspector shrank from him, open-mouthed. "You're not *wounded?*"

154

"Of course I'm not wounded, Dad."

"But—that shot, son! Fired at a range of five feet!"

"A child couldn't have missed you," cried Sheila.

"He *must* have hit you, Ellery," said Charley. "Maybe it was just a flesh wound, a scratch somewhere, but—"

Ellery lit a cigaret with slightly shaking fingers. "Do I have to do a strip-tease to convince you?" He ripped open his shirt front. Something metallic shone in the lamplight.

"A bullet-proof vest!" gasped the Inspector.

"Told you I'd taken precautions, Dad. I didn't depend merely on Velie. This is that steel-mesh vest the Commissioner of Scotland Yard presented to you last year." He grinned. "What the well-dressed dilettante of detection will wear." Ellery clapped his father on the shoulder and helped the old gentleman to his feet.

The Inspector shook off Ellery's hand, becoming gruff. "Sissy," he growled. "Letting me knock the wind out of you. You'd never make a cop."

"And talking about cops," said Charley, "what happened to Sergeant Velie?"

"Velie!" exclaimed Ellery. "Knocked my brains out, too, Dad. Gangway!"

"Be careful, Ellery! Whoever that was took the gun with him!"

"Oh, *that* character's made his exit from the script long ago," snapped Ellery; and he dived through the nearest French door. "Sheila, turn the lights on out here, will you?" he called back.

Sheila ran for the foyer. A moment later the terrace was flooded with light.

"No sign of whoever it was," panted Charley Paxton.

"Here's the gun," cried the Inspector. "Dropped it on the terrace just outside the study. Velie! Where are you, damn your idiot's hide?"

"Velie!" shouted Ellery.

Detective Flint stamped out of the house by way of the foyer, his big hand on Sheila's arm. "I caught this gal in the foyer, Inspector. Monkeying with the light switch."

"Start looking for the Sergeant, you dumb ox," snarled the Inspector. "Ellery sent Miss Brent!"

"Yes, sir," said Flint startled, and at once he began to search among the empty chairs of the terrace, as if he expected Sergeant Velie to materialize in one of them.

"Here he is." Ellery's voice was faint. They found him at the far end of the terrace. He was kneeling by the Sergeant's still, supine figure, slapping the big man's cheeks without mercy. As they ran up, Velie gurgled deep in his throat and blinked his eyes open.

"Glug," said Sergeant Velie.

"He's still dizzy," Inspector Queen bent over him. "Velie!"

"Huh?" The Sergeant turned glassy eyes on his superior.

"Are you all right, Sergeant?" asked Ellery Queen anxiously. "What happened?"

"Oh," Velie groaned and sat up, feeling his head.

"What happened, Velie?" roared the Inspector.

"Take it easy, will ya? Here I am hidin' behind one of these pillars," rumbled Velie, "and—ouch! The roof comes down on my conk. Say," he said excitedly, "I'm wounded. I got a lump on the back of my head!"

"Slugged from behind," said Ellery, rising. "Sees nothing, hears nothing, knows nothing. Come along. Sergeant. It's a miracle you're alive."

There was no clue to Velie's assailant. Detective Flint had seen nothing. They agreed it was the same person who had attempted to assassinate Ellery.

"It was a good trap while you set it," laughed Charley as they returned to the library. Then he shook his head.

"Smart," said Ellery through his teeth. "And quick. Slippery customer. Have to use grappling hooks." He fell into a fierce study. The Inspector examined his clothes while Sergeant Velie groped in the liquor cabinet for first aid.

"Funny," mumbled the Inspector.

"What?" Ellery was scarcely paying attention.

"Nothing, son."

The Inspector then examined the room under full light. The longer he searched, the more perplexed he seemed. And finally he stopped searching and said, "It's impossible."

"What's impossible?" asked Sergeant Velie. He had administered two glasses of first aid and was himself again.

"What are you talking about, Dad?"

"You're still slug-nutty from that fall you took," said the Inspector, "or you'd know without my having to tell you. A shot was fired in this room, wasn't it?"

"The bullet!" cried Ellery. "You can't find it?"

"Not a sign of it. Not a mark on the walls or the furniture or, as far as I can see, the floor or ceiling. No bullet, no shell, no nothing."

"It must be here," said Sheila. "It was fired point-blank into the room."

"Ricocheted off, most likely," said Charley. "Maybe took a funny carom and flew out into the garden."

"Maybe," grunted the Inspector. "But where are the marks of the ricochet? Bullet doesn't ricochet off empty space, Charley. It just isn't here."

"My vest!" said Ellery. "If it's anywhere, it's in my bulletproof vest. Or at least some mark of it, if it bounced off." He opened his shirt again and he and his father together examined the steel vest covering his torso. But there was no indication of a bullet's having struck—no dent in the fabric, no powder burns, no glittering line of abrasion. Moreover, his shirt and jacket were clean and whole.

"But we heard the shot," cried Inspector Queen. "We saw it fired. What is this, another magic trick? Another gob of Mother Goose nonsense?"

Ellery buttoned his shirt slowly. Sergeant Velie was frowning in a mighty, dutiful effort at concentration, a bottle of Irish whisky in his fist. The Inspector was glaring at the Colt which he had recovered from the terrace floor. And then Ellery chuckled. As he was buttoning the top button of his shirt. He chuckled: "Of course. Oh, of course."

"What are you patting yourself on the back about?" demanded the Inspector peevishly.

"That confirms everything."

"*What* confirms everything?"

Sergeant Velie set the whisky bottle down and began to shuffle toward the Queens, a curious look on his rocky face.

"Dad, I know who killed Robert and Maclyn Potts."

PART FIVE

26 . . . The Identity of the Sparrow

"You really know?" said Inspector Queen. "It's not guess-work?"

"I really know," said Ellery with wonder, as if he were surprised himself at the simplicity of it all.

"But how can you?" cried Sheila. "What's happened so suddenly that tells you?"

"Who cares what's happened?" said Charley Paxton grimly. "I want to know who it is!"

"Me, too," said Sergeant Velie, feeling his head. "Put the finger on him once for all, Maestro, so we can stop shadow-boxin' and get in there and punch."

Inspector Queen was regarding his eminent son with suspicion. "Ellery, is this another 'trap' of yours?"

Ellery sighed, and sat down in the straight-backed chair to lean forward with his elbows on his knees. "It rather reminds me," he began, "of *Mother Goose*—"

"Oh, my gosh," groaned the Sergeant.

"Who killed Robert and Maclyn? 'I,' said the Sparrow," murmured Mr. Queen, unabashed. "Wonderful how those jingles which were originally political and social satires keep cropping up in this case. I don't know if the Cock Robin thing was one of those, but I do know the identity of the Sparrow. Except, Charley, that I can't tell you the 'who' without first telling you the 'how.' You wouldn't believe me otherwise."

"Tell it any way you please," begged Sheila. "But tell it, Ellery!"

Ellery lit a cigaret slowly. "Thurlow bought fourteen guns when he launched his dueling career. Fourteen . . . Sergeant, how many of those did you manage to round up?"

Velie started. "Who, me? Twelve."

"Yes. Specifically, the two used in the duel with Bob Potts, the one the Old Woman stole from Thurlow's hoard in that false closet of his, and the nine you found there afterwards, Sergeant. Twelve in all. Twelve out of the fourteen we knew Thurlow had purchased from the small-arms department of Cornwall & Ritchey. So two were missing."

Ellery looked about absently for an ashtray. Sheila jumped up and brought him one. He smiled at her, and she ran back to her chair. "Two were missing," he resumed, "and subsequently we discovered which two. They were exact duplicates in manufacture and type of the two guns Thurlow had produced for his duel with Bob: a .25-caliber Colt Pocket Model automatic, and a Smith & Wesson number unknown as the S. & W. .38/32 revolver, with a 2-inch barrel.

"That struck me as a curious fact. For what were the first twelve weapons?" Ellery took his inventory from his wallet. "A Colt .25 automatic, Pocket Model; a Smith & Wesson .38—the .38/32 revolver with 2-inch barrel; a Harrington & Richardson .22, Trapper Model; an Iver Johnson .32 Special, safety hammerless automatic; a Schmeisser .25 automatic, safety Pocket Model; a Stevens .22 Long Rifle, single-shot Target pistol; an I. J. Champion .22 Target single action; a Stoeger Luger, 7.65 millimeter, refinished; a New Model Mauser of 7.63 millimeter caliber with a ten-shot magazine; a High Standard hammerless automatic Short, .22 caliber; a Browning 1912 of 9-millimeter caliber; and an Ortgies of 6.35-millimeter caliber."

Ellery tucked away his memorandum. "I even remarked at the time that every one of the twelve guns listed was *of different manufacture.* I might have added what was evident from the list itself: that not only were the twelve utterly different in manufacture, but they were as nearly varied in caliber and type as one could reasonably gather in a gun shop.

"*Yet the thirteenth and fourteenth weapons—the two missing ones—were exact duplicates of the first two on the list; not merely similar, but identical.*" Ellery stared at them. "In other words, there were two *pairs* of guns in the fourteen items Thurlow bought at Cornwall & Ritchey's. Why? Why *two* Colt .25 automatics of the Pocket Model type, whose overall length is only four and a half inches, as we pointed out at the time? Why *two* S. & W. .38/32's, whose overall length is only six and one-quarter inches? Hardly dueling pistols, by the way!—although of course they could serve that purpose. There were much larger and longer pistols in Thurlow's arsenal for such romantic bravura as a duel at dawn. Why *those*, and such little fellows, too?"

"Coincidence?" asked Sheila.

"It might have been coincidence," admitted Ellery. "But the weight of logic was against it, Sheila. Because what happened? In giving Bob his choice of weapons at the dinner table the evening before the duel, Thurlow didn't offer Bob one of a *pair* of guns—one of the pair of Colt .25 automatics we know he had at that time, or one of the pair of Smith & Wessons—which would have been the natural thing to do in a duel. No, Thurlow offered Bob his choice of two quite *dissimilar* weapons. Coincidence? Hardly. I could only say to myself: There must have been some purpose, some motive, some plan behind this."

"But what?" Inspector Queen frowned.

"Well, Dad, what was the effect of Bob's choosing one of the two dissimilar guns Thurlow offered him? This: *that no matter which weapon Bob chose*—whether he chose the Colt automatic or the Smith & Wesson revolver— *Thurlow was left not with one gun for himself, but a pair.*"

"A pair!" exclaimed Charley. "Of course! Since Bob picked the Smith & Wesson, Thurlow was left with two identical Colts!"

"And it would have been the same if Bob had selected the Colt," nodded Ellery. "Thurlow couldn't lose, you see—he *had* to be left with a pair of identical weapons. The question was: What was the advantage to Thurlow in this? I couldn't answer it then; but I can now!"

"Wait a minute, son," said the Inspector irritably. "I don't see what difference it would have made if Thurlow'd been left with a dozen identical guns."

"Why not?"

"Why not? Because Thurlow couldn't have murdered Bob Potts, that's why not. From the time you left that Colt .25 in Thurlow's bedroom with a blank in it till you handed Thurlow that same gun the next morning at the duel, Thurlow couldn't possibly have touched it. You said so yourself!"

"That's right, Maestro," said Sergeant Velie. "He never could of got into his bedroom during the night to take the blank out and put the live bullet in the gun—he was with Miss Brent and Charley Paxton, and later you, all the time."

"Either here in the study with us," nodded Charley, "or in Club Bongo, where all four of us went that night after you came downstairs from putting the blank-loaded gun in Thurlow's room, Ellery."

"Not only that," added Inspector Queen, "but you told me yourself, Ellery, that the only ones who positively did *not* have opportunity to switch bullets in that gun in Thurlow's room were Charley, Miss Brent, and Thurlow."

"From the facts, Maestro," chided the Sergeant. "From the facts."

Ellery smiled sadly. "How you all belabor the 'facts'! Although I shouldn't cast the first stone—I did a bit of belaboring myself. I agree: Thurlow could not have replaced the blank cartridge with the live one in that Colt I left on his highboy."

"Then what are you talking about?" expostulated his father.

"Just this," said Ellery crisply. *"Thurlow murdered his brother Bob deliberately nevertheless."*

"Huh?" Sergeant Velie reamed his right ear doubtfully.

"Thurlow murdered—" Sheila stopped.

"But Ellery," protested Charley Paxton, "you just got through admitting—"

"That Thurlow couldn't have replaced the blank with the live cartridge, Charley? So I did. And I still do. But don't you people see that by having two identical guns, Thurlow not only prepared a colossal alibi for himself but pulled off a seemingly impossible murder, too? Look!" Ellery jumped up, grinding out his cigaret. "We all assumed that the killer replaced the blank in the Colt with a live bullet; we all assumed that this was the only possible way in which Bob Potts could have been murdered. *But suppose that blank had never been replaced?"*

They gaped at him.

"Suppose the blank-loaded Colt was not used in the duel at all, but the other Colt was used—the duplicate Colt?"

At that the Inspector groaned and clapped his palms to his gray head in an agony of realization.

"Very fundamental," said Mr. Queen, lighting a fresh cigaret. "Thurlow didn't use the Colt .25 we'd put the blank cartridge in. He simply used the other Colt .25, loaded with a live bullet. The attack on me a few minutes ago proved this—proves that *Thurlow switched the two Colt .25's just before his duel with Bob,* switched them right under our noses. How does the attempt on my life in this room prove this?

"Well, ever since Bob's death, the Colt that killed him—

the one we know had a live bullet in it *because* it killed
him, the Colt that Thurlow aimed at him—has been in
your possession, Dad, as the murder weapon, the vital
piece of evidence. Today Horatio Potts found the *duplicate* Colt .25 in the sycamore tree on the estate. A few
minutes ago that duplicate Colt was fired at me at point-
blank range. Yet there was no mark on me, no bullet
hole, no abrasion on my steel vest, no powder burn; and
no bullet or bullet hole or sign of ricochet anywhere in
this room. Only possible explanation: That duplicate Colt
fired at me tonight *was loaded with a blank cartridge*. But
we'd loaded a Colt .25 with a blank cartridge for Thurlow
to use in his duel with Robert!

"Conclusion: The weapon fired at me tonight *was that
first gun*, the gun that had been on Thurlow's highboy the
whole night before the duel, the gun I'd run up to fetch
for him, the gun I'd handed him at dawn and which he
immediately put, you'll recall, into the right-hand pocket
of his tweed jacket . . . The gun he did *not* take out of
that pocket a few moments later! Yes, Thurlow switched
guns on us under our eyes; and how he did it becomes
childishly apparent once you recognize the basic fact that
he *did* switch guns. The fact that, having *two* guns, he had
no need to switch *bullets* was the strongest and wiliest part
of Thurlow's plan. It made it possible for him to create an
unassailable alibi. He must have eavesdropped and overheard our plan to replace the live bullet with a blank in
the only Colt .25 we knew at the time he possessed. But
he knew he had a duplicate Colt. So why not let us go
through with our plan to draw the death out of the first
Colt, give himself that powerful alibi, and still manage to
kill Robert? Moreover, under such circumstances that he'd
seem the witless tool of some mysterious other person?

"Thurlow snatched his opportunity. Sheila, he permitted
you to get him 'out of the way.' Charley, he welcomed
your joining him and Sheila here in the study later. And
he must have been beside himself with delight when I
came down, too, to join the party. Then what did he do?
If you'll recall, it was *Thurlow* who suggested going to
Club Bongo; it was *Thurlow* who managed things so that
we stayed out all night and didn't get back until it was
time for the duel—whereupon it could never be said that
he'd had opportunity to switch bullets in that gun in his
room at any time after I placed the blank-loaded weapon
there. How were we to know that all the previous evening, all that night at Club Bongo, all the early morning

coming back to the grounds, Thurlow had the duplicate Colt .25, loaded with a lethal bullet, in his right-hand pocket?

"And now observe how cunning he is. We get back, and he sends *me* upstairs to his room to fetch the blank-loaded Colt, under the 'artless' pretense that I'm his second! For it must not be said afterwards that Thurlow Potts for even two minutes was alone with that gun . . .

"I fetched the gun, playing the dupe, handed it to Thurlow in sight of numerous witnesses, and he slipped it at once into his coat pocket.

"The dueling silliness began. Thurlow took a Colt .25 from that pocket. How were we to know that it was not the same weapon, loaded with a blank? How were we to know that the Colt he took out of that pocket was a duplicate of the one I had just handed him, a weapon identical in shape and size and appearance, and that the one just handed him was still in his pocket? And remained there?"

Inspector Queen groaned. "Who'd ever think to search the nut? We didn't even know at the time that there *were* duplicate Colt .25's!"

"No, we did not. And Thurlow knew we didn't. He was running no risks. Later, he simply disposed of the first Colt—hid it in that starling's nest in the sycamore tree, the blank cartridge still in it."

"And then, of course," muttered the Inspector, "he pulled that second challenge—to Mac—as a fake and a cover-up. By that time we were sure to pass his part in the killing off as irresponsible craziness. So he murders Mac in an ordinary way during the night, while we're expecting a duel in the morning. Clever is right."

"But *why'd* he kill the twins?" demanded Sergeant Velie.

Sheila said: "Because he hated them," and began to cry.

"Stop it, darling," said Charley, putting his arms about her. "Or I'll take you out of here."

"It's just that it's the same old story—hate, insanity—" Sheila sobbed.

"Not at all," said Mr. Queen dryly. She looked up quickly; they were all startled. "There's no insanity in Thurlow's murder plan, believe me. It was cold, brutal, logical, criminal ruthlessness."

"Now how do you figure that?" demanded Paxton.

"Yes, what in time did he gain by killing the twins?" echoed the Inspector.

"What did he gain?" Ellery nodded. "Very pointed question, Dad. Let's explore it a bit. But first let's state an interesting fact: This is not a case of one murder; it's a case of two. ALL RIGHT. Who gained most by the deaths of *both* Bob and Mac?"

They were silent.

"Thurlow, and only Thurlow," Ellery answered himself. "Let me show you why I say that.

"What would have happened if Bob and Mac had not been murdered? When the Old Woman died, there'd automatically be an election to determine the new President of the Board of Directors of the Potts Shoe Company. Seven people would have the right to vote in that election, as everyone knew from her will, which we were told was a matter of common knowledge in the household for years.

"With Robert and Maclyn alive, one of them would necessarily have been nominated to take full charge of the huge shoe enterprise. This was brought out at the actual election the day after the Old Woman's death; you said it yourself, Sheila, rather bitterly." Sheila nodded in a puzzled way. "Now suppose the twins had not been murdered? Suppose at your mother's death, Sheila, the twins were still alive? One of them would have been nominated, and he would have been sure of the following votes: his own, his twin's, Sheila's, and Mr. Underhill's. Neither Louella nor Horatio had the desire or capacity to head the business. Thurlow, then, would have been the opposing candidate. Now, who would have voted for Thurlow?

"Well, who *did* vote for Thurlow—in the election that was held? Louella, Horatio and Thurlow himself. In other words, had the twins remained alive, *one of them would have been elected over Thurlow by a vote of four to three.*"

"That's it," said Charley softly.

"By a plurality of one," exclaimed Velie.

"Thurlow would have lost . . ." mused the Inspector.

"Yes, Thurlow would have lost by a vote of four to three," murmured Ellery. "Knowing Thurlow's sensitivity, what wouldn't this have meant to him! Deflated, 'disgraced' in his own eyes, forced to take a back seat to the two younger men when all his adult life he had been waiting for his mother to die so that he could reign supreme in the family! Yes, defeat in the election would have been the supreme insult of Thurlow's life. And not only that. He knew that as soon as his mother passed on, Sheila and the twins and their father intended to take back Steve's real name, Brent. This meant that the Potts business might eventually lose even its name. At best, it would be in the hands of those whom Thurlow had always considered outsiders—not true Pottses.

"Knowing to what lengths Thurlow has gone in the past to avenge fancied insults and ridicule where the name of Potts was concerned, it's easy to believe that his intensely concentrated ego dictated a plan whereby he would seize control of the business on his mother's hourly expected death (page Dr. Innis) and avert the 'catastrophe' of seeing the Potts name possibly lost to a grieving posterity. And what was the only way he could accomplish this? The *only* way? By eliminating the two brothers who stood in his path, the two who not alone controlled two vital votes but who, both of them, were logical candidates to head the firm on the Old Woman's death.

"And so—Bob and Mac died by Thurlow's hand, and in the election, instead of losing by a vote of four to three, he won by a vote of three to two. Oh, no," said Mr. Queen, shaking his head, "there was no madness in Thurlow when he hatched this little mess of eggs. Or should I say the crime was sane if the criminal was not. . . . Granted Thurlow's obsession with the name of Potts, everything he planned and executed afterwards was severely logical."

"Yes," said Sheila slowly. "I was stupid not to have seen it. Louella, Horatio—why should they care? All they've ever asked was to be let alone. But Thurlow—he's been a frustrated little shadow of my mother all his life."

"What do you think, Dad," asked Ellery, "of my Sparrow?"

"I buy it, son," the Inspector said simply. "But there's one little detail you haven't supplied."

"What's that?"

"Proof. Proof that District Attorney Sampson'll cock an eye at," continued the Inspector, "and say: 'Dick, we've got a case for the courts.' "

And there fell upon them the long silence.

"You'll have to dig up the proof yourself, Dad," said Ellery at last, uncoiling his long legs. "All I can do is supply the truth."

"Yeah. The trouble is," said Sergeant Velie, dryly, "they ought to fix up a new set o' laws for you, Maestro. The kind of case you make out—it puts the finger on murderers but it don't put 'em where they can get a hot foot in the seat."

Ellery shrugged. "Not my province, Sergeant. Ordinarily at this stage I'd say to hell with it and go home to my orphaned typewriter. But I must admit—" his eye wandered to Sheila Brent— "in this case I'd feel better seeing Thurlow safely behind bars before I retire, like his sister Louella, to my ivory tower."

"Wait," said Charley Paxton. He was shaking his head. "I think I can supply one important fact that'll tie Thurlow up to at least one of the murders—Bob's. I'm a fool!"

"Two-times killer isn't any the less dead for being burned for only one," said the Inspector. "What have you got, Charley?"

"I should have told you long ago, Inspector, only it didn't mean anything to me till Ellery just explained about the duplicate guns. Some time ago—you'll be able to check the exact date—Thurlow asked me the name of my tailor."

"Your tailor!" Ellery's brows rose. "Never a dull moment. What about it, Charley?"

"I gave it to him, assuming he wanted to order a suit. Next thing I knew, I got a bill from the tailor—I still have it somewhere, and that's evidence for the D.A.—charging me for repairs made on 'a tweed suit jacket.'"

"*Tweed?*"

"I never wear tweeds, so I knew there was a mistake. Then I remembered Thurlow's quizzing me about my tailor. So I asked Thurlow about the tweed jacket my tailor'd billed me for and he said, yes, it must have been his jacket the man meant, because he'd had my tailor make some repairs on it and hadn't received a bill. So Thurlow asked me to pay for the repairs and said he'd reimburse me. He did, too," added Charley grimly, "in cash, the cagey devil!"

"Repairs," exclaimed Ellery softly. "What kind of repairs, Charley, did Thurlow say?"

"No, Thurlow didn't say," retorted the lawyer. "But I smelled a little mouse, I can't tell you why. I asked my tailor when I paid the bill. And he said Mr. Potts had asked him to change the right-hand outside pocket of the tweed jacket into a double pocket—"

"*Double pocket!*" The Inspector leaped to his feet.

"With a partition lining between."

"Charley, that's it," whispered Sheila.

"Double pocket," grinned the Sergeant, "double guns, double bye Mr. Potts!"

"If that won't establish premeditation, I don't know what will," said the Inspector, rubbing his hands briskly. "Charley, I thank you."

"Yes, that's it," said Ellery. "I should have seen it myself. Of course he'd have to take the precaution of preventing a mix-up in the two guns during the short time he had them both in the same pocket. But with a double pocket, he could put the live-loaded Colt in one half, say the half at the front of the pocket; and the Colt with the blank in the half at the back. That made it easy to locate the live-loaded Colt with his fingers when the time came to withdraw the gun for the duel."

"Better get hold of that coat immediately, Inspector," advised Charley. "Thurlow thinks he's safe, so he's done nothing about it. But if he suspects you're looking for evidence, he'll burn the coat and you'll never have a case for Sampson."

A dark figure flung itself through one of the French doors off the terrace and stumbled into the study.

It was Thurlow Potts.

One glimpse of his contorted features was proof enough that Thurlow had overheard every word of the analysis by which Ellery Queen had relegated him to the Death House, and of the testimony of Charley Paxton's which was to provide the switch.

For the second time that evening they were paralyzed by the inhuman quickness of Thurlow's appearance. This was a Sparrow possessed of demons. Before any of them could stir, he had flung himself at Charley Paxton's throat.

"I'll kill you for telling them about that pocket," Thurlow shouted, digging his fingers into Charley's flesh. The young lawyer, taken completely by surprise, had not even had time or presence to rise from his seat; the force of Thurlow's assault had sent him hurtling over backward, and his head had struck the floor with a soggy thud. Thurlow's fingers dug deeper. "I'll kill you," he kept screaming. "That pocket. I'll kill you."

"He's unconscious," Sheila was shrieking. "He hit his head. Thurlow, stop it! Stop, you dirty butcher—*stop!*"

The Queens, father and son, and Sergeant Velie hit the little man simultaneously from three directions. Velie scooped up Thurlow's legs, which instantly began kicking. Ellery grabbed one arm and yanked, and the Inspector the other. Even so, they found it difficult to pluck him from

Paxton's throat. It was only by main force that Ellery was able to tear those stubby, suddenly iron fingers away.

Then they had him loose, and Sheila dropped hysterically by Charley's side to chafe his swollen neck, where the bite of Thurlow's fingers was deep and clear.

Sergeant Velie got Thurlow's throat from behind in the crook of his arm, but the little man kept kicking viciously even as his eyes bugged from his head. They were red, wild eyes. "I'll kill him," he kept screaming. "I killed the twins, and I'll kill Paxton, too, and I'll kill, I'll kill, kill . . ."

And suddenly he went soft all over, like a rag doll. His head draped itself over the Sergeant's arm. His legs stopped kicking.

"On the davenport," said Inspector Queen curtly. "Miss Brent, is Charley all right?"

"I think so, Inspector! He's coming to. Charley, Charley darling . . ."

Velie picked up the little man and carried him to the studio couch. He did not drop Thurlow; he laid him down carefully almost tenderly.

"Cunning as they come," grunted the Inspector. "Well, son, you heard him say he did it. So you're right, and we've got plenty of witnesses, and Thurlow's a gone rattlesnake."

Ellery brushed himself off. "Yes, Dad, premeditated purchase of two pairs of guns, premeditated manufacture of a double pocket, premeditated build-up of a perfect alibi, a clear motive—I think you've got a case for the District Attorney."

"He won't need it," said Sergeant Velie. There was something so sharply strange in Velie's tone that they looked at him in inquiry. He jerked his big jaw in the direction of the man on the couch.

Thurlow Potts lay quiet, with a stare at right angles to sanity. There was nothing in his eyes now, nothing. They were lifeless marbles. The face was putty patted into vertical lines. He was staring up at Sergeant Velie without resentment or hatred, without pain—without recognition.

"Velie, call Bellevue," said Inspector Queen soberly.

Ave atque vale, Thurlow, thought Ellery Queen as he looked down at that stricken flesh of the Old Woman's flesh. For you there will be no arrest, no arraignment, no Grand Jury, no trial, no conviction, no electric chair. For you there will be a cell and bars, and green fields to watch with eyes that see crookedly, and jailers in starched white uniforms.

27 . . . The Beginning of the End

It cannot be stated that Ellery Queen was satisfied to the point of exaltation with his role in the Potts murder case.

Heretofore, Ellery's pursuit of truth in the hunt of human chicanery had been attended by a sort of saddle irritation which magically disappeared when the hunter returned to his hearth. But now, a week after Thurlow Potts had confessed his crime and lapsed into burbling insanity, Ellery's intellectual seat still smarted.

He wondered at himself, thinking over the horrid fantasy of the past week. That he had succeeded, there could be no question. Thurlow Potts had murdered Robert Potts with his own hand. Thurlow Potts had murdered Maclyn Potts similarly. Logic had triumphed, the miscreant had confessed, the case was closed. Where, then, had he failed?

King James had said to the fly, "Have I three kingdoms and thou must needs fly into my eye?"

What was the nature of the fly?

And suddenly, at breakfast with his father that morning, he saw that there were two flies, as it were, in his eye. One was Thurlow Potts himself. Thurlow was still a conundrum, logic and confession notwithstanding. Mr. Queen was uncomfortably aware that he had never known the true nature of Thurlow, and that he still did not know it. The man had been too rich a mixture of sense and nonsense, a mixture too thoroughly mixed. But the recipe for Thurlow was preponderantly madness, and for some reason this annoyed Mr. Queen no end. The man had been mostly mad, and his crime had been mostly sane; perhaps this was the source of the smart. And yet there could be no doubt whatever that Thurlow had murdered his twin brothers, knowing exactly what he was doing.

Ellery gave it up.

The other fly was equally obvious, and equally pestiferous. It had dimples, and its name was Sheila. At this point, Ellery quickly resumed the attack on his breakfast under his father's inquiring eye. Sometimes it is wiser, he thought, not to probe too deeply into certain branches of entomology.

By coincidence Sheila and Charley Paxton dropped into

the Queen apartment before that uneasy breakfast was concluded; and it must be said that Mr. Queen rose heroically to the occasion, the more so since the young couple had come to announce their approaching marriage.

"The best of everything," he said bravely, pressing their hands.

"If ever two snooks deserved happiness in this world," said the Inspector, shaking his head, "it's you two. When's it coming off?"

"Tomorrow," said Sheila. She was radiant.

"Tomorrow!" Mr. Queen blinked.

Charley was plainly embarrassed. "I told Sheila you'd probably be pretty busy catching up on your book," he mumbled. "But you know how women are."

"Indeed I do, and I'd never have forgiven you if you'd taken any such silly excuse for not dropping in."

"There, you see, dear?" said Sheila.

Charley grinned feebly.

"Tomorrow," smiled Inspector Queen. "That's as fine a day as any."

"Then we're going on a honeymoon," said Sheila, hugging Charley's arm, "and when we get back—work, and peace."

"Work?" said Ellery. "Oh, of course. The business."

"Yes. Mr. Underhill's going to manage the production end—he's far and away the best man for it, and of course the office staff will keep on as before."

"How about the executive set-up?" asked the Inspector curiously. "With Thurlow out of circulation—"

"Well, we've tried to get Sheila's father to change his mind about taking an active part in the business," said Charley, "but Steve just won't. Says he's too old and wants only to live the rest of his life out playing checkers with that old scalawag Gotch. So that sort of leaves it up to Sheila. Of course, Louella and Horatio are out of the question, and now that Thurlow's gone, they'll do as Sheila says."

"We've had a long talk with Louella and Horatio," said Sheila, "and they've agreed to accept incomes and not stand in the way of the reorganization. They'll live on at the old house on the Drive. But Daddy and Major Gotch are taking an apartment, and of course Charley and I will take our own place, too." She shivered the least bit. "I can't wait to get out of the house."

"Amen," said Charley in a low voice.

Ellery smiled. "Then from now on I'm going to have to address you as Madam President, Sheila?"

"Looks that way," retorted Sheila. "Actually, I'll be President only for the record. With Mr. Underhill handling production and Charley the business end—he insists on it—I won't have anything to do but clip coupons."

"What a life," groaned the Inspector.

"And of course," said Sheila in an altered tone, gazing at the floor, "of course, Ellery, I can't tell you how grateful I am for everything you've done for us—"

"Spare me," pleaded Ellery.

"And Sheila and I sort of thought," said Charley, "that we'd be even more grateful if you sort of finished the job—"

"Beg pardon?"

"What's the matter with you two?" laughed Sheila. "Charley, can't you even extend a simple invitation? Ellery, Charley would like you to be best man tomorrow, and—well, I think you know how thrilled *I'd* be."

"On one condition."

Charley looked relieved, "Anything!"

"Don't be so rash, Charley. I'd like to kiss the bride." That'll hold you, brother! thought Mr. Queen uncharitably.

"Sure," said Charley with a weak grin. "Help yourself."

Mr. Queen did so, liberally.

Now this was strange, that even in the peace of the church, with Dr. Crittenden smilingly holding his Book open before him, and Sheila standing before him straight and still and tense to the left, her father a little behind and to one side of her, and Charley Paxton standing just as solemnly to the right, Ellery behind *him* . . . even here, even now, the flies buzzed about Ellery's eye.

"*Dearly beloved, we are gathered together here in the sight of God, and in the face of this company . . .*"

Inspector Queen stood behind Ellery. With his father's quiet breathing in his ear, the son was suddenly seized with an irrelevance, so unpredictable is the human mind in its crises of desperation. He slipped his hand into his coat pocket to feel for the ring of which he was honored custodian, and also to finger absently the three documents that lay there. The Inspector had given them to Ellery that morning.

"Give them back to Charley for his files, or hold them

for him," the Inspector had said. "Lord knows I can't get rid of 'em fast enough."

One was the Old Woman's will. His fingers knew that by the thickness of the wrapper. The Old Woman . . .

"*. . . to join together this Man and this Woman in holy Matrimony; which is an honorable estate, instituted of God . . .*"

The Old Woman's confession. Her notepaper. Only one left, anyhow, so it must be. He found it outside his pocket, in his hand. Now how did that happen? Ellery thought innocently. He glanced down at it.

"*. . . and therefore is not by any to be entered into unadvisedly or lightly . . .*"

Forged confession. Never written by the Old Woman. That signature—traced off in the same soft pencil . . . Ellery found himself turning the closely typed sheet over. It was perfectly clean. Not a pencil mark, not the sign of an erasure.

"*. . . but reverently, discreetly, advisedly, soberly and in the fear of God.*"

Something clicked in the Queen brain. Swiftly he took the slip of flimsy from his pocket, the stock memorandum from which he had decided—how long ago it seemed!— the signature of Cornelia Potts had been traced onto the "confession."

He turned it over. On the back of the memorandum he now noticed, for the first time, the faint but clean pencil impression in reverse of the words "Cornelia Potts."

He shifted his position so that he might hold the memorandum up to a ruffle of sunlight skirting Charley's arm. The pencil impression on the reverse of the memorandum lay directly over the signature on the face, with no slightest blurring.

"*Into this holy estate these two persons present come now to be joined.*"

Ellery turned, groped for his father's arm.

Inspector Queen looked at him blankly. Then, scanning Ellery's face, he leaned forward and whispered: "Ellery! Don't you feel well? What's the matter?"

Ellery wet his lips.

"*If any man can show just cause, why they may not lawfully be joined together, let him speak now—*"

"Damn it!" blurted Ellery.

Dr. Crittenden almost dropped the Book.

Ellery's face was convulsed. He was pale and in a rage,

the two documents in his hand rustling like rumors. Later, he said he did not remember having blasphemed.

"Stop," he said a little hoarsely. "Stop the wedding."

28 . . . The End of the Beginning

Inspector Queen whispered: "El, are you crazy? This is a wedding!"

They'll never believe me, thought Ellery painfully. Why did I get mixed up in this fandango? "Please forgive me," he said to Dr. Crittenden, whose expression of amazement had turned to severity. "Believe me, Doctor, I'd never have done this if I hadn't considered it imperative."

"I'm sure, Mr. Queen," replied the pastor coldly, "I can't understand how anything could be more important than a solemnization of marriage between two worthy young people."

"What's happened? What's the matter, Ellery?" cried Charley. "Dr. Crittenden, please—would you be kind enough to leave us alone for five minutes with Mr. Queen?"

Sheila was looking fixedly at Ellery. "Yes, Doctor, please."

"B-but Sheila," began her father. Sheila took old Steve's arm and took him aside, whispering to him.

Dr. Crittenden looked appalled. Then he left the chapel with agitated steps to retire to his vestry.

"Well?" said Sheila, when the vestry door had closed. Her tone was arctic.

"Please understand. This can't wait. You two can always be married; but this can't wait."

"What can't wait, Ellery?" demanded Charley.

"The undoing of the untruth." Ellery cleared his throat; it seemed full of frogs and bulrushes. "The telling of the truth. I don't see it clearly yet, but something's wrong—"

His father was stern. "What are you talking about? This isn't like you, son."

"I'm not like myself—nothing is as it should be." Ellery shook his head as he had shaken it that night on the floor of the Potts study after Thurlow had shot at him. "We've made a mistake, that's all. I've made a mistake. One thing I do see: *the case is still unsolved.*"

Sheila gave voice to a little whimper, so tired, so without hope, that Ellery almost decided to say he had slipped a gear somewhere and that this was all, all a delusion of a brain fallen ill. Almost; not quite.

"You mean Thurlow Potts is *not* our man?" cried the Inspector. "But that can't be, Ellery. He admitted it. You heard him admit the killings!"

"No, no, that's not it," muttered Ellery. "Thurlow did commit those murders—it was his hand that took the lives of Bob and Mac Potts."

"Then what *do* you mean?"

"There's someone else, Dad. *Someone behind Thurlow.*"

"Behind Thurlow?" repeated his father stupidly.

"Yes, Dad. Thurlow was merely the hand. Thurlow pulled the triggers. But he pulled them at the dictation, and according to the plan, of a brain, a boss—the real murderer!"

Major Gotch retreated into a corner of the chapel, like a cautious bear, and it was curious that thenceforth he kept his old puff eyes fixed upon the pale blinking eyes of his crony, Stephen Brent.

"Let me analyze this dreary, distressing business aloud," continued Ellery wearily. "I'll work it out step by step, Dad, as I see it now. If I'm wrong, call Bellevue. If I'm right—" He avoided looking at the others. Throughout most of what followed, he kept addressing his father, as if they had been alone with only the quiet walls of the chapel to keep them company.

"Remember how I proved the Old Woman's signature on that typewritten confession we found on her body was a forgery? I placed the stock memorandum against a windowpane; I placed the confession over the stock memorandum; and I worked the confession about on the memo until the signature of the one lay directly over the signature of the other. Like this." Ellery went to a clear sunny window of the chapel and with the two documents illustrated his thesis.

"Since both signatures were identical in every curve and line," he went on, "I concluded—and correctly—that one of the signatures had been traced off the other. No one ever writes his name exactly the same way twice."

"Well?" The Inspector was inching toward the chapel door.

"Now since the stock memo was handed to Charley Paxton in our presence by the Old Woman herself—in fact, we saw her sign it—we had every right to assume that the signature on the *memorandum* was genuine, and that therefore the signature on the *confession* had been traced from it and was the forgery.

"But see how blind I was." Ellery rapped the knuckles of his free hand against the superimposed documents his other hand held plastered against the window. "When a signature is traced off by using light through a window-pane, in what position must the genuine signature be in relation to the one that's to be traced from it?"

"You've got to put the document being forged *above* the genuine signature, of course," replied the Inspector. He was looking around, restlessly.

"Or in other words, first you lay down on the window-pane the genuine signature, then you place the document to be forged *over* it. Or to put it still another way, it's the genuine document that lies against the glass, and the fake document that lies against the genuine one. Therefore," said Ellery, stepping back from the window, "if the signature on the confession was the traced one, as we believed, then the confession must have been lying *upon* the stock memo, and the stock memo must have been lying against the windowpane. Is that clear so far?"

"Sure. But what of it?"

"Just a minute, Dad. Now, all the Old Woman's signatures were written with a heavy, softleaded pencil." The Inspector looked puzzled by this irrelevance.

"Such pencils leave impressions so thick and soft that when they are pressed on and written over, as would have to be done in the tracing of a signature written by one of them, *they necessarily act like a sheet of carbon paper.* That is, when two sheets are pressed together, one on top of the other, and a soft-pencil signature on the bottom sheet is traced onto the top sheet, the very act of tracing, the very pressure exerted by the tracing agent, *will produce a faint pencil impression on the back of the top sheet,* because it's that back surface on the top sheet which is *in direct contact* with the soft lead of the original signature on the bottom sheet. Is *that* clear?"

"Go on."

"I've already shown that, in order to have been a forgery, the confession must have been the top sheet of the two. But if the confession was the top sheet, there should be a faint pencil impression of Cornelia Potts's signature (in reverse, of course, as if seen in a mirror) *on the back of the confession sheet.*

"Is there?"

Ellery walked over to his father, who by this time was standing, alert, against the chapel door. "Look Dad."

The Inspector looked, quickly. The reverse side of the confession was clean, without smudge.

"That's what I saw a few moments ago, for the first time. There is not the slightest trace of a pencil mark on the back of this confession. Of course, there could have been such an impression and for some reason it might have been erased; but if you examine the surface sheet carefully, you'll find no signs of erasure, either. On the other hand, look at the back of the stock memorandum! Here—" Ellery held it up— "here is the clear, if light, impression of the signature 'Cornelia Potts' on the back of the memo, in reverse. And if you'll hold it up to the light, Dad, you'll see—as I saw—that the reverse impression of the signature lies directly behind the signature on the face of the memo, proving that the impression was made at the same time as the forgery.

"What does all this mean?" Ellery tapped the stock memorandum sharply. "It means that *the stock memo was the top sheet* of the two employed in the forgery. It means that *the confession was the bottom sheet*, lying flat against the windowpane.

"But if the confession was the bottom sheet, *then it was the signature on the confession which was being used as a guide* and it was the signature on the stock memo which was traced from it!

"But if the signature on the confession was being used as a guide then that signature was the *genuine* one, and the one on the stock memo was the forgery. Or, to put it in a capsule," said Mr. Queen grimly, "*the Old Woman's confession was not a forgery as we believed, but was actually written and signed by her own hand.*"

"But El," spluttered the Inspector, "that would make the Old Woman the killer in this case!"

"One would think so," said his son. "But strangely enough, while Cornelia Potts actually wrote that confession of guilt, and signed it, she did *not* murder her two sons, nor could she have been the person behind Thurlow who used Thurlow as a tool in the commission of the murders."

"How can you know that?" asked the Inspector in despair.

"For one thing, Dad, we now know that there never was a substitution of *bullets* in that first Colt .25—we know that there was a substitution of *guns*. Yet in her confession the Old Woman wrote—" Ellery consulted the confession hastily— "the following: 'It was I who substituted a lethal bullet for the blank cartridge the police had put into Thurlow's weapon.' But no bullet *was* substituted! In other words, the Old Woman thought the same thing we thought at the time—that a substitution of bullets had been made. So she didn't even know how the first murder was really committed! How, then, could she have been in any way involved in it?

"And look at this." Ellery waved the confession again. "'Later it was I who stole one of Thurlow's other guns and hid it from the police and went with it into my son Maclyn's bedroom in the middle of the night and shot him with it,' and so on. Stop and think, Dad: Cornelia Potts couldn't have done that, either! Dr. Innis told me, just before he left the Old Woman's bedside that night—shortly before Mac was shot to death—that he had given the Old Woman a sedative by hypodermic injection *which would keep her asleep all night.*

"No, the Old Woman didn't have a thing to do with the murder of the twins, even though she wrote out a confession of guilt and signed it with her own hand. So apparently, knowing she was about to die and had nothing more to lose in this life, she wrote out a false confession to protect whichever whelp of her first litter was guilty. She was a wonderfully shrewd woman, that old lady; I shouldn't be surprised that she suspected it was Thurlow, her pet. By confessing on her deathbed, she believed the case would be officially closed and, with its close, Thurlow would be safe."

The Inspector nodded slowly. "That makes sense. But if it wasn't the Old Woman who was masterminding Thurlow, who was it, son?"

"Obviously, *the person who made us believe the signature on the confession was false when it wasn't.* And, by the way, that was a very clever piece of business. It was necessary to make us think the confession was false, for reasons I'll go into in a moment. In order to accomplish that, what did our criminal require? A signature which would be identical with the signature on the confession. No true signature of Cornelia's could possibly be *identical* with the confession signature, so our criminal had to manufacture one. In doing so, he could only use for tracing purposes the confession signature itself. He chose the stock memo he knew we remembered having seen the Old Woman sign, typed off its message exactly on similar paper, destroyed the genuine memo, and then traced the confession signature onto the spurious stock memo. Very clever indeed."

"But who was it, Ellery?" The Inspector glared about. They were all so quiet one would have thought them in the grip of a paralyzing gas.

"We can get to that only obliquely, Dad. Having established that the real criminal, the brains behind Thurlow, wanted us to believe the Old Woman's confession a forgery, the inevitable question is: Why?

"The reason must be evident. It could only be because he did not want us to accept the Old Woman as the killer, he did not want the case closed—he wanted someone other than Cornelia Potts to be arrested and convicted for the murder of the twins.

"When I proved the case against Thurlow, I thought the series of crimes had come to an end. Well, I was wrong. One more puppet in the play had to be eliminated— *Thurlow himself.*" The Inspector looked befogged. "Yes, Dad, Thurlow was a victim, too. Oh, this is as fancy a plot as any that ever came out of Hollywood. It's not double murder, it's triple murder. First Bob, then Mac—and now Thurlow. For, as we know now, Thurlow was the instrument of the crime, and his being caught doesn't solve it. There's still the person behind him. Then since we see that the criminal wanted someone other than Cornelia to be caught and tried and convicted for the murders, and we've actually pinned it on Thurlow—isn't it clear that *Thurlow's capture, too, was part of the criminal's plan?*"

The Inspector blinked. "You mean—he wanted to get not only the twins, but Thurlow, whom he used to kill 'em, out of the way?"

"Exactly. And here's why I say that. Ask the question: Who benefits most by the elimination of the twins *and* Thurlow? Can you answer that?"

"Well," muttered the Inspector, "the twins were killed for control of the Potts Shoe Company—as a result of their murder. Thurlow became President and got control . . ."

"But with Thurlow out of the way as well, who has control now?"

"Sheila."

It was not the Inspector's voice which answered Ellery.

It was Stephen Brent's.

Stephen Brent was staring at his daughter with the feeble error of a parent who sees his child, for the first time, as others see her.

29 . . . *The End of the End*

"Yes, Sheila," said Ellery Queen, in the saddest voice imaginable.

And now he looked at her, with remorse, and with pity, and with something else that was neither. Sheila was glaring from her father to Ellery in a jerky arc, her lips parted and her breath jerky, too.

Major Gotch made a little whimpering noise in his corner.

Charley was glaring, too—glaring at Ellery, his hands beginning to curl into fists. "Idiot!" he shouted, lunging forward. "The Potts craziness has gone to your head!"

"Charley, cut it out," said Inspector Queen in a tired voice.

Charley stopped impotently. It was plain that he dared not glance at Sheila; he dared not. And Sheila simply stood there, her head jerking to and fro.

The Inspector asked quietly: "You mean this girl with the dimples is the brains behind this nasty business? *She* used Thurlow as a tool? *She* the real killer?" He shook his head. "Charley's right, Ellery. You've gone haywire."

And then Ellery said an odd thing. He said: "Thank you, Dad. For Sheila." And at this they were still with wonder again.

"Because, from the facts, it couldn't be Sheila," Ellery went on in a faraway voice. "All Sheila wants to be is . . . somebody's wife."

"Somebody's wife?" Charley Paxton's head started the pendulum now—from Ellery Queen to Sheila, from Sheila to Ellery.

Mr. Queen looked full upon Mr. Paxton. "This was all planned by the man who missed a brilliant career in criminal law—you told me that yourself, Dad, that very first morning in the Courthouse. The man whose every effort has been to get Sheila to marry him. The man who knew that, married to Sheila and with her twin brothers and Thurlow out of the way, he could control the rich Potts enterprises. That's what was behind your 'insistence,' as Sheila said only yesterday, Charley, on 'running the business' in the reorganization, while she sat back to be your figurehead—wasn't it?"

Charley's skin turned claret.

"Don't you see?" Ellery avoided Sheila's eyes. "Charley Paxton planned every move, every countermove. Charley Paxton played on Thurlow's susceptible mind, on Thurlow's psychopathic obsession with the honor and name of Potts. Charley Paxton convinced Thurlow that he had to murder the twins to protect himself, the business, and the family name. Charley Paxton planned every step of the crime for Thurlow—showed him how to commit two daring murders with safety, planned the scene before the Courthouse, the purchase of the fourteen guns, the duel—everything, no doubt rehearsing Thurlow patiently. A furiously vacillating brain like Thurlow's might have conceived murder, but Thurlow scarcely possessed the cunning and the application necessary to have planned and carried it out as these subtle crimes were planned and carried out. Only a sane mind could have planned these crimes. And that was why I was dissatisfied with Thurlow as the criminal even though all the evidence indicated that his hands and his person had performed the physical acts required to pull the crimes off . . . No, no, Charley, I can assure you you wouldn't stand a chance. Just stand still and refrain from unnecessary movements."

The Inspector took a small police pistol from his shoulder holster and released its safety mechanism.

Ellery continued in a murmur: "You'll recall I conjectured that Thurlow had found out by eavesdropping that we intended to substitute a blank cartridge for the live one in the first Colt automatic. But now perceive. Who suggested the device of substituting a blank? Whose plan was it? *Charley Paxton's.*"

Sheila's eyes grew wider; she began to tremble.

"So now we have a much more reasonable answer to how Thurlow knew about the blank. *Charley, his master, told him.* Paxton waited for me or someone else to suggest the ruse, and when none of us did, he jumped in himself with the suggestion. He had to, for he'd already told Thurlow that was what was going to happen—he'd see to it.

"All along this fine, smart young lawyer who had missed a brilliant career in criminal law set traps—in particular for me. If I fell into them—excellent. But if I hadn't seen the significance of the two pairs of Colt and Smith & Wessons, if I hadn't worked out Thurlow's motive, if I hadn't deduced just how Thurlow switched the guns before our eyes on the lawn that morning—if I hadn't seen through all these things, you may be sure Mr. Charles Hunter Paxton would have managed to suggest the 'truth' to me.

"Think. How closely Paxton clung to me! How often he was there to put in a word, a suggestion, to lead me along the path of speculation he had planned for me to take! I, too, have been a pawn of Counsellor Paxton's from the beginning, thinking exactly what he wanted me to think, eking out enough of the truth, point by point, to pin it on Thurlow and so accomplish the final objective of the Paxton campaign—the elimination of Thurlow."

"You can't be serious," said Charley. "You can't really believe—"

"And that isn't all. When he needed proof against Thurlow—when you specifically asked for it, Dad—who told us about the tailor and the double pocket in Thurlow's tweed jacket?"

"Mr. Paxton."

"And when Thurlow came tearing into the study from the terrace, whom did he attack—me? The man who had worked out the solution? Oh, no. He jumped for *Charley's* throat, mouthing frenzied threats to kill. Isn't it obvious that Thurlow went mad of rage because he had just heard Charley *double-cross* him? The man who had planned the crimes and no doubt promised to protect Thurlow—now giving the vital evidence that would convict him! Luckily for Counsellor Paxton, Thurlow's last link to sanity snapped at that point, or we should have heard him pour out the whole story of Paxton's complicity. But even this was a small risk for Paxton to take, although from the ideal standpoint it was the weakest part of his plot ... that Thurlow would blab. But Paxton must have thought: 'Who'd believe the ravings of a man already well established as a lunatic in face of the incontrovertible evidence against him?' "

"Poor Thurlow," whispered Sheila. And for the first time since the truth had come from Ellery's lips she turned and regarded the man she had been about to marry. She regarded him with such loathing that Steve Brent quickly put his hand on her arm.

"Yes, poor Thurlow," said Ellery grimly. "We broke him before his time—although no matter what had happened, Thurlow would have come to the same end—a barred cell and white-coated attendants. ... It's Sheila I was most concerned about. Seeing the truth, I had to stop this wedding."

And now Sheila turned to look upon Ellery, and he flushed slightly under her gaze.

"Of course, that's it," said Charley Paxton, clearing his throat. His hand came up in a spontaneous little gesture. "You see what's happened, Inspector, don't you? This son of yours—he's in love with Sheila himself—he practically admitted as much to me not long ago—"

"Shut up," said the Inspector.

"He's trying to frame me so he can have her himself—"

"I said shut up, Paxton."

"Sheila, you certainly don't believe these malicious lies?"

Sheila turned her back on him.

"Anything you say—" began the Inspector.

"Oh, don't lecture me!" snarled Charley Paxton. "I know the law." And now he actually smiled. "Stringing a lot of pretty words together is one thing, Mr. Queen. Proving them in court's another."

"The old story," growled the Inspector.

"Oh, no," said Mr. Queen, returning smile for smile. "Quite the new story. There's your proof, Dad—the forged stock memorandum and the Old Woman's confession."

"I don't get it."

"I told you he's talking through his hat," snapped Paxton. He shrugged and turned to the clear window of the chapel. "Dr. Crittenden will be getting impatient, waiting in the vestry," he remarked, without turning. "Sheila, you can't give me up on this man's unsupported word. He's bluffing, because as I said—"

"Bluffing, Paxton?" cried Ellery. "Then let me disabuse that clever mind of yours. I'll clear up a few untouched points first.

"If no one had interfered with this chap's original plans, Dad, Paxton would have got away with the whole scheme. But someone did interfere, the last man in the world Paxton had dreamed would interfere—his own creature, Thurlow."

Charley Paxton's back twitched, and was still.

"Thurlow did things—and then one other did things—which Mr. Paxton in his omniscience hadn't anticipated and therefore couldn't prepare counter-measures against. And it was this interference by others that forced our clever gentleman to make his only serious mistake."

"Keep talking," said Charley's voice. But it was a

choked voice. "You always were good in the gab department."

"The first interference wasn't serious," Ellery went on, paying no attention to the interruption. "Thurlow, flushed with his success in getting away with the murder of his brother Robert, began to think of himself—dangerous, Mr. Paxton, dangerous, but then your egocentric type of mind is so blind that it overlooks the obvious in its labor toward the subtle.

"Thurlow began to think. And instead of following his master's instructions in the second murder, he was so tickled with himself that he decided to add a touch or two of his own.

"In reconstructing what happened, we can ascribe these things to Thurlow because they are the kind of fantastic nonsense an addled brain like Thurlow's would conceive and are precisely not the things a cold and practical brain like Paxton's would conceive."

"What are you referring to?" The Inspector's pistol was pointed at Paxton's back.

"Thurlow shot Mac Potts in his bed in the middle of the night," replied Ellery with a curl and a twist to his tone that snapped Paxton's head up as if he had been touched with a live wire. "Shot him, whipped him with his riding crop, and left a bowl of chicken broth near by. Why? Deliberately to make the murder look like a Mother Goose crime. How sad!" said Mr. Queen mockingly. "How sad for master-minding Mr. Paxton. Upset the orderly creation, you see . . ."

"I d-don't understand that," stuttered Steve Brent. His arm was about Sheila's shoulders; she was clinging to him.

"Well, sir," retorted Ellery in a cheerful way, "all your late wife's first brood have been fed Mother Goose nonsense ever since she was first dubbed the Old Woman Who Lived in a Shoe. Mother Goose squatted on your rooftree, as it were, Mr. Brent, and her shadow was heavy and inescapable. Thurlow must have said to himself, in the ecstasy following his first successful homicide: 'I'm safe, but a little more safety can't do any harm. No one even suspects me for the murder of Robert in the duel. If the police and this fellow Queen see these Mother Goose clues—the whipping, the broth—they'll think of my brother Horatio, the Boy Who Never Grew Up. They'll certainly never think of *me!*'

"It was precisely the murky sort of smoke screen a psychopathic personality like Thurlow's would send up.

But it had a far greater significance for Paxton than for us. For it warped Charley's plot, which had been planned on a straight, if long, line. Charley Paxton didn't *want* suspicion directed toward Horatio. Charley Paxton wanted suspicion directed toward, and to land plumb and squarely upon, chubby little Thurlow. How annoyed you must have been, Charley! But I'll hand it to you: the foolishness being done, you took the wisest course—did nothing, hoping the authorities wouldn't recognize, or would be thrown off the scent by, the Mother Goose rigmarole. When I spotted it, you could only hope I'd dismiss it and get back on the Thurlow spoor."

"You said something about proof," said Paxton in crisp tones.

"Mmm. In good time, Charley. You're a patient animal, as you've proved.

"The next unanticipated interference came from what must have been a shocking source, Charley—the Old Woman. And here's where we hang you . . . no, burn you, to use the more accurate vernacular of the State of New York.

"What did the Old Woman do? She wrote out a confession of guilt, which was untrue. Most unreasonable of her, Charley; that *was* a blow to your plans. So serious a blow that it forced you into activities which you couldn't control, which controlled *you*. Oh, you made the most of your material, I'll give you that. You were ingenious and versatile, you overlooked no bet—but that false confession of Cornelia Potts's controlled you, Charley, and what it made you do is going to make you pay for your crimes by due process of law."

"Talk," sneered Paxton. But then he added: "And what did it make me do, Mr. Queen?"

"It made you say to yourself: 'If the police believe that meddling Old Woman's confession, my whole scheme is shot. They won't pin it on Thurlow, and Thurlow will take the reins of the Potts enterprises, and I'll never get to control them through Sheila.' Very straight thinking, Charley; and quite true, too. So you had to do something, or give up all hope of eating the great big enormous pie you'd set your appetite on."

"Get on with it!" snarled Mr. Paxton.

"You were clever. But cleverness is not wisdom, as Euripides said a couple of thousand years ago; you'd have been better advised to be wiser and less clever, Charley."

"How long do I have to listen to this drivel?"

"You couldn't destroy the large sealed envelope containing the Old Woman's will and smaller envelope with the confession in it, for the absurd reason—"

"That we all saw the envelope in the dead woman's hand," snapped the Inspector. "Go on, son!"

"Nor could you destroy the confession itself—"

"Because," said the Inspector, "the Old Woman had typed at the bottom of the will a paragraph saying that in the smaller sealed envelope was a paper which would tell us who'd murdered the twins."

"Nor could you destroy the will which contained that paragraph—"

"Because we knew it existed and after I gave it to you to hold till the formal reading," snapped the Inspector, "you were responsible for it, Paxton!"

"Nor could you substitute another revelation," Ellery's monotone persisted, "for if you had, the revelation to further your plans could only accuse Thurlow, and no one would believe that the Old Woman, on her deathbed, would accuse her favorite son of murder—she who had shielded him from the consequences of his aberrations all his life.

"No, indeed," continued the great man, "you were trapped by the trap of circumstance, Charley. You did the only possible thing: *you tried to make us believe the Old Woman's confession was untrue*. The simplest way to do that was to make it appear a forgery. If we could be led to believe it was a forgery then logically we'd conclude the Old Woman had not been the killer at all, we would continue the investigation, and eventually, following the trail you were so carefully laying down, we would arrive at Thurlow."

And now Charles Hunter Paxton turned from the window and stood black and stormy against it, rocking a little on the balls of his feet and glaring at the revolver in the Inspector's hand which was aimed steadily at his belly.

"I referred a few moments ago," said Ellery amiably, "to the only serious mistake you made, Charley my boy—the mistake that gives the D.A. his evidence and will bring your career to a fitting climax.

"What was your mistake? You had to prove the Old Woman's confession a forgery. To accomplish this, two series of actions on your part were mandatory:—

"One: You had to get hold of some document which the authorities knew of their own knowledge had been signed by Cornelia Potts. You remembered the stock memorandum, the signing and discussing of which had taken place before our eyes and ears. That would serve admirably, so you decided to get the original stock memo—"

"Sure!" said the Inspector. "It was in that kneehole desk in the Potts library Paxton always used for business."

"Yes. You had to get hold of it, Charley, prepare an exact duplicate on the Old Woman's portable, and then you had to trace onto the duplicate memo the signature at the bottom of the Old Woman's confession."

"Just a minute, Ellery." The Inspector seemed troubled. "Since the original stock memo was in this fellow's desk in the library, anybody in the house could have got to it. It doesn't necessarily pin anything on Paxton."

"How true," said Paxton.

"Yes, Dad," said Ellery patiently, "but what was the second thing Professor Moriarty had to do? He had to get hold of the *confession* in order to trace its signature onto the faked stock memo. *And who had access to the Old Woman's confession?* One person. Of all the people in the world, one person only. And that's how I know Charles Hunter Paxton forged the stock memorandum. That's why I say there's evidence to convict him."

"Only Paxton had possession of Cornelia's confession?" muttered the Inspector.

"It's a tight little question of knowledge and opportunity," smiled his son. "All capable of confirmation. First, the confession in its envelope lay in the larger sealed envelope which also contained the will. When we found that large sealed envelope in Cornelia's hand, not only *didn't* we know that it contained a confession, we *couldn't* have known. It was just a large sealed envelope with the words on it: *Last Will and Testament,* and signed *Cornelia Potts.*

"Second step: You, Dad, hand that large sealed envelope, contents thought to be only a will, to Mr. Paxton. The envelope is still sealed; it hasn't been opened or tampered with. You hand it to him in that bedroom, over the still warm corpse of old Cornelia, only a few minutes after we found it in her dead hand. And you ask Mr. Paxton to hold that large sealed envelope containing what we can only think is the dead woman's will—to hold it until the formal reading after the funeral."

Mr. Paxton began to breathe quickly, and the Inspector's weapon waved a little.

"Third: At the formal reading Mr. Paxton produces the large sealed envelope. It is opened, we discover the confession as well as the will . . . and from that instant you, the officer in charge of the case, Dad, take possession of that confession as important new evidence in the case. It becomes part of an official file.

"Now we know," said Ellery with a cold smile, "we can prove, that some time *before* the opening of that envelope at the formal reading of the will, the envelope had been secretly opened by someone, because we have proved that the Cornelia Potts signature on the confession had been used as a guide to forge a signature on the fake stock memorandum, and it couldn't possibly have been done *after* it got into your possession, Dad, and the police files. When, then specifically, could that envelope have been opened? *Only in the interim between the finding of it in the dead woman's hand and the opening of it before us all in the library for purposes of the will reading. Who* could have done it in that interim? *Only the person who had possession of the large sealed envelope.*

"Who had possession of the large sealed envelope during that interim? *Only one person: Charles Hunter Paxton.* Mr. Paxton, who when you originally handed him the envelope at the dead woman's bedside, Dad, couldn't contain his curiosity and at the first opportunity steamed it open, found the will, found the note at the bottom of the will, found the smaller sealed envelope purporting to contain a revelation of the murderer's identity—who naturally steamed *that* envelope open, read the Old Woman's confession, realized that he couldn't destroy it, saw that he could only make it seem a forgery, and thereupon went through all the motions necessary to achieve that end; and when he had forged the stock memo, he resealed the small envelope with the confession in it, resealed the large envelope with the small envelope and will in *it*, and then produced the sealed large envelope at the formal reading, as if its contents had never been disturbed at all." Mr. Queen's voice became a whip. "You're a fool, Paxton, to think you could get away with any such involved stupidity!"

For a moment Inspector Queen thought the young lawyer would spring at Ellery's throat. But then Paxton's shoulders seemed to collapse, and he dropped into a chair to cover his face with his hands. "I'm tired. It's true. Everything he said is true. I'm glad it's over. I'm tired of being clever."

Mr. Queen thought this last remark might very well be added to the distinguished list of native American epitaphs.

30 . . . *There Was a Young Woman*

"Say, Maestro," said Sergeant Velie the next day, stretching his legs halfway across the Queen living room, "I always seem to miss the third act. Why didn't you send me an Annie Oakley?"

"Because I didn't know myself," grinned Ellery. The lines of anxiety had disappeared from his lean face and he seemed passably pleased with himself.

"Seems to me," chuckled the Inspector, "you didn't know a whole lot of things, my son."

"True, how true," mourned Ellery.

"When you really take a look at it, your 'proof' was pretty much a matter of slats, cardboard, and spit."

"Mmm," said Mr. Queen. "Well, yes. But remember, I was working it out extempore. I'd no chance to prepare my attack; I couldn't let that wedding proceed; I had to do what I could on the spot, working my way from point to point."

"What a man," said Sergeant Velie. "He works his way from point to point. Sort of like a mountain goat, huh?"

"But I had certain advantages, too. Charley was caught offguard in the middle of his wedding—at a time when he thought he'd pulled the whole thing off and had got away with it."

"And now he's chewing his fingernails off in the hoosegow," said the Sergeant. "Such a life."

"Circumstantial evidence," persisted the Inspector.

"But very strong circumstantial evidence, Dad. That last point—about the possession of the sealed envelope—powerful. It was my silver bullet. And it caught Charley Paxton dead center. Yes, he cracked and confessed. But I knew he would. No man can stand up under a confident attack at a time when he's unprepared, after a long period of strain. Charley's the intellectual type of killer, the type that will always crack under blows an ordinary desperado wouldn't even feel."

"Yes, sir," nodded Sergeant Velie, "here yesterday, in the hoosegow today. It makes you think."

"It makes *me* think I've never been so happy to see the end of a case," yawned the Inspector. "*What* a case!"

"You haven't quite seen the end of it," suggested his son respectfully.

"Huh?" The Inspector bounced to his feet. "Don't tell me you just realized you've made *another* mistake!"

"In a way, yes," mused Ellery. But his eyes were twinkling. "Sheila Brent phoned me. She's on her way over."

"What for?" Inspector Queen stuck his little jaw out. But then he shook his head. "Still got a hangover, I guess. Poor girl's taken a bad beating. What's she want, Ellery?"

"I don't know. But I know what *I* want."

"What?"

"To help her. I don't know just why—"

"Aha," said his father. "Velie, let's get out of here."

"And why not?" The Sergeant rose, stretching. "*I'll* tell you what you can do for Miss Brent Maestro. You can help her spend some of those millions of bucks." And the Sergeant left, grumbling that the policeman's lot is not a lucrative one.

"I don't think, Velie," Mr. Queen called after him, "that that's quite what the doctor ordered for Miss Brent."

And he sat musing on various therapeutic matters until his doorbell rang.

"It's good to see you minus a hunted look," said Ellery. "I'd begun to be afraid it was permanent."

But Sheila was not looking too well. She was pale and her dimples spiritless this morning. "Thanks. Could you give a woman a drink of something wet and cold?"

"For a dry and thirsty day—certainly." And Ellery promptly set about mixing something wet and cold. He was nervous, and Sheila remarked it.

"I hope I'm not getting in your hair," she sighed. "I seem to have been hanging onto you—in a way—since . . . Oh. Thanks, Mr. Queen."

"Ellery."

He watched her sip the frosty drink and thought how pleasant it might be to repeat the service *ad infinitum*.

"I can't tell you how sorry I am about what I had to do yesterday, Sheila—"

"Sorry!" She set down the drink. "And here I've been so grateful—"

"You weren't too shocked?" he asked anxiously. "You see, I had no time to warn you—"

"I understand."

"Naturally I couldn't let you go through with it."

"Naturally." She even smiled. "If that isn't just like a

man. Save a woman from—" she shuddered— "from the most horrible kind of mistake . . . and apologize for it!"

"Well, but I thought—"

"Well, but you're a love," said Sheila queerly. "And I can never thank you enough. That's why I asked if I might drop in. I had to tell you in person."

"Don't say another word about it," said Ellery in a nettled tone. "I don't know why you should thank me. I must be associated in your mind almost entirely with nastinesses, and clues, and policemen, and brutal revelations—"

"Oh, don't be an idiot!" cried Sheila. And then she said, blushing: "I'm sorry, Mr. Queen."

"Ellery." Ellery felt vastly pleased. "Sheila, why don't you start a new life?"

She stared. "If you aren't the suddenest man!"

"Well, I mean—you ought to leave that nest of blubbering imbeciles on Riverside Drive, put yourself into a new and cheerful environment, get a real interest in life—"

"Of course you're right." Sheila frowned. "And I'm certainly going to get out into the world and try to forget everything I ever . . . I've found that having money doesn't solve anything important. I've always wanted to do something useful, but Mother wouldn't let me. If I could only find work of some sort—work I'd enjoy doing . . ."

"Ah," said Mr. Queen. "That brings up an important question, Miss Brent." He fingered his ear. "Would you—uh—consider that I come under the heading of enjoyable occupations?"

"You?" Sheila looked blank.

"How would you like to come to work for me?" Ellery added hastily: "On a salary, of course. That's understood. I'm not trying to take advantage of your millions."

"Work for *you?*" Sheila propped one elbow on her knee and put her fist under her chin and stared at him thoughtfully. "Tell me more, Mr. Queen."

"You're not offended? Wonderful woman!" Ellery beamed. "Sheila, forget the past. Break every tie you've ever had. Except with your father, of course. But even in that case I think you should live alone. Change everything. Surroundings, way of living, clothes, habits. Pretend you've been born all over again."

Sheila's eyes had begun to sparkle. But then they clouded over. "Listens good, Ellery, but it's impossible."

"Nothing's impossible."

But Sheila shook her head. "You forget I'm a marked

woman. I'm Sheila Potts, or Sheila Brent—it doesn't matter; they know both names." *They* as she uttered the word sounded ugly. "I'd only mess your life up with a lot of notoriety, and I'd never be allowed to forget who I was ... who my mother was ... my half brother Thurlow ... the man I almost married ..."

"Nonsense."

She looked curious. "But it's true."

"It's true only if you let it be true. There's a perfectly simple way of making it not true."

"How?" she cried. "Anything—tell me how! You don't know how I've wanted to lose myself in crowds and crowds of ordinary, decent, sane people. ... *How* Ellery?"

"Change your name," said Ellery calmly. "And with it your life. If Mr. Queen, the scrivener of detective stories, suddenly hires a secretary named Susie McGargle, a nice young woman from, say, Kansas City—"

"Secretary," whispered Sheila. "Oh, yes! But ..." Her voice became lifeless again. "It's out of the question. You're a dear to make the offer, but I'm not equipped, I don't know how to type, I can't take shorthand—"

"You can learn. That's what secretarial schools are for."

"Yes ... I suppose ..."

"And I think you'll find me an understanding employer."

"But I'd be a liability for such a long time!"

"Six weeks," said Ellery reflectively. "Two months at the outside—to become as efficient a stenographer as ever drew a pothook or made a typewriter sing for its supper. I give you two months, no more."

"Do you think I ... really could?"

"Shucks."

Almost rapturously, Sheila said: "If I could ... a new life ... It would be fun with you! If you really meant it—"

"I really mean it," said Mr. Queen simply.

"Then I'll do it!" She jumped from the sofa. "By golly, I'll do it!" In her excitement she began to race up and down, flying from place to place. "Is this where you work? Is it hard? Doesn't anyone ever clean this desk? That's a terrible photo of you. Light's bad in here. Where's your typewriter? Maybe I could start today. I mean, the school ... Oh, gosh, a new life, a new name, working with Ellery Queen ... A new name," she said damply. "But I don't *like* Susie McGargle."

"That," said Ellery, watching her skim about with a delight that surprised him, "that was a low inspiration of the moment, chosen merely for illustration."

"How you talk!" Sheila laughed and for the first time in a long time Mr. Queen thought how delicious can be a woman's laughter. "Well, then, what's my name going to be? It's your idea—you baptize me."

Ellery closed his eyes. "Name . . . Pretty problem. Pretty problem for a pretty subject. Red hair, dimples . . ." He sat up, beaming. "D'ye know, here's a remarkable coincidence!"

"What, Ellery?"

"The heroine of my new book has red hair and dimples!"

"Really? What's her name? Whatever it is—even if it's Grimalkin—or Pollywog—I'll take it for my own!"

"You will?"

"Certainly."

"Well, you're in luck," said Ellery, grinning. "It's a darned sweet name, if I do say so as shouldn't."

"What is it?"

Mr. Queen told her.

"Nicky?" Sheila looked doubtful.

"Spelled N-i-k-k-i."

"Nikki! Oh, wonderful, wonderful. That's a *beautiful* name. Nikki . . . Mr. Queen, I buy it!"

"As for a last name," murmured that gentleman, "I can't give you my heroine's . . . it's Dempsey . . . perfectly good name, but inappropriate for you, somehow. Let me see. What would go well with 'Nikki' and you?"

"Nikki . . . Nikki Jones? Nikki Brown? Nikki Green—"

"Heavens no. No poetry. Nikki Keats? Nikki Lowell? Nikki Fowler? . . . Fowler. *E-r* ending. *Er.* Yes, that would be good. An *er* ending in a two-syllable name. Parker. Farmer. Porter . . . Porter! Nikki Porter!" Ellery sprang to his feet. "That's it," he cried. *"Nikki Porter."*

"Yes," said Nikki Porter, all soft and tender and merry and grateful at once. "Yes, Mr. Queen."

"Ellery to you, Miss Porter," beamed Mr. Queen.

"Nikki to *you* . . . Ellery."

THE ORIGIN
OF EVIL

One

ELLERY WAS SPREAD over the ponyskin chair before
the picture window, *huarachos* crossed on the typewriter
table, a ten-inch frosted glass in his hand, and the corpse
at his feet. He was studying the victim between sips and
making not too much out of her. However, he was not
concerned. It was early in the investigation, she was of
unusual proportions, and the *ron* consoled.

He took another sip.

It was a curious case. The victim still squirmed; from
where he sat he could make out signs of life. Back in
New York they had warned him that these were an illusion, reflexes following the death rattle. Why, you won't
believe it, they had said, but corruption's set in already and
anyone who can tell a stinkweed from a camellia will
testify to it. Ellery had been skeptical. He had known deceased in her heyday—a tumid wench, every man's day-
dream, and the laughing target of curses and longing. It
was hard to believe that such vitality could be extermi-
nated.

On the scene of the crime—or rather above it, for the
little house he had taken was high over the city, a bird's
nest perched on the twig tip of an upper branch of the
hills—Ellery still doubted. There she lay under a thin
blanket of smog, stirring a little, and they said she was
dead.

Fair Hollywood.

Murdered, ran the post-mortem, by Television.

He squinted down at the city, sipping his rum and enjoying his nakedness. It was a blue-white day. The hill ran
green and flowered to the twinkled plain, simmering in the
sun.

There had been no technical reason for choosing Hollywood as the setting for his new novel. Mystery stories
operate under special laws of growth; their beginnings may

5

lie in the look in a faceless woman's eye glimpsed in a crowd for exactly the duration of one heartbeat, or in the small type on page five of a life insurance policy; generally the writer has the atlas to pick from. Ellery had had only the gauziest idea of where he was going; at that stage of the game it could as well have been Joplin, Missouri, or the kitchens of the Kremlin. In fact, his plot was in such a cloudy state that when he heard about the murder of Hollywood he took it as a sign from the heavens and made immediate arrangements to be present at the autopsy. His trade being violent death, a city with a knife in its back seemed just the place to take his empty sample cases.

Well, there was life in the old girl yet. Of course, theaters with *MOVIES ARE BETTER THAN EVER* on their marquees had crossbars over their portals saying *CLOSED;* you could now get a table at the Brown Derby without waiting more than twenty minutes; that eminent haberdasher of the Strip, Mickey Cohen, was out of business; movie stars were cutting their prices for radio; radio actors were auditioning tensely for television as they redesigned their belts or put their houses up for sale; shopkeepers were complaining that how could anybody find money for yard goods or nail files when the family budget was mortgaged to Hoppy labels, the new car, and the television set; teen-age gangs, solemnly christened "wolf packs" by the Los Angeles newspapers, cruised the streets beating up strangers, high school boys were regularly caught selling marijuana, and "Chicken!" was the favorite highway sport of the hot-rodders; and you could throttle a tourist on Hollywood Boulevard between Vine and La Brea any night after 10:30 and feel reasonably secure against interruption.

But out in the San Fernando Valley mobs of little cheap stuccos and redwood fronts were beginning to elbow the pained hills, paint-fresh signal lights at intersections were stopping cars which had previously known only the carefree California conscience, and a great concrete ditch labeled "Flood Control Project" was making its way across the sandy valley like an opening zipper.

On the ocean side of the Santa Monica Mountains, from Beverly Glen to Topanga Canyon, lordlier mansions were going up which called themselves "estates"—disdaining the outmoded "ranch" or "rancho," which more and more out-of-state ex-innocents were learning was a four-or-five-and-den on a 50×100 lot containing three callow apricot trees.

Beverly Hills might be biting its perfect fingernails, but Glendale and Encino were booming, and Ellery could detect no moans from the direction of Brentwood, Flint-ridge, Sunland, or Eagle Rock. New schools were assembling; more oldsters were chugging in from Iowa and Michigan, flexing their arthritic fingers and practicing old age pension-check-taking; and to drive a car in downtown Los Angeles at noontime the four blocks from 3rd to 7th along Broadway, Spring, Hill, or Main now took thirty minutes instead of fifteen. Ellery heard tell of huge factories moving in; of thousands of migrants swarming into Southern California through Blythe and Indio on 60 and Needles and Barstow on 66—latter-day pioneers to whom the movies still represented Life and Love and "television" remained a highfalutin word, like "antibiotic." The carhops were more beautiful and numerous than ever; more twenty-foot ice cream cones punctuated the skyline; Tchaikovsky under the stars continued to fill Hollywood Bowl with brave-bottomed music lovers; Grand Openings of hardware stores now used two giant searchlights instead of one; the Farmers' Market on Fairfax and 3rd chittered and heaved like an Egyptian bazaar in the tourist season; Madman Muntz had apparently taken permanent possession of the skies, his name in mile-high letters drifting expensively away daily; and the newspapers offered an even more tempting line of cheesecake than in the old days—Ellery actually saw one photograph of the routine well-stacked cutie in a Bikini bathing suit perched zippily on a long flower-decked box inscribed *Miss National Casket Week*. And in three days or so, according to the reports, the Imperial Potentate would lead a six-hour safari of thirteen thousand red-fezzed, capering, elderly Penrods, accompanied by fifty-one bands, assorted camels, clowns, and floats, along Figueroa Street to the Memorial Coliseum to convene the seventy-umpth Imperial Session of the Ancient Arabic Order of the Nobles of the Mystic Shrine —a civic event guaranteed to rouse even the dead.

It became plain in his first few days in Hollywood and environs that what the crapehangers back East were erroneously bewailing was not the death of the angelic city but its exuberant rebirth in another shape. The old order changeth. The new organism was exciting, but it was a little out of his line; and Ellery almost packed up and flew back East. But then he thought, It's all hassle and hurly-burly, everybody snarling or making hay; and there's still the twitching nucleus of the old Hollywood bunch—stick around, old boy, the atmosphere is murderous and it may well inspire a collector's item or two for the circulating library shelves.

Also, there had been the press and its agents. Ellery had thought to slip into town by dropping off at the Lockheed field in Burbank rather than the International Airport in Inglewood. But he touched Southern California soil to a bazooka fire of questions and lenses, and the next day his picture was on the front page of all the papers. They had even got his address in the hills straight, although his pal the real estate man later swore by the beard of Nature Boy that he'd had nothing to do with the leak. It had been that way for Ellery ever since the publicity explosion over the Cat case. The newspaper boys were convinced that, having saved Manhattan from a fate equivalent to death, Ellery was in Los Angeles on a mission at least equally large and torrid. When he plaintively explained that he had come to write a book they all laughed, and their printed explanations ascribed his visit to everything from a top-secret appointment by the Mayor as Special Investigator to Clean Up Greater L.A. to the turning of his peculiar talents upon the perennial problem of the Black Dahlia.

How could he run out?

At this point Ellery noticed that his glass was as empty as his typewriter.

He got up from the ponyskin chair and found himself face to face with a pretty girl.

AS HE JUMPED nudely for the bedroom doorway Ellery thought, The *huarachos* must look ridiculous. Then he thought, Why didn't I put on those ten pounds Barney prescribed? Then he got angry and poked his head around the door to whine, "I told Mrs. Williams I wasn't seeing anybody today, not even her. How did you get in?"

"Through the garden," said the girl. "Climbed up from the road below. I tried not to trample your marigolds. I hope you don't mind."

"I do mind. Go away."

"But I've got to see you."

"Everybody's got to see me. But I don't have to see everybody. Especially when I look like this."

"You are sort of pale, aren't you? And your ribs stick out, Ellery." She sounded like a debunked sister. Ellery suddenly remembered that in Hollywood dress is a matter of free enterprise. You could don a parka and drive a team of Siberian huskies from Schwab's Drugstore at the foot of Laurel Canyon to NBC at Sunset and Vine and never turn a head. Fur stoles over slacks are acceptable if not *de rigueur,* the exposed navel is considered conservative, and at least one man dressed in nothing but Waikiki trunks may be found poking sullenly among the avocados at any vegetable stand. "You ought to put on some weight, Ellery. And get out in the sun."

"Thank you," Ellery heard himself saying.

His Garden of Eden costume meant absolutely nothing to her. And she was even prettier than he had thought. Hollywood prettiness, he thought sulkily; they all look alike. Probably Miss Universe of Pasadena. She was dressed in zebra-striped culottes and bolero over a bra-like doodad of bright green suède. Green open-toed sandals on her tiny feet. A matching suède jockey cap on her cinnamon hair. Skin toast-colored where it was showing, and *no* ribs. A small and slender number, but three-dimensional where it counted. About nineteen years old. For no reason at all she reminded him of Meg in Thorne Smith's *The Night Life of the Gods,* and he pulled his head back and banged the door.

When he came out safe and suave in slacks, Shantung shirt, and burgundy corduroy jacket, she was curled up in his ponyskin chair smoking a cigaret.

"I've fixed your drink," she said.

"Kind of you. I suppose that means I must offer you one." No point in being too friendly.

"Thanks. I don't drink before five." She was thinking of something else.

Ellery leaned against the picture window and looked down at her with hostility. "It's not that I'm a prude, Miss—"

"Hill. Laurel Hill."

"—Miss Laurel Hill, but when I receive strange young things *au naturel* in Hollywood I like to be sure no confederate with a camera and an offer to do business is skulking behind my drapes. Why do you think you have to see me?"

"Because the police are dummies."

"Ah, the police. They won't listen to you?"

"They listen, all right. But then they laugh. I don't think there's anything funny in a dead dog, do you?"

9

"In a what?"

"A dead dog."

Ellery sighed, rolling the frosty glass along his brow. "Your pooch was poisoned, of course?"

"Guess again," said the set-faced intruder. "He wasn't my pooch, and I don't know what caused his death. What's more, dog-lover though I am, I don't care a curse. . . . They said it was somebody's idea of a rib, and I know they're talking through their big feet. I don't know what it meant, but it was no rib."

Ellery had set the glass down. She stared back. Finally he shook his head, smiling. "The tactics are primitive, Laurel. E for Effort. But no dice."

"No tactics," she said impatiently. "Let me tell you—"

"Who sent you to me?"

"Not a soul. You were all over the papers. It solved my problem."

"It doesn't solve mine, Laurel. My problem is to find the background of peaceful isolation which passeth the understanding of the mere, dear reader. I'm here to do a book, Laurel—a poor thing in a state of arrested development, but writing is a habit writers get into and my time has come. So, you see, I can't take any cases."

"You won't even listen." Her mouth was in trouble. She got up and started across the room. He watched the brown flesh below the bolero. Not his type, but nice.

"Dogs die all the time," Ellery said in a kindly voice.

"It wasn't the dog, I tell you. It was the way it happened." She did not turn at the front door.

"The way he died?" Sucker.

"The way we found him." The girl suddenly leaned against the door, sidewise to him, staring down at her cigaret. "He was on our doorstep. Did you ever have a cat who insisted on leaving tidily dead mice on your mat to go with your breakfast eggs? He was a . . . gift." She looked around for an ashtray, went over to the fireplace. "And it killed my father."

A dead dog killing anybody struck Ellery as worth a tentative glance. And there was something about the girl —a remote, hardened purpose—that interested him.

"Sit down again."

She betrayed herself by the quick way in which she came back to the ponyskin chair, by the way she folded her tense hands and waited.

"How exactly, Laurel, did a dead dog 'kill' your father?"

10

"It murdered him."

He didn't like the way she sat there. He said deliberately, "Don't build it up for me. This isn't a suspense program. A strange dead hound is left on your doorstep and your father dies. What's the connection?"

"It frightened him to death!"

"And what did the death certificate say?" He now understood the official hilarity.

"Coronary something. I don't care what it said. Getting the dog did it."

"Let's go back." Ellery offered her one of his cigarets, but she shook her head and took a pack of Dunhills from her green pouch bag. He held a match for her; the cigaret between her lips was shaking. "Your name is Laurel Hill. You had a father. Who was he? Where do you live? What did he do for a living? And so on." She looked surprised, as if it had not occurred to her that such trivia could be of any interest to him. "I'm not necessarily taking it, Laurel. But I promise not to laugh."

"Thank you . . . Leander Hill. Hill & Priam, Wholesale Jewelers."

"Yes." He had never heard of the firm. "Los Angeles?"

"The main office is here, though Dad and Roger have —I mean had . . ." She laughed. "What tense *do* I use? . . . branch offices in New York, Amsterdam, South Africa."

"Who is Roger?"

"Roger Priam. Dad's partner. We live off Outpost, not far from here. Twelve acres of lopsided woods. Formal gardens, with mathematical eucalyptus and royal palms, and plenty of bougainvillea, bird-of-paradise, poinsettia— all the stuff that curls up and dies at a touch of frost, which we get regularly every winter and which everybody says can't possibly happen again, not in Southern California. But Dad liked it. Made him feel like a Caribbean pirate, he used to say. Three in help in the house, a gardener who comes in every day, and the Priams have the adjoining property." From the carefully scrubbed way in which she pronounced the name Priam it might have been Hatfield. "Daddy had a bad heart, and we should have lived on level ground. But he liked hills and wouldn't hear of moving."

"Mother alive?" He knew she was not. Laurel had the motherless look. The self-made female. A man's girl, and there were times when she would insist on being a man's

11

man. Not Miss Universe of Pasadena or anywhere else, he thought. He began to like her. "She isn't?" he said, when Laurel was silent.

"I don't know." A sore spot. "If I ever knew my mother, I've forgotten."

"Foster mother, then?"

"He never married. I was brought up by a nurse, who died when I was fifteen—four years ago. I never liked her, and I think she got pneumonia just to make me feel guilty. I'm—I was his daughter by adoption." She looked around for an ashtray, and Ellery brought her one. She said steadily as she crushed the cigaret, "But really his daughter. None of that fake pal stuff, you understand, that covers contempt on one side and being unsure on the other. I loved and respected him, and—as he used to say —I was the only woman in his life. Dad was a little on the old-school side. Held my chair for me. That sort of thing. He was . . . solid." And now, Ellery thought, it's jelly and you're hanging on to the stuff with your hard little fingers. "It happened," Laurel Hill went on in the same toneless way, "two weeks ago. June third. We were just finishing breakfast. Simeon, our chauffeur, came in to tell Daddy he'd just brought the car around and there was something 'funny' at the front door. We all went out, and there it was—a dead dog lying on the doorstep with an ordinary shipping tag attached to its collar. Dad's name was printed on it in black crayon: *Leander Hill.*"

"Any address?"

"Just the name."

"Did the printing look familiar? Did you recognize it?"

"I didn't really look at it. I just saw one line of crayon marks as Dad bent over the dog. He said in a surprised way, 'Why, it's addressed to me.' Then he opened the little casket."

"Casket?"

"There was a tiny silver box—about the size of a pill-box—attached to the collar. Dad opened it and found a wad of thin paper inside, folded over enough times so it would fit into the box. He unfolded it and it was covered with writing or printing—it might have been typewriting; I couldn't really see because he half turned away as he read it.

"By the time he'd finished reading his face was the color of bread dough, and his lips looked bluish. I started to ask him who'd sent it to him and what was wrong, when he

12

crushed the paper in a sort of spasm and gave a choked cry and fell. I'd seen it happen before. It was a heart attack."

She stared out the picture window at Hollywood.

"How about a drink, Laurel?"

"No. Thanks. Simeon and—"

"What kind of dog was it?"

"Some sort of hunting dog, I think."

"Was there a license tag on his collar?"

"I don't remember seeing any."

"An anti-rabies tag?"

"I saw no tag except the paper one with Dad's name on it."

"Anything special about the dog collar?"

"It couldn't have cost more than seventy-five cents."

"Just a collar." Ellery dragged over a chartreuse latticed blond chair and straddled it. "Go on, Laurel."

"Simeon and Ichiro, our houseman, carried him up to his bedroom while I ran for the brandy and Mrs. Monk, our housekeeper, phoned the doctor. He lives on Castilian Drive and he was over in a few minutes. Daddy didn't die —that time."

"Oh, I see," said Ellery. "And what did the paper in the silver box on the dead dog's collar say, Laurel?"

"That's what I don't know."

"Oh, come."

"When he fell unconscious the paper was still in his hand, crumpled into a ball. I was too busy to try to open his fist, and by the time Dr. Voluta came, I'd forgotten it. But I remembered it that night, and the first chance I got—the next morning—I asked Dad about it. The minute I mentioned it he got pale, mumbled, 'It was nothing, nothing,' and I changed the subject fast. But when Dr. Voluta dropped in, I took him aside and asked him if he'd seen the note. He said he had opened Daddy's hand and put the wad of paper on the night table beside the bed without reading it. I asked Simeon, Ichiro, and the housekeeper if they had taken the paper, but none of them had seen it. Daddy must have spotted it when he came to, and when he was alone he took it back."

"Have you looked for it since?"

"Yes, but I haven't found it. I assume he destroyed it."

Ellery did not comment on such assumptions. "Well, then, the dog, the collar, the little box. Have you done anything about them?"

"I was too excited over whether Daddy was going to live or die to think about the dog. I recall telling Itchie or Sim to get it out of the way. I only meant for them to get it off the doorstep, but the next day when I went looking for it, Mrs. Monk told me she had called the Pound Department or some place and it had been picked up and carted away."

"Up the flue," said Ellery, tapping his teeth with a fingernail. "Although the collar and box . . . You're sure your father didn't react to the mere sight of the dead dog? He wasn't afraid of dogs? Or," he added suddenly, "of dying?"

"He adored dogs. So much so that when Sarah, our Chesapeake bitch, died of old age last year he refused to get another dog. He said it was too hard losing them. As far as dying is concerned, I don't think the prospect of death as such bothered Daddy very much. Certainly not so much as the suffering. He hated the idea of a lingering illness with a lot of pain, and he always hoped that when his time came he'd pass away in his sleep. But that's all. Does that answer your question?"

"Yes," said Ellery, "and no. Was he superstitious?"

"Not especially. Why?"

"You said he was frightened to death. I'm groping."

Laurel was silent. Then she said, "But he was. I mean frightened to death. It wasn't the dog—at first." She gripped her ankles, staring ahead. "I got the feeling that the dog didn't mean anything till he read the note. Maybe it didn't mean anything to him even then. But whatever was in that note terrified him. It came as a tremendous shock to him. I'd never seen him look *afraid* before. I mean the real thing. And I could have sworn he died on the way down. He looked really dead lying there . . . . That note did something devastating." She turned to Ellery. Her eyes were greenish, with brown flecks in them; they were a little bulgy. "Something he'd forgotten, maybe. Something so important it made Roger come out of his shell for the first time in fifteen years."

"What?" said Ellery. "What was that again?"

"I told you—Roger Priam, Dad's business partner. His oldest friend. Roger left his house."

"For the first time in fifteen years?" exclaimed Ellery.

"Fifteen years ago Roger became partly paralyzed. He's lived in a wheelchair ever since, and ever since he's refused to leave the Priam premises. All vanity; he was a

14

large hunk of man in his day, I understand, proud of his build, his physical strength; he can't stand the thought of having people see him helpless, and it's turned him into something pretty unpleasant.

"Through it all Roger pretends he's as good as ever and he brags that running the biggest jewelry business on the West Coast from a wheelchair in the hills proves it. Of course, he doesn't do any such thing. Daddy ran it all, though to keep peace he played along with Roger and pretended with him—gave Roger special jobs to do that he could handle over the phone, never took an important step without consulting him, and so on. Why, some of the people at the office and showrooms downtown have been with the firm for years and have never even laid eyes on Roger. The employes hate him. They call him 'the invisible God,'" Laurel said with a smile. Ellery did not care for the smile. "Of course—being employes—they're scared to death of him."

"A fear which you don't share?"

"I can't stand him." It came out calmly enough, but when Ellery kept looking at her she glanced elsewhere.

"You're afraid of him, too."

"I just dislike him."

"Go on."

"I'd notified the Priams of Dad's heart attack the first chance I got, which was the evening of the day it happened. I spoke to Roger myself on the phone. He seemed very curious about the circumstances and kept insisting he had to talk to Daddy. I refused—Dr. Voluta had forbidden excitement of any kind. The next morning Roger phoned twice, and Dad seemed just as anxious to talk to *him*. In fact, he was getting so upset I let him phone. There's a private line between his bedroom and the Priam house. But after I got Roger on the phone Dad asked me to leave the room."

Laurel jumped up, but immediately she sat down again, fumbling for another Dunhill. Ellery let her strike her own match; she failed to notice.

She puffed rapidly. "Nobody knows what he said to Roger. Whatever it was, it took only a few minutes, and it brought Roger right over. He'd been lifted, wheelchair and all, into the back of the Priams' station wagon, and Delia—Roger's wife—drove him over herself." And Laurel's voice stabbed at the name of Mrs. Priam. So another Hatfield went with this McCoy. "When he was

15

carried up to Dad's bedroom in his chair, Roger locked the door. They talked for three hours."

"Discussing the dead dog and the note?"

"There's no other possibility. It couldn't have been business—Roger had never felt the necessity of coming over before on business, and Daddy had had two previous heart attacks. It was about the dog and note, all right. And if I had any doubts, the look on Roger Priam's face when he wheeled himself out of the bedroom killed them. He was as frightened as Daddy had been the day before, and for the same reason.

"And that was something to see," said Laurel softly. "If you were to meet Roger Priam, you'd know what I mean. Frightened looks don't go with his face. If there's any fright around, he's usually dishing it out . . . . He even talked to me, something he rarely bothers to do. 'You take good care of your father,' he said to me. I pleaded with him to tell me what was wrong, and he pretended not to have heard me. Simeon and Itchie lifted him into the station wagon, and Delia drove off with him.

"A week ago—during the night of June tenth—Daddy got his wish. He died in his sleep. Dr. Voluta says that last shock to his heart did it. He was cremated, and his ashes are in a bronze drawer fifteen feet from the floor at Forest Lawn. But that's what he wanted, and that's where he is. The sixty-four dollar question, Ellery, is: Who murdered him? And I want it answered."

ELLERY RANG FOR Mrs. Williams. When she did not appear, he excused himself and went downstairs to the miniature lower level to find a note from his housekeeper describing minutely her plan to shop at the supermarket on North Highland. A pot of fresh coffee on the range and a deep dish of whipped avocado and bacon bits surrounded by crackers told him that Mrs. Williams had overheard all, so he took them upstairs.

Laurel said, surprised, "How nice of you," as if niceness these days were a quality that called for surprise. She refused the crackers just as nicely, but then she changed her mind and ate ten of them without pausing, and she drank three cups of coffee. "I remembered I hadn't eaten anything today."

"That's what I thought."

She was frowning now, which he regarded as an improvement over the stone face she had been wearing. "I've

16

tried to talk to Roger Priam half a dozen times since then, but he won't even admit he and Dad discussed anything unusual. I told him in words of one syllable where I thought his obligations lay—certainly his debt to their life-long friendship and partnership—and I explained my belief that Daddy was murdered by somebody who knew how bad his heart was and deliberately shocked him into a heart attack. And I asked for the letter. He said innocently, 'What letter?' and I realized I'd never get a thing out of him. Roger's either over his scare or he's being his usual Napoleonic self. There's a big secret behind all this and he means to keep it."

"Do you think," asked Ellery, "that he's confided in Mrs. Priam?"

"Roger doesn't confide in anybody," replied Laurel grimly. "And if he did, the last person in the world he'd tell anything to would be Delia."

"Oh, the Priams don't get along?"

"I didn't say they don't get along."

"They do get along?"

"Let's change the subject, shall we?"

"Why, Laurel?"

"Because Roger's relationship with Delia has nothing to do with any of this." Laurel sounded earnest. But she was hiding something just the same. "I'm interested in only one thing—finding out who wrote that note to my father."

"Still," said Ellery, "what was your father's relationship with Delia Priam?"

"Oh!" Laurel laughed. "Of course you couldn't know. No, they weren't having an affair. Not possibly. Besides, I told you Daddy said I was the only woman in his life."

"Then they were hostile to each other?"

"Why do you keep on the subject of Delia?" she asked, a snap in her voice.

"Why do you keep off it?"

"Dad got along with Delia fine. He got along with everybody."

"Not everybody, Laurel," said Ellery.

She looked at him sharply.

"That is, if your theory that someone deliberately scared him to death is sound. You can't blame the police, Laurel, for being fright-shy. Fright is a dangerous weapon that doesn't show up under the microscope. It takes no fingerprints and it's the most unsatisfactory kind of legal evidence. Now the letter . . . if you had the letter, that would be different. But you don't have it."

"You're laughing at me." Laurel prepared to rise.

"Not at all. The smooth stories are usually as slick as their surface. I like a good rough story. You can scrape away at the uneven places, and the dust tells you things. Now I know there's something about Delia and Roger Priam. What is it?"

"Why must you know?"

"Because you're so reluctant to tell me."

"I'm not. I just don't want to waste any time, and to talk about Delia and Roger is wasting time. Their relationship has nothing to do with my father."

Their eyes locked.

Finally, with a smile, Ellery waved.

"No, I don't have the letter. And that's what the police said. Without the letter, or some evidence to go on, they can't come into it. I've asked Roger to tell them what he knows—knowing that what he knows *would* be enough for them to go on—and he laughed and recommended Arrowhead or Palm Springs as a cure for my 'pipe dream,' as he called it. The police point to the autopsy report and Dad's cardiac history and send me politely away. Are you going to do the same?"

Ellery turned to the window. To get into a live murder case was the last thing in the world he had bargained for. But the dead dog fascinated him. Why a dead dog as a messenger of bad news? It smacked of symbolism. And murderers with metaphoric minds he had never been able to resist. If, of course, there was a murder. Hollywood was a playful place. People produced practical jokes on the colossal scale. A dead dog was nothing compared with some of the elaborations on record. One he knew of personally involved a race horse in a bathroom, another the employment for two days of seventy-six extras. Some wit had sent a cardiac jeweler a recently deceased canine and a fake Mafia note, and before common sense could set in the victim of the dogplay had a heart attack. Learning the unexpected snapper of his joke, the joker would not unnaturally turn shy. The victim, ill and shaken, summoned his oldest friend and business partner to a conference. Perhaps the note threatened Sicilian tortures unless the crown jewels were deposited in the oily crypt of the pterodactyl pit in Hancock Park by midnight of the following day. For three hours the partners discussed the note,

Hill nervously insisting it might be legitimate, Priam reasonably poohing and boshing the very notion. In the end Priam came away, and what Laurel Hill had taken to be fear was probably annoyance at Hill's womanish obduracy. Hill was immobilized by his partner's irritation, and before he could rouse himself his heart gave out altogether. End of mystery. Of course, there were a few dangling ends . . . But you could sympathize with the police. It was a lot likelier than a wild detective-story theory dreamed up by deceased's daughter. They had undoubtedly dismissed her as either a neurotic girl tipped over by grief or a publicity hound with a yen for a starlet contract. She was determined enough to be either.

Ellery turned about. She was leaning forward, the forgotten cigaret sending up question marks.

"I suppose," said Ellery, "your father had a closetful of bony enemies?"

"Not to my knowledge."

This astonished him. To run true to form she should have come prepared with names, dates, and vital statistics.

"He was an easy, comfortable sort of man. He liked people, and people liked him. Dad's personality was one of the big assets of Hill & Priam. He'd have his moments like everybody else, but I never knew anyone who could stay mad at him. Not even Roger."

"Then you haven't the smoggiest notion who could be behind this . . . fright murder?"

"Now you *are* laughing." Laurel Hill got to her feet and dropped her cigaret definitely into the ashtray. "Sorry I've taken up so much of your time."

"You might try a reliable agency. I'll be glad to—"

"I've decided," she smiled at him, "to go into the racket personally. Thanks for the avocado—"

"Why, Laurel."

Laurel turned quickly.

A tall woman stood in the doorway.

"Hello, Delia," said Laurel.

19

Two

NOTHING IN LAUREL Hill's carefully edited remarks had prepared him for Delia Priam. Through his only available windows—the narrow eyes of Laurel's youth—he had seen Delia's husband as a pompous and tyrannical old cock, crippled but rampant, ruling his roost with a beak of iron; and from this it followed that the wife must be a gray-feathered hennypenny, preening herself emptily in corners, one of Bullock's elderly barnyard trade . . . a dumpy, nervous, insignificant old biddy.

But the woman in his doorway was no helpless fowl, to be plucked, swallowed, and forgotten. Delia Priam was of a far different species, higher in the ranks of the animal kingdom, and she would linger on the palate.

She was so much younger than his mental sketch of her that only much later was Ellery to recognize this as one of her routine illusions, among the easiest of the magic tricks she performed as professionally as she carried her breasts. At that time he was to discover that she was forty-four, but the knowledge remained as physically meaningless as—the figure leaped into his mind—learning the chronological age of Ayesha. The romantic nonsense of this metaphor was to persist. He would even be appalled to find that he was identifying himself in his fantasy with that hero of his adolescence, Allan Quatermain, who had been privileged to witness the immortal strip-tease of She-Who-Must-Be-Obeyed behind her curtain of living flame. It was the most naked juvenility, and Ellery was duly amused at himself. But there she was, a glowing end in herself; it took only imagination, a commodity with which he was plentifully provided, to supply the veils.

Delia Priam was big game; one glance told him that. His doorway framed the most superbly proportioned woman he had ever seen. She was dressed in a tawny peasant blouse of some sheer material and a California print skirt

20

of bold colors. Her heavy black hair was massed to one side of her head, sleekly, in the Polynesian fashion; she wore plain broad hoops of gold in her ears. Head, shoulders, bust, hips—he could not decide which pleased him more. She stood there not so much in an attitude as in an atmosphere—an atmosphere of intense repose, watchful and disquieting.

By Hollywood standards she was not beautiful: her eyes were too deep and light-tinted, her eyebrows too lush; her mouth was too full, her coloring too high, her figure too heroic. But it was this very excessiveness that excited—a tropical quality, humid, brilliant, still, and overpowering. Seeing her for the first time was like stepping into a jungle. She seized and held the senses; everything was leashed, lovely, and dangerous. He found his ears trying to recapture her voice, the sleepy growl of something heard from a thicket.

Ellery's first sensible thought was, *Roger, old cock, you can have her.* His second was, *But how do you keep her?* He was on his third when he saw the chilly smile on Laurel Hill's lips.

Ellery pulled himself together. This was evidently an old story to Laurel.

"Then Laurel's . . . mentioned me." A dot-dot-dot talker. It had always annoyed him. But it prolonged the sound of that bitch-in-a-thicket voice.

"I answered Mr. Queen's questions," said Laurel in a warm, friendly voice. "Delia, you don't seem surprised to see me."

"I left my surprise outside with your car." Those lazy throat tones were warm and friendly, too. "I could say . . . the same to you, Laurel."

"Darling, you never surprise me."

They smiled at each other.

Laurel turned suddenly and reached for another cigaret.

"Don't bother, Ellery. Delia always makes a man forget there's another woman in the room."

"Now, Laurel." She was indulgent. Laurel slashed the match across the packet.

"Won't you come in and sit down, Mrs. Priam?"

"If I'd had any idea Laurel was coming here . . ."

Laurel said abruptly, "I came to see the man about the dog, Delia. *And* the note. Did you follow me?"

"What a ridiculous thing to say."

"Did you?"

21

"Certainly not, dear. I read about Mr. Queen in the papers and it coincided with something that's been bothering me."

"I'm sorry, Delia. I've been upset."

"I'll come back, Mr. Queen."

"Mrs. Priam, does it concern Miss Hill's father's death?"

"I don't know. It may."

"Then Miss Hill won't mind your sitting in. I repeat my invitation."

She had a trick of moving slowly, as if she were pushing against something. As he brought the chartreuse chair around he watched her obliquely. When she sat down she was close enough so that he could have touched her bare back with a very slight movement of his finger. He almost moved it.

She did not seem to have taken him in at all. And yet she had looked him over; up and down, as if he had been a gown in a dress shop. Perhaps he didn't interest her. As a gown, that is.

"Drink, Mrs. Priam?"

"Delia doesn't drink," said Laurel in the same warm, friendly voice. Two jets spurted from her nostrils.

"Thank you, darling. It goes to my head, Mr. Queen."

And you wouldn't let anything go to your head, wherefore it stands to reason, thought Ellery, that one way to get at you is to pour a few extra-dry Martinis down that red gullet . . . He was surprised at himself. A married woman, obviously a lady, and her husband was a cripple. But that wading walk was something to see.

"Laurel was about to leave. The facts interest me, but I'm in Hollywood to do a book . . ."

The shirring of her blouse rose and fell. He moved off to the picture window, making her turn her head.

"If, however, you have something to contribute, Mrs. Priam . . ." He suspected there would be no book for some time.

DELIA PRIAM'S STORY penetrated imperfectly. Ellery found it hard to concentrate. He tended to lose himself in details. The curves of her blouse. The promise of her skirt, which molded her strongly below the waist. Her large, shapely hands rested precisely in the middle of her lap, like compass points. *"Mistresses with great smooth marbly limbs . . ."* Right out of Browning's Renaissance.

22

She would have brought joy to the dying Bishop of Saint Praxed's.

"Mr. Queen?"

Ellery said guiltily, "You mean, Mrs. Priam, the same day Leander Hill received the dead dog?"

"The same morning. It was a sort of gift. I don't know what else you'd call it."

Laurel's cigaret hung in the air. "Delia, you didn't tell me Roger had got something, too!"

"He told me not to say anything, Laurel. But you've forced my hand, dear. Kicking up such a fuss about that poor dog. First the police, now Mr. Queen."

"Then you did follow me."

"I didn't have to." The woman smiled. "I saw you looking at Mr. Queen's photo in the paper."

"Delia, you're wonderful."

"Thank you, darling." She sat peaceful as a lady tiger, smiling over secrets . . . Here, Brother Q!

"Oh. Oh, yes, Mrs. Priam. Mr. Priam's been frightened—"

"Ever since the day he got the box. He won't admit it, but when a man keeps roaring that he won't be intimidated it's pretty clear that he is. He's broken things, too, some of his own things. That's not like Roger. Usually they're mine."

Delightful. What a pity.

"What was in the box, Mrs. Priam?"

"I haven't any idea."

"A dead dog," said Laurel. "Another dead dog!" Laurel looked something like a little dog herself, nose up, testing the air. It was remarkable how meaningless she was across from Delia Priam. As sexless as a child.

"It would have to have been an awfully small one, Laurel. The box wasn't more than a foot square of cardboard."

"Unmarked?" asked Ellery.

"Yes. But there was a shipping tag attached to the string that was tied around the box. 'Roger Priam' was printed on it in crayon." The beautiful woman paused. "Mr. Queen, are you listening?"

"In crayon. Yes, certainly, Mrs. Priam. Color?" What the devil difference did the color make?

"Black, I think."

"No address?"

"No. Nothing but the name."

23

"And you don't know what was in it. No idea."

"No. But whatever it was, it hit Roger hard. One of the servants found the box at the front door and gave it to Alfred—"

"Alfred."

"Roger's . . . secretary."

"Wouldn't you call him more of a . . . companion, Delia?" asked Laurel, blowing a smoke ring.

"I suppose so, dear. Companion, nurse, handyman, secretary—what-have-you. My husband, you know, Mr. Queen, is an invalid."

"Laurel's told me. All things to one man, eh, Mrs. Priam? I mean Alfred. We now have the versatile Alfred with the mysterious box. He takes it to Mr. Priam's room. And then?" Why was Laurel laughing? Not outwardly. But she was. Delia Priam seemed not to notice.

"I happened to be in Roger's room when Alfred came in. We didn't know then about . . . Leander and *his* gift, of course. Alfred gave Roger the box, and Roger lifted a corner of the lid and looked inside. He looked angry, then puzzled. He slammed the lid down and told me to get out. Alfred went out with me, and I heard Roger lock his door. And that's the last . . . I've seen of the box or its contents. Roger won't tell me what was in it or what he's done with it. Won't talk about it at all."

"When did your husband begin to show fear, Mrs. Priam?"

"After he talked to Leander in the Hill house the next day. On the way back home he didn't say a word, just stared out the window of the station wagon. Shaking. He's been shaking . . . ever since. It was especially bad a week later when Leander died . . ."

Then what was in Roger Priam's box had little significance for him until he compared gifts with Leander Hill, perhaps until he read the note Hill had found in the collar of the dog. Unless there had been a note in Priam's box as well. But then . . .

Ellery fidgeted before the picture window, sending up a smoke screen. It was ridiculous, at his age . . . pretending to be interested in a case because a respectable married woman had the misfortune to evoke the jungle. Still, he thought, what a waste.

He became conscious of the two women's eyes and expelled a mouthful of smoke, trying to appear professional. "Leander Hill received a queer gift, and he died.

24

Are you afraid, Mrs. Priam, that your husband's life is in danger, too?"

Now he was more than a piece of merchandise; he was a piece of merchandise that interested her. Her eyes were so empty of color that in the sunlight coming through the window she looked eyeless; it was like being looked over by a statue. He felt himself reddening and it seemed to him she was amused. He immediately bristled. She could take her precious husband and her fears elsewhere.

"Laurel darling," Delia Priam was saying with an apologetic glance, "Would you mind terribly if I spoke to Mr. Queen . . . alone?"

Laurel got up. "I'll wait in the garden," she said, and she tossed her cigaret into the tray and walked out.

Roger Priam's wife waited until Laurel's slim figure appeared beyond the picture window, among the shaggy asters. Laurel's head was turned away. She was switching her thigh with her cap.

"Laurel's sweet," said Delia Priam. "But so young, don't you think? Right now she's on a crusade and she's feeling ever so knightly. She'll get over it. . . . Why, about your question, Mr. Queen. I'm going to be perfectly frank with you. I haven't the slightest interest in my husband. I'm not afraid that he may die. If anything, it's the other way around."

- Ellery stared. For a moment her eyes slanted to the sun and they sparkled in a mineral way. But her features were without guile. The next instant she was eyeless again.

"You're honest, Mrs. Priam. Brutally so."

"I've had a rather broad education in brutality, Mr. Queen."

So there was that, too. Ellery sighed.

"I'll be even franker," she went on. "I don't know whether Laurel told you specifically . . . Did she say what kind of invalid my husband is?"

"She said he's partly paralyzed."

"She didn't say what part?"

"What part?" said Ellery.

"Then she didn't. Why, Mr. Queen, my husband is paralyzed," said Delia Priam with a smile, "from the waist down."

You had to admire the way she said that. The brave smile. The smile that said *Don't pity me.*

"I'm very sorry," he said.

25

"I've had fifteen years of it."

Ellery was silent. She rested her head against the back of the chair. Her eyes were almost closed and her throat was strong and defenseless.

"You're wondering why I told you that."

Ellery nodded.

"I told you because you can't understand why I've come to you unless you understand that first. Weren't you wondering?"

"All right. Why have you come to me?"

"For appearance's sake."

Ellery stared. "You ask me to investigate a possible threat against your husband's life, Mrs. Priam, for appearance's sake?"

"You don't believe me."

"I do believe you. Nobody would invent such a reason!" Seating himself beside her, he took one of her hands. It was cool and secretive, and it remained perfectly lax in his. "You haven't had much of a life."

"What do you mean?"

"You've never done any work with these hands."

"Is that bad?"

"It could be." Ellery put her hand back in her lap. "A woman like you has no right to remain tied to a man who's half-dead. If he were some saintly character, if there were love between you, I'd understand it. But I gather he's a brute and that you loathe him. Then why haven't you done something with your life? Why haven't you divorced him? Is there a religious reason?"

"There might have been when I was young. Now . . ." She shook her head. "Now it's the way it would look. You see, I'm stripping myself quite bare."

Ellery looked pained.

"You're very gallant to an old woman." She laughed. "No, I'm serious, Mr. Queen. I come from one of the old California families. Formal upbringing. Convent-trained. Duennas in the old fashion. A pride of caste and tradition. I could never take it as seriously as they did . . .

"My mother had married a heretic from New England. They ostracized her and it killed her when I was a little girl. I'd have got away from them completely, except that when my mother died they talked my father into giving me into their custody. I was brought up by an aunt who wore a mantilla. I married the first man who came along just to get away from them. He wasn't their

26

choice—he was an 'American,' like my father. I didn't love him, but he had money, we were very poor, and I wanted to escape. It cut me off from my family, my church, and my world. I have a ninety-year-old grandmother who lives only three miles from this spot. I haven't seen her for eighteen years. She considers me dead."

Her head rolled. "Harvey died when we'd been married three years, leaving me with a child. Then I met Roger Priam. I couldn't go back to my mother's family, my father was off on one of his jaunts, and Roger attracted me. I would have followed him to hell." She laughed again. "And that's exactly where he led me.

"When I found out what Roger really was, and then when he became crippled and I lost even that, there was nothing left. I've filled the vacuum by trying to go back where I came from.

"It hasn't been easy," murmured Delia Priam. "They don't forget such things, and they never forgive. But the younger generation is softer-bottomed and corrupted by modern ways. Their men, of course, have helped . . . Now it's the only thing I have to hang on to."

Her face showed a passion not to be shared or relished. Ellery was glad when the moment passed. "The life I lead in Roger Priam's house isn't even suspected by these people. If they knew the truth, I'd be dropped and there'd be no return. And if I left Roger, they'd say I deserted my husband. Upper caste women of the old California society don't do that sort of thing, Mr. Queen; it doesn't matter what the husband is. So . . . I don't do it.

"Now something is happening, I don't know what. If Laurel had kept her mouth shut, I wouldn't have lifted a finger. But by going about insisting that Leander Hill was murdered, Laurel's created an atmosphere of suspicion that threatens my position. Sooner or later the papers will get hold of it—it's a wonder they haven't already—and the fact that Roger is apparently in the same danger might come out. I can't sit by and wait for that. My people will expect me to be the loyal wife. So that's what I'm being. Mr. Queen, I ask you to proceed as if I'm terribly concerned about my husband's safety." Delia Priam shrugged. "Or is this all too involved for you?"

"It would seem to me far simpler," said Ellery, "to clear out and start over again somewhere else."

"This is where I was born." She looked out at Hollywood. Laurel had moved over to a corner of the garden.

27

"I don't mean all that popcorn and false front down there. I mean the hills, the orchards, the old missions. But there's another reason, and it has nothing to do with me, or my people, or Southern California."

"What's that, Mrs. Priam?"

"Roger wouldn't let me go. He's a man of violence, Mr. Queen. You don't—you can't—know his furious possessiveness, his pride, his compulsion to dominate, his . . . depravity. Sometimes I think I'm married to a maniac."

She closed her eyes. The room was still. From below Ellery heard Mrs. Williams's Louisiana-bred tones complaining to the gold parakeet she kept in a cage above the kitchen sink about the scandalous price of coffee. An invisible finger was writing in the sky above the Wilshire district: MUNTZ TV. The empty typewriter nudged his elbow.

But there she sat, the jungle in batiste and colored cotton. His slick and characterless Hollywood house would never be the same again. It was exciting just to be able to look at her lying in the silly chair. It was dismaying to imagine the chair empty.

"Mrs. Priam."

"Yes?"

"Why," asked Ellery, trying not to think of Roger Priam, "didn't you want Laurel Hill to hear what you just told me?"

The woman opened her eyes. "I don't mind undressing before a man," she said, "but I do draw the line at a woman."

She said it lightly, but something ran up Ellery's spine. He jumped to his feet. "Take me to your husband."

28

Three

WHEN THEY CAME out of Ellery's house Laurel said pleasantly, "Has a contract been drawn up, Ellery? And if so, with which one of us? Or is the question incompetent and none of my business?"

"No contract," said Ellery testily. "No contract, Laurel. I'm just going to take a look around."

"Starting at the *Priam* house, of course."

"Yes."

"In that case, since we're all in this together—aren't we, Delia?—I suppose there's no objection if I trail along?"

"Of course not, darling," said Delia. "But do try not to antagonize Roger. He always takes it out on me afterwards."

"What do you think he's going to say when he finds out you've brought a detective around?"

"Oh, dear," said Delia. Then she brightened. "Why, darling, *you're* bringing Mr. Queen around, don't you see? Do you mind very much? I know it's yellow, but I have to live with him. And you did get to Mr. Queen first."

"All right," said Laurel with a shrug. "We'll give you a head start, Delia. You take Franklin and Outpost, and I'll go around the long way, over Cahuenga and Mulholland. Where have you been, shopping?"

Delia Priam laughed. She got into her car, a new cream Cadillac convertible, and drove off down the hill.

"Hardly a substitute," said Laurel after a moment. Ellery started. Laurel was holding open the door of her car, a tiny green Austin. Either car *or* driver. Can you see Delia in an Austin? Like the Queen of Sheba in a rowboat. Get in."

"Unusual type," remarked Ellery absently, as the little car shot off.

"The adjective, yes. But as to the noun," said Laurel, "there is only one Delia Priam."

29

"She seems remarkably frank and honest."

"Does she?"

"I thought so. Don't you?"

"It doesn't matter what I think."

"By which you tell me what you think."

"No, you don't! But if you must know . . . You never get to the bottom of Delia. She doesn't lie, but she doesn't tell the truth, either—I mean the whole truth. She always keeps something in reserve that you dig out much, much later, if you're lucky to dig it out at all. Now I'm not going to say anything more about Delia, because whatever I say you'll hold, not against her, but against me. Delia bowls over big shots especially . . . I suppose it's no use asking you what she wanted to talk to you alone about?"

"Take—it—easy," said Ellery, holding his hat. "Another bounce like that and my knees will stab me to death."

"Nice try, Laurel," said Laurel; and she darted into the Freewaybound traffic on North Highland with a savage flip of her exhaust.

After a while Ellery remarked to Laurel's profile: "You said something about Roger Priam's 'never' leaving his wheelchair. You didn't mean that literally, by any chance?"

"Yes. Not ever. Didn't Delia tell you about the chair?"

"No."

"It's fabulous. After Roger became paralyzed he had an ordinary wheelchair for a time, which meant he had to be lifted into and out of it. Daddy told me about it. It seems Roger the Lion-Hearted couldn't take that. It made him too dependent on others. So he designed a special chair for himself."

"What does it do, boost him in and out of bed on mechanical arms?"

"It does away with a bed altogether."

Ellery stared.

"That's right. He sleeps in it, eats in it, does his work in it—everything. A combination office, study, living room, dining room, bedroom and bathroom on wheels. It's quite a production. From one of the arms of the chair hangs a small shelf which he can swing around to the front and raise; he eats on that, mixes drinks, and so on. Under the shelf are compartments for cutlery, napkins, cocktail things, and liquor. There's a similar shelf on

30

the other arm of the chair which holds his typewriter, screwed on, of course, so it won't fall off when it's swung aside. And under that shelf are places for paper, carbon, pencils and Lord knows what else. The chair is equipped with two phones of the plug-in type—the regular line and a private wire to our house—and with an intercom system to Wallace's room."

"Who's Wallace?"

"Alfred Wallace, his secretary-companion. Then—let's see." Laurel frowned. "Oh, he's got compartments and cubbyholes all around the chair for just about everything imaginable—magazines, cigars, his reading glasses, his toothbrush; everything he could possibly need. The chair's built so that it can be lowered and the front raised, making a bed out of it for daytime napping or sleeping at night. Of course, he needs Alfred to help him sponge-bathe and dress and undress and so on, but he's made himself as self-sufficient as possible—hates help of any kind, even the most essential. When I was there yesterday his typewriter had just been sent into Hollywood to be repaired and he had to dictate business memoranda to Alfred instead of doing them himself, and he was in such a foul mood because of it that even Alfred got mad. Roger in a foul mood can be awfully foul . . . I'm sorry, I thought you wanted to know."

"What?"

"You're not listening."

"I am, though not with both ears." They were on Mulholland Drive now, and Ellery was clutching the side of the Austin to avoid being thrown clear as Laurel zoomed the little car around the hairpin curves. "Tell me, Laurel. Who inherits your father's estate? I mean besides yourself?"

"Nobody. There isn't anyone else."

"He didn't leave anything to Priam?"

"Why should he? Roger and Daddy were equal partners. There are some small cash bequests to people in the firm and to the household help. Everything else goes to me. So you see, Ellery," said Laurel, soaring over a rise, "I'm your big suspect."

"Yes," said Ellery, "and you're also Roger Priam's new partner. Or are you?"

"My status isn't clear. The lawyers are working on that now. Of course I don't know anything about the jewelry business and I'm not sure I want to. Roger can't chisel me out of anything, if that's what's in your mind. One of the biggest law firms in Los Angeles is protecting my interests. I must say Roger's been surprisingly decent about that end of it—for Roger, I mean. Maybe Daddy's death hit him harder than he expected—made him realize how important Dad was to the business and how unimportant *he* is. Actually, he hasn't much to worry about. Dad trained a very good man to run things, a Mr. Foss, in case anything happened to him . . . Anyway, there's one item on my agenda that takes priority over everything else. And if you won't clear it up for me, I'll do it myself."

"Because you loved Leander Hill very much?"

"Yes!"

"And because, of course," remarked Ellery, "you *are* the big suspect?"

Laurel's little hands tightened on the wheel. Then they relaxed. "That's the stuff, Ellery," she laughed. "Just keep firing away at the whites of our eyes. I love it.—There's the Priam place."

THE PRIAM PLACE stood on a private road, a house of dark round stones and blackish wood wedged into a fold of the hills and kept in forest gloom by a thick growth of overhanging sycamore, elm, and eucalyptus. Ellery's first thought was that the grounds were neglected, but then he saw evidences of both old and recent pruning on the sides away from the house and he realized that nature had been coaxed into the role she was playing. The hopeless matting of leaves and boughs was deliberate; the secretive gloom was wanted. Priam had dug into the hill and pulled the trees over him. Who was it who had defied the sun?

It was more like an isolated hunting lodge than a Hollywood house. Most of it was hidden from the view of passers-by on the main road, and by its character it transformed a suburban section of ordinary Southern California canyon into a wild Scottish glen. Laurel told Ellery that the Priam property extended up and along the hill for four or five acres and that it was all like the area about the house.

"Jungle," said Ellery as Laurel parked the car in the driveway. There was no sign of the cream Cadillac.

"Well, he's a wild animal. Like the deer you flush occasionally up behind the Bowl."

"He's paying for the privilege. His electric bills must be enormous."

"I'm sure they are. There isn't a sunny room in the house. When he wants—you can't say more *light*—when he wants less gloom, and air that isn't so stale, he wheels himself out on that terrace there." To one side of the house there was a large terrace, half of it screened and roofed, the other open not to the sky but a high arch of blue gum eucalyptus leaves and branches which the sun did not penetrate. "His den—den is the word—is directly off the terrace, past those French and screen doors. We'd better go in the front way; Roger doesn't like people barging in on his sacred preserves. In the Priam house you're announced."

"Doesn't Delia Priam have anything to say about the way her house is run?"

"Who said it's her house?" said Laurel.

A uniformed maid with a tic admitted them. "Oh, Miss Hill," she said nervously. "I don't think Mr. Priam . . . He's dictatin' to Mr. Wallace. I better not . . ."

"Is Mrs. Priam in, Muggs?"

"She just got in from shoppin', Miss Hill. She's upstairs in her room. Said she was tired and was not to be disturbed."

"Poor Delia," said Laurel calmly. "I know Mr. Queen is terribly disappointed. Tell Mr. Priam I want to see him."

"But, Miss Hill—"

A muffled roar of rage stopped her instantly. She glanced over her shoulder in a panic.

"It's all right, Muggsy. I'll take the rap. *Vamos*, Ellery."

"I wonder why she—" Ellery began in a mumble as Laurel led him up the hall.

"Yours not to, where Delia is concerned."

The house was even grimmer than he had expected. They passed shrouded rooms with dark paneling, heavy and humorless drapes, massive uncomfortable-looking furniture. It was a house for secrets and for violence.

The roar was a bass snarl now. "I don't give a damn what Mr. *Hill* wanted to do about the Newman-Arco account, Foss! Mr. *Hill's* locked in a drawer in Forest Lawn and he ain't in any condition to give us the benefit of his advice . . . No, I won't wait a minute, Foss! I'm running this —— business, and you'll either handle things my way or get the hell out!"

33

Laurel's lips thinned. She raised her fist and hammered on the door.

"Whoever that is, Alfred—! Foss, you still there?"

A man opened the heavy door and slipped into the hall, pulling the door to and keeping his hand on the knob behind him.

"You picked a fine time, Laurel. He's on the phone to the office."

"So I hear," said Laurel. "Mr. Queen, Mr. Wallace. His other name ought to be Job, but it's Alfred. The perfect man, I call him. Super-efficient. Discreet as all getout. Never slips. One side, Alfred. I've got business with my partner."

"Better let me set him up," said Wallace with a smile. As he slipped back into the room, his eyes flicked over Ellery. Then the door was shut again, and Ellery waved his right hand tenderly. It still tingled from Wallace's grip.

"Surprised?" murmured Laurel.

Ellery was. He had expected a Milquetoast character. Instead Alfred Wallace was a towering, powerfully assembled man with even, rather sharp, features, thick white hair, a tan, and an air of lean distinction. His voice was strong and thoughtful, with the merest touch of . . . superiority? Whatever it was, it was barely enough to impress, not quite enough to annoy. Wallace might have stepped out of a set on the M-G-M lot labeled *High Society Drawing Room;* and, in fact, "well-preserved actor" had been Ellery's impulsive characterization—Hollywood leading-men types with Athletic Club tans were turning up these days in the most unexpected places, swallowing their pride in order to be able to swallow at all. But a moment later Ellery was not so sure. Wallace's shoulders did not look as if they came off with his coat. His physique, even his elegance, seemed homegrown.

"I should think you'd be smitten, Laurel," said Ellery as they waited. "That's a virile character. Perfectly disciplined, and dashing as the devil."

"A little too old," said Laurel. "For me, that is."

"He can't be much more than fifty-five. And he doesn't look forty-five, white hair notwithstanding."

"Alfred would be too old for me if he were twenty. —Oh. Well? Do I have to get Mr. Queen to brush you aside, Alfred, or is the Grand Vizier going to play gracious this morning?"

Alfred Wallace smiled and let them pass.

THE MAN WHO slammed the phone down and spun the steel chair about as if it were a studio production of balsa wood was a creature of immensities. He was all bulge, spread, and thickness. Bull eyes blazed above iron cheekbones; the nose was a massive snout; a tremendous black beard fell to his chest. The hands which gripped the wheels of the chair were enormous; forearms and biceps strained his coat sleeves. And the whole powerful mechanism was in continuous movement, as if even that great frame was unable to contain his energy. Something by Wolf Larsen out of Captain Teach, on a restless quarterdeck. Besides that immense torso Alfred Wallace's strong figure looked frail. And Ellery felt like an underfed boy.

But below the waist Roger Priam was dead. His bulk sat on a withered base, an underpinning of skeletal flesh and atrophied muscle. He was trousered and shod—and Ellery tried not to imagine the labor that went into that operation twice daily—but his ankles were visible, two shriveled bones, and his knees were twisted projections, like girders struck by lightning. The whole shrunken substructure of his body hung useless.

It was all explicable, Ellery thought, on ordinary grounds: the torso overdeveloped by the extraordinary exertions required for the simplest movement; the beard grown to eliminate one of the irksome processes of his daily toilet; the savage manner an expression of his hatred of the fate that had played such a trick on him; and the restlessness a sign of the agony he endured to maintain a sitting position. Those were the reasons; still, they left something unexplained . . . Ferocity—fierce strength, fierce emotions, fierce reaction to pain and people—ferocity seemed his center. Take everything else away, and Ellery suspected it would still be there. He must have been fierce in his mother's womb, a wild beast by nature. What had happened to him merely brought it into play.

"What d'ye want, Laurel? Who's this?" His voice was a coarse, threatening bass, rumbling up from his chest like live lava. He was still furious from his telephone conversation with the hapless Foss; his eyes were filled with hate. "What are you looking at? Why don't you open your mouth?"

"This is Ellery Queen."

"Who?"

Laurel repeated it.

"Never heard of him. What's he want?" The feral glance turned on Ellery. "What d'ye want? Hey?"

"Mr. Priam," said the beautiful voice of Alfred Wallace from the doorway, "Ellery Queen is a famous writer."

"Writer?"

"And detective, Mr. Priam."

Priam's lips pushed out, dragging his beard forward. The great hands on the wheel became clamps.

"I told you I wasn't going to let go, Roger," said Laurel evenly. "My father was murdered. There must have been a reason. And whatever it was, you were mixed up in it as well as Daddy. I've asked Ellery Queen to investigate, and he wants to talk to you."

"He does, does he?" The rumble was distant; the fiery eyes gave out heat. "Go ahead, Mister. Talk away."

"In the first place, Mr. Priam," said Ellery, "I'd like to know—"

"The answer is no," said Roger Priam, his teeth showing through his beard. "What's in the second place?"

"Mr. Priam," Ellery began again, patiently.

"No good, Mister. I don't like your questions. Now you listen to me, Laurel." His right fist crashed on the arm of the chair. "You're a damn busybody. This ain't your business. It's mine. I'll tend to it. I'll do it my way, and I'll do it myself. Can you get that through your head?"

"You're afraid, Roger," said Laurel Hill.

Priam half-raised his bulk, his eyes boiling. The lava burst with a roar.

"Me afraid? Afraid of what? A *ghost*? What d'ye think I am, another Leander Hill? The snivelin' dirt! Shaking in his shoes—looking over his shoulder—creeping on his face! He was born a —— yellowbelly, and he died the same—"

Laurel hit him on the cheek with her fist. His left arm came up impatiently and brushed her aside. She staggered backward halfway across the room into Alfred Wallace's arms.

"Let go of me," she whispered. "Let go!"

"Laurel," said Ellery.

She stopped, breathing from her diaphragm. Wallace silently released her.

Laurel walked out of the room.

36

"Afraid!" A spot swelled on Priam's cheekbone. "You think so?" he bellowed after her. "Well, a certain some-body's gonna find out that *my* pump don't go to pieces at the first blow! Afraid, am I? I'm ready for the god-dam ——! Any hour of the day or night, understand? Any time he wants to show his scummy hand! He'll find out I got a pretty good pair myself!" And he opened and closed his murderous hands, and Ellery thought again of Wolf Larsen.

"Roger. What's the matter?"

And there she was in the doorway. She had changed to a hostess gown of golden silk which clung as if it loved her. It was slit to the knee. She was glancing coolly from her husband to Ellery.

Wallace's eyes were on her. They seemed amused.

"Who is this man?"

"Nobody. Nothing, Delia. It don't concern you." Priam glared at Ellery. "You. Get out!"

She had come downstairs just to establish the fact that she didn't know him. As a point in character, it should have interested him. Instead, it annoyed him. Why, he could not quite make out. What was he to Hecuba? Although she was making clear enough what Hecuba was to *him*. He felt chagrined and challenged, and at the same time he wondered if she affected other men the same way . . . Wallace was enjoying himself discreetly, like a playgoer who has caught a point which escaped the rest of the audience and is too polite to laugh aloud . . . Her attitude toward her husband was calm, without fear or any other visible emotion.

"What are you waiting for? You ain't wanted, Mister. Get out!"

"I've been trying to make up my mind, Mr. Priam," said Ellery, "whether you're a bag of wind or a damned fool."

Priam's bearded lips did a little dance. His range, ap-parently always in shallow water, was surfacing again. Ellery braced himself for the splash. Priam *was* afraid. Wallace—silent, amused, attentive Wallace—Wallace saw it. And Delia Priam saw it; she was smiling.

"Alfred, if this fella shows up again, break his —— back!"

Ellery looked down at his arm. Wallace's hand was on it.

"I'm afraid, Mr. Queen," murmured Wallace, "that I'm man enough to do it, too."

The man's grip was paralyzing. Priam was grinning, a yellow hairy grin that jarred him. And the woman—that animate piece of jungle—watching. To his amazement, Ellery felt himself going blind-mad. When he came to, Alfred Wallace was sitting on the floor chafing his wrist and staring up at Ellery. He did not seem angry; just surprised.

"That's a good trick," Wallace said. "I'll remember it."

Ellery fumbled for a cigaret, decided against it. "I've made up my mind, Mr. Priam. You're a bag of wind and a damned fool."

The doorway was empty . . .

He was furious with himself. Never lose your temper. Rule One in the book; he had learned it on his father's lap. Just the same, she must have seen it. Wallace flying through the air. And the gape on Priam's ugly face. Probably set her up for the week . . .

He found himself searching for her out of the corners of his eyes as he strode down the hall. The place was overcrowded with shadows; she was certainly waiting in one of them. With the shades of her eyes pulled down but everything else showing.

The hall was empty, too . . .

Slit to the knee! That one was older than the pyramids. And how old was his stupidity? It probably went back to the primordial slime.

Then he remembered that Delia Priam was a lady and that he was behaving exactly like a frustrated college boy, and he slammed the front door.

LAUREL WAS WAITING for him in the Austin. She was still white; smoking with energy. Ellery jumped in beside her and growled, "Well, what are we waiting for?"

"He's cracking," said Laurel tensely. "He's going to pieces, Ellery. I've seen him yell and push his weight around before, but today was something special. I'm glad I brought you. What do you want to do now?"

"Go home. Or get me a cab."

She was bewildered. "Aren't you taking the case?"

"I can't waste any time on idiots."

"Meaning me?"

"Not meaning you."

"But we found out something," she said eagerly. "He

admitted it. You heard him. A 'ghost,' he said. A 'certain somebody'—I heard that on my way out. I wasn't being delirious, Ellery. Roger thinks Daddy was deliberately shocked to death, too. And, what's more, he knows what the dog meant—"

"Not necessarily," grunted Ellery. "That's the trouble with you amateurs. Always jumping to conclusions. Anyway, it's too impossible. You can't get anywhere without Priam, and Priam isn't budging."

"It's Delia," said Laurel, "isn't it?"

"Delia? You mean Mrs. Priam? Rubbish."

"Don't tell me about Delia," said Laurel. "Or about men, either. She's catnip for anything in pants."

"Oh, I admit her charms," muttered Ellery. "But they're a bit obvious, don't you think?" He was trying not to look up at the second-story windows, where her bedroom undoubtedly was. "Laurel, we can't park here in the driveway like a couple of adenoidal tourists—" He had to see her again. Just to see her.

Laurel gave him an odd look and drove off. She turned left at the road, driving slowly.

Ellery sat embracing his knees. He had the emptiest feeling that he was losing something with each spin of the Austin's wheels. And there was Laurel, seeing the road ahead and something else, too. Sturdy little customer. And she must be feeling pretty much alone. Ellery suddenly felt himself weakening.

"What do you intend to do, Laurel?"

"Keep poking around."

"You're determined to go through with this?"

"Don't feel sorry for me. I'll make out."

"Laurel, I'll tell you what I'll do."

She looked at him.

"I'll go as far as that note with you—I mean, give you a head start, anyway. If, of course, it's possible."

"What are you talking about?" She stopped the car with a bump.

"The note your father found in that silver box on the dog's collar. You thought he must have destroyed it."

"I told you I looked for it and it wasn't there."

"Suppose I do the looking."

Laurel stared. Then she laughed and the Austin jumped. The Hill house spread itself high on one of the canyon walls, cheerfully exposing its red tiles to the sun. It was a two-story Spanish house, beautifully bleached, with black wrought-iron tracery, arched and balconied and patioed and covered with pyracantha. It was set in two acres of flowers, flowering shrubs, and trees—palm and fruit and nut and bird-of-paradise. Around the lower perimeter ran the woods.

"Our property line runs down the hill," Laurel said as they got out of the car, "over towards the Priams'. A little over nine additional acres meeting the Priam woods. Through the woods it's no distance at all."

"It's a very great distance," mumbled Ellery. "About as far as from an eagle's nest to an undersea cave. True Spanish, I notice, like the missions, not the modern fakes so common out here. It must be a punishment to Delia Priam—born to this and condemned to *that*."

"Oh, she's told you about that," murmured Laurel; then she took him into her house.

It was cool with black Spanish tile underfoot and the touch of iron. There was a sunken living room forty feet long, a great fireplace set with Goya tiles, books and music and paintings and ceramics and huge jars of flowers everywhere. A tall Japanese in a white jacket came in smiling and took Ellery's hat.

"Ichiro Sotowa," said Laurel. "Itchie's been with us for ages. This is Mr. Queen, Itchie. He's interested in the way Daddy died, too."

The houseman's smile faded. "Bad—bad," he said, shaking his head. "Heart no good. You like a drink, sir?"

"Not just now, thanks," said Ellery. "Just how long did you work for Mr. Hill, Ichiro?"

"Sixteen year, sir."

"Oh, then you don't go back to the time of . . . What about that chauffeur—Simeon, was it?"

"Shimmie shopping with Mis' Monk."

"I meant how long Simeon's been employed here."

"About ten years," said Laurel. "Mrs. Monk came around the same time."

"That's that, then. All right, Laurel, let's begin."

"Where?"

"From the time your father had his last heart attack— the day the dog came—until his death, did he leave his bedroom?"

"No. Itchie and I took turns nursing him. Night and day the entire week."

"Bedroom indicated. Lead the way."

AN HOUR AND a half later, Ellery opened the door of Leander Hill's room. Laurel was curled up in a window niche on the landing, head resting against the wall.

"I suppose you think I'm an awful sissy," she said, without turning. "But all I can see when I'm in there is his marbly face and blue lips and the crooked way his mouth hung open . . . not my daddy at all. Nothing, I suppose."

"Come here, Laurel."

She jerked about. Then she jumped off the ledge and ran to him.

Ellery shut the bedroom door.

Laurel's eyes hunted wildly. But aside from the four-poster bed, which was disarranged, she could see nothing unusual. The spread, sheets, and quilt were peeled back, revealing the side walls of the box spring and mattress.

"What—?"

"The note you saw him remove from the dog's collar," Ellery said. "It was on thin paper, didn't you tell me?"

"Very. A sort of flimsy, or onionskin."

"White?"

"White."

Ellery nodded. He went over to the exposed mattress. "He was in this room for a week, Laurel, between his attack and death. During that week did he have many visitors?"

"The Priam household. Some people from the office. A few friends."

"Some time during that week," said Ellery, "your father decided that the note he had received was in danger of being stolen or destroyed. So he took out insurance." His finger traced on the side wall of the mattress one of the perpendicular blue lines of the ticking. "He had no tool but a dull penknife from the night table there. And I suppose he was in a hurry, afraid he might be caught at it. So the job had to be crude." Half his finger suddenly vanished. "He simply made a slit here, where the blue line meets the undyed ticking. And he slipped the paper into it, where I found it."

"The note," breathed Laurel. "You've found the note. Let me see!"

Ellery put his hand in his pocket. But just as he was about to withdraw it, he stopped. His eyes were on one of the windows.

Some ten yards away there was an old walnut tree.

"Yes?" Laurel was confused. "What's the matter?"

"Get off the bed, yawn, smile at me if you can, and then stroll over to the door. Go out on the landing. Leave the door open."

Her eyes widened.

She got off the bed, yawned, stretched, showed her teeth, and went to the door. Ellery moved a little as she moved, so that he remained between her and the window.

When she had disappeared, he casually followed. Smiling in profile at her, he shut the bedroom door.

And sprang for the staircase.

"Ellery—"

"Stay here!"

He scrambled down the black-tiled stairs, leaving Laurel with her lips parted.

A man had been roosting high in the walnut tree, peering in at them through Leander Hill's bedroom window from behind a screen of leaves. But the sun had been on the tree, and Ellery could have sworn the fellow was mother-naked.

Four

THE NAKED MAN was gone. Ellery thrashed about among the fruit and nut trees feeling like Robinson Crusoe. From the flagged piazza Ichiro gaped at him, and a chunky fellow with a florid face and a chauffeur's cap, carrying a carton of groceries, was gaping with him.

Ellery found a large footprint at the margin of the orchard, splayed and deeptoed, indicating running or jumping, and it pointed directly to the woods. He darted into the underbrush and in a moment he was nosing past trees and scrub on a twisting but clear trail. There were numerous specimens of the naked print on the trail, both coming and going.

"He's made a habit of this," Ellery mumbled. It was hot in the woods and he was soon drenched, uncomfortable, and out of temper.

The trail ended unceremoniously in the middle of a clearing. No other footprints anywhere. The trunk of the nearest tree, an ancient, oakish-looking monster, was yards away. There were no vines.

Ellery looked around, swabbing his neck. Then he looked up. The giant limbs of the tree covered the clearing with a thick fabric of small spiny leaves, but the lowest branch was thirty feet from the ground.

The creature must have flapped his arms and taken off.

Ellery sat down on a corrupting log and wiped his face, reflecting on this latest wonder. Not that anything in Southern California ever really surprised him. But this was a little out of even God's country's class. Flying nudes!

"Lost?"

Ellery leaped. A little old man in khaki shorts, woolen socks, and a T-shirt was smiling at him from a bush. He wore a paper topee on his head and he carried a

43

butterfly net; a bright red case of some sort was slung over one skinny shoulder. His skin was a shriveled brown and his hands were like the bark of the big tree, but his eyes were a bright young blue and they seemed keen.

"I'm not lost," said Ellery irritably. "I'm looking for a man."

"I don't like the way you say that," said the old man, stepping into the clearing. "You're on the wrong track, young fellow. People mean trouble. Know anything about the Lepidoptera?"

"Not a thing. Have you seen—?"

"You catch 'em with this dingbat. I just bought the kit yesterday—passed a toy shop on Hollywood Boulevard and there it was, all new and shiny, in the window. I've caught four beauties so far." The butterfly hunter began to trot down the trail, waving his net menacingly.

"Wait! Have you seen anyone running through these woods?"

"Running? Well, now, depends."

"Depends? My dear sir, it doesn't depend on a thing! Either you saw somebody or you didn't."

"Not necessarily," replied the little man earnestly, trotting back. "It depends on whether it's going to get him—or you—in trouble. There's too much trouble in this world, young man. What's this runner look like?"

"I can't give you a description," snapped Ellery, "inasmuch as I didn't see enough of him to be able to. Or rather, I saw the wrong parts.—Hell. He's naked."

"Ah," said the hunter, making an unsuccessful pass at a large, paint-splashed butterfly. "Naked, hm?"

"And there was a lot of him."

"There was. You wouldn't start any trouble?"

"No, no, I won't hurt him. Just tell me which way he went."

"I'm not worried about your hurting him. He's much more likely to hurt you. Powerful build, that boy. Once knew a stoker built like him—could bend a coal shovel. That was in the old *Susie Belle,* beating up to Alaska—"

"You sound as if you know him."

"Know him? I darned well ought to. He's my grandson. There he is!" cried the hunter.

"Where?"

But it was only the fifth butterfly, and the little old man hopped between two bushes and was gone.

Ellery was morosely studying the last footprint in the

44

trail when Laurel poked her head cautiously into the clearing.

"There you are," she said with relief. "You scared the buttermilk out of me. What happened?"

"Character spying on us from the walnut tree outside the bedroom window. I trailed him here—"

"What did he look like?" frowned Laurel.

"No clothes on."

"Why, the lying mugwump!" she said angrily. "He promised on his honor he wouldn't do that any more. It's got so I have to undress in the dark."

"So you know him, too," growled Ellery. "I thought California had a drive on these sex cases."

"Oh, he's no sex case. He just throws gravel at my window and tries to get me to talk drool to him. I can't waste my time on somebody who's preparing for Armageddon at the age of twenty-three. Ellery, let's see that note!"

"Whose grandson is he?"

"Grandson? Mr. Collier's."

"Mr. Collier wouldn't be a little skinny old gent with a face like a sun-dried fig?"

"That's right."

"And just who is Mr. Collier?"

"Delia Priam's father. He lives with the Priams."

"Her *father*." You couldn't keep her out of anything. "But if this Peeping Tom is Delia Priam's father's grandson, then he must be—"

"Didn't Delia tell you," asked Laurel with a *soupçon* of malice, "that she has a twenty-three year old son? His name is Crowe Macgowan. Delia's child by her first husband. Roger's stepson. But let's not waste any time on him—"

"How does he disappear into thin air? He pulled that miracle right here."

"Oh, that." Laurel looked straight up. So Ellery looked straight up, too. But all he could see was a leafy ceiling where the great oak branched ten yards over his head.

"Mac!" said Laurel sharply. "Show your face."

To Ellery's amazement, a large young male face appeared in the middle of the green mass thirty feet from the ground. On the face there was a formidable scowl.

"Laurel, who is this guy?"

"You come down here."

"Is he a reporter?"

"Heavens, no," said Laurel disgustedly. "He's Ellery Queen."

"Who?"

"Ellery Queen."

"You're kidding!"

"I wouldn't have time."

"Say. I'll be right down."

The face vanished. At once something materialized where it had been and hurtled to the ground, missing Ellery's nose by inches. It was a rope ladder. A massive male leg broke the green ceiling, then another, then a whole young man, and in a moment the tree man was standing on the ground on the exact spot where the trail of naked footprints ended.

"I'm certainly thrilled to meet you!"

Ellery's hand was seized and the bones broken before he could cry out. At least, they felt broken. It was a bad day for the Master's self-respect: he could not decide which had the most powerful hands, Roger Priam, Alfred Wallace, or the awesome brute trying to pulverize him. Delia's son towered six inches above him, a handsome giant with an impossible spread of shoulder, an unbelievable minimum of waist, the muscular development of Mr. America, the skin of a Hawaiian—all of which was on view except a negligible area covered by a brown loincloth—and a grin that made Ellery feel positively aged.

"I thought you were a newshound, Mr. Queen. Can't stand those guys—they've made my life miserable. But what are we standing here for? Come on up to the house."

"Some other time, Mac," said Laurel coldly, taking Ellery's arm.

"Oh, that murder foolitchness. Why don't you relax, Laur?"

"I don't think I'd be exactly welcome at your stepfather's, Mac," said Ellery.

"You've already had the pleasure? But I meant come up to *my* house."

"He really means 'up,' Ellery," sighed Laurel. "All right, let's get it over with. You wouldn't belive it secondhand."

"House? Up?" Feebly Ellery glanced aloft; and to his horror the young giant nodded and sprang up the rope ladder, beckoning them hospitably to follow.

46

IT REALLY WAS a house, high in the tree. A one-room house, to be sure, and not commodious, but it had four walls and a thatched roof, a sound floor, a beamed ceiling, two windows, and a platform from which the ladder dangled—this dangerous-looking perch young Macgowan referred to cheerfully as his "porch," and perfectly safe if you didn't fall off.

The tree, he explained, was *Quercus agrifolia,* with a bole circumference of eighteen feet, and "watch those leaves, Mr. Queen, they bite." Ellery, who was gingerly digging several of the spiny little devils out of his shirt, nodded sourly. But the structure was built on a foundation of foot-thick boughs and seemed solid enough underfoot.

He poked his head indoors at his host's invitation and gaped like a tourist. Every foot of wall- and floor-space was occupied by—it was the only phrase Ellery could muster—aids to tree-living.

"Sorry I can't entertain you inside," said the young man, "but three of us would bug it out a bit. We'd better sit on the porch. Anybody like a drink? Bourbon? Scotch?" Without waiting for a reply Macgowan bent double and slithered into his house. Various liquid sounds followed.

"Laurel, why don't they put the poor kid away?" whispered Ellery.

"You have to have grounds."

"What do you call this?" cried Ellery. "Sanity?"

"Don't blame you, Mr. Queen," said the big fellow amiably, appearing with two chilled glasses. "Appearances are against me. But that's because you people live in a world of fantasy." He thrust a long arm into the house and it came out with another glass.

"Fantasy. We." Ellery gulped a third of the contents of his glass. "You, of course, live in a world of reality?"

"Do we have to?" asked Laurel wearily. "If he gets started on this, Ellery, we'll be here till sundown. That note—"

"I'm the only realist I know," said the giant, lying down at the edge of his porch and kicking his powerful legs in space. "Because, look. What are you people doing? Living in the same old houses, reading the same old newspapers, going to the same old movies or looking at the same old television, walking on the same old sidewalks, riding in the same old new cars. That's a dream world, don't

47

you realize it? What price business-as-usual? What price, well, sky-writing, Jacques Fath, Double-Crostics, murder? Do you get my point?"

"Can't say it's entirely clear, Mac," said Ellery, swallowing the second third. He realized for the first time that his glass contained bourbon, which he loathed. However.

"We are living," said young Mr. Macgowan, "in the crisis of the disease commonly called human history. You mess around with your piddling murders while mankind is being set up for the biggest homicide since the Flood. The atom bomb is already fuddy-duddy. Now it's hydrogen bombs, guaranteed to make the nuclear chain reaction —or whatever the hell it is—look like a Fourth of July firecracker. Stuff that can poison all the drinking water on a continent. Nerve gases that paralyze and kill. Germs there's no protection against. And only God knows what else. They won't use it? My friend, those words constitute the epitaph of Man. Somebody'll pull the cork in a place like Yugoslavia or Iran or Korea and, whoosh! that'll be that.

"It's all going to go," said Macgowan, waving his glass at the invisible world below. "Cities uninhabitable. Crop soil poisoned for a hundred years. Domestic animals going wild. Insects multiplying. Balance of nature upset. Ruins and plagues and millions of square miles radioactive and maybe most of the earth's atmosphere. The roads crack, the lines sag, the machines rust, the libraries mildew, the buzzards fatten, and the forest primeval creeps over Hollywood and Vine, which maybe isn't such a bad idea. But there you'll have it. Thirty thousand years of primate development knocked over like a sleeping duck. Civilization atomized and annihilated. Yes, there'll be some survivors—I'm going to be one of them. But what are we going to have to do? Why, go back where we came from, brother—to the trees. That's logic, isn't it? So here I am. All ready for it."

"Now let's have the note," said Laurel.

"In a moment." Ellery polished off the last third, shuddering. "Very logical, Mac, except for one or two items."

"Such as?" said Crowe Macgowan courteously. "Here, let me give you a refill."

"No, thanks, not just now. Why, such as these." Ellery pointed to a network of cables winging from some hidden

48

spot to the roof of Macgowan's tree house. "For a chap who's written off thirty thousand years of primate development you don't seem to mind tapping the main power line for such things as—" he craned, surveying the interior—"electric lights, a small electric range and refrigerator, and similar primitive devices; not to mention—" he indicated a maze of pipes—"running water, a compact little privy connected with—I assume—a septic tank buried somewhere below, and so on. These things—forgive me, Mac—blow bugs through your logic. The only essential differences between your house and your stepfather's are that yours is smaller and thirty feet in the air."

"Just being practical," shrugged the giant. "It's my opinion it'll happen any day now. But I can be wrong—it may not come till next year. I'm just taking advantage of the civilized comforts while they're still available. But you'll notice I have a .22 rifle hanging there, a couple of .45s, and when my ammunition runs out or I can't rustle any more there's a bow that'll bring down any deer that survives the party. I practice daily. And I'm getting pretty good running around these treetops—"

"Which reminds me," said Laurel. "Use your own trees after this, will you, Mac? I'm no prude, but a girl likes her privacy sometimes. Really, Ellery—"

"Macgowan," said Ellery, eying their host, "what's the pitch?"

"Pitch? I've just told you."

"I know what you've just told me, and it's already out the other ear. What character are you playing? And in what script by whom?" Ellery set the glass down and got to his feet. The effect he was trying to achieve was slightly spoiled, as he almost fell off the porch. He jumped to the side of the house, a little green. "I've been to Hollywood before."

"Go ahead and sneer," said the brown giant without rancor. "I promise to give you a decent burial if I can find the component parts."

Ellery eyed the wide back for a moment. It was perfectly calm. He shrugged. Every time he came to Hollywood something fantastic happened. This was the screwiest yet. He was well out of it.

But then he remembered that he was still in it.

He put his hand in his pocket.

"Laurel," he said meaningfully, "shall we go?"

"If it's about that piece of paper I saw you find in Leander's mattress," said young Macgowan, "I wouldn't mind knowing myself what's in it."

"It's all right, Ellery," said Laurel with an exasperated laugh. "Crowe is a lot more interested in the petty affairs of us dreamers than he lets on. And in a perverted sort of way I trust him. May I *please* see that note?"

"IT ISN'T THE note you saw your father take from the collar of the dog," said Ellery, eying Macgowan disapprovingly as he took a sheet of paper from his pocket. "It's a copy. The original is gone." The sheet was folded over once. He unfolded it. It was a stiff vellum paper, tinted green-gray, with an embossed green monogram.

"Daddy's personal stationery."

"From his night table. Where I also found this bi-colored pencil." Ellery fished an automatic pencil from his pocket. "The blue lead is snapped. The note starts in blue and ends in red. Evidently the blue ran out halfway through his copying and he finished writing with the red. So the pencil places the copying in his bedroom, too." Ellery held out the sheet. "Is this your father's handwriting?"

"Yes."

"No doubt about it?"

"No."

In a rather peculiar voice, Ellery said, "All right, Laurel. Read it."

"But it's not signed." Laurel sounded as if she wanted to punch somebody.

"Read it."

Macgowan knelt behind her, nuzzling her shoulder with his big chin. Laurel paid no attention to him; she read the note with a set face.

You believed me dead. Killed, murdered. For over a score of years I have looked for you—for you and for him. And now I have found you. Can you guess my plan? You'll die. Quickly? No, very slowly. And so pay me back for my long years of searching and dreaming of revenge. Slow dying . . . unavoidable dying. For you and for him. Slow and sure—dying in mind and in body. And for each pace forward a warning . . . a warning of special meaning for you—and for him. Meanings for pondering and puzzling. Here is warning number one.

Laurel stared at the notepaper.

"That," said Crowe Macgowan, taking the sheet, "is the unfunniest gag of the century." He frowned over it.

"Not just that." Laurel shook her head. "Warning number one. Murder. Revenge. Special meanings . . . It—it has a long curly mustache on it. Next week *Uncle Tom's Cabin.*" She looked around with a laugh. "Even in Hollywood."

"Why'd the old scout take it seriously?" Crowe watched Laurel a little anxiously.

Ellery took the sheet from him and folded it carefully. "Melodrama is a matter of atmosphere and expression. Pick up any Los Angeles newspaper and you'll find three news stories running serially, any one of which would make this one look like a work by Einstein. But they're real because they're couched in everyday terms. What makes this note incredible is not the contents. It's the wording."

"The wording?"

"It's painful. Actually archaic in spots. As if it were composed by someone who wears a ruff, or a tricorn. Someone who speaks a different kind of English. Or writes it. It has a . . . bouquet, an archive smell. A something that would never have been put into it purely for deception, for instance . . . like the ransom note writers who deliberately misspell words and mix their tenses to give the impression of illiteracy. And yet—I don't know." Ellery slipped the note into his pocket. "It's the strangest mixture of genuineness and contrivance. I don't understand it."

"Maybe," suggested the young man, putting his arm carelessly around Laurel's shoulders, "maybe it's the work of some psycho foreigner. It reads like somebody translating from another language."

"Possible." Ellery sucked his lower lip. Then he shrugged. "Anyway, Laurel, there's something to go on. Are you sure you wouldn't rather discuss this—?"

"You mean because it involves Roger?" Laurel laughed again, removing Macgowan's paw. "Mac isn't one of Roger's more ardent admirers, Ellery. It's all right."

"What did he do now?" growled Roger Priam's stepson.

"He said he wasn't going to be scared by any 'ghost,' Mac. Or rather roared it. And here's a clue to someone from his past and, apparently, Leander Hill's. 'For you and for him . . .' Laurel, what do you know of your father's background?"

"Not much. He'd led an adventurous life, I think, but whenever I used to ask him questions about it— especially when I was little—he'd laugh, slap me on the bottom, and send me off to Mad'moiselle."

"What about his family?"

"Family?" said Laurel vaguely.

"Brothers, sisters, uncle, cousins—family. Where did he come from? Laurel, I'm fishing. We need some facts."

"I'm no help there. Daddy never talked about himself. I always felt I couldn't pry. I can't remember his ever having any contact with relatives. I don't even know if any exist."

"When did he and Priam go into business together?"

"It must have been around twenty, twenty-five years ago."

"Before Delia and he got married," said Crowe. "Delia —that's my mother, Mr. Queen."

"I know," said Ellery, a bit stiffly. "Had Priam and Hill known each other well before they started the jewelry business, Macgowan?"

"I don't know." The giant put his arm about Laurel's waist.

"I suppose they did. They must have," Laurel said in a helpless way, absently removing the arm. "I realize now how little I know about Dad's past."

"Or I about Roger's" said Crowe, marching two fingers up Laurel's back. She wriggled and said, "Oh, stop it, Mac." He got up. "Neither of them ever talked about it." He went over to the other end of the platform and stretched out again.

"Apparently with reason. Leander Hill and Roger Priam had a common enemy in the old days, someone they thought was dead. *He* says they tried to put him out of the way, and he's spent over twenty years tracking them down."

Ellery began to walk about, avoiding Crowe Macgowan's arms.

"Dad tried to murder somebody?" Laurel bit her thumb.

"When you yell bloody murder, Laurel," said Ellery, "you've got to be prepared for a certain echo of nastiness. This kind of murder," he said, lighting a cigaret and placing it between her lips, "is never nice. It's usually rooted

52

in pretty mucky soil. Priam means nothing to you, and your father is dead. Do you still want to go through with this? *You're* my client, you know, not Mrs. Priam. At her own suggestion."

"Did Mother come to you?" exclaimed Macgowan.

"Yes, but we're keeping it confidential."

"I didn't know she cared," muttered the giant.

Ellery lit a cigaret for himself.

Laurel was wrinkling her nose and looking a little sick.

Ellery tossed the match overside. "Whoever composed that note is on a delayed murder spree. He wants revenge badly enough to have nursed it for over twenty years. A quick killing doesn't suit him at all. He wants the men who injured him to suffer, presumably, as he's suffered. To accomplish this he starts a private war of nerves. His strategy is all plotted. Working from the dark, he makes his first tactical move . . . the warning, the first of the 'special meanings' he promises. Number one is—of all things—a dead pooch, number two whatever was in the box to Roger Priam—I wonder what it was, by the way! You wouldn't know, Mac, would you?"

"I wouldn't know *anything* about my mother's husband," replied Macgowan.

"And he means to send other warnings with other 'gifts' which have special meanings. To Priam exclusively now—Hill foxed him by dying at once. He's a man with a fixed idea, Laurel, and an obsessive sense of injury. I really think you ought to keep out of his way. Let Priam defy him. It's his skin, and if he needs help he knows where he can apply for it."

Laurel threw herself back on the platform, blowing smoke to the appliquéd sky.

"Don't you feel you have to act like the heroine of a magazine serial?"

Laurel did not reply.

"Laurel, drop it. Now."

She rolled her head. "I don't care what Daddy did. People make mistakes, even commit crimes, who are decent and nice. Sometimes events force you, or other people. I knew him—as a human being—better than anyone in creation. If he and Roger Priam got into a mess it was Roger who thought up the dirty work . . . The fact that he wasn't my real father makes it even more important. I owe him everything." She sat up suddenly. "I'm not going to stay out of this, Ellery. I can't."

53

"You'll find, Queen," scowled young Macgowan in the silence that followed, "that this is a very tough number."

"Tough she may be, my Tarzanian friend," grumbled Ellery, "but this sort of thing is a business, not an endurance contest. It takes knowhow and connections and a technique. And experience. None of which Miss Strongheart has." He crushed his cigaret out on the platform vindictively. "Not to mention the personal danger . . . Well, I'll root around a little, Laurel. Do some checking back. It shouldn't be too much of a job to get a line on those two and find out what they were up to in the Twenties. And who got caught in the meat-grinder . . . You driving me back to the world of fantasy?"

Five

THE NEXT MORNING Ellery called the Los Angeles Police Department and asked to speak to the officer in charge of the Public Relations Department.

"Sergeant Lordetti."

"Sergeant, this is Ellery Queen . . . Yes, how do you do. Sergeant, I'm in town to write a Hollywood novel—oh, you've seen that . . . no, I can't make the newspapers believe it and, frankly, I've given up trying. Sergeant Lordetti, I need some expert advice for background on my book. Is there anyone in, say, the Hollywood Division who could give me a couple hours of his time? Some trouble-shooter with lots of experience in murder investigation and enough drag in the Department so I could call on him from time to time? . . . Exposé? So you fell for that, too, haha! Me, the son of a cop? No, no, Sergeant, nothing like that, believe me . . . Who? . . . K-e-a-t-s. Thanks a lot . . . Not at all, Sergeant. If you can make a little item out of it, you're entirely welcome."

Ellery called the Hollywood Division on Wilcox below Sunset and asked to speak to Lieutenant Keats. Informed that Lieutenant Keats was on another phone, Ellery left his telephone number with the request that Lieutenant Keats call back as soon as he was free.

Twenty minutes later a car drew up to his house and a big lean man in a comfortable-looking business suit got out and rang the bell, glancing around at Ellery's pint-sized garden curiously. Hiding behind a drape, Ellery decided he was not a salesman, for he carried nothing and his interest had something amused in it. Possibly a reporter, although he seemed too carefully dressed for that. He might have been a sports announcer or a veteran airline pilot off duty.

"It's a policeman, Mr. Queen," reported Mrs. Williams nervously. "You done something?"

"I'll keep you out of it, Mrs. Williams. Lieutenant Keats? The service staggers me. I merely left a message for you to phone back."

"Sergeant Lordetti phoned and told me about it," said the Hollywood detective, filling the doorway. "Thought I'd take the shortcut. No, thanks, don't drink when I'm working."

"Working—? Oh, Mrs. Williams, close the door, will you? . . . Working, Lieutenant? But I explained to Lordetti—"

"He told me." Keats placed his hat neatly on the chartreuse chair. "You want expert advice for a mystery novel. Such as what, Mr. Queen? How a homicide is reported in Los Angeles? That was for the benefit of the *Mirror* and *News*. What's really on your mind?"

Ellery stared. Then they both grinned, shook hands, and sat down like old friends.

Keats was a sandy-haired man of thirty-eight or forty with clear, rather distant gray eyes below reddish brows. His hands were big and well-kept, with a reliable look to them; there was a gold band on the fourth finger of the left. His eyes were intelligent and his jaw had been developed by adversity. His manner was slightly stand-offish. A smart cop, Ellery decided, and a rugged one.

"Let me light that for you, Lieutenant."

"The nail?" Keats laughed, taking a shredded cigaret from between his lips. It was unlit. "I'm a dry smoker, Mr. Queen. Given up smoking." He put the ruin on an ashtray and fingered a fresh cigaret, settling back. "Some case you're interested in? Something you don't want to get around?"

"It came my way yesterday morning. Do you know anything about the death of a wholesale jeweler named Leander Hill?"

"So she got to you." Keats lipped the unlit cigaret. "It passed through our Division. The girl made a pest of herself. Something about a dead dog and a note that scared her father to death. But no note. An awfully fancy yarn. More in your line than ours."

Ellery handed Keats the sheet of Leander Hill's stationery.

Keats read it slowly. Then he examined the notepaper, front and back.

"That's Hill's handwriting, by the way. Obviously a copy he made. I found it in a slit in his mattress."

"Where's the original of this, Mr. Queen?"

"Probably destroyed."

"Even if this were the McCoy." Keats put the sheet down. "There's nothing here that legally connects Hill's death with a murder plot. Of course, the revenge business . . ."

"I know, Lieutenant. It's the kind of case that gives you fellows a hard ache. Every indication of a psycho, and a possible victim who won't co-operate."

"Who's that?"

"The 'him' of the note." Ellery told Keats about Roger Priam's mysterious box, and of what Priam had let slip during Ellery's visit. "There's something more than a gangrenous imagination behind this, Lieutenant. Even though no one's going to get anywhere with Priam, still . . . it ought to be looked into, don't you agree?"

The detective pulled at his unlit cigaret.

"I'm not sure I want any part of it myself," Ellery said, glancing at his typewriter and thinking of Delia Priam. "I'd like a little more to go on before I commit myself. It seemed to me that if we could find something in Hill's past, and Priam's, that takes this note out of the ordinary crackpot class . . ."

"On the q.t.?"

"Yes. Could you swing it?"

For a moment Keats did not reply. He picked up the note and read it over again.

"I'd like to have this."

"Of course. But I want it back."

"I'll have it photostated. Tell you what I'll do, Mr. Queen." Lieutenant Keats rose. "I'll talk to the Chief and if he thinks it's worth my time, I'll see what I can dig up."

"Oh, Keats."

"Yes, sir?"

"While you're digging . . . Do a little spadework on a man who calls himself Alfred Wallace. Roger Priam's secretary-general."

DELIA PRIAM PHONED that afternoon. "I am surprised you're in."

"Where did you think I'd be, Mrs. Priam?" The moment he heard her throaty purr his blood began

57

stewing. Damn her, she was like the first cocktail after a hard day.

"Out detecting, or whatever it is detectives do."

"I haven't taken the case." He was careful to keep his voice good-humored. "I haven't made up my mind."

"You're angry with me about yesterday."

"Angry? Mrs. Priam!"

"Sorry. I thought you were." Oh, were you? "I'm afraid I'm allergic to messes. I usually take the line of least resistance."

"In everything?"

"Give me an example." Her laugh was soft.

He wanted to say, *I'd be glad to specify if you'd drop in on me, say, this afternoon.* Instead, he said innocuously, "Who's questioning whom?"

"You're such a careful man, Mr. Queen."

"Well, I haven't taken the case—yet, Mrs. Priam."

Do you suppose I could help you make up your mind?" There's the nibble. Reel 'er in . . .

"You know, Mrs. Priam, that might be a perilous offer . . . Mrs. Priam? . . . Hello!"

She said in a low voice, quickly, "I must stop," and the line went dead.

Ellery hung up perspiring. He was so annoyed with himself that he went upstairs and took a shower.

LAUREL HILL DROPPED in on him twice in the next twenty-four hours. The first time she was "just passing by" and thought she would report that nothing was happening, nothing at all. Priam wouldn't see her and as far as she could tell he was being his old bullying, beastly self. Delia had tried to pump her about Ellery and what he was doing, and as a matter of fact she couldn't help wondering herself if . . .

Ellery's glance kept going to his typewriter and after a few moments Laurel left abruptly.

She was back the next morning, recklessly hostile.

"Are you taking this case, or aren't you?"

"I don't know, Laurel."

"I've talked to my lawyers. The estate isn't settled, but I can get the money together to give you a retainer of five thousand dollars."

"It isn't the money, Laurel."

"If you don't want to bother, say so and I'll get someone else."

"That's always the alternative, of course."

"But you're just sitting here!"

"I'm making a few preliminary inquiries," he said patiently.

"From this—this ivory tower?"

"Stucco. What I'll do, Laurel, depends entirely on what I find out."

"You've sold out to Delia, that's what you've done," Laurel cried. "She doesn't really want this investigated at all. She only followed me the other day to see what I was up to—the rest was malarkey! She *wants* Roger murdered! And that's all right with me, you understand—all I'm interested in is the case of Leander Hill. But if Delia's standing in the way—"

"You're being nineteen, Laurel." He tried not to let his anger show.

"I'll admit I can't offer you what she can—"

"Delia Priam hasn't offered me a thing, Laurel. We haven't even discussed my fee."

"And I don't mean money!" She was close to tears.

"Now you're hysterical." His voice came out sharp, not what he intended at all. "Have a little patience, Laurel. Right now there's nothing to do but wait."

She strode out.

The next morning Ellery spread his newspaper behind a late breakfast tray to find Roger Priam, Leander Hill, and Crowe Macgowan glaring back at him. Mac was glaring from a tree.

$$$aire Denies Murder Threat;

Says Partner Not Slain

Denying that he has received a threat against his life, Roger Priam, wealthy wholesale gem merchant of L.A., barred himself behind the doors of his secluded home above Hollywood Bowl this morning when reporters investigated a tip that he is the intended victim of a murder plot which allegedly took the life of his business partner, Leander Hill, last week . . .

Mr. Priam, it appeared, after ousting reporters had issued a brief statement through his secretary, Alfred Wallace, repeating his denial and adding that the cause of Hill's death was "a matter of official record."

Detectives at the Hollywood Division of the L.A.P.D. admitted this morning that Hill's daughter, Laurel, had charged her father was "frightened to death," but said that they had found no evidence to support the charge, which they termed "fantastic."

Miss Hill, interviewed at her home adjoining the Priam property, said: "If Roger Priam wants to bury his head in the sand, it's his head." She intimated that she "had reason to believe" both her father and Priam were slated to be murdered "by some enemy out of their past."

The story concluded with the reminder that "Mr. Priam is the stepfather of twenty-three year old Crowe Macgowan, the Atomic Age Tree Boy, who broke into print in a big way recently by taking off his clothes and bedding down in a tree house on his stepfather's estate in preparation for the end of the world."

Observing to himself that Los Angeles journalism was continuing to maintain its usual standards, Ellery went to the phone and called the Hill home.

"Laurel? I didn't expect you'd be answering the phone in person this morning."

"I've got nothing to hide." Laurel laid the slightest stress on her pronoun. Also, she was cold, very cold.

"One question. Did you tip off the papers about Priam?"

"No."

"Cross your heart and —?"

"I said no!" There was a definite *snick!*

It was puzzling, and Ellery puzzled over it all through breakfast, which Mrs. Williams with obvious disapproval persisted in calling lunch. He was just putting down his second cup of coffee when Keats walked in with a paper in his pocket.

"I was hoping you'd drop around," said Ellery, as Mrs. Williams set another place. "Thanks, Mrs. W, I'll do the rest . . . Not knowing exactly what is leaking where, Keats, I decided not to risk a phone call. So far I've been kept out of it."

"Then you didn't feed the kitty?" asked Keats. "Thanks. No cream or sugar."

"Of course not. I was wondering if it was you."

"Not me. Must have been the Hill girl."

"Not she. I 've asked her."

"Funny."

"Very. How was the tip tipped?"

"By phone call to the city room. Disguised voice, and they couldn't trace it."

"Male or female?"

"They said male, but they admitted it was pitched in a queer way and might have been female. With all the actors floating around this town you never know." Keats automatically struck a match, but then he shook his head and put it out. "You know, Mr. Queen," he said, scowling at his cigaret, "if there's anything to this thing, that tip might have come . . . I know it sounds screwy . . ."

"From the writer of the note? I've been dandling that notion myself, Lieutenant."

"Pressure, say."

"In the war on Priam's nerves."

"If he's got an iron nerve himself." Keats rose. "Well, this isn't getting us anywhere."

"Anything yet on Hill and Priam?"

"Not yet." Keats slowly crumpled his cigaret. "It might be a toughie, Mr. Queen. So far I haven't got to first base."

"What's holding you up?"

"I don't know yet. Give me another few days."

"What about Wallace?"

"I'll let you know."

LATE THAT AFTERNOON—it was the twenty-first, the day after the Shriners parade—Ellery looked around from his typewriter to see the creamy nose of Delia Priam's convertible in profile against his front window.

He deliberately forced himself to wait until Mrs. Williams answered the door.

As he ran his hand over his hair, Mrs. Williams said: "It's a naked man. You in?"

Macgowan was alone. He was in his Tree Boy costume —one loincloth, flame-colored this time. He shook Ellery's hand limply and accepted a Scotch on the Rocks, settling himself on the sofa with his bare heels on the sill of the picture window.

"I thought I recognized the car," said Ellery.

"It's my mother's. Mine was out of gas. Am I inconvenient?" The giant glanced at the typewriter. "How do you knock that stuff out? But I had to see you." He seemed uneasy.

"What about, Mac?"

"Well . . . I thought maybe the reason you hadn't

61

made up your mind to take the case was that there wasn't enough money in it for you."

"Did you?"

"Look. Maybe I could put enough more in the pot to make it worth your while."

"You mean *you* want to hire me, too, Mac?"

"That's it." He seemed relieved that it was out. "I got to thinking . . . that note, and then whatever it was Roger got in that box the morning old man Hill got the dead dog . . . I mean, maybe there's something in it after all, Mr. Queen."

"Suppose there is." Ellery studied him with curiosity. "Why are you interested enough to want to put money into an investigation?"

"Roger's my mother's husband, isn't he?"

"Touching, Mac. When did you two fall in love?"

Young Macgowan's brown skin turned mahogany. "I mean . . . It's true Roger and I never got along. He's always tried to dominate me as well as everybody else. But he means well, and—"

"And that's why," smiled Ellery, "you call yourself Crowe Macgowan instead of Crowe Priam."

Crowe laughed. "Okay, I detest his lazy colon. We've always fought like a couple of wild dogs. When Delia married him he wouldn't adopt me legally; the idea was to keep me dependent on him. I was a kid, and it made me hate him. So I kept my father's name and I refused to take any money from Roger. I wasn't altogether a hero—I had a small income from a trust fund my father left for me. You can imagine how that set with Mr. Priam." He laughed again. But then he finished lamely, "The last few years I've grown up, I guess. I tolerate him for Mother's sake. That's it," he added, brightening, "Mother's sake. That's why I'd like to get to the bottom of this. You see, Mr. Queen?"

"Your mother loves Priam?"

"She's married to him, isn't she?"

"Come off it, Mac. I intimated to you myself the other day, in your tree, that your mother had already offered to engage my services. Not to mention Laurel. What's this all about?"

Macgowan got up angrily. "What difference does my reason make? It's an honest offer. All I want is this damned business cleaned up. Name your fee and get going on it!"

"As they say in the textbooks, Mac," said Ellery, "I'll leave you know. It's the best I can do."

"What are you waiting for?"

"Warning number two. If this business is on the level, Mac, there will be a warning number two, and I can't do a thing till it comes. With Priam being pigheaded, you and your mother can be most useful by simply keeping your eyes open. I'll decide then."

"What do we watch for," sneered the young man, "another mysterious box?"

"I've no idea. But whatever it turns out to be—and it may not be a thing, Mac, but an event—whatever happens out of the ordinary, no matter how silly or trivial it may seem to you—let me know about it right away. You," and Ellery added, as if in afterthought, "or your mother."

THE PHONE WAS ringing. He opened his eyes, conscious that it had been ringing for some time.

He switched on the light, blinking at his wristwatch. 4:35. He hadn't got to bed until 1:30.

"Hello?" he mumbled.

"Mr. Queen—"

Delia Priam.

"Yes?" He had never felt so wakeful.

"My son Crowe said to call you if—" She sounded far away, a little frightened.

"Yes? Yes?"

"It's probably nothing at all. But you told Crowe—"

"Delia, what's happened?"

"Roger's sick, Ellery. Dr. Voluta is here. He says it's ptomaine poisoning. But—"

"I'll be right over!"

DR. VOLUTA WAS a floppy man with jowls and a dirty eye, and it was a case of hate at first sight. The doctor was in a bright blue yachting jacket over a yellow silk undershirt and his greasy brown hair stuck up all over his head. He wore carpet slippers. Twice Ellery caught himself about to address him as Captain Bligh and it would not have surprised him if, in his own improvised costume of soiled white ducks and turtleneck sweater, he had inspired Priam's doctor to address him in turn as Mr. Christian.

"The trouble with you fellows," Dr. Voluta was saying

63

as he scraped an evil mess from a rumpled bedsheet into a specimen vial, "is that you really enjoy murder. Otherwise you wouldn't see it in every bellyache."

"Quite a bellyache," said Ellery. "The stopper's right there over the sink, Doctor."

"Thank you. Priam is a damn pig. He eats too much for even a well man. His alimentary apparatus is a medical problem in itself. I've warned him for years to lay off bedtime snacks, especially spicy fish."

"I'm told he's fond of spicy fish."

"I'm fond of spicy blondes, Mr. Queen," snapped Dr. Voluta, "but I keep my appetite within bounds."

"I thought you said there's something wrong with the tuna."

"Certainly there's something wrong with it. I tasted it myself. But that's not the point. The point is that if he'd followed my orders he wouldn't have eaten any in the first place."

They were in the butler's pantry, and Dr. Voluta was looking irritably about for something to cover a plastic dish into which he had dumped the remains of the tuna.

"Then it's your opinion, Doctor—?"

"I've given you my opinion. The can of tuna was spoiled. Didn't you ever hear of spoiled canned goods, Mr. Queen?" He opened his medical bag, grabbed a surgical glove, and stretched it over the top of the dish.

"I've examined the empty tin, Dr. Voluta." Ellery had fished it out of the tin can container, thankful that in Los Angeles you had to keep cans separate from garbage. "I see no sign of a bulge, do you?"

"You're just assuming that's the tin it came from," the doctor said disagreeably. "How do you know?"

"The cook told me. It's the only tuna she opened today. She opened it just before she went to bed. And I found the tin at the top of the waste can."

Dr. Voluta threw up his hands. "Excuse me. I want to wash up."

Ellery followed him to the door of the downstairs lavatory. "Have to keep my eye on that vial and dish, Doctor," he said apologetically. "Since you won't turn them over to me."

"You don't mean a thing to me, Mr. Queen. I still think it's all a lot of nonsense. But if this stuff has to be analyzed, I'm turning it over to the police personally. Would you mind stepping back? I'd like to close this door."

"The vial," said Ellery.

"Oh, for God's sake." Dr. Voluta turned his back and opened the tap with a swoosh.

They were waiting for Lieutenant Keats. It was almost six o'clock and through the windows a pale farina-like world was taking shape. The house was cold. Priam was purged and asleep, his black beard jutting from the blankets on his reclining chair with a moribund majesty, so that all Ellery had been able to think of—before Alfred Wallace shut the door politely in his face—was Sennacherib the Assyrian in his tomb; and that was no help. Wallace had locked Priam's door from the inside. He was spending what was left of the night on the day-bed in Priam's room reserved for his use during emergencies.

Crowe Macgowan had been snappish. "If I hadn't made that promise, Queen, I'd never have had Delia call you. All this stench about a little upchucking. Leave him to Voluta and go home." And he had gone back to his oak, yawning.

Old Mr. Collier, Delia Priam's father, had quietly made himself a cup of tea in the kitchen and trotted back upstairs with it, pausing only long enough to chuckle to Ellery: "A fool and his gluttony are soon parted."

Delia Priam . . . He hadn't seen her at all. Ellery had rather built himself up to their middle-of-the-night meeting, although he was prepared to be perfectly correct. Of course, she couldn't know that. By the time he arrived she had returned to her room upstairs. He was glad, in a way, that her sense of propriety was so delicately tuned to his state of mind. It was, in fact, astoundingly perceptive of her. At the same time, he felt a little empty.

Ellery stared gritty-eyed at Dr. Voluta's blue back. It was an immense back, with great fat wrinkles running across it.

He could, of course, get rid of the doctor and go upstairs and knock on her door. There was always a question or two to be asked in a case like this.

He wondered what she would do.

And how she looked at six in the morning.

He played with this thought for some time.

"Ordinarily," said the doctor, turning and reaching for a towel, "I'd have told you to go to hell. But a doctor with a respectable practice has to be cagey in this town,

Mr. Queen, and Laurel started something when she began to talk murder at Leander Hill's death. I know your type. Publicity-happy." He flung the towel at the bowl, picked up the vial and the plastic dish, holding them firmly. "You don't have to watch me, Mr. Queen. I'm not going to switch containers on you. Where the devil is that detective? I haven't had any sleep at all tonight."

"Did anyone ever tell you, Doctor," said Ellery through his teeth, "that you look like Charles Laughton in *The Beachcomber?*"

They glared at each other until a car drew up outside and Keats hurried in.

AT FOUR O'CLOCK that afternoon Ellery pulled his rented Kaiser up before the Priam house to find Keats's car already there. The maid with the tic, which was in an active state, showed him into the living room. Keats was standing before the fieldstone fireplace, tapping his teeth with the edge of a sheet of paper. Laurel Hill, Crowe Macgowan, and Delia Priam were seated before him in a student attitude. Their heads swiveled as Ellery came in, and it seemed to him that Laurel was coldly expectant, young Macgowan uneasy, and Delia frightened.

"Sorry, Lieutenant. I had to stop for gas. Is that the lab report?"

Keats handed him the paper. Their eyes followed. When Ellery handed the paper back, their eyes went with it.

"Maybe you'd better line it up for these folks, Mr. Queen," said the detective. "I'll take it from there."

"When I got here about five this morning," nodded Ellery, "Dr. Voluta was sure it was food poisoning. The facts were these: Against Voluta's medical advice, Mr. Priam invariably has something to eat before going to sleep. This habit of his seems to be a matter of common knowledge. Since he doesn't sleep too well, he tends to go to bed at a late hour. The cook, Mrs. Guittierez, is on the other hand accustomed to retiring early. Consequently, Mr. Priam usually tells Mr. Wallace what he expects to feel like having around midnight, and Mr. Wallace usually transmits this information to the cook before she goes to bed. Mrs. Guittierez then prepares the snack as ordered, puts it into the refrigerator, and retires.

"Last night the order came through for tuna fish, to

which Mr. Priam is partial. Mrs. Guittierez got a can of tuna from the pantry—one of the leading brands, by the way—opened it, prepared the contents as Mr. Priam likes it—with minced onion, sweet green pepper, celery, lots of mayonnaise, the juice of half a freshly squeezed lemon, freshly ground pepper and a little salt, a dash of Worcestershire sauce, a half-teaspoon of dried mustard, and a pinch of oregano and powdered thyme—and placed the bowl, covered, in the refrigerator. She then cleaned up and went to bed. Mrs. Guittierez left the kitchen at about twenty minutes of ten, leaving a night light burning.

"At about ten minutes after midnight," continued Ellery, speaking to the oil painting of the Spanish grandee above the fireplace so that he would not be disturbed by a certain pair of eyes, "Alfred Wallace was sent by Roger Priam for the snack. Wallace removed the bowl of tuna salad from the refrigerator, placed it on a tray with some caraway-seed rye bread, sweet butter, and a sealed bottle of milk, and carried the tray to Mr. Priam's study. Priam ate heartily, although he did not finish the contents of the tray. Wallace then prepared him for bed, turned out the lights, and took what remained on the tray back to the kitchen. He left the tray there as it was, and himself went upstairs to his room.

"At about three o'clock this morning Wallace was awakened by the buzzer of the intercom from Mr. Priam's room. It was Priam, in agony. Wallace ran downstairs and found him violently sick. Wallace immediately phoned Dr. Voluta, ran upstairs and awakened Mrs. Priam, and the two of them did what they could until Dr. Voluta's arrival, which was a very few minutes later."

Macgowan said irritably, "Damned if I can see why you tell us—"

Delia Priam put her hand on her son's arm and he stopped.

"Go on, Mr. Queen," she said in a low voice. When she talked, everything in a man tightened up. He wondered if she quite realized the quality and range of her power.

"On my arrival I found the tray in the kitchen, where Wallace said he had left it. When I had the facts I phoned Lieutenant Keats. While waiting for him I got together everything that had been used in the preparation

67

of the midnight meal—the spices, the empty tuna tin, even the shell of the lemon, as well as the things on the tray. There was a quantity of the salad, some rye bread, some of the butter, some of the milk. Meanwhile Dr. Voluta preserved what he could of the regurgitated matter. When Lieutenant Keats arrived, we turned everything over to him."

Ellery stopped and lit a cigaret.

Keats said: "I took it all down to the Crime Laboratory and the report just came through." He glanced at the paper. "I won't bother you with the detailed report. Just give you the highlights.

"Chemical analysis of the regurgitated matter from Mr. Priam's stomach brought out the presence of arsenic.

"Everything is given a clean bill—spices, tuna tin, lemon, bread, butter, milk—everything, that is, but the tuna salad itself.

"Arsenic of the same type was found in the remains of the tuna salad.

"Dr. Voluta was wrong," said Keats. "This is not a case of ptomaine poisoning caused by spoiled fish. It's a case of arsenical poisoning caused by the introduction of arsenic into the salad. The cook put the salad in the refrigerator about 9:40 last night. Mr. Wallace came and took it to Mr. Priam around ten minutes after midnight. During that period the kitchen was empty, with only a dim light burning. During those two and a half hours someone sneaked into the kitchen and poisoned the salad."

"There can't have been any mistake," added Ellery. "There is a bowl of something for Mr. Priam in the refrigerator every night. It's a special bowl, used only for his snacks. It's even more easily identified than that—it has the name *Roger* in gilt lettering on it, a gift to Roger Priam from Alfred Wallace last Christmas."

"The question is," concluded Keats, "who tried to poison Mr. Priam."

He looked at the three in a friendly way.

Delia Priam, rising suddenly, murmured, "It's so incredible," and put a handkerchief to her nose.

Laurel smiled at the older woman's back. "That's the way it's seemed to me, darling," she said, "ever since Daddy's death."

"Oh, for Pete's sake, Laur," snapped Delia's son, "don't keep smiling like Lady Macbeth, or Cassandra, or who-

68

ever it was. The last thing in the world Mother and I want is a mess."

"Nobody's accusing you, Mac," said Laurel. "My only point is that now maybe you'll believe I wasn't talking through clouds of opium."

"All *right!*"

Delia turned to Keats. Ellery saw Keats look her over uncomfortably, but with that avidity for detail which cannot be disciplined in the case of certain women. She was superb today, all in white, with a large wooden crucifix on a silver chain girdling her waist. No slit in this skirt; long sleeves; and the dress came up high to the neck. But her back was bare to the waist. Some Hollywood designer's idea of personalized fashion; didn't she realize how shocking it was? But then women, even the most respectable, have the wickedest innocence in this sort of thing, mused Ellery; it really wasn't fair to a hardworking police officer who wore a gold band on the fourth finger of his left hand. "Lieutenant, do the police have to come into this?" she asked.

"Ordinarily, Mrs. Priam, I could answer a question like that right off the bat." Keats's eyes shifted; he put an unlit cigaret between his lips and rolled it nervously to the corner of his mouth. A note of stubbornness crept into his voice. "But this is something I've never run into before. Your husband refuses to co-operate. He won't even discuss it with me. All he said was that he won't be caught that way again, that he could take care of himself, and that I was to pick up my hat on the way out."

Delia went to a window. Studying her back, Ellery thought that she was relieved and pleased. Keats should have kept her on a hook; he'd have to have a little skull session with Keats on the best way to handle Mrs. Priam. But the back *was* disturbing.

"Tell me, Mrs. Priam, is he nuts?"

"Sometimes, Lieutenant," murmured Delia without turning, "I wonder."

"I'd like to add," said Keats abruptly, "that Joe Doakes and his Ethiopian brother could have dosed that tuna. The kitchen back door wasn't locked. There's gravel back there, and woods beyond. It would have been a cinch for anyone who'd cased the household and found out about the midnight snack routine. There seems to be a tie-up with somebody from Mr. Priam's and Mr. Hill's past—

somebody who's had it in for both of them for a long time. I'm not overlooking that. But I'm not overlooking the possibility that that's a lot of soda pop, too. It could be a cover-up. In fact, I think it is. I don't go for this revenge-and-slow-death business. I just wanted everybody to know that. Okay, Mr. Queen, I'm through."

He kept looking at her back.

Brother, thought Ellery with compassion.

And he said, "You may be right, Keats, but I'd like to point out a curious fact that appears in this lab report. The quantity of arsenic apparently used, says the report, was 'not sufficient to cause death.' "

"A mistake," said the detective. "It happens all the time. Either they use way too much or way too little."

"Not all the time, Lieutenant. And from what's happened so far I don't see this character—whoever he is—as the impulsive, emotional type of killer. If this is all tied up, it has a pretty careful and coldblooded brain behind it. The kind of criminal brain that doesn't make simple mistakes like underdosing. 'Not sufficient to cause death' . . . that was deliberate."

"But why?" howled young Macgowan.

" 'Slow dying,' Mac!" said Laurel triumphantly. "Remember?"

"Yes, it connects with the note to Hill," said Ellery in a glum tone. "Nonlethal dose. Enough to make Priam very sick, but not fatally. 'Slow and sure . . . For each pace forward a warning.' The poisoning attack is a warning to Roger Priam to follow up whatever was in the box he received the morning Hill got the dead dog. Priam's warning number one—unknown. Warning number two—poisoned tuna. Lovely problem."

"I don't admire your taste in problems," said Crowe Macgowan. "What's it mean? All this—this stuff?"

"It means, Mac, that I'm forced to accept your assignment," replied Ellery. "And yours, Delia. I shouldn't take the time, but what else can I do?"

Delia Priam came to him and took his hands and looked into his eyes and said, with simplicity, "Thank you, Ellery. It's such a . . . relief knowing it's going to be handled . . . by you."

She squeezed, ever so little. It was all impersonally friendly on her part; he felt that. It had to be, with her own son present. But he wished he could control his sweat glands.

Keats lipped his unlit cigaret.

Macgowan looked down at them, interested.

Laurel said, "Then we're all nicely set," in a perfectly flat voice, and she walked out.

Six

THE NIGHT WAS chilly, and Laurel walked briskly along the path, the beam of her flashlight bobbing before her. Her legs were bare under the long suède coat and they felt goose-pimply.

When she came to the great oak she stabbed at the green ceiling with her light.

"Mac. You awake?"

Macgowan's big face appeared in her beam.

"Laurel?" he said incredulously.

"It's not Esther Williams."

"Are you crazy, walking alone in these woods at night?" The rope ladder hurtled to her feet. "What do you want to be, a sex murder in tomorrow's paper?"

"You'd be the natural suspect." Laurel began to climb, her light streaking about the clearing.

"Wait, will you! I'll put on the flood." Macgowan disappeared. A moment later the glade was bright as a studio set. "That's why I'm nervous," he grinned, reappearing. His long arm yanked her to the platform. "Boy, is this cosy. Come on in."

"Turn off the flood, Mac. I'd like some privacy."

"Sure!" He was back in a moment, lifting her off her feet. She let him carry her into his tree house and deposit her on the rollaway bed, which was made up for the night. "Wait till I turn the radio off." When he straightened up his head barely missed the ceiling. "*And* the light."

"Leave the light."

"Okay, okay. Aren't you cold, baby?"

"That's the only thing you haven't provided for, Mac. The California nights."

"Didn't you know I carry my own central heating? Shove over."

"Sit down, Mac."

"Huh?"

"On the floor. I want to talk to you."

"Didn't you ever hear of the language of the eyes and so forth?"

"Tonight it has to come out here." Laurel leaned back on her arms, smiling at him. He was beginning to glower. But then he folded up at her feet and put his head on her knees. Laurel moved him, drew her coat over her legs, and replaced his head.

"All right, then, let it out!"

"Mac," said Laurel, "why did *you* hire Ellery Queen?"

He sat still for a moment. Then he reached over to a shelf, got a cigaret, lit it, and leaned back.

"That's a hell of a question to ask a red-blooded man in a tree house at twelve o'clock at night."

"Just the same, answer it."

"What difference does it make? You hired him, Delia hired him, everybody was doing it, so I did it too. Let's talk about something else. If we've got to talk."

"Sorry. That's my subject for tonight."

He encircled his mammoth legs, scowling through the smoke at his bare feet. "Laurel, how long have we known each other?"

"Since we were kids." She was surprised.

"Grew up together, didn't we?"

"We certainly did."

"Have I ever done anything out of line?"

"No," Laurel laughed softly, "but it's not because you haven't tried."

"Why, you little squirt, I could break you in two and stuff both halves in my pants pocket. Don't you know I've been in love with you ever since I found out where babies come from?"

"Why, Mac," murmured Laurel. "You've never said that to me before. Used that word, I mean."

"Well, I've used it," he growled. "Now let me hear your side of it."

"Say it again, Mac?"

"Love! I love you!"

"In that tone of voice?"

She found herself off the bed and on the floor, in his arms. "Damn you," he whispered, "I love you."

She stared up at him. "Mac—"

"I love you . . ."

"Mac, let go of me!" She wriggled out of his arms and jumped to her feet. "I suppose," she cried, "that's the reason you hired him! Because you love me, or—or

73

something like that. Mac, what's the *reason?* I've got to know!"

"Is that all you have to say to a guy who tells you he loves you?"

"The reason, Mac."

Young Macgowan rolled over on his back and belched smoke. Out of the reek his voice mumbled something ineffectual. Then it stopped. When the smoke cleared, he was lying there with his eyes shut.

"You won't tell me."

"Laur, I can't. It's got . . . nothing to do with anything. Just some cockeyed thing of my own."

Laurel seated herself on the bed again. He was very long, and broad, and brown and muscular and healthy-looking. She took a Dunhill from her coat pocket and lit it with shaky fingers. But when she spoke, she sounded calm. "There are too many mysteries around here, Chesty. I know there's one about you, and where you're concerned . . ."

His eyes opened.

"No, Mac, stay there. I'm not entirely a fool. There's something behind this tree house and all this learned bratwurst about the end of civilization, and it's not the hydrogen bomb. Are you just lazy? Or is it a new thrill for some of your studio girls—the ones who want life with a little extra something they can't get in a motel?" He flushed, but his mouth continued sullen. "All right, we'll let that go. Now about this love business."

She put her hand in his curly hair, gripping. He looked up at her thoroughly startled. She leaned forward and kissed him on the lips.

"That's for thanks. You're such a beautiful man, Mac . . . you see, a girl has her secrets, too—No! Mac, no. If we ever get together, it's got to be in a clean house. On the ground. Anyway, I have no time for love now."

"No time!"

"Darling, something's happening, and it's ugly. There's never been any ugliness in my life before . . . That I can remember, that is. And he was so wonderful to me. The only way I can pay him back is by finding whoever murdered him and seeing him die. How stupid does that sound? And maybe I'm kind of bloodthirsty myself. But it's all in the world I'm interested in right now. If the law gets him, fine. But if . . ."

"For God's sake!" Crowe scrambled to his feet, his

face bilious. A short-nosed little automatic had materialized in Laurel's hand and it was pointing absently at his navel.

"If they don't, I'll find him myself. And when I do, Mac, I'll shoot him as dead as that dog. If they send me to the gas chamber for it."

"Laurel, put that blamed thing back in your pocket!"

"No matter who it is." Her green, brown-flecked eyes were bright. The gun did not move. "Even if it turned out to be you, Mac. Even if we were married—had a baby. If I found out it was you, Mac, I'd kill you, too."

"And I thought Roger was tough." Macgowan stared at her. "Well, if you find out it was me, it'll serve me right. But until you do—"

Laurel cried out. The gun was in his hand. He turned it over curiously.

"Nasty little beanshooter. Until you do, Red, don't let anybody take this away from you," and he dropped it politely into her pocket, picked her up, and sat down on the bed with her.

A little later Laurel was saying faintly, "Mac, I didn't come here for this."

"Surprise."

"Mac, what do you think of Ellery Queen?"

"I think he's got a case on Ma," said the giant. "Do we have to talk?"

"How acute of you. I think he has, too. But that's not what I meant. I meant professionally."

"Oh, he's a nice enough guy . . ."

"Mac!"

"Okay, okay," He got up sullenly, dumping her. "If he's half as good as his rep—"

"That's just it. Is he?"

"Is he what? What are we talking about?" He poured himself a drink.

"Is he even *half* as good?"

"How should I know? You want one?"

"No. I've dropped in on him twice and phoned him I don't know how many times in the past couple of days, and he's always there. Sitting in his crow's nest, smoking and scanning the horizon."

"Land ho. It's a way of life, Laurel." Macgowan tossed if off and made a face. "That's the way these big-shot dicks work sometimes. It's all up here."

"Well, I'd like to see a little activity on the other

75

end." Laurel jumped up suddenly. "Mac, I can't stand this doing nothing. How about you and me taking a crack at it? On our own?"

"Taking a crack at what?"

"At what he ought to be doing."

"Detecting?" The big fellow was incredulous.

"I don't care what you call it. Hunting for facts, if that sounds less movie-ish. Anything that will get somewhere."

"Red Hill, Lady Dick, and Her Muscle Man," said young Macgowan, touching the ceiling with both hands. "You know? It appeals to me."

Laurel looked up at him coldly. "I'm not gagging, Mac."

"Who's gagging? Your brain, my sinews—"

"Never mind. Good night."

"Hey!" His big hand caught her in the doorway. "Don't be so half-cocky. I'm really going birdy up here, Laurel. It's tough squatting in this tree waiting for the big boom. How would you go about it?"

She looked at him for a long time. "Mac, don't try to pull anything cute on me."

"My gosh, what would I pull on *you!*"

"This isn't a game, like your apeman stunt. We're not going to have any code words in Turkish or wear disguises or meet in mysterious bistros. It's going to be a lot of footwork and maybe nothing but blisters to show for it. If you understand that and still want to come in, all right. Anything else, I go it solo."

"I hope you'll put a skirt on, or at least long pants," the giant said morosely. "Where do we start?"

"We should have started on that dead dog. Long ago. Where it came from, who owned it, how it died, and all that. But now that's as cold as I am . . . I'd say, Mac," said Laurel, leaning against the jamb with her hands in her pockets, "the arsenic. That's fresh, and it's something to go on. Somebody got into the kitchen over there and mixed arsenic in with Roger's tuna. Arsenic can't be too easy to get hold of. It must leave a trail of some sort."

"I never thought of that. How the dickens would you go about tracing it?"

"I've got some ideas. But there's one thing we ought to do before that. The tuna was poisoned in the house. So that's the place to start looking."

"Let's go." Macgowan reached for a dark blue sweater.

"Now?" Laurel sounded slightly dismayed.

"Know a better time?"

MRS. WILLIAMS CAME in and stumbled over a chair. "Mr. Queen? You in here?"

"Present."

"Then why don't you put on a light?" She found the switch. Ellery was bunched in a corner of the sofa, feet on the picture window, looking at Hollywood. It looked like a fireworks display, popping lights in all colors. "Your dinner's cold."

"Leave it on the kitchen table, Mrs. Williams. You go on home."

She sniffed. "It's that Miss Hill and the naked man, only he's got clothes on this evening."

"Why didn't you say so!" Ellery sprang from the sofa. "Laurel, Mac! Come in."

They were smiling, but Ellery thought they both looked a little peaked. Crowe Macgowan was in a respectable suit; he even wore a tie.

"Well, well, still communing with mysterious thoughts, eh, Queen? We're not interrupting anything momentous?"

"As far as I can see," said Laurel, "he hasn't moved from one spot in sixty hours. Ellery," she said abruptly, "we have some news for you."

"News? For me?"

"We've found out something."

"I wondered why Mac was dressed," said Ellery. "Here, sit down and tell me all about it. You two been on the trail?"

"There's nothing to this detective racket," said the giant, stretching his legs. "You twerps have been getting away with mayhem. Tell him, Red."

"We decided to do a little detecting on our own—"

"That sounds to me," murmured Ellery, "like the remark of a dissatisfied client."

"That's what it is." Laurel strode around smoking a cigaret. "We'd better have an understanding, Ellery. I hired you to find a killer. I didn't expect you to produce him in twenty-four hours necessarily, but I did expect *something—some* sign of interest, maybe even a twitch or two of activity. But what have you done? You've sat here and smoked!"

"Not a bad system, Laurel," said Ellery, reaching for a pipe. "I've worked that way for years."

"Well, I don't care for it!"

"Am I fired?"

"I didn't say that—"

"I think all the lady wants to do," said young Macgowan, "is give you a jab, Queen. She doesn't think thinking is a substitute for footwork."

"Each has its place," Ellery said amiably—"sit down, Laurel, won't you? Each has its place, and thinking's place can be very important. I'm not altogether ignorant of what's been going on, seated though I've remained. Let's see if I can't—er—think this out for you . . ." He closed his eyes. "I would say," he said after a moment, "that you two have been tracking down the arsenic with which Priam's tuna was poisoned." He opened his eyes. "Is that right so far?"

"That's right," cried Macgowan.

Laurel glared. "How did you know?"

Ellery tapped his forehead. "Never sell cerebration short. Now! What exactly have you accomplished? I look into my mental ball and I see . . . you and Mac . . . discovering a . . . can of . . . a can of rat poison in the Priam cellar." They were open-mouthed. "Yes. Rat poison. And you found that this particular rat poison contains arsenic . . . arsenic, the poison which was also found in Priam's salad. How'm I doin'?"

Laurel said feebly, "But I can't imagine how you . . ."

Ellery had gone to the blondewood desk near the window and pulled a drawer open. Now he took out a card and glanced over it. "Yes. You traced the purchase of that poison, which bears the brand name of D-e-t-h hyphen o-n hyphen R-a-t-z. You discovered that this revoltingly named substance was purchased on May the thirteenth of this year at . . . let me see . . . at Kepler's Pharmacy at 1723 North Highland."

Laurel looked at Macgowan. He was grinning. She glared at him and then back at Ellery.

"You questioned either Mr. Kepler himself," Ellery went on, "or his clerk, Mr. Candy—unfortunately my crystal ball went blank at this point. But one of them told you that the can of Deth-on-Ratz was bought by a tall, handsome man whom he identified—probably from a set of snapshots you had with you—as Alfred Wallace. Correct, Laurel?"

Laurel said tightly, "How did you find out?"

"Why, Red, I leave these matters to those who can attend to them far more quickly and efficiently than I—

78

or you, Red. Or the Atomic Age Tree Boy over here. Lieutenant Keats had all that information within a few hours and he passed it along to me. Why should I sauté myself in the California sun when I can sit here in comfort and think?"

Laurel's lip wiggled and Ellery burst into laughter. He shook up her hair and tilted her chin. "Just the same, that was enterprising of you, Laurel. That was all right."

"Not so all right." Laurel sank into a chair, tragic. "I'm sorry, Ellery. You must think I'm an imbecile."

"Not a bit of it. It's just that you're impatient. This business is a matter of legs, brains, and bottoms, and you've got to learn to wait on the last-named with philosophy while the other two are pumping away. What else did you find out?"

"Nothing," said Laurel miserably.

"I thought it was quite a piece," said Crowe Macgowan. "Finding out that Alfred bought the poison that knocked Roger for a loop . . . that ought to mean something, Queen."

"If you jumped to that kind of conclusion," said Ellery dryly, "I'm afraid you're in for a bad time. Keats found out something else."

"What's that?"

"It was your mother, Mac, who thought she heard mice in the cellar. It was your mother who told Wallace to buy the rat poison."

The boy gaped, and Laurel looked down at her hands suddenly.

"Don't be upset, Mac. No action is going to be taken. Even though the mice seem to have been imaginary—we could find no turds or holes . . . The fact is, we have nothing positive. There's no direct evidence that the arsenic in Priam's tuna salad came from the can of rat poison in the cellar. There's no direct evidence that either your mother or Wallace did anything but try to get rid of mice who happen not to have been there."

"Well, of course not." Macgowan had recovered; he was even looking pugnacious. "Stupid idea to begin with. Just like this detective hunch of yours, Laurel. Everything's under control. Let's leave it that way."

"All right," said Laurel. She was still studying her hands.

But Ellery said, "No. I don't see it that way. It's not a bad notion at all for you two to root around. You're on the scene—"

"If you think I'm going to rat on my mother," began Crowe angrily.

"We seem to be in a rodent cycle," Ellery complained. "Are you worried that your mother may have tried to poison your stepfather, Mac?"

"No! I mean—you know what I mean! What kind of rat —skunk do you think I am?"

"I got you into this, Mac," Laurel said. "I'm sorry. You can back out."

"I'm *not* backing out! Seems to me you two are trying to twist every word I say!"

"Would you have any scruples," asked Ellery with a smile, "where Wallace is concerned?"

"Hell, no. Wallace doesn't mean anything to me. Delia does." Her son added, with a sulky shrewdness, "I thought she did to you, too."

"Well, she does." The truth was, Keats's information about Delia Priam and the rat poison had given him a bad time. "But let's stick to Wallace for the moment. Mac, what do you know about him?"

"Not a thing."

"How long has he been working for your stepfather?"

"About a year. They come and go. Roger's had a dozen stooges in the last fifteen years. Wallace is just the latest."

"Well, you keep your eye on him. And Laurel—"

"On Delia," said Macgowan sarcastically.

"Laurel on everything. Keep giving me reports. Anything out of the ordinary. This case may prove to be a series of excavations, with the truth at the bottom level. Dig in."

"I could go back to the beginning," mumbled Laurel, "and try to trace the dead dog . . ."

"Oh, you don't know about that, do you?" Ellery turned to the writing desk again.

"About the *dog?*"

He turned around with another card. "The dog belonged to somebody named Henderson who lives on Clybourn Avenue in the Toluca Lake district. He's a dwarf who gets occasional work in films. The dog's name was Frank. Frank disappeared on Decoration Day. Henderson reported his disappearance to the Pound Department, but his description was vague and unfortunately Frank had no license—Henderson, it seems, is against bureaucracy and regimentation. When the dog's body was

80

picked up at your house, Laurel, in view of its lack of identification it was disposed of in the usual way. It was only afterward that Henderson identified the collar, which was returned to him.

"Keats has seen the collar, although Henderson refuses to part with it for sentimental reasons. Keats doubts, though, that anything can be learned from it. There's no trace of the little silver box which was attached to the collar. The receipt Henderson signed at the Pound Department mentions it, but Henderson says he threw it away as not belonging to him.

"As for what the dog died of, an attendant at the Pound remembered the animal and he expressed the opinion that Frank had died of poisoning. Asked if it could have been arsenic poisoning, the man said, yes, it could have been arsenic poisoning. In the absence of an analysis of the remains, the opinion is worthless. All we can do is speculate that the dog was fed something with arsenic in it, which is interesting as speculation but meaningless as evidence. And that's the story of the dead dog, Laurel. You can forget it."

"I'll help wherever I can," said Laurel in a subdued voice. "And again, Ellery—I'm sorry."

"No need to be. My fault for not having kept you up to date." Ellery put his arm around her, and she smiled faintly. "Oh, Mac," he said. "There's something personal I want to say to Laurel. Would you mind giving me a couple of minutes with her alone?"

"Seems to me," grumbled the giant, rising, "as a bloodhound you've got a hell of a wolf strain in you, Queen." His jaw protruded. "Lay off my mother, hear me? Or I'll crack your clavicles for soup!"

"Oh, stop gibbering, Mac," said Laurel quickly.

"Laur, do you want to be alone with this character?"

"Wait for me in the car."

Mac almost tore the front door off its hinges.

"Mac is something like a great Dane himself," Laurel murmured, her back to the door. "Huge, honest, and a little dumb. What is it, Ellery?"

"Dumb about what, Laurel?" Ellery eyed her. "About me? That wasn't dumb. I admit I've found Delia Priam very attractive."

"I didn't mean dumb about you." Laurel shook her head. "Never mind, Ellery. What did you want?"

"Dumb about Delia? Laurel, you know something about Mac's mother—"

"If it's Delia you want to question me about, I—I can't answer. May I go now, please?"

"Right away." Ellery put his hand on the doorknob, looking down at her cinnamon hair. "You know, Laurel, Lieutenant Keats has done some work at your house, too."

Her eyes flew to his. "What do you mean?"

"Questioning your housekeeper, the chauffeur, the houseman."

"They didn't say anything about me!"

"You're dealing with a professional, Laurel, and a very good one. They didn't realize they were being pumped." His eyes were grave. "A few weeks ago you lost or mislaid a small silver box, Laurel. A sort of pillbox."

She had gone pale, but her voice was steady. "That's right."

"From the description Mrs. Monk, Simeon, and Ichiro gave—you'd asked them to look for it—the box must have been about the same size and shape as the one you told me contained the warning note to your father. Keats wanted to quiz you about it immediately, but I told him I'd handle it myself. Laurel, was it your silver box that was attached to the collar of Henderson's defunct dog?"

"I don't know."

"Why didn't you mention to me the fact that a box of the same description belonging to you had disappeared shortly before June second?"

"Because I was sure it couldn't have been the same one. The very idea was ridiculous. How could it have been my box? I got it at the May Company, and I think The Broadway and other department stores have been carrying it, too. It's advertised for carrying vitamin tablets and things like that. There must have been thousands of them sold all over Los Angeles. I really bought it to give to Daddy. He had to take certain pills and he could have carried this around in his watch pocket. But I mislaid it—"

"Could it have been your pillbox?"

"I suppose it could, but—"

"And you never found the one you lost?"

She looked at him, worried. "Do you suppose it was?"

"I'm not supposing much of anything yet, Laurel. Just trying to get things orderly. Or just trying to get things." Ellery opened the door and looked out cautiously. "Be sure to tell your muscular admirer that I'm returning you to him *virgo intacto*. I'm sort of sentimental about my clavicles." He smiled and squeezed her fingers.

He watched until they were out of sight around the lower curve of the hill, not smiling at all.

ELLERY WENT DOWN to his cold supper and chewed away. The cottage was cheerlessly silent. His jaws made sounds.

Then there was a different sound.

A tap on the kitchen door?

Ellery stared. "Come in?"

And there she was.

"Delia." He got out of his chair, still holding the knife and fork.

She was in a long loose coat of some dark blue material. It had a turned-up collar which framed her head. She stood with her back against the door, looking about the room.

"I've been waiting in the back garden in the dark. I saw Laurel's car. And after Laurel and . . . Crowe drove away I thought I'd better wait a little longer. I wasn't sure that your housekeeper was gone."

"She's gone."

"That's good." She laughed.

"Where is your car, Delia?"

"I left it in a side lane at the bottom of the hill. Walked up. Ellery, this is a darling kitchen—"

"Discreet," said Ellery. He had not stirred.

"Aren't you going to ask me in?"

He said slowly, "I don't think I'm going to."

Her smile withered. But then it burgeoned again. "Oh, don't sound so serious. I was passing by and I thought I'd drop in and see how you were getting on—"

"With the case."

"Of course." She had dimples. Funny, he had never noticed them before.

"This isn't a good idea, Delia."

"*What* isn't?"

"This is a small town, Delia, and it's all eyes and ears. It doesn't take much in Hollywood to destroy a woman's reputation."

"Oh, that." She was silent. Then she showed her teeth. "Of course, you're right. It was stupid of me. It's just that sometimes . . ." She stopped, and she shivered suddenly.

"Sometimes what, Delia?"

"Nothing. I'm going.—Is there anything new?"

"Just that business about the rat poison."

She shrugged. "I really thought there were mice."

"Of course."

"Good night, Ellery."

"Good night, Delia."

He did not offer to walk her down the hill and she did not seem to expect it.

He stared at the kitchen door for a long time.

Then he went upstairs and poured himself a stiff drink.

AT THREE IN the morning Ellery gave up trying to sleep and crawled out of bed. He turned on the lights in the living room, loaded and fired his brier, turned the lights out, and sat down to watch Hollywood glimmer scantily below. Light always disturbed him when he was groping in the dark.

And he was groping, and this was darkness.

Of course, it was a puzzling case. But puzzle was merely the absence of answer. Answer it, and the puzzle vanished. Nor was he bothered by the nimbus of fantasy which surrounded the case like a Los Angeles daybreak fog. All crimes were fantastic insofar as they expressed what most people merely dreamed about. The dream of the unknown enemy had been twenty years or more in the making . . .

He clucked to himself in the darkness. Back to the writer of the note.

The wonder was not that he made gifts of poisoned dogs and wrote odd notes relishing slow death and promising mysterious warnings with special meanings. The wonder was that he had been able to keep his hatred alive for almost a generation; and that was not fantasy, but sober pathology.

Fantasy was variance from normal experience, a matter of degree. Hollywood had always attracted its disproportionate quota of variants from the norm. In Vandalia, Illinois, Roger Priam would have been encysted in the community like a foreign substance, but in the Southern California canyons he was peculiarly soluble. There might be Delia Priams in Seattle, but in the houri paradise of Hollywood she belonged, the female archetype from whom all desire sprang. And Tree Boy, who in New York would have been dragged off to the observation ward of Bellevue Hospital, was here just another object of civic admiration, rating columns of good-natured newspaper space.

No, it wasn't the fantasy.

It was the hellish scarcity of facts.

Here was an enemy out of the past. What past? No data. The enemy was preparing a series of warnings. What were they? A dead dog had been the first. Then the unknown contents of a small cardboard box. Then a deliberately nonlethal dose of arsenic. The further warnings, the warnings that were promised, had not yet come forth. How many would there be? They were warnings of "special meaning." A series, then. A pattern. But what connection could exist between a dead dog and an arsenic-salted tunafish salad? It would help, help greatly, to know what had been in that box Roger Priam had received at the same moment that Leander Hill was stooping over the body of the dog and reading the thin, multi-creased note. Yes, greatly. But . . . no data. It was probable that, whatever it was, Priam had destroyed it. But Priam knew. How could the man be made to talk? He must be made to talk.

The darkness was darker than even that. Ellery mused, worrying his pipe. There was a pattern, all right, but how could he be sure it was the only pattern? Suppose the dead hound had been the first warning of special meaning in a proposed series to Hill, the other warnings of which were forever lost in the limbo of an unknown mind because of Hill's premature death? And suppose whatever was in Priam's box was the first warning of a *second* series, of which the second warning was the poisoning—a series having no significant relation to the one aborted by Hill's heart attack? It was possible. It was quite possible that there was no connection in *meaning* between Hill's and Priam's warnings.

The safest course for the time being was to ignore the dead dog received by Hill and to concentrate on the living Priam, proceeding on the assumption that the unknown contents of Priam's box and the poisoning of his salad constituted a separate series altogether. . . .

Ellery went back to bed. His last thought was that he must find out at any cost what had been in that box, and that he could only wait for the third warning to Priam.

But he dreamed of Delia Priam in a jungle thicket, showing her teeth.

Seven

AS ELLERY WAS able to put it together when he arrived at Delia Priam's summons that fabulous Sunday morning—from the stories of Delia, Alfred Wallace, and old Mr. Collier—Delia had risen early to go to church. Beyond remarking that her church attendance was "spotty," she was reticent about this; Ellery gathered that she could not go as regularly as she would like because of the peculiar conditions of her life, and that only occasionally was she able to slip away and into one of the old churches where, to "the blessed mutter of the mass," she returned to her childhood and her blood. This had been such a morning, five days after the poisoning attack on her husband, two after her strange visit to Ellery's cottage.

While Delia had been up and about at an early hour, Alfred Wallace had risen late. He was normally an early riser, because Priam was a demanding charge and Wallace had learned that if he was to enjoy the luxury of breakfast he must get it over with before Priam awakened. On Sundays, however, Priam preferred to lie in bed until midmorning, undisturbed, and this permitted Wallace to sleep until nine o'clock.

Delia's father was invariably up with the birds. On this morning he had breakfasted with his daughter, and when she drove off to Los Angeles Mr. Collier went out for his early morning tramp through the woods. On his way back he had stopped before the big oak and tried to rouse his grandson, but as there was no answer from the tree house beyond Crowe's Brobdingnagian snores the old man had returned to the Priam house and gone into the library. The library was downstairs off the main hall, directly opposite the door to Roger Priam's quarters, with the staircase between. This was shortly after eight, Mr. Collier told Ellery; his son-in-law's door was shut and there was no light visible under the door; all seemed as it always was at that hour of a Sunday morning; and the old man had got his postage stamp albums out of a drawer of the library desk, his stamp hinges, his tongs, and his Scott's catalogue, and he had set to work mounting his latest mail purchases of stamps. "I've done a lot of knocking about the world," he told Ellery, "and it's corking fun to collect stamps from places I've actually been in. Want to see my collection?" Ellery had declined; he was rather busy at the time.

At a few minutes past nine Alfred Wallace came downstairs. He exchanged greetings with Delia's father—the library door stood open—and went in to his breakfast without approaching Priam's door.

Mrs. Guittierez served him, and Wallace read the Sunday papers, which were always delivered to the door, as he ate. It was the maid's and chauffeur's Sunday off and the house was unusually quiet. In the kitchen the cook was getting things ready for Roger Priam's breakfast.

Shortly before ten o'clock Alfred Wallace painstakingly restored the Sunday papers to their original state, pushed back his chair, and went out into the hall carrying the papers. Priam liked to have the newspapers within arm's reach when he awakened Sunday mornings, and he flew into a rage if they were crumpled or disarranged.

Seeing a line of light beneath Priam's door, Wallace quickened his step.

He went in without knocking.

The first *he* knew anything out of the ordinary had occurred, said Mr. Collier, he heard Wallace's cry from Roger Priam's room: "Mr. Collier! Mr. Collier! Come here!" The old man jumped up from his stamp albums and ran across the hall. Wallace was rattling the telephone, trying to get the operator. Just as he was shouting to Collier, "See about Mr. Priam! See if he's all right!" the operator responded, and Wallace—who seemed in a panic—babbled something about the police and Lieutenant Keats. Collier picked his way across the room to his son-in-law's wheelchair, which was still made up as a bed. Priam, in his night clothes, was up on one elbow, glaring about with a sort of vitreous horror. His mouth was open and his beard was in motion, but no sound passed them. As far as the old man could see, there was nothing wrong with Priam but stupefying fright. Collier eased the paralyzed man backward until he was supine, trying to

87

soothe him; but Priam lay rigid, as if in a coma, his eyes tightly shut to keep out what he had seen, and the old man could get no response from him.

At this moment, Delia Priam returned from church.

Wallace turned from the phone and Collier from Priam at a choked sound from the doorway. Delia was staring into the room with eyes sick with disbelief. She was paler than her husband and she seemed about to faint.

"All this . . . all these . . ."

She began to titter.

Wallace said roughly, "Get her out of here."

"He's dead. He's dead!"

Collier hurried to her. "No, no, daughter. Just scared. Now you go upstairs. We'll take care of Roger."

"He's not dead? Then why—? How do these—?"

"Delia." The old man stroked her hand.

"Don't touch anything. Anything!"

"No, no, daughter—"

"Nothing must be touched. It's got to be left exactly as you found it. *Exactly*." And Delia stumbled up the hall to the household telephone and called Ellery.

WHEN ELLERY PULLED up before the Priam house a radio patrol car was already parked in the driveway. A young officer was in the car, making a report to head-quarters by radio, his mouth going like a faucet. His mate was apparently in the house.

"Here, you." He jumped out of the car. "Where you going?" His face was red.

"I'm a friend of the family, Officer. Mrs. Priam just telephoned me." Ellery looked rather wild himself. Delia had been hysterical over the phone and the only word he had been able to make out, "fogs," had conveyed nothing reasonable. "What's happened?"

"I wouldn't repeat it," said the patrolman excitedly. "I wouldn't lower myself. They think I'm drunk. What do you think I am? Sunday morning! I've seen a lot of crosseyed things in this town, but—"

"Here, get hold of yourself, Officer. Has Lieutenant Keats been notified, do you know?"

"They caught him at home. He's on his way here now."

Ellery bounded up the steps. As he ran into the hall he saw Delia. She was dressed for town, in black and modest dress, hat, and gloves, and she was leaning against

a wall bloodlessly. Alfred Wallace, disheveled and unnerved, was holding one of her gloved hands in both
of his, whispering to her. The tableau dissolved in an
instant; Delia spied Ellery, said something quickly to Wallace, withdrawing her hand, and she ran forward. Wallace
turned, rather startled. He followed her with a hasty
shuffle, almost as if he were afraid of being left alone.

"Ellery."

"Is Mr. Priam all right?"

"He's had a bad shock."

"Can't say I blame him," Wallace mumbled. The handsome man passed a trembling handkerchief over his
cheeks. "The doctor's on his way over. We can't seem
to snap Mr. Priam out of it."

"What's this about 'fogs,' Delia?" Ellery hurried up
the hall, Delia clinging to his arm. Wallace remained
where he was, still wiping his face.

"Fogs? I didn't say fogs. I said—"

Ellery stopped in the doorway.

The other radio car patrolman was straddling a chair,
cap pushed back on his head, looking about helplessly.

Roger Priam lay stiffly on his bed staring at the ceiling.

And all over Priam's body, on his blanket, on his sheet,
in the shelves and compartments of his wheelchair, on
his typewriter, strewn about the floor, the furniture, Wallace's emergency bed, the window sills, the cornices, the
fireplace, the mantelpiece—everywhere—were frogs.

Frogs and toads.

Hundreds of frogs and toads.

Tiny tree toads.

Yellow-legged frogs.

Bullfrogs.

Each little head was twisted.

The room was littered with their corpses.

ELLERY HAD TO confess to himself that he was
thrown. There was a nonsense quality of the frogs that
crossed over the line of laughter into the darker regions
of the mind. Beyond the black bull calf of the Nile with
the figure of an eagle on his back and the beetle upon
his tongue stood Apis, a god; beyond absurdity loomed
fear. Fear was the timeless tyrant. At mid-twentieth
century it took the shape of a gigantic mushroom. Why
not frogs? With frogs the terrible Wrath of the Hebrews

had plagued the Egyptian, with frogs and blood and wild beasts and darkness and the slaying of the first-born ... He could hardly blame Roger Priam for lying frozen. Priam knew something of the way of gods; he was by way of being a minor one himself.

While Keats and the patrolmen tramped about the house, Ellery drifted around the Priam living room trying to get a bearing. The whole thing irritated and enchanted him. It made no sense. It related to nothing. There lay its power over the uninitiated; that was its appearance for the mob. But Priam was of the inner temple. He knew something the others did not. He knew the sense this nonsense made. He knew the nature of the mystery to which it related. He knew the nature of this primitive god and he grasped the meaning of the god's symbolism. Knowledge is not always power; certainty does not always bring peace. This knowledge was paralyzing and this certainty brought terror.

Keats found him nibbling his thumb under the Spanish grandee.

"Well, the doctor's gone and the frogs are all collected and maybe you and I had better have a conference about this."

"Sure."

"This is what you'd call Priam's third warning, isn't it?"

"Yes, Keats."

"Me," said the detective, seating himself heavily on a heavy chair, "I'd call it broccoli."

"Don't make that mistake."

Keats looked at him in a resentful way. "I don't go for this stuff, Mr. Queen. I don't believe it even when I see it. Why does he go to all this trouble?" His tone said he would have appreciated a nice, uncomplicated bullet.

"How is Priam?"

"He'll live. The problem was this doctor, Voluta. It seems we took him away from a party—a blonde party—at Malibu. He took the frogs as a personal insult. Treated Priam for shock, put him to sleep, and dove for his car."

"Have you talked to Priam?"

"I talked to Priam, yes. But he didn't talk to me."

"Nothing?"

"He just said he woke up, reached for that push-button-on-a-cord arrangement he's got for turning on the lights, saw the little beasties, and knew no more."

"No attempt at explanation?"

"You don't think he knows the answer to *this* one!"

"The strong man type represented by our friend Priam, Lieutenant," said Ellery, "doesn't pass out at the sight of a few hundred frogs, even when they're strewn all over his bed. His reaction was *too* violent. Of course he knows the answer. And it scares the wadding out of him."

Keats shook his head. "What do we do now?"

"What did you find out?"

"Not a thing."

"No sign of a point of entry?"

"No. But what sign would there be? You come from the suspicious East, Mr. Queen. This is the great West, where men are men and nobody locks his door but Easterners." Keats rolled a tattered cigaret to the other side of his mouth. "Not even," he said bitterly, "taxpayers who are on somebody's knock-off list." He jumped up with a frustrated energy. "The trouble is, this Priam won't face the facts. Poison him, and he looks thoughtful. Toss a couple hundred dead frogs around his bedroom and he shakes his head doubtfully. You know what I think? I think everybody in this house, present company excepted, is squirrel food."

But Ellery was walking a tight circle, squinting toward some hidden horizon. "All right, he got in without any trouble—simply by walking in. Presumably in the middle of the night. Priam's door isn't locked at night so that Wallace or the others can get at him in an emergency, consequently he enters Priam's room with equal facility. So there he is, with a bag or a suitcase full of murdered frogs. Priam is asleep—not dead, mind you, just asleep. But he might just as well have been dead, because his visitor distributed two or three hundred frogs about the premises—in the dark, mind you—without disturbing Priam in the least. Any answers, Lieutenant?"

"Yes," said Keats wearily. "Priam polished off a bottle last night. He *was* dead—dead to the world."

Ellery shrugged and resumed his pacing. "Which takes us back to the frogs. A cardboard box containing . . . we don't know what; that's warning number one. Food poisoning . . . that's warning number two. Warning number three . . . a zoo colony of dead frogs. One, unknown;

91

two, poisoned food; three, strangled frogs. It certainly would help to know number one."

"Suppose it was a fried coconut," suggested Keats. "Would it help?"

"There's a connection, Lieutenant. A pattern."

"I'm listening."

"You don't just pick frogs out of your hat. Frogs *mean* something."

"Yeah," said Keats, "warts." But his laugh was unconvincing. "Okay, so they mean something. So this *all* means something. I don't give a damn what it means. I said, what kind of maniac is this Priam? Does he *want* to shove off? Without putting up a battle?"

"He's putting up a battle, Lieutenant," frowned Ellery. "In his peculiar way, a brave one. To ask for help, even to accept help without asking for it, would be defeat for Priam. Don't you understand that? He has to be top man. He has to control his own destiny. He *has* to, or his life has no meaning. Remember, Keats, he's a man who's living his life away in a chair. You say he's asleep now?"

"With Wallace guarding him. I offered a cop, and I nearly got beaned with the *Examiner*. It was all I could do to make Priam promise he'd keep his doors locked from now on. At that, he didn't promise."

"How about that background stuff? On the partners?"

The detective crushed the stained butt in his fist and flipped it in the fireplace. "It's like pulling teeth," he said slowly. "I don't get it. I put two more men on it yesterday." He snapped a fresh cigaret into his mouth. "The way I see it, Mr. Queen, we're doing this like a couple of country constables. We've got to go right to the horse's mouth. Priam's got to talk. He knows the whole story, every answer. Who his enemy is. Why the guy's nursed a grudge for so many years. Why the fancy stuff—"

"And what was in the box," murmured Ellery.

"Correct. I promised Dr. Voluta I'd lay off Priam today." Keats clapped his hat on his head. "But tomorrow I think I'm going to get tough."

WHEN THE DETECTIVE had left, Ellery wandered out into the hall. The house was moody with silence. Crowe Macgowan had gone loping over to the Hill house to tell Laurel all about the amphibian invasion. The door to Priam's quarters was shut.

92

There was no sign or sound of Delia. She was going to her room to lock herself in, she had said, and lie down. She had seemed to have no further interest in her husband's condition. She had looked quite ill.

Ellery turned disconsolately to go, but then—or perhaps he was looking for an excuse to linger—he remembered the library, and he went back up the hall to the doorway opposite Priam's.

Delia's father sat at the library desk intently examining a postage stamp for its watermark.

"Oh, Mr. Collier."

The old man looked up. Immediately he rose, smiling. "Come in, come in, Mr. Queen. Everything all right now?"

"Well," said Ellery, "the frogs are no longer with us."

Collier shook his head. "Man's inhumanity to everything. You'd think we'd restrict our murderous impulses to our own kind. But no, somebody had to take his misery out on some harmless little specimens of *Hyla regilla,* not to mention—"

"Of what?" asked Ellery.

"*Hyla regilla.* Tree toads, Mr. Queen, or tree frogs. That's what most of those little fellows were." He brightened. "Well, let's not talk about that any more. Although why a grown man like Roger Priam should be afraid of them—with their necks wrung, too!—I simply don't understand."

"Mr. Collier," said Ellery quietly, "have you any idea what this is all about?"

"Oh, yes," said the old man. "I'll tell you what this is all about, Mr. Queen." He waved his stamp tongs earnestly. "It's about corruption and wickedness. It's about greed and selfishness and guilt and violence and hatred and lack of self-control. It's about black secrets and black hearts, cruelty, confusion, fear. It's about not making the best of things, not being satisfied with what you have, and always wanting what you haven't. It's about envy and suspicion and malice and lust and nosiness and drunkenness and unholy excitement and a thirst for hot running blood. It's about man, Mr. Queen."

"Thank you," said Ellery humbly, and he went home.

AND THE NEXT morning Lieutenant Keats of the Hollywood Division put on his tough suit and went at Roger Priam as if the fate of the city of Los Angeles hung on Priam's answers. And nothing happened except that Keats lost his temper and used some expressions not recommended in the police manual and had to retreat under a counterattack of even harder words, not to mention objects, which flew at him and Ellery like mortar fire. Priam quite stripped his wheelchair of its accessories in his furious search for ammunition.

Overnight the bearded man had bounced back. Perhaps not all the way: his eyes looked shaft-sunken and he had a case of the trembles. But the old fires were in the depths and the shaking affected only his aim, not his strength—he made a bloodless shambles of his quarters.

Keats had tried everything in ascending order—reason, cajolery, jokes, appeals to personal pride and social responsibility, derision, sarcasm, threats, curses, and finally sheer volume of sound. Nothing moved Priam but the threats and curses, and then he responded in kind. Even the detective, who was left livid with fury, had to admit that he had been out-threatened, out-cursed, and out-shouted.

Through it all Alfred Wallace stood impeccably by his employer's wheelchair, a slight smile on his lips. Mr. Wallace, too, had ricocheted. It occurred to Ellery that in Wallace's make-up there was a great deal of old Collier's *Hyla regilla*—a chameleon quality, changing color to suit his immediate background. Yesterday Priam had been unnerved, Wallace had been unnerved. Today Priam was strong, Wallace was strong. It was a minor puzzle, but it annoyed him.

Then Ellery saw that he might be wrong and that the phenomenon might have a different explanation altogether. As he crossed the threshold to the echo of Priam's last blast, with Wallace already shutting the door, Ellery glimpsed for one second a grotesquely different Priam. No belligerent now. No man of wrath. His beard had fallen to his chest. He was holding on to the arms of his wheelchair as if for the reassurance of contact with reality. And his eyes were tightly closed. Ellery saw his lips moving; and if the thought had not been blasphemous, Ellery would have said Priam was praying. Then Wallace slammed the door.

"That was all right, Keats." Ellery was staring at the door. "That got somewhere."

"Where?" snarled the detective. "You heard him. He wouldn't say what was in the cardboard box, he wouldn't say who's after him, he wouldn't say why—he wouldn't say anything but that he'll handle this thing himself and let the blanking so-and-so come get him if he's man enough. So where did we get, Mr. Queen?"

"Closer to the crackup."

"What crackup?"

"Priam's. Keats, all that was the bellowing of a frightened steer in the dark. He's even more demoralized than I thought. He played a big scene just now for our benefit—a very good one, considering the turmoil he's in.

"Maybe one more, Keats," murmured Ellery. "One more."

Eight

LAUREL SAID THE frogs were very important. The enemy had slipped. So many hundreds of the warty beasts must have left a trail. All they had to do was pick it up.

"What trail? Pick it up where?" demanded Macgowan.

"Mac, where would you go if you wanted some frogs?"

"I wouldn't want some frogs."

"To a pet shop, of course!"

The giant looked genuinely admiring. "Why can't I think of things like that?" he complained. "To a pet shop let us go."

But as the day wore on young Macgowan lost his air of levity. He began to look stubborn. And when even Laurel was ready to give up, Macgowan jeered, "Chicken!" and drove on to the next shop on their list. As there are a great many pet emporia in Greater Los Angeles, and as Greater Los Angeles includes one hundred towns and thirty-six incorporated cities, from Burbank north to Long Beach south and Santa Monica west to Monrovia east, it became apparent by the end of an endless day that the detective team of Hill and Macgowan had assigned themselves an investigation worthy of their high purpose, if not their talents.

"At this rate we'll be at it till Christmas," said Laurel in despair as they munched De Luxe Steerburgers at a drive-in in Beverly Hills.

"You can give up," growled Crowe, reaching for his Double-Dip Giant Malted. "Me, I'm not letting a couple of hundred frogs throw me. I'll go it alone tomorrow."

"I'm not giving up," snapped Laurel. "I was only going to say that we've gone at this like the couple of amateurs we are. Let's divide the list and split up tomorrow. That way we'll cover twice the territory in the same time."

"Functional idea," grunted the giant. "Now how about getting something to eat? I know a good steak joint not far from here where the wine is on the house."

Early next morning they parceled the remaining territory and set out in separate cars, having arranged to meet at 6:30 in the parking lot next to Grauman's Chinese. At 6:30 they met and compared notes while Hollywood honked its homeward way in every direction.

Macgowan's notes were dismal. "Not a damn lead, and I've still got a list as long as your face. How about you?"

"One bite," said Laurel gloomily. "I played a hunch and went over to a place in Encino. They even carry zoo animals. A man in Tarzana had ordered frogs. I tore over there and it turned out to be some movie star who'd bought two dozen—he called them 'jug-o'-rums'—for his rock pool. All I got out of it was an autograph, which I didn't ask for, and a date, which I turned down."

"What's his name?" snarled Crowe.

"Oh, come off it and let's go over to Ellery's. As long as we're in the neighborhood."

"What for?"

"Maybe he'll have a suggestion."

"Let's see what the Master has to say, hey?" hissed her assistant. "Well, I won't wash his feet!"

He leaned on his horn all the way to the foot of the hill.

When Laurel got out of her Austin, Crowe was already bashing Ellery's door.

"Open up, Queen! What do you lock yourself in for?"

"Mac?" came Ellery's voice.

"And Laurel," sang out Laurel.

"Just a minute."

When he unlocked the front door Ellery looked rumpled and heavy-eyed. "Been taking a nap, and Mrs. Williams must have gone. Come in. You two look like the shank end of a hard day."

"Brother," scowled Macgowan. "Is there a tall, cool drink in this oasis?"

"May I use your bathroom, Ellery?" Laurel started for the bedroom door, which was closed.

"I'm afraid it's in something of a mess, Laurel. Use the downstairs lavatory . . . Right over there, Mac. Help yourself."

When Laurel came back upstairs her helper was showing Ellery their lists. "We can't seem to get anywhere,"

Crowe was grumbling. "Two days and nothing to show for them."

"You've certainly covered a lot of territory," applauded Ellery. "There are the fixings, Laurel—"

"Oh, *yes*."

"You'd think it would be easy," the giant went on, waving his glass. "How many people buy frogs? Practically nobody. Hardly one of the pet shops even handles 'em. Canaries, yes. Finches, definitely. Parakeets, by the carload. Parakeets, macaws, dogs, cats, tropical fish, monkeys, turkeys, turtles, even snakes. And I know now where you can buy an elephant, cheap. But no frogs to speak of. And toads—they just look at you as if you were balmy."

"Where did we go wrong?" asked Laurel, perching on the arm of Crowe's chair.

"In not analyzing the problem before you dashed off. You're not dealing with an idiot. Yes, you could get frogs through the ordinary channels, but they'd be special orders, and special orders leave a trail. Our friend is not leaving any trails for your convenience. Did either of you think to call the State Fish and Game Commission?"

They stared.

"If you had," said Ellery with a smile, "you'd have learned that most of the little fellows we found in Priam's room are a small tree frog or tree toad—*Hyla regilla* is the scientific name—commonly called spring peepers, which are found in great numbers in this part of the country in streams and trees, especially in the foothills. You can even find bullfrogs here, though they're not native to this part of the country—they've all been introduced from the East. So if you wanted a lot of frogs and toads, and you didn't want to leave a trail, you'd go out hunting for them."

"Two whole days," groaned Macgowan. He gulped what was left in his glass.

"It's my fault, Mac," said Laurel miserably. But then she perked up. "Well, it's all experience. Next time we'll know better."

"Next time he won't use frogs!"

"Mac." Ellery was tapping his teeth with the bit of his pipe. "I've been thinking about your grandfather."

"Is that good?" Mac immediately looked bellicose.

"Interesting man."

"You said it. And a swell egg. Keeps pretty much to

98

himself, but that's because he doesn't want to get in anybody's way."

"How long has he been living with you people?"

"A few years. He knocked around all his life and when he got too old for it he came back to live with Delia. Why this interest in my grandfather?"

"Is he very much attached to your mother?"

"Well, I'll put it this way," said Crowe, squinting through his empty glass. "If Delia was God, Gramp would go to church. He's gone on her and she's the only reason he stays in Roger's vicinity. And I'm not gone on these questions," said Crowe, looking at Ellery, "so let's talk about somebody else, shall we?"

"Don't you like your grandfather, Mac?"

"I love him! Will you change the subject?"

"He collects stamps," Ellery went on reflectively. "And he's just taken to hunting and mounting butterflies. A man of Mr. Collier's age, who has no business or profession and takes up hobbies, Mac, usually doesn't stop at one or two. What other interests has he?"

Crowe set his glass down with a smack. "Damned if I'm going to say another word about him. Laurel, you coming?"

"Why the heat, Mac?" asked Ellery mildly.

"Why the questions about Gramp?"

"Because all I do is sit here and think, and my thoughts have been covering a lot of territory. Mac, I'm feeling around."

"Feel in some other direction!"

"No," said Ellery, "you feel in all directions. That's the first lesson you learn in this business. Your grandfather knew the scientific name of those spring peepers. It suggests that he may have gone into the subject. So I'd like to know: In those long tramps he takes in the foothill woods, has he been collecting tree frogs?"

Macgowan had gone rather pale and his handsome face looked pained and baffled. "I don't know."

"He has a rabbit hutch somewhere near the house, Mac," said Laurel in a low voice. "We could look."

"We could, but we're not going to! *I'm* not going to! What do you think I am?" His fists were whistling over their heads. "Anyway, suppose he did? It's a free country, and you said yourself there's lots of these peepers around!"

"True, true," Ellery soothed him. "Have another drink.

99

I've fallen in love with the old gent myself. Oh, by the way, Laurel."

"Do I brace myself?" murmured Laurel.

"Well," grinned Ellery. "I'll admit my thoughts have sauntered in your direction too, Laurel. The first day you came to me you said you were Leander Hill's daughter by adoption."

"Yes."

"And you said something about not remembering your mother. Don't you know anything at all about your real parents, where you came from?"

"No."

"I'm sorry if this distresses you—"

"You know what you are?" yelled Macgowan from the sideboard. "You're equally divided between a bottom and a nose!"

"It doesn't distress me, Ellery," said Laurel with a rather unsuccessful smile. "I don't know a thing about where I came from. I was one of those storybook babies—really left on a doorstep. Of course, Daddy had no right to keep me—a bachelor and all. But he hired a reliable woman and kept me for about a year before he even reported me. Then he had a lot of trouble. They took me away from him and there was a long court squabble. But in the end they couldn't find out a thing about me, nobody claimed me, and he won out in court and was allowed to make it a legal adoption. I don't remember any of that, of course. He tried for years afterwards to trace my parents, because he was always afraid somebody would pop up and want me back and he wanted to settle the matter once and for all. But," Laurel made a face, "he never got anywhere and nobody ever did pop up."

Ellery nodded. "The reason I asked, Laurel, was that it occurred to me that this whole business . . . the circumstances surrounding your foster father's death, the threats to Roger Priam . . . may somehow tie in with your past."

Laurel stared.

"Now there," said Macgowan, "there is a triumph of the detective science. How would that be, Chief? Elucidate."

"I toss it into the pot for what it's worth," shrugged Ellery, "admitting as I toss that it's probably worth little or nothing. But Laurel," he said, "whether that's a cockeyed theory or not, your past may enter this problem. In another way. I've been a little bothered by *you* in this thing. Your drive to get to the bottom of this, your wanting revenge—"

"What's wrong with that?" Laurel sounded sharp.

"What's wrong with it is that it doesn't seem altogether normal. No, wait, Laurel. The drive is overintense, the wish for revenge almost neurotic. I don't get the feeling that it's like you—like the you I think you are."

"I never lost my father before."

"Of course, but—"

"You don't know me." Laurel laughed.

"No, I don't." Ellery tamped his pipe absently. "But one possible explanation is that the underlying motivation of your drive is not revenge on a murderer at all, but the desire to find yourself. It could be that you're nursing a subconscious hope that finding this killer will somehow clear up the mystery of your own background."

"I never thought of that." Laurel cupped her chin and was silent for some time. Then she shook her head. "No, I don't think so. I'd like to find out who I am, where I came from, what kind of people and all that, but it wouldn't mean very much to me. They'd be strangers and the background would be . . . not home. No, I loved him as if he were my father. He *was* my father. And I want to see the one who drove him into that fatal heart attack get paid back for it."

WHEN THEY HAD gone, Ellery opened his bedroom door and said, "All right, Delia."

"I thought they'd never go."

"I'm afraid it was my fault. I kept them."

"You wanted to punish me for hiding."

"Maybe." He waited.

"I like it here," she said slowly, looking around at the pedestrian blond furniture.

She was seated on his bed, hands gripping the spread. She had not taken her hat off, or her gloves.

She must have sat that way all during the time they were in the other room, Ellery thought. Hanging in midair. Like her probable excuse for leaving the Priam house. A visit somewhere in town. Among the people who wore hats and gloves.

"Why do you feel you have to hide, Delia?"

"It's not so messy that way. No explanations to give. No lies to make up. No scenes. I hate scenes." She

101

seemed much more interested in the house than in him. "A man who lives alone. I can hardly imagine it."

"Why did you come again?"

"I don't know. I just wanted to." She laughed. "You don't sound any more hospitable this time than you did the last. I'm not very quick, but I'm beginning to think you don't like me."

He said brutally, "When did you get the idea that I did?"

"Oh, the first couple of times we met."

"That was barnyard stuff, Delia. You make every man feel like a rooster."

"And what's your attitude now?" She laughed again. "That you don't feel like a rooster any more?"

"I'll be glad to answer that question, Delia, in the living room."

Her head came up sharply.

"You don't have to answer any questions," she said. She got up and strolled past him. "In your living room or anywhere else." As he shut the bedroom door and turned to her, she said, "You really don't like me?" almost wistfully.

"I like you very much, Delia. That's why you mustn't come here."

"But you just said in there—"

"That was in there."

She nodded, but not as if she really understood. She went to his desk, ignoring the mirror above it, and picked up one of his pipes. She stroked it with her forefinger. He concentrated on her hands, the skin glowing under the sheer nylon gloves.

He made an effort. "Delia—"

"Aren't you ever lonely?" she murmured. "I think I die a little every day, just from loneliness. Nobody who talks to you really *talks*. It's just words. People listening to themselves. Women hate me, and men . . . At least when they talk to me!" She wheeled, crying, "Am I that stupid? You won't talk to me, either! Am I?"

He had to make the effort over again. It was even harder this time. But he said through his teeth, "Delia, I want you to go home."

"Why?"

"Just because you're lonely, and have a husband who's half-dead—in the wrong half—and because I'm not a skunk, Delia, and you're not a tramp. Those are the reasons,

102

Delia, and if you stay here much longer I'm afraid I'll forget all four of them."

She hit him with the heel of her hand. The top of his head flew off and he felt his shoulderblades smack against the wall.

Through a momentary mist he saw her in the doorway.

"I'm sorry," she said in an agonized way. "You're a fool, but I'm sorry. I mean about coming here. I won't do it again."

Ellery watched her go down the hill. There was fog, and she disappeared in it.

That night he finished most of a bottle of Scotch, sitting at the picture window in the dark and fingering his jaw. The fog had come higher and there was nothing to see but a chaos. Nothing made sense.

But he felt purged, and safe, and wryly noble.

Nine

JUNE TWENTY-NINTH WAS a Los Angeles special.
The weather man reported a reading of ninety-one and
the newspapers bragged that the city was having its warm-
est June twenty-ninth in forty-three years.

But Ellery, trudging down Hollywood Boulevard in a
wool jacket, was hardly aware of the roasting desert
heat. He was a man in a dream these days, a dream entirely filled with the pieces of the Hill-Priam problem.
So far it was a meaningless dream in which he mentally
chased cubist things about a crazy landscape. In that
dimension temperature did not exist except on the ther-
mometer of frustration.

Keats had phoned to say that he was ready with the
results of his investigation into the past of Hill and Priam.
Well, it was about time.

Ellery turned south into Wilcox, passing the post office.

You could drift about in your head for just so long
recognizing nothing. There came a point at which you
had to find a compass and a legible map or go mad.

This ought to be it.

HE FOUND KEATS tormenting a cigaret, the knot of
his tie on his sternum and his sandy hair bristling.

"I thought you'd never get here."

"I walked down." Ellery took a chair, settling himself.
"Well, let's have it."

"Where do you want it," asked the detective, "between
the eyes?"

"What do you mean?" Ellery straightened.

"I mean," said Keats, plucking shreds of tobacco from
his lips—"damn it, they pack cigarets looser all the time!
—I mean we haven't got a crumb."

"A crumb of what?"

"Of information."

"You haven't found out *anything?*" Ellery was incredulous.

"Nothing before 1927, which is the year Hill and Priam went into business in Los Angeles. There's nothing that indicates they lived here before that year; in fact, there's reason to believe they didn't, that they came here that year from somewhere else. But from where? No data. We've tried everything from tax records to the Central Bureau fingerprint files. I'm pretty well convinced they had no criminal record, but that's only a guess. They certainly had no record in the State of California.

"They came here in '27," said Keats bitterly, "started a wholesale jewelry business as partners, and made a fortune before the crash of '29. They weren't committed to the market and they rode out the depression by smart manipulation and original merchandising methods. Today the firm of Hill & Priam is rated one of the big outfits in its line. They're said to own one of the largest stocks of precious stones in the United States. And that's a lot of help, isn't it?"

"But you don't come into the wholesale jewelry business from outer space," protested Ellery. "Isn't there a record somewhere of previous connections in the industry? At least of one of them?"

"The N.J.A. records don't show anything before 1927."

"Well, have you tried this? Certainly Hill, at least, had to go abroad once in a while in connection with the firm's foreign offices—Laurel told me they have branches in Amsterdam and South Africa. That means a passport, a birth certificate—"

"That was my ace in the hole." Keats snapped a fresh cigaret to his lips. "But it turns out that Hill & Priam don't own those branches, although they do own the one in New York. They're simply working arrangements with established firms abroad. They have large investments in those firms, but all their business dealings have been, and still are, negotiated by and through agents. There's no evidence that either Hill or Priam stepped off American soil in twenty-three years, or at least during the twenty-three years we have a record of them." He shrugged. "They opened the New York branch early in 1929, and for a few years Priam took care of it personally. But it was only to get it going and train a staff. He left it in charge of a man who's still running it there, and came back here. Then Priam met and married Delia Collier

Macgowan, and the next thing that happened to him was the paralysis. Hill did the transcontinental hopping for the firm after that."

"Priam's never had occasion to produce a birth certificate?"

"No, and in his condition there's no likelihood he ever will. He's never voted, for instance, and while he might be challenged to prove his American citizenship—to force him to loosen up about his place of birth and so on—I'm afraid that would take a long, long time. Too long for this merry-go-round."

"The war—"

"Both Priam and Hill were over the military age limit when World War II conscription began. They never had to register. Search of the records on World War I failed to turn up their names."

"You're beginning to irritate me, Lieutenant. Didn't Leander Hill carry any insurance?"

"None that antedated 1927, and in the photostats connected with what insurance he did take out after that date his place of birth appears as Chicago. I've had the Illinois records checked, and there's none of a Leander Hill; it was a phony. Priam carries no insurance at all. The industrial insurance carried by the firm, of course, is no help.

"In other words, Mr. Queen," said Lieutenant Keats, "there's every indication that both men deliberately avoided leaving, or camouflaged, the trail to their lives preceding their appearance in L.A. It all adds up to one thing—"

"That there was no Leander Hill or Roger Priam in existence before 1927," muttered Ellery. "Hill and Priam weren't their real names."

"That's it."

Ellery got up and went to the window. Through the glass, darkly, he saw the old landscape again.

"Lieutenant." He turned suddenly. "Did you check Roger Priam's paralysis?"

Keats smiled. "Got quite a file on that if you want to read a lot of medical mumbo jumbo. The sources are some of the biggest specialists in the United States. But if you want it in plain American shorthand, his condition is on the level and it's hopeless. By the way, they were never able to get anything out of Priam about his previous medical history, if that's what you had in mind."

106

"You're disgustingly thorough, Keats. I wish I could find the heart to congratulate you. Now tell me you couldn't find anything on Alfred Wallace and I'll crown you."

Keats picked up an inkstand and offered it to Ellery. "Start crowning."

"Nothing on Wallace *either?*"

"That's right." Keats spat little dry sprigs of tobacco. "All I could dig up about Mr. Alfred W. dates from the day Priam hired him, just over a year ago."

"Why, that can't be!" exploded Ellery. "Not three in the same case."

"He's not an Angeleno, I'm pretty well convinced of that. But I can't tell you what he *is*. I'm still working on it."

"But . . . it's such a short time ago, Keats!"

"I know," said Keats, showing his teeth without dropping the cigaret, "you wish you were back in New York among the boys in the big league. Just the same, there's something screwy about Wallace, too. And I thought, Mr. Queen, having so little to cheer you up with today, I'd cut out the fancy stuff and try a smash through the center of the line. I haven't talked to Wallace. How about doing it now?"

"You've got him here?" exclaimed Ellery.

"Waiting in the next room. Just a polite invitation to come down to the station here and have a chat. He didn't seem to mind—said it was his day off anyway. I've got one of the boys keeping him from getting bored."

Ellery pulled a chair into a shadowed corner of the office and snapped, "Produce."

ALFRED WALLACE CAME in with a smile, the immaculate man unaffected by the Fahrenheit woes of lesser mortals. His white hair had a foaming wave to it; he carried a debonair slouch hat; there was a small purple aster in his lapel.

"Mr. Queen," said Wallace pleasantly. "So you're the reason Lieutenant Keats has kept me waiting over an hour."

"I'm afraid so." Ellery did not rise.

But Keats was polite. "Sorry about that, Mr. Wallace. Here, have this chair . . . But you can't always time yourself in a murder investigation."

"You mean what *may* be a murder investigation, Lieutenant," said Wallace, seating himself, crossing his legs, and setting his hat precisely on his knee. "Or has something new come up?"

"Something new could come up, Mr. Wallace, if you'll answer a few questions."

"Me?" Wallace raised his handsome brows. "Is that why you've placed this chair where the sun hits my face?" He seemed amused.

Keats silently pulled the cord of the Venetian blind.

"Thanks, Lieutenant. I'll be glad to answer any questions you ask. If, of course, I can."

"I don't think you'll have any trouble answering this one, Mr. Wallace: Where do you come from?"

"Ah." Wallace looked thoughtful. "Now that's just the kind of question, Lieutenant, I can't answer."

"You mean you won't answer."

"I mean I can't answer."

"You don't know where you come from, I suppose."

"Exactly."

"If that's going to be Mr. Wallace's attitude," said Ellery from his corner, "I think we can terminate the interview."

"You misunderstand me, Mr. Queen. I'm not being obstructive." Wallace sounded earnest. "I can't tell you gentlemen where I come from because I don't know myself. I'm one of those interesting cases you read about in the papers. An amnesia victim."

Keats glanced at Ellery. Then he rose. "Okay, Wallace. That's all."

"But that's not all, Lieutenant. This isn't something I can't prove. In fact, now that you've brought it up, I insist on proving it. You're making a recording of this, of course? I would like this to go into the record."

Keats waved his hand. His eyes were intent and a little admiring.

"One day about a year and a half ago—the exact date was January the sixteenth of last year—I found myself in Las Vegas, Nevada, on a street corner," said Alfred Wallace calmly. "I had no idea what my name was, where I came from, how I had got there. I was dressed in filthy clothing which didn't fit me and I was rather banged up. I looked through my pockets and found nothing—no wallet, no letters, no identification of any kind. There was no money, not even coins. I went up to a policeman and told him of the fix I was in, and he took me to a police station. They asked me questions and had a doctor in to examine me. The doctor's name was Dr. James V. Cutbill, and his address was 515 North Fifth Street, Las Vegas. Have you got that, Lieutenant?

"Dr. Cutbill said I was obviously a man of education and good background, about fifty years old or possibly older. He said it looked like amnesia to him. I was in perfect physical condition, and from my speech a North American. Unfortunately, Dr. Cutbill said, there were no identifying marks of any kind on my body and no operation scars, though he did say I'd had my tonsils and adenoids out probably as a child. This, of course, was no clue. There were some fillings in my teeth, of good quality, he thought, but I'd had no major dental work done. The police photographed me and sent my picture and a description to all Missing Persons Bureaus in the United States. There must be one on file in Los Angeles, Lieutenant Keats."

Keats grew fiery red. "I'll check that," he growled. "And lots more."

"I'm sure you will, Lieutenant," said Wallace with a smile. "The Las Vegas police fixed me up with some clean clothes and found me a job as a handyman in a motel, where I got my board and a place to sleep, and a few dollars a week. The name of the motel is the 711, on Route 91 just north of town. I worked there for about a month, saving my pay. The Las Vegas police told me no one of my description was listed as missing anywhere in the country. So I gave up the job and hitchhiked into California.

"In April of last year I found myself in Los Angeles. I stayed at the Y, the Downtown Branch on South Hope Street; I'm surprised you didn't run across my name on their register, Lieutenant, or haven't you tried to trace me?—and I got busy looking for employment. I'd found out I could operate a typewriter and knew shorthand, that I was good at figures—apparently I'd had business training of some sort as well as a rather extensive education—and when I saw an ad for a secretarial companion-nurse job to an incapacitated businessman, I answered it. I told Mr. Priam the whole story, just as I've told it to you. It seems he'd been having trouble keeping people in recent years and, after checking back on my story, he took me on for a month's trial. And here," said Wallace with the same smile, "here I am, still on the job."

"Priam took you on without references?" said Keats, doodling. "How desperate was he?"

"As desperate as he could be, Lieutenant. And then Mr. Priam prides himself on being a judge of character. I was really glad of that, because to this day I'm not entirely sure what my character is."

Ellery lit a cigaret. Wallace watched the flame of the match critically. When Ellery blew the flame out, Wallace smiled again. But immediately Ellery said, "How did you come to take the name Alfred Wallace if you remembered nothing about your past? Or did you remember that?"

"No, it's just a name I plucked out of the ether, Mr. Queen. Alfred, Wallace—they're very ordinary names and more satisfying than John Doe. Lieutenant Keats, aren't you going to check my story?"

"It's going to be checked," Keats assured him. "And I'm sure we'll find it happened exactly as you've told it, Wallace—dates, names, and places. The only thing is, it's all a dodge. That's something I feel in my bones. As one old bone-feeler to another, Mr. Queen, how about it?"

"Did this doctor in Las Vegas put you under hypnosis?" Ellery asked the smiling man.

"Hypnosis? No, Mr. Queen. He was just a general practitioner."

"Have you seen any other doctor since? A psychiatrist, for example?"

"No, I haven't."

"Would you object to being examined by a psychiatrist of—let's say—Lieutenant Keats's choosing?"

"I'm afraid I would, Mr. Queen," murmured Wallace. "You see, I'm not sure I want to find out who I really am. I might discover, for example, that I'm an escaped thief, or that I have a bowlegged wife and five idiot children somewhere. I'm perfectly happy where I am. Of course, Roger Priam isn't the easiest employer in the world, but the job has its compensations. I'm living in royal quarters. The salary Priam pays me is very large—he's a generous employer, one of his few virtues. Old, fat Mrs. Guittierez is an excellent cook, and even though Muggs, the maid, is a straitlaced virgin with halitosis who's taken an unreasonable dislike to me, she does keep my room clean and polishes my shoes regularly. And the position even solves the problem of my sex life—oh, I shouldn't have mentioned that, should I?" Wallace looked distressed; he waved his muscular hand gently. "A slip of the tongue, gentlemen. I do hope you'll forget I said it."

Keats was on his feet. Ellery heard himself saying, "Wallace. Just what did you mean by that?"

"A gentleman, Mr. Queen, couldn't possibly have the bad taste to pursue such a question."

"A gentleman couldn't have made the statement in the first place. I ask you again, Wallace: How does your job with Priam take care of your sex life?"

Wallace looked pained. He glanced up at Keats. Lieutenant, must I answer that question?"

Keats said slowly, "You don't have to answer anything. You brought this up, Wallace. Personally, I don't give a damn about your sex life unless it has something to do with this case. If it has, you'd better answer it."

"It hasn't, Lieutenant. How could it have?"

"I wouldn't know."

"Answer the question," said Ellery in a pleasant voice.

"Mr. Queen seems more interested than you, Lieutenant."

"Answer the question," said Ellery in a still pleasanter voice.

Wallace shrugged. "All right. But you'll bear witness, Lieutenant Keats, that I've tried my best to shield the lady in the case." He raised his eyes suddenly to Ellery and Ellery saw the smile in them, a wintry shimmer. "Mr. Queen, I have the great good luck to share my employer's wife's bed. As the spirit moves. And the flesh being weak, and Mrs. Priam being the most attractive piece I've yet seen in this glorious state, I must admit that the spirit moves several times a week and has been doing so for about a year. Does that answer your question?"

"Just a minute, Wallace," Ellery heard Keats say.

And Keats was standing before him, between him and Wallace. Keats was saying in a rapid whisper, "Queen, look, let me take it from here on in. Why don't you get out of here?"

"Why should I?" Ellery said clearly.

Keats did not move. But then he straightened up and stepped aside.

"You're lying, of course," Ellery said to Wallace. "You're

111

counting on the fact that no decent man could ask a decent woman a question like that, and so your lie won't be exposed. I don't know what slimy purpose your lie serves, but I'm going to step on it right now. Keats, hand me that phone."

And all the time he was speaking Ellery knew it was true. He had known it was true the instant the words left Wallace's mouth. The story of the amnesia was true only so far as the superficial facts went; Wallace had prepared a blind alley for himself, using the Las Vegas police and a mediocre doctor to seal up the dead end. But this was all true. He knew it was all true and he could have throttled the man who sat halfway across the room smiling that iced smile.

"I don't see that that would accomplish anything," Keats was saying. "She'd only deny it. It wouldn't prove a thing."

"He's lying, Keats."

Wallace said with delicate mockery, "I'm happy to hear you take that attitude, Mr. Queen. Of course. I'm lying. May I go, Lieutenant?"

"No, Wallace." Keats stuck his jaw out. "I'm not letting it get this far without knowing the whole story. You say you've been cuckolding Priam for almost a year now. Is Delia Priam in love with you?"

"I don't think so," said Wallace. "I think it's the same thing with Delia that it is with me. A matter of convenience."

"But it stopped some time ago, didn't it?" Keats had a wink in his voice; man-to-man stuff. "It's not still going on."

"Certainly it's still going on. Why should it have stopped?"

Keats's shoulders bunched. "You must feel plenty proud of yourself, Wallace. Eating a man's food, guzzling his liquor, taking his dough, and sleeping with his wife while he's helpless in a wheelchair on the floor below. A cripple who couldn't give you what you rate even if he knew what was going on."

"Oh, didn't I make that clear, Lieutenant?" said Alfred Wallace, smiling. "Priam does know what's going on. In fact, looking back, I can see that he engineered the whole thing."

"What are you giving me!"

"You gentlemen apparently don't begin to understand

the kind of man Priam is. And I think you ought to know the facts of life about Priam, since it's his life you're knocking yourselves out to save."

Wallace ran his thumb tenderly around the brim of his hat. "I don't deny that I didn't figure Priam right myself in the beginning, when Delia and I first got together. I sneaked it, naturally. But Delia laughed and told me not to be a fool, that Priam knew, that he wanted it that way. Although he'd never admit it or let on—to me, or to her.

"Well," said Wallace modestly. "Of course I thought she was kidding me. But then I began to notice things. Looks in his eye. The way he kept pushing us together. That sort of thing. So I did a little investigating on the quiet.

"I found out that in picking secretaries Priam had always hired particularly virile-looking men.

"And I remembered the questions he asked me when I applied for the job—how he kept looking me over, like a horse." Wallace took a cigar from his pocket and lit it. Puffing with enjoyment, he leaned back. "Frankly, I've been too embarrassed to put the question to Delia directly. But unless I'm mistaken, and I don't think I am, Priam's secretaries have always done double duty. Well, for the last ten years, anyway. It also explains the rapid turnover. Not every man is as virile as he looks," Wallace said with a laugh, "and then there are always some mushy-kneed lads who'd find a situation like that uncomfortable . . . But the fact remains. Priam's hired men to serve not only the master of the house, you might say, but the mistress too."

"Get him out of here," Ellery said to Keats. But to his surprise no words came out.

"Roger Priam," continued Alfred Wallace, waving his cigar, "is an exaggerated case of crudity, raw power, and frustration. The clue to his character—and, gentlemen, I've had ample opportunity to judge it—is his compulsive need to dominate everything and everyone around him. He tried to dominate old Leander Hill through the farce of pretending he, Roger Priam, was running a million-dollar business from a wheelchair at home. He tried to dominate Crowe Macgowan before Crowe got too big for him, according to Delia. And he's always dominated Delia, who doesn't care enough about anything to put up a scrap—dominated her physically until he became paralyzed, Delia's told me, with the most incredible vulgarities and brutalities.

"Now imagine," murmured Wallace, "what paralysis from the waist down did to Priam's need to dominate his woman. Physically he was no longer a man. And his wife was beautiful; to this day every male who meets her begins strutting like a bull. Priam knew, knowing Delia, that it was only a question of time before one of them made the grade. And then where would he be? He might not even know about it. It would be entirely out of his control. Unthinkable! So Priam worked out the solution in his warped way—to dominate Delia by proxy.

"By God, imagine that! He deliberately picks a virile man—the substitute for himself physically and psychologically—and flings them at each other's heads, letting nature take its course."

Wallace flicked an ash into the tray on Keats's desk. "I used to think he'd taken a leaf out of Faulkner's *Sanctuary,* or Krafft-Ebing, except that I've come to doubt if he's read a single book in forty-five years. No, Priam couldn't explain all this—to himself least of all. He's an ignorant man; he wouldn't even know the words. Like so many ignorant men, he's a man of pure action. He throws his wife and handpicked secretary together, thus performing the function of a husband vicariously, and by pretending to be deaf to what goes on with domestic regularity over his head he retains his mastery of the situation. He's the god of the machine, gentlemen, and there is no other god but Roger Priam. That is, to Roger Priam." Wallace blew a fat ring of cigar smoke and rose. "And now, unless there's something else, Lieutenant, I'd like to salvage what's left of my day off."

Keats said in a loud voice, "Wallace, you're a fork-tongued female of a mucking liar. I don't believe one snicker of this dirty joke. And when I prove you're a liar, Wallace, I'm going to leave my badge home with my wife and kids, and I'm going to haul you into some dark alley, and I'm going to kick the —— out of you."

Wallace's smile thinned. His face reassembled itself and looked suddenly old. He reached over Keats's desk and picked up the telephone.

"Here," he said, holding the phone out to the detective. "Or do you want me to get the number for you?"

"Scram."

"But you want proof. Delia will admit it if you ask her in the right way, Lieutenant. Delia's a very civilized woman."

"Get out."

Wallace laughed. He replaced the phone gently, adjusted his fashionable hat on his handsome head, and walked out humming.

KEATS INSISTED ON driving Ellery home. The detective drove slowly through the five o'clock traffic.

Neither man said anything.

He had seen them for that moment in the Priam hallway, the day he had come at her summons to investigate the plague of dead frogs. Wallace had been standing close to her, far closer than a man stands to a woman unless he knows he will not be repulsed. And she had not repulsed him. She had stood there accepting his pressure while Wallace squeezed her hand and whispered in her ear . . . He remembered one or two of Wallace's glances at her, the glances of a man with a secret knowledge, glances of amused power . . . "I always take the line of least resistance . . ." He remembered the night she had hidden herself in his bedroom at the sound of her son's and Laurel's arrival. She had come to him that night for the purpose to which her life in the Priam house had accustomed her. Probably she had a prurient curiosity about "celebrities" or she was tired of Wallace (And this was Wallace's revenge?) He would have read the signs of the nymph easily enough if he had not mistaken her flabbiness for reserve—

"We're here, Mr. Queen," Keats was saying.

They were at the cottage.

"Oh. Thanks." Ellery got out automatically. "Good night."

Keats failed to drive away. Instead he said, "Isn't that your phone ringing?"

"Yes. Why doesn't Mrs. Williams answer it?" Ellery said with irritation. Then he laughed. "She isn't answering it because I gave her the afternoon off. I'd better go in."

"Wait." Keats turned his motor off and vaulted to the road. "Maybe it's my office. I told them I might be here."

Ellery unlocked the front door and went in. Keats straddled the threshold.

"Hello?"

Keats saw him stiffen.

"Yes, Delia."

Ellery listened in silence. Keats heard the vibration of the throaty tones, faint and warm and humid.

"Keats is with me now. Hide it till we get there, Delia. We'll be right over."

Ellery hung up.

"What does the lady want?" asked Keats.

"She says she's just found another cardboard box. It was in the Priam mailbox on the road, apparently left there a short time ago. Priam's name handprinted on it. She hasn't told Priam about it, asked what she ought to do. You heard what I told her."

"Another warning!"

Keats ran for his car.

Ten

KEATS STOPPED HIS car fifty feet from the Priam mailbox and they got out and walked slowly toward it, examining the road. There were tire marks in profusion, illegibly intermingled. Near the box they found several heelmarks of a woman's shoe, but that was all.

The door of the box hung open and the box was empty.

They walked up the driveway to the house. Keats neither rang nor knocked. The maid with the tic came hurrying toward them as he closed the door.

"Mrs. Priam said to come upstairs," she whispered. "To her room." She glanced over her shoulder at the closed door of Roger Priam's den. "And not to make any noise, she said, because *he's* got ears like a dog."

"All right," said Keats.

Muggs fled on tiptoe. The two men stood there until she had disappeared beyond the swinging door at the rear of the hall. Then they went upstairs, hugging the balustrade.

As they reached the landing, a door opposite the head of the stairs swung in. Keats and Ellery went into the room.

Delia Priam shut the door swiftly and sank back against it.

She was in brief tight shorts and a strip of sun halter. Her thighs were long and heavy and swelled to her trunk; her breasts spilled over the halter. The glossy black hair lay carelessly piled; she was barefoot—her high-heeled shoes had been kicked off. The rattan blinds were down and in the gloom her pale eyes glowed sleepily.

Keats looked her over deliberately.

"Hello, Ellery." She sounded relieved.

"Hello, Delia." There was nothing in his voice, nothing at all.

"Don't you think you'd better put something on, Mrs. Priam?" said Keats. "Any other time this would be a privilege and a pleasure, but we're here on business." He grinned with his lips only. "I don't think I could think."

She glanced down at herself, startled. "I'm sorry, Lieutenant. I was up on the sun deck before I walked down to the road. I'm very sorry." She sounded angry and a little puzzled.

"No harm done, Delia," said Ellery. "This sort of thing is all in the eye of the beholder."

She glanced at him quickly. A frown appeared between her heavy brows.

"Is something wrong, Ellery?"

He looked at her.

The color left her face. Her hands went to her naked shoulders and she hurried past them into a dressing room, slamming the door.

"Bitch," said Keats pleasantly. He took a cigaret out of his pocket and jammed it between his lips. The end tore and he spat it out, turning away.

Ellery looked around.

The room was overpowering, with dark Spanish furniture and wallpaper and drapes which flaunted masses of great tropical flowers. The rug was a sullen Polynesian red with a two-inch pile. There were cushions and hassocks of unusual shapes and colors. Huge majolicas stood about filled with lilies. On the wall hung heroic Gauguin reproductions and above the bed a large black iron crucifix that looked very old. Niches were crowded with ceramics, woodcarvings, metal sculptures of exotic subjects, chiefly modern in style and many of them male nudes. There was an odd bookshelf hanging by an iron chain, and Ellery strolled over to it, his legs brushing the bed. Thomas Aquinas, Kinsey, Bishop Berkeley, Pierre Loti, Havelock Ellis. *Lives of the Saints* and *Fanny Hill* in a Paris edition. The rest were mystery stories; there was one of his, his latest. The bed was a wide and herculean piece set low to the floor, covered with a cloth-of-gold spread appliquéd, in brilliant colors of metallic thread, with a vast tree of life. In the ceiling, directly above the bed and of identical dimensions, glittered a mirror framed in fluorescent tubing.

"For some reason," remarked Lieutenant Keats in the silence, "this reminds me of that movie actor, What's-

His-Name, of the old silent days. In the wall next to his john he had a perforated roll of rabbit fur." The dressing room door opened and Keats said, "Now that's a relief, Mrs. Priam. Thanks a lot. Where's this box?"

She went to a trunk-sized teak chest covered with brasswork chased intricately in the East Indian manner, which stood at the foot of the bed, and she opened it. She had put on a severe brown linen dress and stockings as well as flat-heeled shoes; she had combed her hair back in a knot. She was pale and frigid, and she looked at neither man.

She took out of the chest a white cardboard box about five inches by nine and an inch deep, bound with ordinary white string, and handed it to Keats.

"Have you opened this, Mrs. Priam?"

"No."

"Then you don't know what's in it?"

"No."

"You found it exactly where and how, again?"

"In our mailbox near the road. I'd gone down to pick some flowers for the dinner table and I noticed it was open. I looked in and saw this. I took it upstairs, locked it in my chest, and phoned."

The box was of cheap quality. It bore no imprint. To the string was attached a plain Manila shipping tag. The name "Roger Priam" was lettered on the tag in black crayon, in carefully characterless capitals.

"Dime store stock," said Keats, tapping the box with a fingernail. He examined the tag. "And so is this."

"Delia." At the sound of his voice she turned, but when she saw his expression she looked away. "You saw the box your husband received the morning Hill got the dead dog. Was it like this? In quality, kind of string, tag?"

"Yes. The box was bigger, that's all." There was a torn edge to the furry voice.

"No dealer's imprint?"

"No."

"Does the lettering on this tag look anything like the lettering on the other tag?"

"It looks just like it." She put her hand on his arm suddenly, but she was looking at Keats. "Lieutenant, I'd like to speak to Mr. Queen privately for a minute."

"I don't have any secrets from Keats." Ellery was glancing down at his arm.

"Please?"

Keats walked over to one of the windows with the box. He lifted the blind, squinting along the slick surface of the box.

"Ellery, is it what happened the other night?" Her voice was at its throatiest, very low.

"Nothing happened the other night."

"Maybe that's the trouble." She laughed.

"But a great deal has happened since."

She stopped laughing. "What do you mean?"

He shrugged.

"Ellery. Who's been telling you lies about me?"

Ellery glanced again at her hand. "It's my experience, Delia, that to label something a lie before you've heard it expressed is to admit it's all too true."

He took her hand between his thumb and forefinger as if it were something sticky, and he dropped it.

Then he turned his back on her.

Keats had the box to his ear and he was shaking it with absorption. Something inside rustled slightly. He hefted the box.

"Nothing loose. Sounds like a solid object wrapped in tissue paper. And not much weight." He glanced at the woman. "I don't have any right to open this, Mrs. Priam. But there's nothing in the statutes to stop *you* . . . here and now."

"I wouldn't untie that string, Lieutenant Keats," said Delia Priam in a trembling voice, "for all the filth in your mind."

"What did I do?" Keats raised his reddish brows as he handed the box to Ellery. "That puts it up to you, Mr. Queen. What do you want to do?"

"You can both get out of my bedroom!"

Ellery said, "I'll open it, Keats, but not here. And not now. I think this ought to be opened before Roger Priam, with Mrs. Priam there, and Laurel Hill, too."

"You can get along without me," she whispered. "Get out."

"It's important for you to be there," Ellery said to her.

"You can't tell me what to do."

"In that case I'll have to ask the assistance of someone who can."

"No one can."

"Not Wallace?" smiled Ellery. "Or one of his numerous predecessors?"

Delia Priam sank to the chest, staring.

"Come on, Keats. We've wasted enough time in this stud pasture."

LAUREL WAS OVER in ten minutes, looking intensely curious. Padding after her into the cavelike gloom of the house came the man of the future. Young Macgowan had returned to the Post-Atomic Age.

"What's the matter now?" he inquired plaintively.

No one replied.

By a sort of instinct, he put a long arm about his mother and kissed her. Delia smiled up at him anxiously, and when she straightened she kept her grasp on his big hand. Macgowan seemed puzzled by the atmosphere. He fixed on Keats as the cause, and he glared murderously from the detective to the unopened box.

"Loosen up, boy," said Keats. "Tree life is getting you. Okay, Mr. Queen?"

"Yes."

Young Macgowan didn't know. Laurel knew—Laurel had known for a long time—but Delia's son was wrapped in the lamb's wool of mother-adoration. I'd hate to be the first one, Ellery thought, to tell him.

As for Laurel, she had glanced once at Delia and once at Ellery, and she had become mousy.

Ellery waited on the threshold to the hall as Keats explained about the box.

"It's the same kind of tag, same kind of crayon lettering, as on the dead dog," Laurel said. She eyed the box grimly. "What's inside?"

"We're going to find that out right now." Ellery took the box from Keats and they all followed him up the hall to Priam's door.

"Furl your mains'l," said a voice. It was old Mr. Collier, in the doorway across the hall.

"Mr. Collier. Would you care to join us? There's something new."

"I'll sit up in the rigging," said Delia's father. "Hasn't there been enough trouble?"

"We're trying to prevent trouble," said Keats mildly.

"So you go looking for it. Doesn't make sense to me," said the old man, shaking his head. "Live and let live. Or die and let die. If it's right one way, it's right the other." He stepped back and shut the library door emphatically.

Ellery tried Priam's door. It was locked. He rapped loudly.

"Who is it?" The bull voice sounded slurry.

Ellery said, "Delia, you answer him."

She nodded mechanically. "Roger, open the door, won't you?" She sounded passive, almost bored.

"Delia? What d'ye want?" They heard the trundling of his chair and some glassy sounds. "Damn this rug! I've told Alfred a dozen times to tack it down—" The door opened and he stared up at them. The shelf before him supported a decanter of whisky, a siphon, and a half empty glass. His eyes were bloodshot. "What's this?" he snarled at Ellery. "I thought I told you two to clear out of my house and stay out." His fierce eyes lighted on the box in Ellery's hand. They contracted, and he looked up and around. His glance passed over his wife and stepson as if they had not been there. It remained on Laurel's face for a moment with a hatred so concentrated that Crowe Macgowan made an unconscious growling sound. Laurel's lips tightened.

He put out one of his furry paws. "Give me the box."

"No, Mr. Priam."

"That tag's got my name on it. Give it to me!"

"I'm sorry, Mr. Priam."

He raised the purplish ensign of his rage, his eyes flaming. "You can't keep another man's property!"

"I have no intention of keeping it, Mr. Priam. I merely want to see what's inside. Won't you please back into the room so that we can come in and do this like civilized people?"

Ellery kept looking at him impassively. Priam glared back, but his hands went to the wheels of his chair. Grudgingly, they pushed backwards.

Keats shut the door very neatly. Then he put his back against it. He remained there, watching Priam.

Ellery began to untie the box.

He seemed in no hurry.

Priam's hands were still at the sides of his chair. He was sitting forward, giving his whole attention to the untying process. His beard rose and fell with his chest. The purple flag had come down, leaving a sort of gray emptiness, like a foggy sky.

Laurel was intent.

Young Macgowan kept shifting from foot to naked foot, uneasily.

Delia Priam stood perfectly still.

"Lieutenant," said Ellery suddenly, as he worked over the last knot, "what do you suppose we'll find in here?"

Keats said, "After those dead frogs I wouldn't stick my chin out." He kept looking at Priam.

"Do you have to take out the knots?" cried Crowe. "Open it!"

"Would anyone care to guess?"

"*Please.*" Laurel, begging.

"Mr. Priam?"

Priam never stirred. Only his lips moved, and the beard around them. But nothing came out.

Ellery whipped the lid off.

Roger Priam threw himself back, almost upsetting the chair. Then, conscious of their shock, he fumbled for the glass of whisky. He tilted his head, drinking, not taking his glance from the box.

All that had been exposed was a layer of white tissue.

"From the way you jumped, Mr. Priam," said Ellery conversationally, "anyone would think you expected a hungry rattler to pop out at you, or something equally live and disagreeable. What is it you're afraid of?"

Priam set the glass down with a bang. His knuckles were livid. "I ain't afraid," he sputtered. "Of anything!" His chest spread. "Stop needling me, you ——! Or I swear——"

He brought his arm up blindly. It struck the decanter and the decanter toppled from the shelf, smashing on the floor.

Ellery was holding the object high, stripped of its tissue wrapping. He held it by its edges, between his palms.

His own eyes were amazed, and Keats's.

Because there was nothing in what he was displaying to make a man cringe.

It was simply a wallet, a man's wallet of breast pocket size made of alligator leather, beautifully grained and dyed forest green. There were no hideous stains on it; it had no history; it was plainly brand-new. And high-priced; it was edged in gold. Ellery flipped it open. Its pockets were empty. There had been no note or card in the box.

"Let me see that," said Keats.

Nothing to make a man cower, or a woman grow pale.

"No initials," said Keats. "Nothing but the maker's name." He scratched his cheek, glancing at Priam again.

123

"What is it, Lieutenant?" asked Laurel.

"What is what, Miss Hill?"

"The maker's name."

"Leatherland, Inc., Hollywood, California."

Priam's beard had sunk to his chest.

Paler than Priam. For Delia Priam's eyes had flashed to their widest at sight of the wallet, all the color running out of her face. Then the lids had come down as if to shut out a ghost.

Shock. But the shock of what? Fear? Yes, there was fear, but fear followed the shock; it did not precede.

Suddenly Ellery knew what it was.

Recognition.

He mulled over this, baffled. It was a new wallet. She couldn't possibly have seen it before. Unless . . . For that matter, neither could Priam. Did it mean the same thing to both of them? Vaguely, he doubted this. Their reactions had thrown off different qualities. Lightning had struck both of them, but it was as if Priam were a meteorologist who understood the nature of the disaster, his wife an ignorant bystander who knew only that she had been stunned. I'm reading too much into this, Ellery thought. You can't judge the truth of anything from a look . . . It's useless to attempt to talk to her now . . . In an indefinable way he was glad. It was remarkable how easily passion was killed by a dirty fact. He felt nothing when he looked at her now, not even revulsion. The sickness in the pit of his stomach was for himself and his gullibility.

"Delia, where you going?"

She was walking out.

"Mother."

So Crowe had seen it, too. He ran after her, caught her at the door.

"What's the matter?"

She made an effort. "It's all too silly, darling. It's getting to be too much for me. A wallet! And such a handsome one, too. Probably a gift from someone who thinks it's Roger's birthday. Let me go, Crowe. I've got to see Mrs. Guittierez about dinner."

"Oh. Sure." Mac was relieved.

And Laurel . . .

"The only thing that would throw me," Keats was drawling, "I mean if I was in Mr. Priam's shoes—"

Laurel had been merely puzzled by the wallet.

124

"—is what the devil I'd be expected to do with it. Like a battleship getting a lawnmower."

Laurel had been merely puzzled by the wallet, but when she had glimpsed Delia's face her own had reflected shock. The shock of recognition. Again. But this was not recognition of the object per se. This was recognition of Delia's recognition. A chain reaction.

"When you stop and think of it, everything we know about these presents so far shows one thing in common—"

"In common?" said Ellery. "What would that be, Keats?"

"Arsenic, dead frogs, a wallet for a man who never leaves his house. They've all been so damned *useless.*"

Ellery laughed. "There's a theory, Mr. Priam, that's in your power to affirm or deny. Was your first gift useless, too? The one in the first cardboard box?"

Priam did not lift his head.

"Mr. Priam. What was in that box?"

Priam gave no sign that he heard.

"What do these things mean?"

Priam did not reply.

"May we have this wallet for examination?" asked Keats.

Priam simply sat there.

"Seems to me I caught the flicker of one eyelash, Mr. Queen." Keats wrapped the wallet carefully in the tissue paper and tucked it back in the box. "I'll drop you off at your place and then take this down to the Lab."

They left Roger Priam in the same attitude of frozen chaos.

KEATS DROVE SLOWLY, handling the wheel with his forearms and peering ahead as if answers lay there. He was chewing on a cigaret, like a goat.

"Now I'm wrong about Priam," laughed Ellery. "Perfect score."

Keats ignored the addendum. "Wrong about Priam how?"

"I predicted he'd blow his top and spill over at warning number four. Instead of which he's gone underground. Let's hope it's only a temporary recession."

"You're sure this thing is a warning."

Ellery nodded absently.

"Me, I'm not," Keats complained. "I can't seem to get the feel of this case. It's like trying to catch guppies with your bare hands. Now the arsenic, that I could hold on

125

to, even though I couldn't go anywhere with it. But all the rest of it . . ."

"You can't deny the existence of all the rest of it, Keats. The dead dog was real enough. The first box Priam got was real, and whatever was in it. There was nothing vapory about those dead frogs and toads, either. Or about the contents of this box. Or, for that matter," Ellery shrugged, "about the thing that started all this, the note to Hill."

"Oh, yes," growled the detective.

"Oh yes what?"

"The note. What do we know about it? Not a thing. It's not a note, it's a copy of a note. Or is it even that? That might be only what it *seems*. Maybe the whole business was dreamed up by Hill."

"The arsenic, froglets, and wallet weren't dreamed up by Hill," said Ellery dryly, "not in the light of his current condition and location. No, Keats, you're falling for the temptation to be a reasonable man. You're not dealing with a reasonable thing. It's a fantasy, and it calls for faith." He stared ahead. "There's something that links these four 'warnings,' as the composer of the note calls them, links them in a series. They constitute a group."

"How?" Bits of tobacco flew. "Poisoned food, dead frogs, a seventy-five dollar wallet! And God knows what was in that first box to Priam—judging by what followed, it might have been a size three Hopalong Cassidy suit, or a bock beer calendar of the year 1897. Mr. Queen, you *can't* connect those things. They're not connectable." Keats waved his arms, and the car swerved. "The most I can see in this is that each one stands on its own feet. The arsenic? That means: Remember how you tried to poison *me?*—this is a little reminder. The frogs? That means . . . Well, you get the idea."

But Ellery shook his head. "If there's one thing in this case I'm sure of, it's that the warnings have related meanings. And the over-all meaning ties up with Priam's past and Hill's past and their enemy's past. What's more, Priam knows its significance, and it's killing him.

"What we've got to do, Lieutenant, is crack Priam, or the riddle, before it's too late."

"I'd like to crack Priam," remarked Keats. "On the nut."

They drove the rest of the way in silence.

KEATS PHONED JUST before midnight.

"I thought you'd like to know what the Lab found out from examination of the wallet and box."

"What?"

"Nothing. The only prints on the box were Mrs. Priam's. There were no prints on the wallet at all. Now I'm going home and see if I'm still married. How do you like California?"

Eleven

OUTSIDE HER GARAGE, Laurel looked aronud. Her look was furtive. He hadn't been in the walnut tree this morning, thank goodness, and there was no sign of him now. Laurel slipped into the garage, blinking as she came out of the sun, and ran to her Austin.

"Morning, Little Beaver."

"Mac! Damn you."

Crowe Macgowan came around the big Packard, grinning. "I had a hunch you had a little something under your armpit last night when you told me how late you were going to sleep this morning. Official business, hm?" He was dressed. Mac looked very well when he was dressed, almost as well as when he wasn't. He even wore a hat, a Swiss yodeler sort of thing with a little feather. "Shove over."

"I don't want you along today."

"Why not?"

"Mac, I just don't."

"You'll have to give me a better reason than that."

"You . . . don't take this seriously enough."

"I thought I was plenty serious on the frog safari."

"Well . . . Oh! all right. Get in."

Laurel drove the Austin down to Franklin and turned west, her chin northerly. Macgowan studied her profile in peace.

"La Brea to Third," he said, "and west on Third to Fairfax. Aye, aye, Skipper?"

"Mac! You've looked it up."

"There's only one Leatherland, Inc., of Hollywood, California, and it's in Farmers' Market."

"I wish you'd let me drop you!"

"Nothing doing. Suppose you found yourself in an opium den?"

"There are no opium dens around Fairfax and Third."

128

"Then maybe a gangster. All the gangsters are coming west, and you know how tourists flock to Farmers' Market."

Laurel said no more, but her heart felt soggy. Between her and the traffic hung a green alligator.

She parked in the area nearest Gilmore Stadium. Early as they were, the paved acres were jammed with cars.

"How are you going to work this?" asked Crowe, shortening his stride as she hurried along.

"There's nothing much to it. Their designs are exclusive, they make everything on the premises, and they have no other outlets. I'll simply ask to see some men's wallets, work my way around to alligator, then to green alligator—"

"And then what?" he asked dryly.

"Why . . . I'll find out who's bought one recently. They certainly can't sell many green alligator wallets with gold trimming. Mac, what's the idea? Let go!"

They were outside The Button Box. Leatherland, Inc., was nearby, a double-windowed shop with a ranchhouse and corral fence décor, bannered with multicolored hides and served by a bevy of well-developed cowgirls.

"And how are *you* going to get one of those babes to open up?" asked Crowe, keeping Laurel's arm twisted behind her back with his forefinger. "In the first place, they don't carry their customers' names around in their heads; they don't have that kind of head. In the second place, they're not going to go through their sales slips —for you, that is. In the third place, what's the matter with me?"

"I might have known."

"All I have to do is flash my genuine Red Ryder sheriff's badge, turn on the charm, and we're in. Laurel, I'm typecasting."

"Take off your clothes," said Laurel bitterly, "and you'll get more parts than you can handle."

"Watch me—fully dressed and lounging-like."

He went into the shop confidently.

Laurel pretended to be interested in a handtooled, silverstudded saddle in the window.

Although the shop was crowded, one of the cowgirls spotted Crowe immediately and cantered up to him. Everything bouncing, Laurel observed, hoping one of the falsies would slip down. But it was well-anchored, and she could see him admiring it. So could the cowgirl.

They engaged in a dimpled conversation for fully two minutes. Then they moved over to the rear of the shop. He pushed his hat back on his head the way they did in the movies and leaned one elbow on the showcase. The rodeo Venus began to show him wallets, bending and sunfishing like a bronc. This went on for some time, the sheriff's man leaning farther and farther over the case until he was practically breathing down her sternum. Suddenly he straightened, looked around, put his hand in his pocket, and withdrew it cupped about something. The range-type siren dilated her eyes . . .

When Crowe strolled out of the shop he passed Laurel with a wink.

She followed him, furious and relieved. The poor goop still didn't catch on, she thought. But then men never noticed anything but women; men like Mac, that is. She turned a corner and ran into his arms.

"Come to popsy," he grinned. "I've got all the dope."

"Are you sure that's all you've got?" Laurel coldly swept past him.

"And I thought you'd give me a gold star!"

"It's no make-up off my skin, but as your spiritual adviser—if you're lining up future mothers of the race for the radioactive new world, pick specimens who look as if they can climb a tree. You'd have to send that one up on a breeches buoy."

"What do you mean, is that all I've got? You saw me through the window. Could anything have been more antiseptic?"

"I saw you take down her phone number!"

"Shucks, gal. That was professional data. Here." He picked Laurel up, dropped her into the Austin, and got in beside her. "They made up a line of men's wallets in alligator leather last year, dyed three or four different colors. All the other colors sold but the green—they only unloaded three of those. Two of the three greens were bought before Christmas, almost seven months ago, as gifts. One by a Broadway actor to be sent to his agent back in New York, the other by a studio executive for some bigshot French producer—the shop mailed that one to Paris. The third and only other one they've sold is unaccounted for."

"It would be," said Laurel morosely, "seeing that that's the one we're interested in. How unaccounted for, Mac?"

"My cowgirl dug out the duplicate sales slip. It was a

130

cash-and-carry and didn't have the purchaser's name on it."

"What was the date?"

"This year. But what month this year, or what day of what month this year, sales slip showeth not. The carbon slipped or something and the date was smudged."

"Well, didn't she remember what the purchaser looked like? That might tell us something."

"It wasn't my babe's customer, because the initials of the salesgirl on the slip were of someone else."

"Who? Didn't you find out?"

"Sure I found out."

"Then why didn't you speak to *her?* Or were you too wrapped up in Miss Falsies?"

"Miss who? Say, I thought those were too good to be true. I couldn't speak to the other gal. The other gal quit last week."

"Didn't you get her name and address?"

"I got her name, Lavis La Grange, but my babe says it wasn't Lavis's real name and she doesn't know what Lavis's real name is. Certainly not Lavis or La Grange. Her address is obsolete, because she decided she'd had enough of the glamorous Hollywood life and went back home. But when I asked my babe where Lavis's home is, she couldn't say. For all she knows it could be Labrador. And anyway, even if we could locate Lavis, my babe says she probably wouldn't remember. My babe says Lavis has the brain of a barley seed."

"So we can't even fix the buyer's sex," said Laurel bitterly. "Some manhunters we are."

"What do we do now, report to the Master?"

"You report to the Master, Mac. What's there to report? He'll probably know all this before the day's out, anyway. I'm going home. You want me to drop you?"

"You've got more sex appeal. I'll stick with you."

YOUNG MACGOWAN STUCK with Laurel for the remainder of the day; technically, in fact, until the early hours of the next, for it was five minutes past two when she climbed down the rope ladder from the tree house to the floodlit clearing. He leaped after her and encircled her neck with his arm all the way to her front door.

"Sex fiends," he said cheerfully.

"You're doing all right," said Laurel, who felt black and blue; but then she put her mouth up to be kissed, and he

131

kissed it, and that was a mistake because it took her another fifteen minutes to get rid of him.

Laurel waited behind the closed door ten minutes longer to be sure the coast was clear.

Then she slipped out of her house and down to the road.

She had her flashlight and the little automatic was in her coat pocket.

Just before she got to the Priam driveway she turned off into the woods. Here she stopped to put a handkerchief over the lens of her flash. Then, directing the feeble beam to the ground, she made her way toward the Priam house.

Laurel was not feeling adventurous. She was feeling sick. It was the sickness not of fear but of self-appraisal. How did the heroines of fiction do it? The answer was, she decided, that they were heroines of fiction. In real life when a girl had to let a man make love to her in order to steal a key from him she was nothing but a tramp. Less than a tramp, because a tramp got something out of her trampery—money, or an apartment, a few drinks, or even, although less likely, fun. It was a fairly forthright transaction. But she . . . she had had to pretend, all the while searching desperately for the key. The worst part of it was trying to dislike it. That damned Macgowan was so purely without guile and he made love so cheerfully—and he was such a darling—that the effort to hate him, it, and herself came off poorly. What a bitchy thing to do, Laurel moaned as her fingers tightened about the key in her pocket.

She stopped behind a French lilac bush. The house was dark. No light anywhere. She moved along the strip of lawn below the terrace.

Even then it wouldn't have been so nasty if it hadn't concerned his *mother*. How could Mac have lived with Delia all these years and remained blind to what she was? Why did Delia have to be *his* mother?

Laurel tried the front door carefully. It was locked, sure enough. She unlocked it with the key, silently thankful that the Priams kept no dogs. She closed the door just as carefully behind her. Wielding the handkerchief-covered flashlight for a moment, she oriented herself; then she snapped it off.

She crept upstairs close to the banisters.

On the landing she used the flash again. It was almost

three o'clock. The four bedroom doors were closed. There was no sound either from this floor or the floor above, where the chauffeur slept. Mrs. Guittierez and Muggs occupied two servants' rooms off the kitchen downstairs.

Laurel tiptoed across the hall and put her ear against a door. Then, quickly and noiselessly, she opened the door and went into Delia Priam's bedroom. How co-operative of Delia to go up to Santa Barbara, where she was visiting "some old Montecito friends" for the weekend. The cloth-of-gold tree of life spread over the bed immaculately. In whose bed was she sleeping tonight?

LAUREL HOOKED THE FLASH to the belt of her coat and began to open dresser drawers. It was the weirdest thing, rummaging through Delia's things in the dead of night by the light of a sort of dark lantern. It didn't matter that you weren't there to take anything. What chiefly made a sneak thief was the technique. If Delia's father, or the unspeakable Alfred, were to surprise her now . . . Laurel held on to the thought of the leaden, blue-lipped face of Leander Hill.

It was not in the dresser. She went into Delia's clothes closet.

The scent Delia used was strong, and it mingled disagreeably with the chemical odor of mothproofing and the cedar lining of the walls. Delia's perfume had no name. It had been created exclusively for her by a British Colonial manufacturer, a business associate of Roger Priam's, after a two-week visit to the Priam house years before. Each Christmas thereafter Delia received a quart bottle of it from Bermuda. It was made from the essence of the passionflower. Laurel had once suggested sweetly to Delia that she name it *Prophetic*, but Delia had seemed not to think that very funny.

It was not in the closet. Laurel came out and shut the door, inhaling.

Had she been wrong after all? Maybe it was an illusion, built on the substructure of her loathing for Delia and that single, startling look on Delia's face as Ellery had held up the green wallet.

But suppose it wasn't an illusion. Then the fact that it wasn't where she would ordinarily have kept such a thing might be significant. Because Delia had hurried out of Roger's den immediately. She might have gone directly upstairs to her bedroom, taken it from among the others, and stowed it away where it was unlikely to be found. By Muggs, for instance.

Where might Delia have hidden it? All Laurel wanted was to see it, to verify its existence . . .

It was not in the brassbound teak chest at the foot of the bed. Laurel took everything out and then put everything back.

After conquering three temptations to give it up and go home and crawl into bed and pull the bedclothes of oblivion over her head, Laurel found it. It was in the clothes closet after all. But not, Laurel felt, in an honest place. It was wedged in the dolman sleeve of one of Delia's winter coats, a luxurious white duvetyn, which in turn was encased in a transparent plastic bag. Innocent and clever. Only a detective, Laurel thought, would have found it. Or another woman.

Laurel felt no triumph, just a shooting pain, like the entry of a hypodermic needle; and then a hardening of everything.

She had been right. She *had* seen Delia carrying one. Weeks before.

It was a woman's envelope bag of forest green alligator leather, with gold initials. The maker's name was Leatherland, Inc., of Hollywood, California.

A sort of Eve to the Adam of the wallet someone had sent to Roger Priam. A mate to the fourth warning.

"I SUPPOSE I should have told you yesterday," Laurel said to Ellery in the cottage on the hill, "that Mac and I were down to Farmers' Market on the trail of the green wallet. But we didn't find out anything, and anyway I knew you'd know about it."

"I've had a full report from Keats." Ellery looked at Laurel quizzically. "We had no trouble identifying Tree Boy from the salesgirl's description, and it stood to reason you'd put him up to it."

"Well, there's something else you don't know."

"The lifeblood of this business is information, Laurel. Is it very serious? You look depressed."

"Me?" Laurel laughed. "It's probably a result of confusion. I've found out something about somebody in this case that *could* mean . . ."

"Could mean what?" Ellery asked gravely, when she paused.

"That we've found the right one!" Laurel's eyes glittered. "But I can't quite put it into place. It seems to mean so much, only . . . Ellery, last night—really in the early hours of this morning—I did something dishonest and—and horrible. Since Roger was poisoned Alfred Wallace has been locking the doors at night. I stole a key from Mac and in the middle of the night I let myself in, sneaked upstairs—"

"And you went into Delia Priam's bedroom and searched it."

"How did you know!"

"Because I caught the look on your face day before yesterday when *you* saw the look on *Delia's* face. That man's alligator wallet meant something to her. She either recognized it or something about it reminded her directly of something like it. And her start of recognition produced some sort of recognition in you, too, Laurel. Delia left the room at once, and before we went away we made sure of where she'd gone. She'd gone right up to her bedroom.

"She left for Santa Barbara yesterday afternoon, and last night—while you were luring the key out of young Macgowan, probably—I pulled a second-story job and gave the bedroom a going-over. Keats, of course, couldn't risk it; the L.A. police have had to lean over backwards lately, and if Keats had been caught housebreaking there might have been a mess that would spoil everything. There wasn't enough, of course, to justify a warrant and an open search.

"I left Delia's alligator bag in the sleeve of the white coat, where I found it. And where, I take it, you found it a few hours later. I hope you left everything exactly as it was."

"Yes," moaned Laurel. "But all that breast-beating for nothing."

Ellery lit a cigaret. "Now let me tell you something *you* don't know, Laurel." His eyes, which had not laughed at all, became as smoky as his cigaret. "That green alligator pocketbook of Delia's was a gift. She didn't buy it herself. Luckily, the salesgirl who sold it remembered clearly what the purchaser looked like, even though it was a cash sale. She gave an excellent and recognizable description, and when she was shown the corresponding photograph she identified it as the man she had described. The purchase was made in mid-April of this year, just

135

before Delia's birthday, and the purchaser was Alfred Wallace."

"Alfred—" Laurel was about to go on, but then her teeth closed on her lower lip.

"It's all right, Laurel," said Ellery. "I know all about Delia and Alfred."

"I wasn't sure." Laurel was silent. Then she looked up. "What do you think it means?"

"It could mean nothing at all," Ellery said slowly. "Coincidence, for example, although coincidence and I haven't been on speaking terms for years. More likely whoever it is we're after may have noticed Delia's bag and, consciously or unconsciously, it suggested to him the nature of the fourth warning to Priam. Delia's suspicious actions can be plausibly explained, in this interpretation, as the fear of an innocent person facing a disagreeable involvement. Innocent people frequently act guiltier than guilty ones.

"It could mean that," said Ellery, "or . . ." He shrugged. "I'll have to think about it."

Twelve

BUT ELLERY'S THOUGHTS were forced to take an unforeseen turn. In this he was not unique. Suddenly something called the 38th Parallel, half a planet away, had become the chief interest in the lives of a hundred and fifty million Americans.

Los Angeles particularly suffered a bad attack of the jitters.

A few days before, Koreans from the north had invaded South Korea with Soviet tanks and great numbers of Soviet 7.63-millimeter submachine guns. The explosive meaning of this act took some time to erupt the American calm. But when United States occupation troops were rushed to South Korea from Japan and were overwhelmed, and the newspapers began printing reports of American wounded murdered by the invaders, conviction burst. The president made unpleasantly reminiscent announcements, reserves were being called, the United Nations were in an uproar, beef and coffee prices soared, there were immediate rumors about sugar and soap scarcities, hoarding began, and everyone in Los Angeles was saying that World War III had commenced and that Los Angeles would be the first city on the North American continent to feel the incinerating breath of the atom bomb—and how do we know it won't be tonight? San Diego, San Francisco, and Seattle were not sleeping soundly, either, but that was no consolation to Los Angeles.

It was impossible to remain unaffected by the general nervousness. And, absurd as the thought was, there was always the possibility that it was only too well grounded.

The novel, which had been sputtering along, coughed and went into a nose dive. Ellery hounded the radio, trying to shut out the prophecies of doom which streaked up from his kitchen like flak in wailing Louisiana accents from eight to five daily. His thoughts kept coming back to Tree Boy. Crowe Macgowan no longer seemed funny.

He had not heard from Lieutenant Keats for days. There was no word from the Priam establishment. He knew that Delia had returned from Montecito, but he had not seen or heard from her.

Laurel phoned once to seek, not give, information. She was worried about Macgowan.

"He just sits and broods, Ellery. You'd think with what's happening in Korea he'd be going around saying I told you so. Instead of which I can't get him to open his big mouth."

"The world of fantasy is catching up with Crowe, and it's probably a painful experience. There's nothing new at the Priams'?"

"It's quiet. Ellery, what do you suppose this lull means?"

"I don't know."

"I'm so confused these days!" Laurel's was something of a wail, too. "Sometimes I think what's going on in the world makes all this silly and unimportant. And I suppose in one way it is. But then I think, no, it's not silly and it is important. Aggressive war is murder, too, and you don't take *that* lying down. You have to fight it on every front, starting with the picayune personal ones. Or else you go down."

"Yes," said Ellery with a sigh, "that makes sense. I only wish this particular front weren't so . . . fluid, Laurel. You might say we've got a pretty good General Staff, and a bang-up army behind us, but our Intelligence is weak. We have no idea where and when the next attack is coming, in what form and strength—or the meaning of the enemy's strategy. All we can do is sit tight and keep on the alert."

Laurel said quickly, "Bless you," and she hung up quickly, too.

THE ENEMY'S NEXT attack came during the night of July 6–7. It was, surprisingly, Crowe Macgowan who notified Ellery. His call came at a little after one in the morning, as Ellery was about to go to bed.

"Queen. Something screwy just happened. I thought you'd want to know." Macgowan sounded tired, not like himself at all.

"What, Mac?"

"The library's been broken in to. One of the windows.

138

Seems like a case of ordinary housebreaking, but I dunno."

"The *library?* Anything taken?"

"Not as far as I can see."

"Don't touch anything. I'll be over in ten minutes." Ellery rang up Keats's home, got a sleepy "What, again?" from the detective, and ran.

He found young Macgowan waiting for him in the Priam driveway. There were lights on upstairs and down, but Roger Priam's French windows off the terrace were dark.

"Before you go in, maybe I'd better explain the set-up..."

"Who's in there now?"

"Delia and Alfred."

"Go on. But make it snappy, Mac."

"Last couple of nights I've been sleeping in my old room here at the house—"

"What? No more tree?"

"You wanted it presto, didn't you?" growled the giant. "I hit the sack early tonight, but I couldn't seem to sleep. Long time later I heard sounds from downstairs. Seemed like the library; my room's right over it. I thought maybe it was Gramp and I felt a yen to talk to him. So I got up and went down the hall and at the top of the stairs I called, 'Gramp?' No answer, and it was quiet down there. Something made me go back up the hall and look in the old gent's room. He wasn't there; bed hadn't been slept in. So I went back to the head of the stairs and there was Wallace."

"Wallace?" repeated Ellery.

"In a robe. He said he'd heard a noise and was just going to go downstairs." Macgowan sounded odd; his eyes were hard in the moonlight. "But you know something, Queen? I got a queer feeling as I spotted Wallace at the head of those stairs. I couldn't make up my mind whether he was about to go down . . . or had just come up."

He stared at Ellery defiantly.

A car was tearing up the road.

Ellery said, "Life is full of these dangling participles, Mac. Did you find your grandfather?"

"No. Maybe I'd better take a look in the woods." Crowe sounded casual. "Gramp often takes a walk in the middle of the night. You know how it is when you're old."

"Yes." Ellery watched Delia's son stride off, pulling a flashlight from his pocket as he went.

Keats's car slammed to a stop a foot from Ellery's rear.

"Hi."

"What is it this time?" Keats had a leather jacket on over an undershirt, and he sounded sore.

Ellery told him, and they went in.

Delia Priam was going through the library desk, looking baffled. She was in a brown monkish negligee of some thick-napped material, girdled by a heavy brass chain. Her hair hung down her back and there were purplish shadows, almost welts, under her eyes. Alfred Wallace, in a Paisley dressing gown, was seated comfortably in a club chair, smoking a cigaret.

Delia turned, and Wallace rose, as the two men came into the library, but neither said anything.

Keats went directly to the only open window. He examined the sash about the catch without touching it.

"Jimmied. Have any of you touched this window?"

"I'm afraid," said Wallace, "we all did."

Keats mumbled something impolite and went out. A few moments later Ellery heard him outside, below the open window, and saw the beam of his flash.

Ellery looked around. It was the kind of library he liked; this was one room in which the prevailing Priam gloom was mellow. Leather shone, and the black oak paneling was a friendly background for the books. Books from floor to ceiling on all four walls, and a fieldstone fireplace with a used look. It was a spacious room, and the lamps were good.

"Nothing missing, Delia?"

She shook her head. "I can't understand it." She turned away, pulling her robe closer about her.

"Crowe and I probably scared him off." Alfred Wallace sat down again, exhaling smoke.

"Your father's stamp albums?" Ellery suggested to Delia's back. He had no idea why he thought of old Collier's treasures, except that they might be valuable.

"As far as I know, they haven't been touched."

Ellery wandered about the room.

"By the way, Crowe tells me Mr. Collier hasn't been to bed. Have you any idea where he is, Delia?"

"No." She wheeled on him, eyes flashing. "My father and I don't check up on each other. And I can't recall,

Mr. Queen, that I ever gave you permission to call me by my first name. Suppose you stop it."

Ellery looked at her with a smile. After a moment she turned away again. Wallace continued to smoke.

Ellery resumed his ambling.

When Keats returned he said shortly, "There's nothing out there. Have you got anything?"

"I think so," said Ellery. He was squatting before the fireplace. "Look here."

Delia Priam turned at that, and Wallace.

The fireplace grate held the remains of a wood fire. It had burned away to a fine ash. On the ashes lay a heat-crimped and badly charred object of no recognizable shape.

"Feel the ashes to the side, Keats."

"Stony cold."

"Now the ashes under that charred thing."

The detective snatched his hand away. "Still hot!"

Ellery said to Delia, "Was there a wood fire in this grate tonight . . . Mrs. Priam?"

"No. There was one in the morning, but it burned out by noon."

"This object was just burned here, Keats. On top of the cold ashes."

The lieutenant wrapped a handkerchief around his hand and cautiously removed the charred thing. He laid it on the hearth.

"What was it?"

"A book, Keats."

"Book?" Keats glanced around at the walls. "I wonder if—"

"Can't tell any more. Pages all burned away and what's left of the binding shows nothing."

"It must have been a special binding." Most of the volumes on the shelves were leatherbound. "Don't they stamp the titles into these fancy jobs?" Keats prodded the remains of the book, turning it over. "Ought to be some indication left."

"There would have been, except that whoever burned this indulged in a little vandalism before he set fire to it. Look at these slashes on the spine—and here. The book was mutilated with a sharp instrument before it was tossed into the grate."

Keats looked up at Delia and Wallace, who were stooping over them. "Any idea what this book was?"

141

"Damn you! Are you two here again?"

Roger Priam's wheelchair blocked the doorway. His hair and beard were threatening. His pajama coat gaped, exposing his simian chest; a button was missing, as if he had torn at himself in a temper. His chair was made up as a bed and the blankets trailed on the floor.

"Ain't nobody going to open his mouth? Man can't get any shut-eye in his own house! Alfred, where the hell have you been? Not in your room, because I couldn't get you on the intercom!" He did not glance at his wife.

"Something's happened down here, Mr. Priam," said Wallace soothingly.

"Happened! What now?"

Ellery and Keats were watching Priam closely. The library desk and a big chair stood between the wheelchair and the fireplace; Priam had not seen the burned book.

"Somebody broke into your library here tonight, Mr. Priam," rasped Keats, "and don't think I'm happy about it, because I'm as sick of you as you are of me. And if you're thinking of blasting me out again, forget it. Breaking and entering is against the law, and I'm the cop on the case. Now you're going to answer questions about this or, by God, I'll pull you in on a charge of obstructing a police investigation. Why was this book cut up and burned?"

Keats stalked across the room carrying the charred remains. He thrust the thing under Priam's nose.

"Book . . . burned?"

All his rage had fled, exposing the putty color beneath. Priam glared down at the twisted cinder in Keats's hand, pulling away a little.

"Do you recognize this?"

Priam's head shook.

"Can't you tell us what it is?"

"No." The word came out cracked. He seemed fascinated by the binding.

Keats turned in disgust. "I guess he doesn't know at that. Well—"

"Just a moment, Lieutenant." Ellery was at the shelves, riffling through books. They were beautiful books, the products of private presses chiefly—handmade paper, lots of gold leaf, colored inks, elaborate endpaper designs, esoteric illustrations, specially designed type fonts; each was hand-bound and expensively hand-tooled. And the

142

titles were impeccable, all the proper classics. The only thing was, after riffling through two dozen books, Ellery had still to find one in which the pages had been cut.

The books had never been read. It was likely, from their stiff pristine condition, that they had not been opened since leaving the hands of the bookbinder.

"How long have you had these books, Mr. Priam?"

"How long?" Priam licked his lips. "How long is it, Delia?"

"Since shortly after we were married."

"Library means books," Priam muttered, nodding. "Called in a fancy dealer and had him measure the running feet of shelf space and told him to go out and get enough books to fill the space. Highbrow stuff, I told him; only the best." He seemed to gain confidence through talking; a trace of arrogance livened his heavy voice. "When he lugged them around, I threw 'em back in his face. 'I said the best!' I told him. 'Take this junk back and have it bound up in the most expensive leather and stuff you can find. It's got to look the money or you don't get a plugged nickel.' "

Keats had dropped his impatience. He edged back.

"And a very good job he did, too," murmured Ellery. "I see they're in the original condition, Mr. Priam. Don't seem to have been opened, any of them."

"Opened! And crack those bindings? This collection is worth a fortune, Mister. I've had it appraised. Won't let *nobody* read 'em."

"But books are made to be read, Mr. Priam. Haven't you ever been curious about what's in these pages?"

"Ain't read a book since I played hooky from public school," retorted Priam. "Books are for women and longhairs. Newspapers, that's different. And picture magazines." His head jerked up with a belligerent reflex. "What are you getting at?"

"I'd like to spend about an hour here, Mr. Priam, looking over your collection. I give you my word, I'll handle your books with the greatest care. Would you have any objection to that?"

Cunning pinpointed Priam's eyes. "You're a book writer yourself, ain't you?"

"Yes."

"Ever write articles like in the Sunday magazine sections?"

"Occasionally."

"Maybe you got some idea about writing up an article on the Priam Book Collection. Hey?"

"You're a shrewd man, Mr. Priam," said Ellery with a smile.

"I don't mind," the bearded man said with geniality. There was color in his cheekbones again. "That bookdealer said no millionaire's library ought to be without its own special catalogue. 'It's too good a collection, Mr. Priam,' he says to me. 'There ought to be a record of it for the use of bib- bib-' "

"Bibliophiles?"

"That's it. Hell, it was little enough, and besides I figured it might come in handy for personal publicity in my jewelry business. So I told him to go ahead. You'll find a copy of the catalogue right there on that stand. Cost me a lot of money—specially designed, y' know, four-color job on special paper. And there's a lot of technical stuff in it, in the descriptions of the books. Words I can't even pronounce," Priam chuckled, "but, God Almighty, you don't have to be able to pronounce it if you can pay for it." He waved a hairy hand. "Don't mind at all, Mister—what was the name again?"

"Queen."

"You go right ahead, Queen."

"Very kind of you, Mr. Priam. By the way, have you added any books since your catalogue was made up?"

"Added any?" Priam stared. "I got all the good ones. What would I want with more? When d'ye want to do it?"

"No time like the present, I always say, Mr. Priam. The night is killed, anyway."

"Maybe tomorrow I'll change my mind, hey?" Priam showed his teeth again in what he meant to be a friendly grin. "That's all right, Queen. Shows you're no dope, even if you do write books. Go to it!" The grin faded as he turned his animal eyes on Wallace. "You push me back, Alfred. And better bunk downstairs for the rest of the night."

"Yes, Mr. Priam," said Alfred Wallace.

"Delia, what are you standing around for? Go back to bed."

"Yes, Roger."

The last they saw of Priam he was waving amiably as Wallace wheeled him across the hall. From his gesture it was apparent that he had talked himself out of his fears, if indeed he had not entirely forgotten their cause.

When the door across the hall had closed, Ellery said: "I hope you don't mind, Mrs. Priam. We've got to know which book this was."

"You think Roger's a fool, don't you?"

"Why don't you go to bed?"

"Don't ever make that mistake. Crowe!" Her voice softened. "Where've you been, darling? I was beginning to worry. Did you find your grandfather?"

Young Macgowan filled the doorway; he was grinning. "You'll never guess where." He yanked, and old Collier appeared. There was a smudge of chemical stain along his nose and he was smiling happily. "Down in the cellar."

"*Cellar?*"

"Gramp's fixed himself up a dark room, Mother. Gone into photography."

"I've been using your Contax all day, daughter. I hope you don't mind. I've got a great deal to learn," said Collier, shaking his head. "My pictures didn't come out very well. Hello there! Crowe tells me there's been more trouble."

"Have you been in the cellar all this time, Mr. Collier?" asked Lieutenant Keats.

"Since after supper."

"Didn't you hear anything? Somebody jimmied that window."

"That's what my grandson told me. No, I didn't hear anything, and if I had I'd probably have locked the cellar door and waited till it was all over! Daughter, you look all in. Don't let this get you down."

"I'll survive, Father."

"You come on up to bed. Good night, gentlemen." The old man went away.

"Crowe." Delia's face set. "Mr. Queen and Lieutenant Keats are going to be working in the library for a while. I think perhaps you'd better stay . . . too."

"Sure, sure," said Mac. He stooped and kissed her. She went out without a glance at either of the older men. Macgowan shut the door after her. "What's the matter?" he asked Ellery in a plaintive tone. "Don't you two get along any more? What's happened?"

"If you must keep an eye on us, Mac," snapped Ellery,

145

"do it from that chair in the corner, where you'll be out of the way. Keats, let's get going."

THE "PRIAM COLLECTION" was a bibliographic monstrosity, but Ellery was in a scientific, not an esthetic, mood and his methodology had nothing to with art or even morals; he simply had the Hollywood detective read off the titles on Priam's shelves and he checked them against the gold-crusted catalogue.

It took them the better part of two hours, during which Crowe Macgowan fell asleep in the leather chair.

When at last Keats stopped, Ellery said: "Hold it," and he began to thumb back along the pages of the catalogue.

"Well?" said Keats.

"You failed to read just one title." Ellery set the catalogue down and picked up the charred corpse of the book. "This used to be an octavo volume bound in laminated oak, with handblocked silk endpapers, of *The Birds*, by Aristophanes."

"The what, by whom?"

"*The Birds*. A play by Aristophanes, the great satirical dramatist of the fifth century before Christ."

"I don't see the joke."

Ellery was silent.

"You mean to tell me," demanded the detective, "that the burning of this book by a playwright dead a couple of dozen centuries is another of these warnings?"

"It must be."

"How can it be?"

"Mutilated and burned, Keats. At least two of the four previous warnings also involved violence in some form: the food poisoning, the murder of the frogs . . ." Ellery sat up.

"What's the matter?"

"Frogs. Another play by Aristophanes has that exact title. *The Frogs*."

Keats looked pained.

"But that's almost certainly a coincidence. The other items wouldn't begin to fit . . . *The Birds*. An unknown what's-it, food poisoning, dead toads and frogs, an expensive wallet, and now a plushy edition of a Greek social satire first performed—unless I've forgotten my Classics II—in 414 B.C."

"And I'm out of cigarets," grunted Keats. Ellery tossed

146

a pack over. "Thanks. You say there's a connection?"

" 'And for each pace forward a warning . . . a warning of special meaning for you—and for him,' " Ellery quoted. "That's what the note said. 'Meanings for pondering and puzzling.' "

"How right he was. I still say, Queen, if this stuff means anything at all, each one stands on its own tootsies."

" 'For each pace forward,' Keats. It's *going* somewhere. No, they're tied. The whole thing's a progression." Ellery shook his head. "I'm not even sure any more that Priam knows what they mean. This one tonight really balls things up. Priam is virtually an illiterate. How could he possibly know what's meant by the destruction of an old Greek play?"

"What's it about?"

"The play? Well . . . to the best of my recollection, two Athenians talk the Birds into building an aerial city, in order to separate the Gods from Man."

"That helps."

"What did Aristophanes call his city in the air? Cloud . . . Cloudland . . . Cloud-Cuckoo-Land."

"That's the first thing I've heard in this case that rings the bell." Keats got up in disgust and went to the window.

A long time passed. Keats stared out at the night, which was beginning to boil and show a froth. But the room was chilly, and he hunched his shoulders under the leather jacket. Young Macgowan snored innocently in the club chair. Ellery said nothing.

Ellery's silence lasted for so long that after a time Keats, whose brain was empty and wretched, became conscious of its duration. He turned around tiredly and there was a gaunt, unshaven, wild-eyed refugee from a saner world staring back at him with uninvited joy, grudgingly delirious, like a girl contemplating her first kiss.

"What in the hell," said the Hollywood detective in alarm, "is the matter with you?"

"Keats, they have something in common!"

"Sure. You've said that a dozen times."

"*Not one thing, but two.*"

Keats came over and took another of Ellery's cigarets. "What do you say we break this up? Go home, take a shower, and hit the hay." Then he said, "*What?*"

"Two things in common, Keats!" Ellery swallowed. His

147

mouth was parched and there was a tuneful fatigue in his head, but he knew he had it, he had it at last.

"You've *got* it?"

"I know what it means, Keats. I know."

"What? What?"

But Ellery was not listening. He fumbled for a cigaret without looking.

Keats struck a match for him and then, absently, held it to his own cirgaret; he went to the window again, inhaling, filling his lungs. The froth on the night had bubbled down, leaving a starchy mass, glimmering like soggy rice. Keats suddenly became aware of what he was doing. He looked startled, then desperate, then defiant. He smoked hungrily, waiting.

"Keats."

Keats whirled. "Yes?"

Ellery was on his feet. "The man who owned the dog. What were his name and address again?"

"Who?" Keats blinked.

"The owner of the dead dog, the one you have reason to believe was poisoned before it was left on Hill's doorstep. What was the owner's name? I've forgotten it."

"Henderson. Clybourn Avenue, in Toluca Lake."

"I'll have to see him as soon as I can. You going home?"

"But why—"

"You go on and get a couple of hours' sleep. Are you going to be at the station later this morning?"

"Yeah. But what—"

But Ellery was walking out of Roger Priam's library with stiff short steps, a man in a dream.

Keats stared after him.

When he heard Ellery's Kaiser drive away, he put Ellery's pack of cigarets in his pocket and picked up the remains of the burned book.

Crowe Macgowan awoke with a snort.

"You still here? Where's Queen?" Macgowan yawned. "Did you find out anything?"

Keats held his smoldering butt to a fresh cigaret, puffing recklessly. "I'll send you a telegram," he said bitterly, and he went away.

SLEEP WAS IMPOSSIBLE. He tossed for a while, not even hopefully.

At a little after six Ellery was downstairs in his kitchen, brewing coffee.

He drank three cups, staring into the mists over Hollywood. A dirty gray world with the sun struggling through. In a short time the mist would be gone and the sun would shine clear.

The thing was sharply brilliant. All he had to do was get rid of the mist.

What he would see in that white glare Ellery hardly dared anticipate. It was something monstrous, and in its monstrous way beautiful; that, he could make out dimly.

But first there was the problem of the mist.

He went back upstairs, shaved, took a shower, changed into fresh clothing, and then he left the cottage and got into his car.

Thirteen

IT WAS ALMOST eight o'clock when Ellery pulled up before a small stucco house tinted cobalt blue on Clybourn Avenue off Riverside Drive.

A handcolored wooden cutout resembling Dopey, the Walt Disney dwarf, was stuck into the lawn on a stake, and on it a flowery artist had lettered the name HENDERSON.

The uniformly closed Venetian blinds did not look promising.

As Ellery went up the walk a woman's voice said, "If you're lookin' for Henderson, he's not home."

A stout woman in an orange wrapper was leaning far over the railing of her red cement stoop next door, groping with ringed fingers for something hidden in a violet patch.

"Do you know where I can reach him?"

Something swooshed, and six sprinklers sent up watery bouquets over the woman's lawn. She straightened, red-faced and triumphant.

"You can't," she said, panting. "Henderson's a picture actor. He's being a pirate mascot on location around Catalina or somewhere. He expected a few weeks' work. You a press agent?"

"Heaven forbid," muttered Ellery. "Did you know Mr. Henderson's dog?"

"His dog? Sure I knew him. Frank, his name was. Always tearin' up my lawn and chasin' moths through my pansy beds—though don't go thinkin'," the fat woman added hastily, "that I had anything to do with poisonin' Frank, because I just can't abide people who do things like that to animals, even the destroyin' kind. Henderson was all broke up about it."

"What kind of dog was Frank?" Ellery asked.

"Kind?"

150

"Breed."

"Well . . . he wasn't very big. Nor so little, neither, when you stop to think of it—"

"You don't know his breed?"

"I think some kind of a hunting dog. Are you from the Humane Society or the Anti-Vivisection League? I'm against experimentin' with animals myself, like the *Examiner's* always sayin'. If the good Lord—"

"You can't tell me, Madam, what kind of hunting dog Frank was?"

"Well . . ."

"English setter? Irish? Gordon? Llewellyn? Chesapeake? Weimaraner?"

"I just guess," said the woman cheerfully, "I don't know."

"What color was he?"

"Well, now, sort of brown and white. No, black. Come to think of it, not really white, neither. More creamy, like."

"More creamy, like. Thank you," said Ellery. And he got into his car and moved fifty feet, just far enough to be out of his informant's range.

After thinking for a few minutes, he drove off again.

He cut through Pass and Olive, past the Warner Brothers studio, into Barham Boulevard to the Freeway. Emerging through the North Highland exit into Hollywood, he found a parking space on McCadden Place and hurried around the corner to the Plover Bookshop.

It was still closed.

He could not help feeling that this was inconsiderate of the Plover Bookshop. Wandering up Hollywood Boulevard disconsolately, he found himself opposite Coffee Dan's. This reminded him vaguely of his stomach, and he crossed over and went in for breakfast. Someone had left a newspaper on the counter and as he ate he read it conscientiously. When he paid his check, the cashier said, "What's the news from Korea this morning?" and he had to answer stupidly, "Just about the same," because he could not remember a word he had read.

Plover was open!

He ran in and seized the arm of a clerk. "Quick," he said fiercely. "A book on dogs."

"Book on dogs," said the clerk. "Any particular kind of book on dogs, Mr. Queen?"

"Hunting dogs! With illustrations! In color!"

Plover did not fail him. He emerged carrying a fat book

and a charge slip for seven and a half dollars, plus tax.

He drove up into the hills rashly and caught Laurel Hill a moment after she stepped into her stall shower.

"GO AWAY," LAUREL said, her voice sounding muffled. "I'm naked."

"Turn that water off and come out here!"

"Why, Ellery."

"Oh . . . ! I'm not the least bit interested in your nakedness—"

"Thanks. Did you ever say that to Delia Priam?"

"Cover your precious hide with this! I'll be in the bedroom." Ellery tossed a bath towel over the shower door and hurried out. Laurel kept him waiting five minutes. When she came out of the bathroom she was swaddled in a red, white, and blue robe of terry cloth.

"I didn't know you cared. But next time would you mind at least knocking? Gads, look at my hair—"

"Yes, yes," said Ellery. "Now Laurel, I want you to project yourself back to the morning when you and your father stood outside your front door and looked at the body of the dead dog. Do you remember that morning?"

"I think so," said Laurel steadily.

"Can you see that dog right now?"

"Every hair of him."

"Hold on to him!" Ellery yanked her by the arm and she squealed, grabbing at the front of her robe. She found herself staring down at her bed. Upon it, open to an illustration in color of a springer spaniel, lay a large book. "Was he a dog like this?"

"N-no . . ."

"Go through the book page by page. When you come to Henderson's pooch, or a reasonable facsimile thereof, indicate same in an unmistakable manner."

Laurel looked at him suspiciously. It was too early in the morning for him to have killed a bottle, and he was shaved and pressed, so it wasn't the tag end of a large night. Unless . . .

"Ellery!" she screamed. "You've found out something!"

"Start looking," hissed Ellery viciously; at least it sounded vicious to his ears, but Laurel only looked overjoyed and began to turn pages like mad.

"Easy, easy," he cried. "You may skip it."

152

"I'll find your old hound." Pages flew like locust petals in a May wind. "Here he is—"

"Ah."

Ellery took the book.

The illustration showed a small, almost dumpy, dog with short legs, pendulous ears, and a wiry upcurving tail. The coat was smooth. Hindlegs and forequarters were an off-white, as was the muzzle; the little dog had a black saddle and black ears with secondary pigmentation of yellowish brown extending into his tail.

The caption under the illustration said: *Beagle.*

"Beagle." Ellery glared. "Beagle . . . Of course. Of *course.* No other possibility. None whatever. If I'd had the brain of a wood louse . . . Beagle, Laurel, beagle!" And he swept her off her feet and planted five kisses on the top of her wet head. Then he tossed her on her unmade bed and before her horrified eyes went into a fast tap— an accomplishment which was one of his most sacred secrets, unknown even to his father. And Ellery chanted, *"Merci,* my pretty one, my she-detective. You have follow ze clue of ze ar-sen-ique, of ze little frog, of ze wallette, of ze everysing but ze sing you know all ze time—zat is to say, ze beagle. Oh, ze beagle!" And he changed to a softshoe.

"But what's the breed of dog got to do with anything, Ellery?" moaned Laurel. "The only connection I can see with the word 'beagle' is its slang meaning. Isn't a 'beagle' a detective?"

"Ironic, isn't it?" chortled Ellery; and he exited doing a Shuffle-Off-to-Buffalo, blowing farewell kisses and almost breaking the prominent nose of Mrs. Monk, Laurel's housekeeper, who had it pressed in absolute terror to the bedroom door.

TWENTY MINUTES LATER Ellery was closeted with Lieutenant Keats at the Hollywood Division. Those who passed the closed door heard the murmur of the Queen voice, punctuated by a weird series of sounds bearing no resemblance to Keats's usual tones.

The conference lasted well over an hour.

When the door opened, a suffering man appeared. Keats looked as if he had just picked himself up from the floor after a kick in the groin. He kept shaking his head and muttering to himself. Ellery followed him briskly. They vanished in the office of Keats's chief.

An hour and a half later they emerged. Keats now looked convalescent, even robust.

"I still don't believe it," he said, "but what the hell, we're living in a funny world."

"How long do you think it will take, Keats?"

"Now that we know what to look for, not more than a few days. What are you going to do in the meantime?"

"Sleep and wait for the next one."

"By that time," grinned the detective, "maybe we'll have a pretty good line on this inmate."

They shook hands solemnly and parted, Ellery to go home to bed and Keats to set the machinery of the Los Angeles police department going on a twenty-four hour a day inquiry into a situation over twenty years old . . . this time with every prospect of success.

IN THREE DAYS not all the moldy threads were gathered in, but those they had been able to pick up by teletype and long distance phone tied snugly around what they already knew. Ellery and Keats were sitting about at the Hollywood Division trying to guess the lengths and textures of the missing ends when Keats's phone rang. He answered it to hear a tense voice.

"Lieutenant Keats, is Ellery Queen there?"

"It's Laurel Hill for you."

Ellery took the phone. "I've been neglecting you, Laurel. What's up?"

Laurel said with a rather hysterical giggle, "I've committed a crime."

"Serious?"

"What's the rap for lifting what doesn't belong to you?"

Ellery said sharply, "Something for Priam again?"

He heard a scuffle, then Crowe Macgowan's voice saying hastily, "Queen, she didn't swipe it. I did."

"He did not!" yelled Laurel. "I don't care, Mac! I'm sick and tired of hanging around not knowing—"

Is it for Roger Priam?

"It is," said Macgowan. "A pretty big package this time. It was left on top of the mailbox. Queen, I'm not giving Roger a hold over Laurel. I took it and that's that."

"Have you opened it, Mac?"

"No."

"Where are you?"

"Your house."

"Wait there and keep your hands off it." Ellery hung up. "Number six, Keats!"

They found Laurel and Macgowan in Ellery's living room, hovering hostilely over a package the size of a man's suit box, wrapped in strong Manila paper and bound with heavy string. The now-familiar shipping tag with Priam's name lettered on it in black crayon—the now-familiar lettering—was attached to the string. The package bore no stamps, or markings of any kind.

"Delivered in person again," said Keats. "Miss Hill, how did you come to get hold of this?"

"I've been watching for days. Nobody tells me anything, and I've got to do *something*. And, darn it, after hours and hours of hiding behind bushes I missed her after all."

"Her?" said Crowe Macgowan blankly.

"Well, her, or him, or whoever it is." Laurel turned old rose.

Crowe stared at her.

"Let's get technical," said Keats. "Go ahead and open it, Macgowan. Then we won't have to lie awake nights with a guilty conscience."

"Very humorous," mumbled Delia's son. He snapped the string and ripped off the wrapping in silence.

The box was without an imprint, white, and of poor quality. It bulged with its contents.

Mac removed the lid.

The box was crammed with printed documents in a great variety of sizes, shapes, and colored inks. Many were engraved on banknote paper.

"What the devil." Keats picked one out at random. "This is a stock certificate."

"So is this," said Ellery. "And this . . ." After a moment they stared at each other. "They all seem to be stock certificates."

"I don't get it." Keats worried his thumbnail. "This doesn't fit in with what you figured out, Queen. It couldn't."

Ellery frowned. "Laurel, Mac. Do these mean anything to you?"

Laurel shook her head, staring at a name on the certificate she had picked up. Now she put it down, slowly, and turned away.

"Why, this must represent a fortune," exclaimed Crowe. "Some warning!"

Ellery was looking at Laurel. "We'd better have a break-

155

down on the contents of this box, Keats, and then we can decide how to handle it.—Laurel, what's the matter?"

"Where you going?" demanded Macgowan.

Laurel turned at the door. "I'm sick of this. I'm sick of the whole thing, the waiting and looking and finding and doing absolutely nothing. If you and the lieutenant have anything, Ellery, what is it?"

"We're not through making a certain investigation, Laurel."

"Will you ever be?" She said it drearily. Then she went out, and a moment later they heard the Austin scramble away.

ABOUT SEVEN O'CLOCK that evening Ellery and Keats drove up to the Priam house in Keats's car, Ellery carrying the box of stock certificates. Crowe Macgowan was waiting for them at the front door.

"Where's Laurel, Mac? Didn't you get my phone message?" said Ellery.

"She's home." Crowe hesitated. "I don't know what's the matter with her. She's tossed off about eight Martinis and I couldn't do a thing with her. I've never seen Laurel act like that. She doesn't take a drink a week. I don't like it."

"Well, a girl's entitled to a bender once in a while," jeered Keats. "Your mother in?"

"Yes. I've told her. What did you find out?"

"Not much. The wrappings and box were a washout. Our friend likes gloves. Did you tell Priam?"

"I told him you two were coming over on something important. That's all."

Keats nodded, and they went to Roger Priam's quarters.

Priam was having his dinner. He was wielding a sharp blade and a fork on a thick rare steak. Alfred Wallace was broiling another on a portable barbecue. The steak was smothered with onions and mushrooms and barbecue sauce from several chafing dishes, and a bottle of red wine showed three-quarters empty on the tray. Priam ate in character: brutally, teeth tearing, powerful jaws crunching, eyes bulging with appetite, flecks of sauce on his agitated beard.

His wife, in a chair beside him, watched him silently, as one might watch a zoo animal at feeding time.

The entrance of the three men caught the meat-laden fork in mid-air. It hung there for a moment, then it completed its journey, but slowly, and Priam's jaws ground away mechanically. His eyes fixed and remained on the box in Ellery's hands.

"Sorry to interrupt your dinner, Mr. Priam," said Keats, "but we may as well have this one out now."

"The other steak, Alfred." Priam extended his plate. Wallace refilled it in silence. "What's this, now?"

"Warning number six, Mr. Priam," said Ellery.

Priam attacked his second steak.

"I see it's no use," he said in almost a friendly tone, "trying to get you two to keep your noses out of my business."

"I took it," said Crowe Macgowan abruptly. "It was left on the mailbox and I lifted it."

"Oh, you did." Priam inspected his stepson.

"I live here, too, you know. I'm getting pretty fed up with this and I want to see it cleaned out."

Priam hurled his plate at Crowe Macgowan's head. It hit the giant a glancing blow above the ear. He staggered, crashed back into the door. His face went yellow.

"Crowe!"

He brushed his mother aside. "Roger, if you ever do that again," he said in a low voice, "I'll kill you."

"Get out!" Priam's voice was a bellow.

"Not while Delia's here. If not for that I'd be in a uniform right now. God knows why she stays, but as long as she does, I do too. I don't owe you a thing, Roger. I pay my way in this dump. And I have a right to know what's going on . . . It's all right, Mother." Delia was dabbing at his bleeding ear with her handkerchief; her face was pinched and old-looking. "Just remember what I said, Roger. Don't do that again."

Wallace got down on his hands and knees and began to clean up the mess.

Priam's cheekbones were a violent purple. He had gathered himself in, bunched and knotted. His glare at young Macgowan was palpable.

"Mr. Priam," said Ellery pleasantly, "have you ever seen these stock certificates before?"

Ellery laid the box on the tray of the wheelchair. Priam looked at the mass of certificates for a long time without touching them—almost, Ellery would have said, without seeing them. But gradually awareness crept over his face and as it advanced it touched the purple like a chemical, leaving pallor behind.

157

Now he seized a stock certificate, another, another. His great hands began to scramble through the box, scattering its contents. Suddenly his hands fell and he looked at his wife.

"I remember these." And Priam added, with the most curious emphasis, "Don't you, Delia?"

The barb penetrated her armor. "I?"

"Look at 'em, Delia." His bass was vibrant with malice. "If you haven't seen them lately, here's your chance."

She approached his wheelchair reluctantly, aware of something unpleasant that was giving him a feeling of pleasure. If he felt fear at the nature of the sixth warning, he showed no further trace of it.

"Go ahead, Delia." He held out an engraved certificate. "It won't bite you."

"What are you up to now?" growled Crowe. He strode forward.

"You saw them earlier today, Macgowan," said Keats. Crowe stopped, uneasy. The detective was watching them all with a brightness of eye he had not displayed for some time . . . watching them all except Wallace, whom he seemed not to be noticing, and who was fussing with the barbecue as if he were alone in the room.

Delia Priam read stiffly, "Harvey Macgowan."

"Sure is," boomed her husband. "That's the name on the stock, Delia. Harvey Macgowan. Your old man, Crowe. He chuckled.

Macgowan looked foolish. "Mother, I didn't notice the name at all."

Delia Priam made an odd gesture. As if to silence him. "Are they all—?"

"Every one of them, Mrs. Priam," said Keats. "Do they mean anything to you?"

"They belonged to my first husband. I haven't seen these for . . . I don't know how many years."

"You inherited these stocks as part of Harvey Macgowan's estate?"

"Yes. If they're the same ones."

"They're the same ones, Mrs. Priam," Keats said dryly. "We've done a bit of checking with the old probate records. They were turned over to you at the settlement of your first husband's estate. Where have you kept them all these years?"

"They were in a box. Not this box . . . It's so long ago, I don't remember."

158

"But they were part of your effects? When you married Mr. Priam, you brought them along with you? Into this house?"

"I suppose so. I brought everything." She was having difficulty enunciating clearly. Roger Priam kept watching her lips, his own parted in a grin.

"Can't you remember exactly where you've kept these, Mrs. Priam? It's important."

"Probably in the storeroom in the attic. Or maybe among some trunks and boxes in the cellar."

"That's not very helpful."

"Stop badgering her, Keats," said young Macgowan. Because he was bewildered, his jaw stuck out. "Do you remember where you put your elementary school diploma?"

"Not quite the same thing," said the detective. "The face value of these stocks amounts to a little over a million dollars."

"That's nonsense," said Delia Priam with a flare of asperity. "These shares are worthless."

"Right, Mrs. Priam. I wasn't sure everybody knew. They're worth far less than the paper they're printed on. Every company that issued these shares is defunct."

"What's known on the stock market," said Roger Priam with every evidence of enjoyment, "as cats and dogs."

"My first husband sank almost everything he had in these pieces of paper," said Delia in a monotone. "He had a genius for investing in what he called 'good things' that always turned out the reverse. I didn't know about it until after Harvey died. I don't know why I've hung on to them."

"Why, to show 'em to your loving second husband, Delia," said Roger Priam, "right after we were married; remember? And remember I advised you to wallpaper little Crowe's little room with them as a reminder of his father? I gave them back to you and I haven't seen them again till just now."

"They've been somewhere in the house, I tell you! Where anyone could have found them!"

"And where someone did," said Ellery. "What do you make of it, Mr. Priam? It's another of these queer warnings you've been getting—in many ways the queerest. How do you explain it?"

"These cats and dogs?" Priam laughed. "I'll leave it to you, my friends, to figure it out."

There was contempt in his voice. He had either

159

convinced himself that the whole fantastic series of events was meaningless, the work of a lunatic, or he had so mastered his fears of what he knew to be a reality that he was able to dissemble like a veteran actor. Priam had the actor's zest; and, shut up in a room for so many years, he may well have turned it into a stage, with himself the star performer.

"Okay," said Lieutenant Keats without rancor. "That seems to be that."

"Do you think so?"

The voice came from another part of the room.

Everyone turned.

Laurel Hill stood inside the screen door to Priam's terrace.

Her face was white, nostrils pinched. Her murky eyes were fixed on Delia Priam.

Laurel wore a suède jacket. Both hands were in the pockets.

"That's the end of that, is it?"

Laurel shoved away from the screen door. She teetered for an instant, regained her balance, then picked her way very carefully half the distance to Delia Priam, her hands still in her pockets.

"Laurel," began Crowe.

"Don't come near me, Mac. Delia, I have something to say to you."

"Yes?" said Delia Priam.

"When that green alligator wallet came, it reminded me of something. Something that belonged to you. I searched your bedroom while you were in Montecito and I found it. One of your bags—alligator, dyed green, and made by the same shop as the wallet. So I was sure you were behind all this, Delia."

"You'd better get her out of here," said Alfred Wallace suddenly. "She's tight."

"Shut up, Alfred." Roger Priam's voice was a soft rumble.

"Miss Hill," said Keats.

"No!" Laurel laughed, not taking her eyes from Delia. "I was sure you were behind it, Delia. But Ellery Queen didn't seem to think so. Of course, he's a great man, so I thought I must be wrong. But these stock certificates belong to you, Delia. You put them away. You knew where they were. You're the only one who could have sent them."

160

"Laurel," began Ellery, "that's not the least bit logical—"

"*Don't come near me!*" Her right hand came out of her pocket with an automatic.

Laurel pointed its snub nose at Delia Priam's heart. Young Macgowan was gaping.

"But if you sent this 'warning'—whatever in your poisoned mind it's supposed to mean—you sent the others too, Delia. And *they* won't do anything about it. It's washed up, they say. Well, I've given them their chance, Delia. You'd have got away with it if only men were involved; your kind always does. But *I'm* not letting you get away with killing my father! You're going to pay for that right now, Delia!—right n . . ."

Ellery struck her arm as the gun went off and Keats caught it neatly as it flew through the air. Crowe made a choking sound, taking a step toward his mother. But Delia Priam had not moved. Roger Priam was looking down at his tray. The bullet had shattered the bottle of wine two inches from his hand.

"By God," snarled Priam, "she almost got me. Me!"

"That was a dumb-bunny stunt, Miss Hill," said Keats. "I'm going to have to take you in for attempted homicide."

Laurel was looking in a glazed way from the gun in the detective's hand to the immobile Delia. Ellery felt the girl shrinking in his grip, in spasms, as if she were trying to compress herself into the smallest possible space.

"I'm sorry, Mrs. Priam," Keats was saying. "I couldn't know she was carrying a gun. She never seemed the type. I'll have to ask you to come along and swear out a complaint."

"Don't be silly, Lieutenant."

"Huh?"

"I'm not making any charge against this girl."

"But Mrs. Priam, she shot to kill—"

"Me!" yelled Roger Priam.

"No, it's me she shot at." Delia Priam's voice was listless. "She's wrong, but I understand how you can bring yourself to do a thing like this when you've lost somebody you've loved. I wish I had Laurel's spunk. Crowe, stop looking like a dead carp. I hope you're not going to be stuffy about this and let Laurel down. It's probably taken her weeks to work herself up to this, and at that she had to get drunk to do it. She's a good girl,

161

Crowe. She needs you. And I know you're in love with her."

Laurel's bones all seemed to melt at once. She sighed, and then she was silent.

"I think," murmured Ellery, "that the good girl has passed out."

Macgowan came to life. He snatched Laurel's limp figure from Ellery's arms, looked around wildly, and then ran with her. The door opened before him; Wallace stood there, smiling.

"She'll be all right." Delia Priam walked out of the room. "I'll take care of her."

They watched her go up the stairs behind her son, back straight, head high, hips swinging.

Fourteen

BY THE NIGHT of July thirteenth all the reports were in.

"If I'm a detective," Keats said unhappily to Ellery, "then you've got second sight. I'm still not sure how you doped this without inside information."

Ellery laughed. "What time did you tell Priam and the others?"

"Eight o'clock."

"We've just got time for a congratulatory drink."

They were in Priam's house on the stroke of eight. Delia Priam was there, and her father, and Crowe Macgowan, and a silent and drained-looking Laurel. Roger Priam had evidently extended himself for the occasion; he had on a green velvet lounging jacket and a shirt with starched cuffs, and his beard and hair had been brushed. It was as if he suspected something out of the ordinary and was determined to meet it full-dress, in the baronial manner. Alfred Wallace hovered in the background, self-effacing and ineffaceable, with his constant mocking, slightly irritating smile.

"This is going to take a little time," said Lieutenant Keats, "but I don't think anybody's going to be bored . . . I'm just along for atmosphere. It's Queen's show."

He stepped back to the terraceward wall, in a position to watch their faces.

"Show? What kind of show?" There was fight in the Priam tones, his old hairtrigger belligerence.

"Showdown would be more like it, Mr. Priam," said Ellery.

Priam laughed. "When are you going to get it through your heads that you're wasting your time, not to mention mine? I didn't ask for your help. I don't want your help, I won't take your help—and I ain't giving any information."

"We're here, Mr. Priam, to give you information."

Priam stared. Of all of them, he was the only one who seemed under no strain except the strain of his own untempered arrogance. But there was curiosity in his small eyes.

"Is that so?"

"Mr. Priam, we know the whole story."

"What whole story?"

"We know your real name. We know Leander Hill's real name. We know where you and Hill came from before you went into business in Los Angeles in 1927, and what your activities were before you both settled in California. We know all that, Mr. Priam, and a great deal more. For instance, we know the name of the person whose life was mixed up with yours and Hill's before 1927—the one who's trying to kill you today."

The bearded man held on to the arms of his wheelchair. But he gave no other sign; his face was iron. Keats, watching from the sidelines, saw Delia Priam sit forward, as at an interesting play; saw the flicker of uneasiness in old Collier's eyes; the absorption of Macgowan; the unchanging smile on Wallace's lips. And he saw the color of life creep back in Laurel Hill's cheeks.

"I can even tell you," continued Ellery, "exactly what was in the box you received the morning Leander Hill got the gift of the dead dog."

Priam exclaimed, "That's bull! I burned that box and what was in it the same day I got it. Right in that fireplace there! Is the rest of your yarn going to be as big a bluff as this?"

"I'm not bluffing, Mr. Priam."

"You know what was in that box?"

"I know what was in that box."

"Out of the zillions of different things it could have been, you know the one thing it was, hey?" Priam grinned. "I like your nerve, Queen. You must be a good poker player. But that's a game I used to be pretty good at myself. So suppose I call you. What was it?"

He raised a glass of whisky to his mouth.

"Something that looked like a dead eel."

Had Ellery said, "Something that looked like a live unicorn," Priam could not have reacted more violently. He jerked against the tray and most of the whisky sprayed out on his beard. He spluttered, swiping at himself.

As far as Keats could see, the others were merely

bewildered. Even Wallace dropped his smile, although he quickly picked it up and put it on again.

"I was convinced from practically the outset," Ellery went on, "that these 'warnings'—to use the language of the original note to Hill—were interconnected; separate but integral parts of an all-over pattern. And they are. The pattern is fantastic—for instance, even now I'm sure Lieutenant Keats still suspects what Hollywood calls a weenie. But fantastic or not, it exists; and the job I set myself was to figure out what it was. And now that I've figured it out, it doesn't seem fantastic at all. In fact, it's straightforward, even simple, and it certainly expresses a material enough meaning. The fantasy in this case, as in so many cases, lies in the mind that evolved the pattern, not in the pattern itself.

"As the warnings kept coming in, I kept trying to discover their common denominator, the cement that was holding them together. When you didn't know what to look for—unlike Mr. Priam, who did know what to look for—it was hard, because in some of them the binding agent was concealed.

"It struck me, after I'd gone over the warnings innumerable times," said Ellery, and he paused to light a cigaret so that nothing in the room was audible but the scratch of the match and Roger Priam's heavy breathing, "it struck me finally that *every warning centrally involved an animal.*"

Laurel said, "What?"

"I'm not counting the dog used to bring the warning note to Hill. Since it conveyed a warning to Hill and not to you, Mr. Priam, we must consider the dead dog entirely apart from the warnings sent to you. Still it's interesting to note in passing that Hill's series of warnings, which never got beyond the first, began with an animal, too.

"Omitting for the moment the contents of the first box you received, Mr. Priam," Ellery said, "let's see how the concept 'animal' derives from the warnings we had direct knowledge of. Your second warning was a poisoning attack, a non-fatal dose of arsenic. The animal? *Tuna fish,* the medium by which the poison was administered.

"The third warning? *Frogs and toads.*

"The fourth warning was one step removed from the concept—a wallet. But the wallet was leather, and the leather came from an *alligator.*

"There was no mistaking the animal in the fifth warning. The ancient Greek comedy by Aristophanes—*The Birds*.

"And the sixth warning, Mr. Priam—some worthless old stock certificates—would have given me a great deal of trouble if you hadn't suggested the connection yourself. There's a contemptuous phrase applied to such stocks by market traders, you said—*'cats and dogs.'* And you were quite right—that's what they're called.

"So . . . fish, frogs, alligator, birds, cats and dogs. The fish, frogs, and alligator suggested literally, the birds and the cats and dogs suggested by allusion. All animals. That was the astonishing fact. What did you say, Mr. Priam?"

But Priam had merely been mumbling in his beard.

"Now the fact that each of the five warnings I'd had personal contact with concealed, like a puzzle, a different animal—astonishing as it was—told me nothing," continued Ellery, throwing his cigarette into Priam's fireplace. "I realized after some skull work that the meaning must go far deeper. It had to be dug out.

"But digging out the deeper meaning was another story.

"You either see it or you don't. It's all there. There's nothing up its sleeve. The trick lies in the fact that, like all great mystifications, it wears the cloak of invisibility. I do not use the word 'great' loosely. It's just that—a great conception—and it wouldn't surprise me if it takes its place among the classic inventions of the criminal mind."

"For God's sake," burst out Crowe Macgowan, "talk something that makes sense!"

"Mac," said Ellery, "what are frogs and toads?"

"What are frogs and toads?"

"That's right. What kind of animals are they?"

Macgowan looked blank.

"Amphibians," said old Mr. Collier.

"Thank you, Mr. Collier. And what are alligators?"

"Alligators are reptiles."

"The wallet derived from a reptile. And to which family of animals do cats and dogs belong?"

"Mammals," said Delia's father.

"Now let's restate our data, still ignoring the first warning, of which none of us had firsthand knowledge but Mr. Priam. The second warning was *fish*. The third warning was *amphibians*. The fourth warning was *reptiles*.

166

The fifth warning was *birds*. The sixth warning was *mammals*.

"Immediately we perceive a change in the appearance of the warnings. From being an apparently unrelated, rather silly conglomeration, they've taken on a related, scientific character.

"Is there a science in which fish, amphibians, reptiles, birds, and mammals are related—what's more, *in exactly that order?*

"In fact, is there a science in which fish are regarded as coming—as it were—second, amphibians third, reptiles fourth, birds fifth, and mammals last?—exactly as the warnings came?

"Any high school biology student could answer the question without straining himself.

"*They are progressive stages in the evolution of man.*"

Roger Priam was blinking steadily, as if there were a growing, rather too bright light.

"So you see, Mr. Priam," said Ellery with a smile, "there was no bluff involved whatever. Since the second warning, fish, represents the second stage in the evolution of man, and the third warning, amphibians, represents the third stage in the evolution of man, and so on, then plainly the first warning could only have represented the first stage in the evolution of man. It's the lowest class of what zoologists call, I believe, craniate vertebrates—the lamprey, which resembles an eel but belongs to a different order. So I knew, Mr. Priam, that when you opened that first box you found in it something that looked like an eel. There was no other possibility."

"I thought it was a dead eel," said Priam rigidly.

"And did you know what the thing that looked like a dead eel meant, Mr. Priam?"

"No, I didn't."

"There was no note in that first box giving you the key to the warnings?"

"No . . ."

"He couldn't have expected you to catch his meaning from the nature of the individual warnings themselves," said Ellery with a frown. "To see through a thing like this calls for a certain minimum of education which—unfortunately, Mr. Priam—you don't have. And he knows you don't have it; he knows you, I think, very well."

"You mean he sent all these things," cried Laurel, "not caring whether they were understood or not?"

The question was in Lieutenant Keats's eyes, too.

"It begins to appear," said Ellery slowly, "as if he preferred that they *weren't* understood. It was terror he was after—terror for its own sake." He turned slightly away with a worried look.

"I never did know what they meant," muttered Roger Priam. "It was not knowing that made me . . ."

"Then it's high time you did, Mr. Priam." Ellery had shrugged his worry off. "The kind of mentality that would concoct such an unusual series of warnings was obviously not an ordinary one. Granted his motive—which was to inspire terror, to punish, to make his victim die mentally over and over—he must still have had a mind which was capable of thinking in these specialized terms and taking this specific direction. Why did he choose the stages of evolution as the basis of his warnings? How did his brain come to take that particular path? Our mental processes are directly influenced by our capacities, training, and experience. To have founded his terror campaign on the evolution theory, to have worked it out in such systematic detail, the enemy of Leander Hill and Roger Priam must have been a man of scientific training—biologist, zoologist, anthropologist . . . or a naturalist.

"When you think of the stages of evolution," continued Ellery, "you automatically think of Charles Darwin. Darwin was the father of the evolutionary theory. It was Darwin's researches over a hundred years ago, his lecture before the Linnaean Society in 1858 on 'The Theory of Evolution,' his publication the following year of the amplification of his 'Theory' which he called *On the Origin of Species*, that opened a new continent of scientific knowledge in man's exploration of his own development.

"So when I saw the outline of a naturalist and accordingly thought of Darwin, the greatest naturalist of all, it was a logical step to think back to Darwin's historic voyage—one of the world's great voyages on perhaps science's most famous ship—the voyage of naturalistic exploration on which Darwin formulated his theory of the origin of species and their perpetuation by natural selection. And thinking back to that produced a really wonderful result." Ellery gripped the back of a chair, leaning over it. "Because the ship on which Charles Darwin set sail from Plymouth, England, in 1831 on that epic voyage was named . . . H.M.S. *Beagle*."

"Beagle." Laurel goggled. "*The dead dog!*"

"There were a number of possibilities," Ellery nodded. "In sending Hill a beagle, the sender might have been providing the master key which was to unlock the door of the warnings to come—beagle, Darwin's ship, Darwin, evolution. But that seemed pretty remote. Neither Hill nor Priam was likely to know the name of the ship on which Darwin sailed more than a hundred years ago, if indeed they knew anything at all about the man who had sailed on it. Or the plotter might have been memorializing in a general way the whole basis of his plot. But this was even unlikelier. Our friend the scientifically minded enemy hasn't wasted his time with purposeless gestures.

"There were other possibilities along the same line, but the more I puzzled over the dead beagle the more convinced I became that it was meant to refer to something specific and significant in the background of Hill, Priam, and their enemy. What could the connection have been? What simple, direct tie-up could have existed among a naturalist and two nonscientific men, and the word or concept 'beagle,' and something that happened about twenty-five years ago?

"Immediately a connection suggested itself, a connection that covered the premises in the simplest, most direct way. Suppose twenty-five years or so ago a naturalist, together with Hill and Priam, planned a scientific expedition. Today they would probably use a plane; twenty-five years ago they would have gone by boat. And suppose the naturalist, conscious of his profession's debt to the great naturalist Darwin, in embarking on this expedition had the problem of naming, or the fancy to rename, the vessel on which he, Hill, and Priam were to be carried on their voyage of naturalistic exploration . . .

"I suggested to Lieutenant Keats," said Ellery, "that he try to trace a small ship, probably of the coastal type, which was either built, bought, or chartered for purposes of a scientific expedition—a ship named, or renamed, *Beagle* which set sail from probably an American port in 1925 or so.

"And Lieutenant Keats, with the co-operation of various police agencies of the coastal cities, succeeded in tracing such a vessel. Shall I go on, Mr. Priam?"

Ellery paused to light a fresh cigaret.

Again there was no sound but the hiss of the match and Priam's breathing.

"Let's take the conventional interpretation of Mr. Priam's

169

silence, Lieutenant," said Ellery, blowing out the match, "and nail this thing down."

Keats pulled a slip of paper from his pocket and came forward.

"THE NAME OF the man we want," the detective began, "is Charles Lyell Adam. Charles Lyell Adam came from a very wealthy Vermont family. He was an only child and when his parents died he inherited all their money. But Adam wasn't interested in money. Or, as far as we know, in women, liquor, or good times. He was educated abroad, he never married, and he kept pretty much to himself.

"He was a gentleman, a scholar, and an amateur scientist. His field was naturalism. He devoted all his time to it. He was never attached to a museum, or a university, or any scientific organization that we've been able to dig up. His money made it possible for him to do as he liked, and what he liked to do most was tramp about the world studying the flora and fauna of out-of-the-way places.

"His exact age," continued Keats, after referring to his notes, "isn't known. The Town Hall where his birth was recorded went up in smoke around 1910, and there was no baptismal record—at least, we haven't located one. Attempts to fix his age by questioning old residents of the Vermont town where he was born have produced conflicting testimony—we couldn't find any kin. We weren't able to find anything on him in the draft records of the First World War—he can't be located either as a draftee or an enlisted man. Probably he got some sort of deferment, although we haven't been able to turn up anything on this, either. About all we can be sure of is that, in the year 1925, when Adam organized an expedition bound for the Guianas, he was anywhere from twenty-seven to thirty-nine years old.

"For this expedition," said Keats, "Adam had a special boat built, a fifty-footer equipped with an auxiliary engine and scientific apparatus of his own design. Exactly what he was after, or what he was trying to prove scientifically, no one seems to know. But in the summer of '25 Adam's boat, *Beagle,* cleared Boston Harbor and headed down the coast.

"It stopped over in Cuba for repairs. There was a long delay. When the repairs were finished, the *Beagle* got under way again. And that was the last anybody saw or heard of the *Beagle*, or Charles Lyell Adam, or his crew. The delay ran them into hurricane weather and, after a thorough search turned up no trace of the vessel, the *Beagle* was presumed to have gone down with all hands.

"The crew," said Lieutenant Keats, "consisted of two men, each about forty years old at the time, each a deepwater sailor of many years' experience, like Adam himself. We've got their names—their real names—but we may as well keep calling them by the names they took in 1927: Leander Hill and Roger Priam."

Keats shot the name at the bearded man in the wheelchair as if it were a tennis ball; and, like spectators at a match, they turned their heads in unison to Priam. And Priam clutched the arms of his chair, and he bit his lip until a bright drop appeared. This drop he licked; another appeared and it oozed into his beard. But he met their eyes defiantly.

"All right," he rumbled. "So now you know it. What about it?"

It was as if he were grounded on a reef and gamely mustering his forces of survival against the winds.

"THE REST," SAID Ellery, squarely to Priam, "is up to you."

"You bet it's up to me!"

"I mean whether you tell us the truth or we try to figure it out, Mr. Priam."

"You're doing the figuring, Mister."

"You still won't talk?"

"You're doing the talking," said Priam.

"We don't have much to go on, as you know very well," said Ellery, nodding as if he had expected nothing else, "but perhaps what we have is enough. You're here, twenty-five years later; and up to recently Leander Hill was here, too. And according to the author of the note that was left in the beagle's collar, Charles Lyell Adam was left for dead twenty-five years ago, under circumstances which justified him—in his own judgment, at any rate—in using the word 'murder,' Mr. Priam . . . except that he didn't die and *he's* here.

"Did you and Hill scuttle the *Beagle*, Mr Priam, when you were Adam's crew and the *Beagle* was somewhere in West Indian water? Attack Adam, leave him for dead, scuttle the *Beagle*, and escape in a dinghy, Mr. Priam?

171

The Haitians sail six hundred miles in cockleshells as a matter of course, and you and Hill were good enough seamen for Adam to have hired in the first place.

"But seamen don't attempt murder and scuttle good ships for no reason, Mr. Priam. What was the reason? If it had been a personal matter, or mutiny, or shipwreck as a result of incompetence or negligence, or any of the usual reasons, you and Hill could always have made your way back to the nearest port and reported what you pleased to explain the disappearance of Adam and his vessel. But you and Hill didn't do that, Mr. Priam. You and Hill chose to vanish along with Adam—to vanish in your sailor personalities, that is, leading the world to believe that Adam's crew had died with him. You went to a great deal of trouble to bury yourselves, Mr. Priam. You spent a couple of years doing it, preparing new names and personalities for your resurrection. Why? Because you had something to conceal— *something you couldn't have concealed had you come back as Adam's crew.*

"That's the most elementary logic, Mr. Priam. Now will you tell us what happened?"

Nothing in Priam stirred, not even the hairs of his beard.

"Then I'll have to tell you. In 1927, you and Hill appeared in Los Angeles and set up a wholesale jewelry business. What did you know about the jewlry business? We know all about you and Hill now, Mr. Priam, from the time you were born until you signed on the *Beagle* for its one and only voyage. You both went to sea as boys. There was nothing in either of your backgrounds that remotely touched jewels or jewelry. And, like most sailors, you were poor men. Still, two years later, here you both were, starting a fabulous business in precious stones. *Was that what you couldn't have concealed had you come back as Adam's crew?* Because the authorities would have said, *Where did these two poor seamen get all this money—or all these jewels?* And that's one question, Mr. Priam, you didn't want asked—either you or Hill.

"So it's reasonable to conjecture, Mr. Priam," said Ellery, smiling, "that the *Beagle* didn't go down in a hurricane after all. That the *Beagle* reached its destination, perhaps an uninhabited island, and that in exploring for the fauna and flora that interested him as a naturalist,

Adam ran across something far afield from his legitimate interests. Like an old treasure chest, Mr. Priam, buried by one of the pirate swarms who used to infest those waters. You can find descendants of those pirates, Mr. Priam, living in the Bahamas today . . . An old treasure chest, Mr. Priam, filled with precious stones. And you and Hill, poor sailors, attacked Adam, took the *Beagle* into blue water, sank her, and got away in her dinghy.

"And there you were, with a pirate's fortune in jewels, and how were you to live to enjoy it? The whole thing was fantastic. It was fantastic to find it, it was fantastic to own it, and it was fantastic to think that you couldn't do anything with it. But one of you got a brilliant idea, and about that idea there was nothing fantastic at all. Bury all trace of your old selves, come back as entirely different men—*and go into the jewelry business*.

"And that's what you and Hill did, Mr. Priam. For two years you studied the jewelers' trade—exactly where, we haven't learned. When you felt you had enough knowledge and experience, you set up shop in Los Angeles . . . and your stock was the chest of precious stones Adam had found on his island, for undisputed possession of which you'd murdered him. And now you *could* dispose of them. Openly. Legitimately. And get rich on them."

Priam's beard was askew on his chest. His eyes were shut, as if he were asleep . . . or gathering his strength.

"But Adam didn't die," said Ellery gently. "You and Hill bungled. He survived. Only he knows how he nursed himself back to health, what he lived on, how he got back to civilization, and where, and where he's been since. But by his own testimony, in the note, he dedicated the rest of his life to tracking you and Hill down. For over twenty years he kept searching for the two sailors who had left him for dead—for his two murderers, Mr. Priam. Adam didn't want the fortune—he had his own fortune; and, anyway, he was never very interested in money. What he wanted, Mr. Priam, was revenge. As his note says.

"And then he found you."

And now Ellery's voice was no longer gentle.

"Hill was a disappointment to him. The shock of learning that Adam, against all reason, was alive—and all that that implied—was too much for Hill's heart. Hill was rather different from you, I think, Mr. Priam; whatever he'd been in the old days at sea, he had grown into the semblance of a solid citizen. And perhaps he'd never been really vicious. You were always the bully-boy of the team, weren't you? Maybe Hill didn't do anything but acquiesce in your crime, dazzled by the reward you dangled before his eyes. You needed him to get away; I think you needed his superior intelligence. In any event, after that one surrender to you and temptation, Hill built himself up into what a girl like Laurel could learn to love and respect . . . and for the sake of whose memory she was even willing to kill.

"Hill was a man of imagination, Mr. Priam, and I think what killed him at the very first blow was as much his dread of the effect on Laurel of the revelation of his old crime as the knowledge that Adam was alive and hot for revenge.

"But you're made of tougher material, Mr. Priam. You haven't disappointed Adam; on the contrary. It's really a pleasure for Adam to work on you. He's still the scientist—his method is as scientifically pitiless as the dissection of an old cadaver. And he's having himself a whale of a time, Mr. Priam, with you providing the sport. I don't think you understand with what wonderful humor Charles Lyell Adam is chasing you. Or do you?"

But when Priam spoke, he seemed not to have been listening. At least, he did not answer the question. He roused himself and he said, "Who is he? What's he calling himself now? Do you know that?"

"That's what you're interested in, is it?" Ellery smiled. "Why, no, Mr. Priam, we don't. All we know about him today is that he's somewhere between fifty-two and sixty-four years of age. I'm sure you wouldn't recognize him; either his appearance has been radically changed by time or he's had it changed for him by, say, plastic surgery. But even if Adam looked today exactly as he looked twenty-five years ago, it wouldn't do you—or us, Mr. Priam—any good. Because he doesn't have to be on the scene in person, you see. He could be working through someone else." Priam blinked and blinked. "You're not precisely a well-loved man, Mr. Priam, and there are people very close to you who might not be at all repelled by the idea of contributing to your unhappiness. So if you have any idea that as long as you protect yourself against a middle-aged male of certain proportions you're all right, you'd better get rid of it as quickly as possible. Adam's unofficial accomplice, working entirely for love of the job, you might say, could be of either

174

sex, of any age . . . and right here, Mr. Priam, in your own household."

Priam sat still. Not wholly in fear—with a reserve of desperate caution, it seemed, even defiance, like a treed cat.

"What a stinking thing to say—!"

"Shut up, Mac." And this was Keats, in a low voice, but there was a note in it that made Delia's son bring his lips together and keep them that way.

"A moment ago," said Ellery, "I mentioned Adam's sense of humor. I wonder if you see the point, Mr. Priam. Where his joke is heading."

"What?" said Priam in a mumble.

"All his warnings to you have had not one, but two, things in common. Not only has each warning involved an animal—*but each animal was dead.*"

Priam's head jerked.

"His first warning was a dead lamprey. His second warning was a dead fish. His third consisted of dead frogs and toads. The next a dead alligator. The next—*The Birds*—a little symbolism here, because he mutilated and destroyed the book . . . the only way in which you can physically 'kill' a book! Even his last warning—the 'cats and dogs'—connotes death; there's nothing quite so 'dead' as the stock of a company that has folded up. Really a humorist, this Adam.

"Right up the ladder of evolution—from the lowest order of vertebrates, the lamprey, to one of the highest, cats and dogs. And every one, in fact or by symbol, was delivered dead.

"But Mr. Priam, Adam isn't finished." Ellery leaned forward. "He hasn't climbed Darwin's ladder to stop at the next-to-the-last rung. The top rung of that ladder is still to be put in evidence. The highest creature in the class of Mammalia.

"So it's perfectly certain that there's an exhibit yet to come, the last exhibit, and by inference from the preceding ones, a dead exhibit. Charles Lyell Adam is going to produce *a dead man,* Mr. Priam, and there wouldn't be much point to his Darwinian joke if that dead man weren't Roger Priam."

Priam remained absolutely motionless.

"WE'VE GONE ALL over this," said Lieutenant Keats sharply, "and we agree there's only one thing to do. You're

tagged for murder, Priam, and it's going to come soon—
tomorrow, maybe tonight, maybe an hour from now.
I've got to have you alive, Priam, and I want Adam
alive, too, if possible, because the law likes us to bring
'em back that way. You're going to have to be guarded
night and day, starting right now. A man in this room.
One on the terrace there. A couple around the grounds—"

Roger Priam filled his chest.

A roar came out that set the crystals in the chandelier
jangling.

"Criminal, am I? On what evidence?" He brandished a
clublike forefinger at Lieutenant Keats. "I'm not admitting
a thing, you can't prove a thing, and I ain't asking for
your protection or taking it!—d'ye get me?"

"What are you afraid of?" jeered the detective. "That
we *will* lay our hands on Adam?"

"I've always fought my own scraps and, by God, I'll
fight this one!"

"From a wheelchair?"

"From a wheelchair! Now get out of my house, you
——, and stay out!"

Fifteen

THEY STAYED OUT. Anyone from the outside would have said they were finished with Roger Priam and all his works. Daily Lieutenant Keats might have been seen going about his business; daily Ellery might have been seen staring at his—a blank sheet of paper in a still typewriter —or at night dining alone, with an ear cocked, or afterwards hovering above the telephone. He rarely left the cottage during the day; at night, never. His consumption of cigarets, pipe tobacco, coffee, and alcohol gave Mrs. Williams a second subject for her interminable monologues; she alternated between predictions of sudden death for the world and creeping ulcers for Ellery.

At one time or another Laurel, Crowe Macgowan, Alfred Wallace, Collier—even Delia Priam—phoned or called in person, either unsolicited or by invitation. But each hung up or went away as worried or perplexed or thoughtful as he had been; and if Ellery unburdened himself to any of them, or vice versa, nothing seemed to come of it.

And Ellery lit another cigaret, or tormented another pipe, or gulped more hot coffee, or punished another highball, and Mrs. Williams's wails kept assailing the kitchen ceiling.

THEN, ONE HUMID night at the beginning of the fourth week in July, just after midnight, the call came for which Ellery was waiting.

He listened, he said a few words, he broke the connection, and he called the number of Keats's house.

Keats answered on the first ring.

"Queen?"

"Yes. As fast as you can."

Ellery immediately hung up and ran out to his car.

He had parked the Kaiser at the front door every night for a week.

He left it on the road near the Priam mailbox. Keats's car was already there. Ellery made his way along the bordering grass to the side of the house. He used no flashlight. In the shadow of the terrace a hand touched his arm.

"Quick." Keats's whisper was an inch from his ear.

The house was dark, but a faint night light was burning in Roger Priam's room off the terrace. The French door was open, and the terrace was in darkness.

They got down on their knees, peered through the screening of the inner door.

Priam's wheelchair was in its bed position, made up for the night. He lay on his back, motionless, beard jutting obliquely to the ceiling.

Nothing happened for several minutes.

Then there was the slightest metallic sound.

The night light was in an electric outlet in the wainscoting near the door which led into the hall. They saw the doorknob clearly; it was in motion. When it stopped, the door began to open. It creaked. Came to rest.

Priam did not move.

The door opened swiftly.

But the night light was beyond the doorway and when the door swung back to the farther wall it cut off most of the slight glow. All they could make out from the terrace was a formless blackness deeper than the darkness at the rear of the room. This gap in the void moved steadily from the doorway to Roger Priam's chair-bed. A tentacular something projected before it. The projection swam into the outermost edge of the night light's orbit and they saw that it was a revolver.

Beside Priam's chair the moving blackness halted.

The revolver came up a little.

Keats stirred. It was more a tightening of his muscles than a true movement; still, Ellery's fingers clamped on the detective's arm.

Keats froze.

AND THEN THE whole room exploded, motion gone wild.

Priam's arm flashed upward and his great hand closed like the jaws of a reptile on the wrist of the hand that held the revolver. The crippled man heaved his bulk upright, bellowing. There was the blurriest of struggles; they

178

looked like two squids locked in battle at the bottom of the sea.

Then there was a soggy report, a smart thud, and quiet.

When Ellery snapped the wall switch Keats was already on his knees by the figure on the floor. It lay in a curl, almost comfortably, one arm hidden and the other outstretched. At the end of the outstretched arm lay the revolver.

"Chest," Keats muttered.

Roger Priam was glaring at the two men.

"It's Adam," he said hoarsely. "Where did you two come from? He came to kill me. It's Adam. I told you I could handle him!" He laughed with his teeth, but at once he began to shake, and he squinted at the fallen figure and rubbed his eyes with a trembling hand. "Who is he? Let me see him!"

"It's Alfred."

"Alfred?" The beard drooped.

Keats rose to go around Priam's chair. He plucked one of Priam's telephones from its hook and dialed a number.

"Alfred is Adam?" Priam sounded dazed, stupid. He recoiled quickly, but it was only Ellery removing his top blanket.

Ellery dropped the blanket over the thing on the floor.

"He's . . . ?" Priam's tongue came out. "Is he dead?"

"Headquarters?" said Keats. "Keats, Hollywood Division, reporting a homicide. The Hill-Priam case. Roger Priam just shot Alfred Wallace, his secretary-nurse-what-have-you, shot him to death . . . That's right. Through the heart. I witnessed the shooting myself, from the terrace—"

"To death," said Priam. "To death. He's dead! . . . But it was self-defense. You witnessed it—if you witnessed it . . . He pussy-footed into my room here. I heard him come in. I made believe I was sleeping. Oh, I was ready for him!" His voice cracked. "Didn't you see him point the gun at me? I grabbed it, twisted his hand! It was self-defense—"

"We saw it all, Mr. Priam," said Ellery in a soothing voice.

"Good, you saw it. He's dead. Damn him, he's dead! Wallace . . . Try to kill me, would he? By God, it's over. It's over."

"Yes," Keats was saying into the phone. "When? Okay, no hurry." He hung up.

179

"You heard Mr. Queen," Priam babbled. "He saw it all, Lieutenant—"

"I know." Keats went over to the blanket and lifted one corner. Then he dropped the blanket and took out a cigaret and lit it. "We'll have to wait." He inhaled.

"Sure, yes, Lieutenant." Priam fumbled with something. The upper half of his bed rose, the lower sank, to form the chair. He groped. "A drink," he said. "You join me? Celebration." He guffawed. "Besides, I'm a little wobbly."

Ellery was wandering around, pulling at an ear, rubbing the back of his neck. There was a ridge between his eyes.

Keats kept smoking and watching him.

"I've got to hand it to him," Priam was saying, busy with a bottle and a glass. "Alfred Wallace . . . Must have had his nose fixed. I never recognized him. Smooth, smooth operator. Gets right on the inside. Laughing up his sleeve all the time! But who's laughing now? Here's to him." He raised the glass, grinning, but the wild animal was still in his eyes. He tossed the whisky off. When he set the glass down, his hand was no longer shaking. "But there he is, and here I am, and it's all over." His head came down, and he was silent.

"Mr. Priam," said Ellery.

Priam did not reply.

"Mr. Priam?"

"Hey?" Priam looked up.

"There's one point that still bothers me. Now that it's over, would you straighten me out on it?"

Priam looked at him. Then, deliberately, he reached for the bottle and refilled his glass.

"Why, Mr. Queen, it all depends," he said. "If you expect me to admit a lot of guff—with maybe a stenographer taking it all down from my terrace—you can save your wind. All right, this man was after me. No idea why, friends, except that he went crazy. On that voyage. Absolutely nuts.

"On the *Beagle* he went after me and my shipmate with a machete. We were off some dirty island and we jumped overboard, swam to the beach, and hid in the woods. Hurricane blew up that night and swept the *Beagle* out to sea. We never saw the ship or Adam again. Shipmate and me, we then found a treasure on that island and we finally got it off on a raft we made.

"Reason we laid low and changed our names to Hill and Priam was so Adam could never come back and claim one third of the treasure—he'd been exploring that island. And maybe he'd still try to kill us even if he didn't claim a third. That's my story, friends. Not a crime in a cargo load." He grinned and tossed off the second glassful. "And I'm sticking to it."

Keats was regarding him with admiration. "It's a lousy story, Priam, but if you stick to it we're stuck with it."

"Anything else, Mr. Queen . . ." Priam waved genially. "All you got to do is ask. What's the point that's been giving you such a bad time?"

"The letter Adam sent to Leander Hill," said Ellery.

"The letter—?" Priam stared. "Why in hell would you be worrying about *that?*"

Ellery took a folded sheet of paper from his breast pocket.

"This is a copy of the note Hill found in the silver box on the beagle's collar," he said. "It's been some time and perhaps I'd better refresh your memory by reading it aloud."

"Go ahead." Priam still stared.

"You believed me dead," read Ellery. *"Killed, murdered. For over a score of years I have looked for you —for you and for him. And now I have found you. Can you guess my plan? You'll die. Quickly? No, very slowly. And so pay me back for my long years of searching and dreaming of revenge. Slow dying . . . unavoidable dying. For you and for him. Slow and sure—dying in mind and in body. And for each pace forward a warning . . . a warning of special meaning for you—and for him. Meanings for pondering and puzzling. Here is warning number one."*

"See?" said Priam. "Crazy as a bug."

"Killed, murdered," said Keats. "By a hurricane, Mr. Priam?" But he was smiling.

"That was his craziness, Lieutenant. I remember when he was steaming after us on deck, waving the machete around his head, how he kept yelling we were trying to murder him. All the time he was trying to murder us. Ask your brain doctors. They'll tell you." Priam swung about. "Is that what's been bothering you, Mr. Queen?"

"What? Oh! No, not that, Mr. Priam." Ellery scowled down at the paper. "It's the phrasing."

"The what?"

"The way the message is worded."

Priam was puzzled. "What's the matter with it?"

181

"A great deal is the matter with it, Mr. Priam. I'll go so far as to say that this is the most remarkable collection of words I've ever been privileged to read. How many words are there in this message, Mr. Priam?"

"How the devil should I know?"

"Ninety-nine, Mr. Priam."

Priam glanced at Keats. But Keats was merely smoking with the gusto of a man who has denied himself too long, and there was nothing on Ellery's face but concern. "So it's got ninety-nine words. I don't get it."

"Ninety-nine words, Mr. Priam, comprising three hundred and ninety-seven letters of the English alphabet."

"I still don't get it." A note of truculence crept into Priam's heavy voice. "What are you trying to prove, that you can count?"

"I'm trying to prove—and I can prove, Mr. Priam—that there's something wrong with this message."

"Wrong?" Priam's beard shot up. "What?"

"The tools of my business, Mr. Priam," said Ellery, "are words. I not only write words of my own, but I read extensively—and sometimes with envy—the words of others. So I consider myself qualified to make the following observation: This is the first time I've ever run across a piece of English prose, deathless or otherwise, made up of as many as ninety-nine words, consisting of almost four hundred individual characters, *in which the writer failed to use a single letter T.*"

"SINGLE LETTER *T*," repeated Priam. His lips moved after he stopped speaking, so that for a moment it looked as if he were chewing something with a foreign and disagreeable taste.

"It took me a long time to spot that, Mr. Priam," continued Ellery, walking around the body of Alfred Wallace. "It's the sort of thing you can't see because it's so obvious. When we read, most of us concentrate on the sense of what we're reading, not its physical structure. Who looks at a building and sees the individual bricks? Yet the secret of the building lies precisely there. There are twenty-six basic bricks in the English language, some of them more important than the rest. There's no guesswork about those bricks, Mr. Priam. Their nature, their usability, their interrelationships, the frequency of their occurrence have been determined as scientifically as the composition of stucco.

"Let me tell you about the letter *T*, Mr. Priam," said Ellery.

"The letter *T* is the second most frequently used letter in the English language. Only *E* occurs more frequently. *T* is the number two brick of the twenty-six.

"*T*, Mr. Priam, is the most frequently used *initial* letter in the English language.

"English uses a great many combinations of two letters representing a single speech sound. These are known as digraphs. The letter *T*, Mr. Priam, is part of the most frequently used digraph—*TH*.

"*T* is also part of the most frequently used trigraph—three letters spelling a single speech sound—*THE*, as in the word *BATHE*.

"*TT*, Mr. Priam, gives ground only to *SS* and *EE* as the most frequently used *double* letter.

"The same letters, *S* and *E*, are the only letters which occur more frequently than *T* as the *last* letters of words.

"But that isn't all, Mr. Priam," said Ellery. "The letter *T* is part of the most frequently used three-letter word in the English language—the word *THE*.

"The letter *T* is part of the most frequently used four-letter word—*THAT*—and also of the second most frequently used four letter word—*WITH*.

"And as if that weren't enough, Mr. Priam," said Ellery, "we find *T* in the second most frequently used two-letter word—*TO*—and in the fourth most frequently used two-letter word—*IT*. Do you wonder now, Mr. Priam," said Ellery, "why I called Charles Adam's note to your partner remarkable?

"It's so remarkable, Mr. Priam, that it's impossible. No conceivable chance or coincidence could produce a communication of almost a hundred English words that was completely lacking in *T's*. *The only way you can get a hundred-word message without a single* T *is by setting out to do so. You have to make a conscious effort to avoid using it.*

"Do you want confirmation, Mr. Priam?" asked Ellery, and now something new had come into his voice; it was no longer thoughtful or troubled. "The writer of this note didn't use a single *TO* or *IT* or *AT* or *THE* or *BUT* or *NOT* or *THAT* or *WITH* or *THIS*. You simply can't escape those words unless you're trying to.

"The note refers to you and Leander Hill; that is, to two people. He says: *I have looked for you and for him.* Why didn't he write: *I have looked for the two of you,*

183

or *I have looked for both of you?*—either of which would have been a more natural expression than *for you and for him?* The fact that in the word *TWO* and in the word *BOTH* the letter *T* occurs can hardly escape us. He just happened to express it that way? Perhaps once; even possibly twice; but he wrote *for you and for him* three times in the same message!

"He writes: *Slow dying . . . unavoidable dying.* And again: *dying in mind and in body.* He's no novelist or poet looking for a different way of saying things. And this is a note, not an essay for publication. Why didn't he use the common phrases: *Slow death . . . inevitable death . . . death mentally and physically?* Even though the whole message concerns death, the word itself—in that form —does not occur even once. If he was deliberately avoiding the letter *T*, the question is answered.

"*You believed me dead . . .* Had he expressed this in a normal, natural way he would have written: *You thought I was dead.* But *thought* contains two *T's.* We find the word *pondering,* for *to think over,* for obviously the same reason.

"And surely *Here is warning number one* is a circumlocution to avoid writing the more natural *This is the first warning.*

"Am I quibbling? Can this still have been a coincidence, dictated by an eccentric style? The odds against this mount astronomically when you consider two other examples from the note.

"*And for each pace forward a warning,* he writes. He's not talking about physical progress, where a *pace* might have a specialized meaning in the context. There is no reason on earth why he shouldn't have written *And for each step forward,* except that *step* contains a *T.*

"My last example is equally significant. He writes: *For over a score of years.* Why use the fancy word *score?* Why didn't he write: *For over twenty years,* or whatever the actual number of years was? Because the word *twenty,* or any combination including the word *twenty* —from twenty-one through twenty-nine—gets him involved in *T's.*"

ROGER PRIAM WAS baffled. He was trying to capture something, or recapture it. All his furrows were deeper with the effort, and his eyes rolled a little. But he said nothing.

And, in the background, Keats smoked; and, in the foreground, Alfred Wallace lay under the blanket.

"The question is, of course," said Ellery, "why the writer of the note avoided using the letter *T*.

"Let's see if we can't reconstruct something useful here.

"How was the original of Leander Hill's copy written? By hand, or by mechanical means? We have no direct evidence; the note has disappeared. Laurel caught a glimpse of the original when Hill took it from the little silver box, but Hill half-turned away as he read it and Laurel couldn't specify the character of the writing.

"But the simplest analysis shows the form in which it must have appeared. The letter could not have been hand-written. It is just as easy to write the letter *T* as any other letter of the alphabet. The writer, considering the theme of his message, could hardly have been playing word games; and no other test but ease or difficulty makes sense.

"If the note wasn't handwritten, then it was typewritten. You saw that note, Mr. Priam—Hill showed it to you the morning after his heart attack. Wasn't it typewritten?"

Priam looked up, frowning in a peculiar way. But he did not answer.

"It was typewritten," said Ellery. "But the moment you assume a typewritten note, the answer suggests itself. The writer was composing his message on a typewriter. He used no *T*'s. Why look for complicated reasons? If he used no *T*'s, it's simply because *T*'s were not available to him. He *couldn't* use *T*'s. The *T* key on the machine he was using wouldn't function. It was broken."

Surprisingly, Priam lifted his head and said, "You're guessing."

Ellery looked pained. "I'm not trying to prove how clever I am, Mr. Priam, but I must object to your verb. Guessing is as obnoxious to me as swearing is to a bishop. I submit that I worked this out; I've had little enough fun in this case! But let's assume it's a guess. It's a very sound guess, Mr. Priam, and it has the additional virtue of being susceptible to confirmation.

"I theorize a typewriter with a broken key. Do we know of a typewriter—in this case—which wasn't in perfect working order?

"Strangely enough, Mr. Priam, we do.

"On my way to your house for the first time, in Laurel Hill's car, I asked Laurel some questions about you. She

185

told me how self-sufficient you've made yourself, how as a reaction to your disability you dislike help of the most ordinary kind. As an example, Laurel said that when she was at your house 'the day before' you were in a foul mood over having to dictate business memoranda to Wallace instead of doing them yourself—*your typewriter had just been sent into Hollywood to be repaired.*"

Priam twisted. Keats stood by his wheelchair, lifting the attached typewriter shelf.

Priam choked a splutter, glancing painfully down at the shelf as Keats swung it up and around.

Ellery and Keats bent over the machine, ignoring the man in the chair.

They glanced at each other.

Keats tapped the *T* key with a fingernail. "Mr. Priam," he said, "there's only one key on this machine that's new. It's the *T*. The note to Hill was typed right here." He spread his fingers over the carriage of Priam's typewriter, almost with affection.

A sound, formless and a little beastly, came out of Priam's throat. Keats stood by him, very close.

"And who could have typed a note on your machine, Mr. Priam?" asked Ellery in the friendliest of voices. "There's no guesswork here. If I'd never seen this typewriter shelf I'd have known the machine is screwed on. It would have to be, to keep it from falling off when the shelf is swung aside and dropped. Besides, Laurel Hill told me so.

"So, except for those times when the typewriter needs a major repair, it's a permanent fixture of your wheelchair. Was the original of the note to Hill typed on your machine after it was removed for repair but before the broken *T* key was replaced? No, because the note was delivered to Hill two weeks *before* you sent the machine into Hollywood. Did someone type the note on your machine while you were out of your wheelchair? No, Mr. Priam, because you're never out of your chair; you haven't left it for fifteen years. Was the note typed on your machine while you were—say—asleep? Impossible; when the chair is a bed the shelf obviously can't come up.

"So I'm very much afraid, Mr. Priam, there's only one conclusion we can reach," said Ellery. *"You typed that warning note yourself.*

"It's you who threatened your partner with death.

"The only active enemy out of your past and Hill's, Mr. Priam, is Roger Priam."

"DON'T MISUNDERSTAND ME," said Ellery. "Charles Adam is not imaginary. He was an actual person, as our investigation uncovered. Adam disappeared in West Indian waters 'over a score of years ago,' as you wrote in the note, and he hasn't been seen or heard of since. It was only the note that made us believe Adam was still alive. Knowing now that you wrote the note, we can only conclude that Adam didn't survive the *Beagle's* voyage twenty-five years ago after all, that you and Hill did succeed in killing him, and that his reappearance here in Southern California this summer was an illusion you deliberately engineered.

"Priam," said Ellery, "you knew what a shock it would be to your partner Hill to learn that Adam was apparently alive after so many years of thinking he was dead. Not only alive but explicitly out for revenge. You knew that Hill would be particularly susceptible to such news. He had built a new life for himself. He was bound up emotionally with Laurel, his adopted daughter, who worshiped the man he seemed to be.

"So Adam's 'reappearance' threatened not only Hill's life but, what was possibly even more important to him, the whole structure of Laurel's love for him. There was a good chance, you felt, that Hill's bad heart—he had had two attacks before—could not survive such a shock. And you were right—your note killed him.

"If Hill had any doubts about the authenticity of the note, you dispelled them the morning after the heart attack, when for the first time in fifteen years you took the trouble of having yourself carted over to Hill's house. The cause could only have been a telephone agreement with Hill to have a confidential, urgent talk about the note. You had, I imagine, another and equally pressing reason for that unprecedented visit: You wanted to be sure the note was destroyed so that it couldn't be traced back to your typewriter. Either Hill gave it to you and you destroyed it then or later, or he destroyed it before your eyes. What you didn't know, Priam, and what he didn't tell you, was that he had already made a copy of the note in his own handwriting and hidden it in his mattress. Why? Maybe after the first shock, when Hill thought it over, he hadn't been *quite* convinced. Maybe a sixth sense told him before you got to him that something was wrong. Whether you convinced him during that visit or not, the note was probably already copied and in his mattress, and a native caution—despite all your arguments

187

—made him leave it there and say nothing about it. We can't know and won't ever know just what went on in Hill's mind.

"But the damage was done by the sheer impact of the shock, Priam. Murder by fright," said Ellery. "Far colder-blooded and more deliberate than killing by gun or knife, or even poison. A murder calling for great pains of premeditation. One wonders why. Not merely why you wanted to kill Hill, but why you splashed your crime so carefully with that elaborate camouflage of 'the enemy out of the past.'

"Your motive must have been compelling. It couldn't have been gain, because Hill's death brought you no material benefits; his share of the business went to Laurel. It couldn't have been to avoid exposure as the murderer of Adam twenty-five years ago, for Hill was neck-deep in that crime with you and had benefited from it equally—he was hardly in a position to hold it over you. In fact, he was in a poorer position than you were to hold it over *him,* because Hill had the additional reason to want to keep it from Laurel. Nor is it likely that you killed him to avoid exposure for any other crime of which he might have gained knowledge, such as—I take the obvious theory —embezzlement of the firm's funds. Because the truth is you have had very little to do with the running of Hill & Priam; it was Hill who ran it, while you merely put up a show of being an equal partner in work and responsibility. Never leaving your house, you could hardly have been so in control of daily events as to have been able to steal funds, or falsify accounts, or anything like that. Nor was it trouble over your wife. Hill's relationship with Mrs. Priam was friendly and correct; besides," said Ellery rather dryly, "he was getting past the age for that sort of thing.

"There's only one thing you accomplished, Priam, by killing Leander Hill. So, in the absence of a positive indication in any other direction, I'm forced to conclude that that's why you wanted Hill out of the way.

"And it's confirmed by your character, Priam, the whole drive of your personality.

"By killing Hill *you got rid of your business partner.* That is one of the facts that emerge from his death. Is it the key fact? I think it is.

"Priam, you have an obsessive need to dominate, to dominate your immediate background and everyone in it. The one thing above all others that you can't stand is dependence on others. With you the alternative is not so much independence of others as making others dependent on you. Because physically you're helpless, you want power. You must be master—even if, as in the case of your wife, you have to use another man to do it.

"You hated Hill because he, not you, was master of Hill & Priam. He ran it and he had run it for fifteen years with no more than token help from you. The firm's employes looked up to him and loathed you. He made policy, purchases, sales; to accounts, big and small, Leander Hill was Hill & Priam and Roger Priam was a forgotten and useless invalid stuck away in a house somewhere. The fact that to Hill you owe your material security and the sound condition of Hill & Priam has festered inside of you for fifteen years. Even while you enjoyed the fruits of Hill's efforts, they left a bitter taste in your mouth that eventually poisoned you.

"You planned his death.

"With Hill out of the way, you would be undisputed master of the business. That you might run it into the ground probably never occurred to you. But if it did, I'm sure the danger didn't even make you hesitate. The big thing was to make everyone involved in or with Hill & Priam come crawling to you. The big thing was to be boss."

ROGER PRIAM SAID nothing. This time he did not even make the beastly sound. But his little eyes roved.

Keats moved even closer.

"Once you saw what you had to do," continued Ellery, "you realized that you were seriously handicapped. You couldn't come and go as you pleased; you had no mobility. An ordinary murder was out of the question. Of course, you could have disposed of Hill right in this room during a business conference by a shot. But Hill's death wasn't the primary objective. He had to die and leave you free to run the business.

"You had to be able to kill him in such a way that you wouldn't be even suspected.

"It occurred to you, as it's occurred to murderers before, that the most effective way of diverting suspicion from yourself was to create the illusion that you were equally in danger of losing your life, and from the same source. In other words, you had to create a fictitious outside threat directed not merely at Hill but at both of you.

"Your and Hill's connection with Charles Lyell Adam

twenty-five years ago provided a suitable, if daring and dangerous, means for creating such an illusion. If Adam were 'alive,' he could have a believable motive to seek the death of both of you. Adam's background could be traced by the authorities; the dramatic voyage of the *Beagle* was traceable to the point of its disappearance with all hands; the facts of your and Hill's existence and present situation in life, plus the hints you could let drop in 'Adam's' note, would lead any competent investigator to the conclusion you wanted him to reach.

"You were very clever, Priam. You avoided the psychological error of making things too obvious. You deliberately told not quite enough in 'Adam's' note. You repeatedly refused on demand to give any information that would help the police or make the investigation easier, although an examination of your 'refusals' show that you actually helped us considerably. But on the surface you made us work for what we got.

"You made us work hard, because you laid a fantastic trail for us to follow.

"But if your theory-of-evolution pattern was on the fancy side, your logic was made curiously more convincing because of it. To nurse a desire for revenge for almost a generation a man has to be a little cracked. Such a mind might easily run to the involved and the fanciful. At the same time, 'Adam' would naturally tend to think in terms of his own background and experience. Adam having been a naturalist, you created a trail such as an eccentric naturalist might leave—a trail you were sure we would sooner or later recognize and follow to its conclusion, which was that Naturalist Charles Adam was 'the enemy out of the past.'

"Your camouflage was brilliantly conceived and stroked on, Priam. You laid it so thickly on this case that, if you had not foolishly used that broken-*T* typewriter, we should probably have been satisfied to pin the crime on a man who's really been dead for a quarter of a century."

Priam's big head wavered a little, almost a nod. But it might have been a momentary trembling of the muscles of his neck. Otherwise, he gave no sign that he was even listening.

"In an odd sort of way, Priam, you were unlucky. You didn't realize quite how bad Hill's heart was, or you miscalculated the impact of your paper bullet. Because Hill died as a result of your very first warning. You had sent yourself a warning on the same morning,

190

intending to divide the other warnings between you and Hill, probably, alternating them. When Hill died so immediately, it was too late to pull yourself out. You were in the position of the general who has planned a complicated battle against the enemy, finds that his very first sortie has accomplished his entire objective, but is powerless to stop his orders and preparation for the succeeding attacks. Had you stopped after sending yourself only one warning the mere stoppage would have been suspect. The warnings to yourself had to continue in order that the illusion of Adam-frightening-Hill-to-death should be completely credible.

"You sent six warnings, including the masterly one of having your tuna salad poisoned so that you could eat some, fall sick, and so call attention to your 'fish' clue. After six warnings you undoubtedly felt you had thoroughly fooled us as to the real source of the crime. On the other hand, you recognized the danger of stopping even at six with yourself still alive. We might begin to wonder why—in your case—'Adam' had given up. Murderers have been caught on a great deal less.

"You saw that, for perfect safety, you had to give us a convincing end to the whole business.

"The ideal, of course, was for us to 'catch' 'Adam.'

"A lesser man, Priam, wouldn't have wasted ten seconds wrestling with the problem of producing a man dead twenty-five years and handing his living body over to the police. But you didn't abandon the problem merely because it seemed impossible to solve. There's a lot of Napoleon in you.

"And you solved it.

"Your solution was tied up with another unhappy necessity of the case. To carry out your elaborate plot against Hill and yourself, you needed help. You have the use of your brain unimpaired, and the use of your hands and eyes and ears in a limited area, but these weren't enough. Your plans demanded the use of legs, too, and yours are useless. You couldn't possibly, by yourself, procure a beagle, poison it, deliver it and the note to Hill's doorstep; get cardboard boxes and string from the dime store, a dead lamprey from God knows where, poison, frogs, and so on. It's true that the little silver box must have been left here, or dropped, by Laurel; that the arsenic undoubtedly came from the can of Deth-on-Ratz in your cellar; that the tree frogs were collected in these very foothills; that the green alligator wallet must have been suggested by your wife's possession of a handbag of the same material and from the same shop; that you found the worthless stock from Mrs. Priam's first husband's estate in some box or trunk stored in this house; that to leave the bird clue you chose a book from your own library. Whenever possible you procured what you needed from as close by as you could manage, probably because in this way you felt you could control them better. But even for the things in and from this house, you needed a substitute for your legs.

"Who found and used these things at your direction?

"Alfred Wallace could. Secretary, nurse, companion, orderly, handyman. . . with you all day, on call all night . . . you could hardly have used anyone else. If for no other reason than that Wallace couldn't possibly have been kept ignorant of what was going on. Using Wallace turned a liability into an asset.

"Whether Wallace was your accomplice willingly because you paid him well or under duress because you had something on him," said Ellery, looking down at the mound under the blanket, "is a question only you can answer now, Priam. I suppose it doesn't really matter any more. However you managed it, you persuaded Alfred to serve as your legs and as extensions of your eyes and hands. You gave Alfred his orders and he carried them out.

"Now you no longer needed Alfred. And perhaps—as other murderers have found out—tools like Alfred have a way of turning two-edged. Wallace was the only one who knew you were the god of the machine, Priam. No matter what you had on him—if anything—Wallace alive was a continuous danger to your safety and peace of mind.

"The more you mulled, the more feasible Wallace's elimination became. His death would remove the only outside knowledge of your guilt; as your wife's lover he ought to die to satisfy your peculiar psychological ambivalence; and, dead, he became a perfect Charles Adam. Wallace was within Adam's age range had Adam lived; Wallace's background was unknown because of his amnesic history; even his personality fitted with what we might have expected Adam to be.

"If you could make us flush Alfred Wallace from the mystery as Charles Adam, you'd be killing three birds with one stone.

"And so you arranged for Wallace's death."

ROGER PRIAM RAISED his head. Color had come back into his cheekbones, and his heavy voice was almost animated.

"I'll have to read some of your books," Priam said. "You sure make up a good story."

"As a reward for that compliment, Priam," said Ellery, smiling, "I'll tell you an even better one.

"A few months ago you ordered Alfred Wallace to go out and buy a gun. You gave Wallace the money for it, but you wanted the gun's ownership traceable to him.

"Tonight you buzzed Wallace on the intercom, directly to his bedroom, and you told Wallace you heard someone prowling around outside the house. You told him to take the gun, make sure it was loaded, and come down here to your room, quietly—"

"That's a lie," said Roger Priam.

"That's the truth," said Ellery.

Priam showed his teeth. "You're a bluffer after all. Even if it was true—which it ain't—how could you know it?"

"Because Wallace told me so."

The skin above Priam's beard changed color again.

"You see," said Ellery, "I took Wallace into my confidence when I saw the danger he was in. I told him just what to expect at your hands and I told him that if he wanted to save his skin he'd be wise to play ball with Lieutenant Keats and me.

"Wallace didn't need much convincing, Priam. I imagine you've found him the sort of fellow who can turn on a dime; or, to change the figure, the sort who always spots the butter side of the bread. He came over to me without a struggle. And he promised to keep me informed; and he promised, when the time came, to follow not your instructions, Priam, but mine.

"When you told him on the intercom tonight to sneak down here with the loaded revolver, Wallace immediately phoned me. I told him to hold up going downstairs for just long enough to allow the lieutenant and me to get here. It didn't take us long, Priam, did it? We'd been waiting nightly for Wallace's phone call for some time now.

"I'm pretty sure you expected someone to be outside on guard, Priam, although of course you didn't know it would be Keats and me in person on Wallace's notification. You've put up a good show about not wanting police guards, in line with your shrewd performance all along, but you've known from the start that we would

193

probably disregard your wishes in a crisis, and that was just what you wanted us to do.

"When Alfred stole into this room armed with a gun, you knew whoever was on guard—you hoped actually watching from the terrace—would fall for the illusion that Wallace was trying to kill you. If no one was watching, but a guard on the grounds heard the shot, within seconds he'd be in the room, and he'd find Wallace dead —in *your* room, with you obviously awakened from sleep, and only your story to listen to. With the previous build-up of someone threatening your life, he'd have no reason to doubt your version of what happened. If there were no guards at all, you would phone for help immediately, and between your version of the events and the fact that the gun was bought by Wallace you had every reason to believe the matter would end there. It was a bold, even a Bonapartist plan, Priam, and it almost worked."

Priam stirred, and with the stir a fluidity came over him, passing like a ripple. Then he said in a perfectly controlled voice, "Whatever Wallace told you was a damn lie. I didn't tell him to buy a gun. I didn't call him down here tonight. And you can't prove I did. You yourself saw him sneak in here a while back with a loaded gun, you saw me fight for my life, you saw him lose, and now he's *dead*." The bearded man put the lightest stress on the last word, as if to underscore Wallace's uselessness as a witness.

"I'm afraid you didn't listen very closely to what I said, Priam," said Ellery. "I said it *almost* worked. You don't think I'd allow Alfred to risk death or serious injury, do you? What he brought downstairs with him tonight, on my instructions, was a gun loaded with blanks. We've put on a show for you, Priam." And Ellery said, *"Get up, Wallace."*

Before Priam's bulging eyes the blanket on the floor rose like the magic carpet, and there, under it, stood Alfred Wallace, smiling.

Roger Priam screamed.

Sixteen

WHAT NO ONE foresaw—including Ellery—was how Roger Priam would react to his arrest, indictment, and trial. Yet from the moment he showed his hand it was impossible to conceive that he might have acted otherwise. Alfred Wallace was a probable sole exception, but Wallace was being understandably discreet.

Priam took the blame for everything. His contempt for Wallace's part in the proceedings touched magnificence. Wallace, Priam said, had been the merest tool, not understanding what he was being directed to do. One would have thought, to hear Priam, that Wallace was an idiot. And Wallace acted properly idiotic. No one was fooled, but the law operates under the rules of evidence, and since there were only two witnesses, the accused and his accomplice, each—for different motives—minimizing Wallace and maximizing Priam, Wallace went scot-free.

As Keats said, in a growl, "Priam's got to be boss, by God, even at his own murder trial."

It was reported that Priam's attorney, a prominent West Coast trial lawyer, went out on the night of the verdict and got himself thoroughly fried, missing the very best part of the show. Because that same night Roger Priam managed to kill himself by swallowing poison. The usual precautions against suicide had been taken, and those entrusted with the safety of the condemned man until his execution were chagrined and mystified. Roger Priam merely lay there with his bearded mouth open in a grin, looking as fiercely joyful as a pirate cut down on his own quarter-deck. No one could dictate to *him,* his grin seemed to say, not even the sovereign State of California. If he had to die, he was picking the method and the time.

He had to be dominant even over death.

TO EVERYONE'S SURPRISE, Alfred Wallace found a new employer immediately after the trial, an Eastern writer by the name of Queen. Wallace and his suitcase moved into the little cottage on the hill, and Mrs. Williams and her two uniforms moved out, the cause leading naturally to the effect.

Ellery could not say that it was a poor exchange, for Wallace turned out a far better cook than Mrs. Williams had ever been, an accomplishment in his new employe Ellery had not bargained for, since he had hired Wallace to be his secretary. The neglected novel was still the reason for his presence in Southern California, and now that the Hill-Priam case was closed Ellery returned to it in earnest.

Keats was flabbergasted. "Aren't you afraid he'll put arsenic in your soup?"

"Why should he?" Ellery asked reasonably. "I'm paying him to take dictation and type my manuscript. And talking about soup, Wallace makes a mean *sopa de almendras, à Mallorquiña*. From Valldemosa—perfectly delicious. How about sampling it tomorrow night?"

Keats said thanks a lot but he didn't go for that gourmet stuff himself, his speed was chicken noodle soup, besides his wife was having some friends for television, and he hung up hastily.

To the press Mr. Queen was lofty. He had never been one to hound a man for past errors. Wallace needed a job, and he needed a secretary, and that was that.

Wallace merely smiled.

DELIA PRIAM SOLD the hillside property and disappeared.

The usual guesses, substantiated by no more than "a friend of the family who asks that her name be withheld" or "Delia Priam is rumored," had her variously in Las Vegas at the dice tables with a notorious underworld character; in Taos, New Mexico, under an assumed name, where she was said to be writing her memoirs for newspaper and magazine syndication; flying to Rome heavily veiled; one report insisted on placing her on a remote shelf in India as the "guest" of some wild mountain rajah well-known for his peculiar tastes in Occidental women.

That none of these pleasantly exciting stories was true everyone took for granted, but authoritative information was lacking. Delia Priam's father was not available for comment; he had stuffed some things in a duffel bag and gone off to Canada to prospect, he said, for uranium ore. And her son simply refused to talk to reporters.

To Ellery, privately, Crowe Macgowan confided that

196

his mother had entered a retreat near Santa Maria; he spoke as if he never expected to see her again.

Young Macgowan was cleaning up his affairs preparatory to enlisting in the Army. "I've got ten days left," he told Ellery, "and a thousand things to do, one of which is to get married. I said it was a hell of a preliminary to a trip to Korea, but Laurel's stuck her chin out, so what can I do?"

Laurel looked as if she were recuperating from a serious illness. She was pale and thin but at peace. She held on to Macgowan's massive arm with authority. "I won't lose you, Mac."

"What are you afraid of, the Korean women?" jeered Crowe. "I'm told their favorite perfume is garlic."

"I'm joining the WACs," said Laurel, "if they'll ship me overseas. I suppose it's not very patriotic to put a condition to it, but if my husband is in Asia I want to be in the same part of the world."

"You'll probably wind up in West Germany," growled the large young man. "Why don't you just stay home and write me long and loving letters?"

Laurel patted his arm.

"Why don't *you* just stay home," Ellery asked Crowe, "and stick to your tree?"

"Oh, that." Crowe reddened. "My tree is sold."

"Find another."

"Listen, Queen," snarled Delia's son, "you tend to your crocheting and I'll tend to mine. I'm no hero, but there's a war on—beg pardon, a United Nations police action. Besides, they'll get me anyway."

"I understand that," said Ellery with gravity, "but your attitude seems so different these days, Mac. What's happened to the Atomic Age Tree Boy? Have you decided, now that you've found a mate, that you're not worth preserving for the Post-Atomic Era? That's hardly complimentary to Laurel."

Mac mumbled, "You let me alone . . . Laurel, no!"

"Laurel yes," said Laurel. "After all, Mac, you owe it to Ellery. Ellery, about that Tree Boy foolishness . . ."

"Yes," said Ellery hopefully. "I've been rather looking forward to a solution of that mystery."

"I finally worried it out of him," said Laurel. "Mac, you're fidgeting. Mac was trying to break into the movies. He'd heard that a certain producer was planning a series of Jungle Man pictures to compete with the Tarzan series, and he got the brilliant idea of becoming a jungle man

197

in real life, right here in Hollywood. The Atomic Age silliness was bait for the papers. It worked, too. He got so much publicity that the producer approached him, and he was actually negotiating a secret contract when Daddy Hill died and I began to yell murder. The murder talk, and the newspaper stories involving Mac's stepfather— which I suppose Roger planted himself, or had Alfred plant for him—scared the producer and he called off the negotiations. Crowe was awfully sore at me, weren't you, darling?"

"Not as sore as I am right now. For Pete's sake, Laur, do you have to expose my moral underwear to the whole world?"

"I'm only a very small part of it, Mac," grinned Ellery. "So that's why you tried to hire me to solve the case. You thought if I could clear it up pronto, you could still have the deal with the movie producer."

"I did, too," said young Macgowan forlornly. "He came back at me only last week, asking questions about my draft status. I offered him the services of my grandfather, who'd have loved to be a jungle man, but the ungrateful guy told me to go to hell. And here I am, en route. Confidentially, Queen, does Korea smell as bad as they say it does?"

Laurel and Crowe were married by a Superior Court judge in Santa Monica, with Ellery and Lieutenant Keats as witnesses, and the wedding supper was ingested and imbibed at a drive-in near Oxnard, the newlyweds thereafter scooting off in Laurel's Austin in the general direction of San Luis Obispo, Paso Robles, Santa Cruz, and San Francisco. Driving back south on the Coast Highway, Ellery and Keats speculated as to their destination.

"I'd say Monterey," said Keats emotionally. "That's where I spent my honeymoon."

"I'd say, knowing Mac," said Ellery, "San Juan Capistrano or La Jolla, seeing that they lie in the opposite direction."

They were both misty-eyed on the New York State champagne which Ellery had traitorously provided for the California nuptials, and they wound up on a deserted beach at Malibu with their arms around each other, harmonizing "Ten Little Fingers and Ten Little Toes" to the silver-teared Pacific.

AFTER DINNER ONE night in late September, just as Alfred Wallace was touching off the fire he had laid in the living room, Keats dropped in. He apologized for not having phoned before coming, saying that only five minutes before he had had no idea of visiting Ellery; he was passing by on his way home and he had stopped on impulse.

"For heaven's sake, don't apologize for an act of Christian mercy," exclaimed Ellery. "I haven't seen any face but Wallace's now for more than a week. The lieutenant takes water in his Scotch, Wallace."

"Go easy on it," Keats said to Wallace. "I mean the water. May I use your phone to call my wife?"

"Wonderful. You're going to stay." Ellery studied Keats. The detective looked harassed.

"Well, for a while." Keats went to the phone.

When he came back, a glass was waiting for him on the coffee table before the fire, and Ellery and Wallace were stretching their legs in two of the three armchairs around it. Keats dropped between them and took a long sip. Ellery offered him a cigaret and Wallace held a match to it, and for a few moments Keats frowned into the fire.

"Something wrong, Keats?" Ellery asked finally.

"I don't know." Keats picked up his glass. "I'm an old lady, I guess. I've wanted to chin with you for a long time now. I kept resisting the temptation, feeling stupid. Tonight . . ." He raised his glass and gulped.

"What's bothering you?"

"Well . . . the Priam case. Of course, it's all over—"

"What about the Priam case?"

Keats made a face. Then he set the glass down with a bang. "Queen, I've been over that spiel of yours—to me at the Hollywood Division, to Priam that night in his room—it must be a hundred times. I don't know, I can't explain it . . ."

"You mean my solution to the case?"

"It never seems to come out as pat when I go over it as it did when you . . ." Keats stopped and rather deliberately turned to look at Alfred Wallace. Wallace looked back politely.

"It's not necessary for Wallace to leave, Keats," said Ellery with a grin. "When I said that night at Priam's that I'd taken Wallace into my confidence, I meant just that. I took him into my confidence completely. He knows everything I know, including the answers to the questions that I take it have been giving you a bad time."

The detective shook his head and finished what was left

199

in his glass. When Wallace rose to refill it, Keats said, "No more now," and Wallace sat down again.

"It's not the kind of thing I can put my mitt on," said the detective uncomfortably. "No *mistakes*. I mean mistakes that you can . . ." He drew on his cigaret for support, started over. "For instance, Queen, a lot of the hoopla you attributed to Priam just doesn't *fit*."

"Doesn't fit what?" asked Ellery mildly.

"Doesn't fit Priam. I mean, what Priam was. Take that letter he typed on the broken machine and put in the collar of the dead beagle for delivery to Hill . . ."

"Something wrong with it?"

"Everything wrong with it! Priam was an uneducated man. If he ever used a fancy word, I wasn't around to hear it. His talk was crude. But when he wrote that letter . . . How could a man like Priam have made such a letter up? To avoid using the letter T, to invent roundabout ways of saying things—that takes . . . a *feel* for words, doesn't it? A certain amount of practice in—in composition? And punctuation—the note was dotted and dashed and commaed and everything perfectly."

"What's your conclusion?" asked Ellery.

Keats squirmed.

"Or haven't you arrived at one?"

"Well . . . I have."

"You don't believe Priam typed that note?"

"He typed it, all right. Nothing wrong with your reasoning on that . . . Look." Keats flipped his cigaret into the fire. "Call me a halfwit. But the more I think about it, the less I buy the payoff. Priam typed that letter, but somebody else dictated it. Word for word. Comma for comma." Keats jumped out of the chair as if he felt the need of being better prepared for the attack that was sure to come. But when Ellery said nothing, merely looked thoughtful and puffed on his pipe, Keats sat down again. "You're a kindhearted character. Now tell me what's wrong with *me*."

"No, you keep going, Keats. Is there anything else that's bothering you?"

"Lots more. You talked about Priam's shrewd tactics, his cleverness; you compared him to Napoleon. Shrewd? Clever? A tactician? Priam was about as shrewd as a bull steer in heat and as clever as a punch in the nose. He couldn't have planned a menu. The only weapon Priam knew was a club.

"He figured out a series of related clues, you said, that

200

added up—for our benefit—to a naturalist. Evolution. The steps in the ladder. Scientific stuff. How could a roughneck smallbrain like Priam have done that? A man who bragged he hadn't read a book since he was in knee pants! You'd have to have a certain amount of technical knowledge even to *think* of that evolutionary stuff as the basis of a red herring, let alone get all the stages correct and in the right order. Then picking a fancy-pants old Greek drama to tie in birds! No, sir, I don't purchase it. Not Priam.

"Oh, I don't question his guilt. He murdered his partner, all right. Hell, he confessed. But he wasn't the bird who figured out the method and thought up the details. That was the work of somebody with a lot better equipment than Roger Priam ever hoped to have."

"In other words, if I get your thought, Keats," murmured Ellery, "you believe Priam needed not only someone else's legs but someone else's gray matter, too."

"That's it," snapped the detective. "And I'll go whole hog. I say the same man who supplied the legs supplied the know-how!" He glared at Alfred Wallace, who was slumped in the chair, hands clasped loosely about the glass on his stomach, eyes gleaming Keats's way. "I mean you, Wallace! You got a lucky break, my friend, Priam sloughing you off as a moron who trotted around doing what you were told—"

"Lucky nothing," said Ellery. "That was in the cards, Keats. Priam *did* believe Wallace was a stupid tool and that the whole brilliant plot was the product of his own genius; being Priam, he couldn't believe anything else—as Wallace, who knew him intimately, accurately foresaw. Wallace made his suggestions so subtly, led Priam about by his large nose so tactfully, that Priam never once suspected that *he* was the tool, being used by a master craftsman."

Keats glanced again at Wallace. But the man lay there comfortably, even looking pleased.

Keats's head ached. "Then—you mean—"

Ellery nodded. "The real murderer in this case, Keats, was not Priam. It's Wallace. Always was."

WALLACE EXTENDED A lazy arm and snagged one of Ellery's cigarets. Ellery tossed him a packet of matches, and the man nodded his thanks. He lit up, tossed the packet back, and resumed his hammocky position.

The detective was confused. He glanced at Ellery, at

Wallace, at Ellery again. Ellery was puffing peacefully away at his pipe.

"You mean," said Keats in a high voice, "Hill wasn't murdered by Priam after all?"

"It's a matter of emphasis, Keats. Gangster A, a shot big enough to farm out his dirty work, employs Torpedo C to kill Gangster B. Torpedo C does so. Who's guilty of B's murder? A *and* C. The big shot and the little shot. Priam and Alfred were both guilty."

"Priam hired Wallace to do his killing for him," said Keats foolishly.

"No." Ellery picked up a pipe cleaner and inserted it in the stem of his pipe. "No, Keats, that would make Priam the big shot and Wallace the little. It was a whole lot subtler than that. Priam *thought* he was the big shot and that Wallace was a tool, but he was wrong; it was the other way around. Priam *thought* he was using Wallace to murder Hill, when all the time Wallace was using Priam to murder Hill. And when Priam planned the clean-up killing of Wallace—planned it on his own—Wallace turned Priam's plan right around against Priam and used it to make Priam kill himself."

"Take it easy, will you?" groaned Keats. "I've had a hard week. Let's go at this in words of one syllable, the only kind I can understand.

"According to you, this monkey sitting here, this man you call a murderer—who's taking your pay, drinking your liquor, and smoking your cigarets, all with your permission——this Wallace planned the murders first of Hill, then of Priam, using Priam without Priam's realizing that he was being used—in fact, in such a way that Priam thought *he* was the works. All my pea-brain wants to know is: *Why?* Why should *Wallace* want to kill Hill and Priam? What did *he* have against 'em?"

"You know the answer to that, Lieutenant."

"Me?"

"Who's wanted to murder Hill and Priam from the start?"

"Who?"

"Yes, who's had that double motive throughout the case?"

Keats sat up gripping the arms of his chair. He looked at Alfred Wallace in a sickly way. "You're kidding," he said feebly. "This whole thing is a rib."

"No rib, Keats," said Ellery. "The question answers itself. The only one who had motive to kill both Hill *and*

202

Priam was Charles Adam. Ditto Wallace? Then why look for two? Things equal to the same thing are equal to each other. Wallace is Adam. Refill now?"

Keats swallowed.

Wallace got up and amiably did the honors, Keats watching as if he half-expected to catch the tall man slipping a white powder into the glass. He drank, and afterward gazed glumly into the brown liquid.

"I'm not being specially obtuse," Keats said finally. "I'm just trying to wriggle out of this logic of yours. Let's forget logic. You say that proves this smoothie is Charles Adam. How about coincidence? Of all the millions of nose-wipers who *could* have been Priam's man Friday, it turns out to be the one man in the universe who wanted to kill him. Too neat, Queen, not to say gaudy."

"Why do you call it coincidence? There was nothing coincidental about Charles Adam's becoming Priam's wet nurse. *Adam planned it that way.*

"For twenty-five years he looked for Priam and Hill. One day he found them. Result: He became Priam's secretary-nurse-companion . . . not as Adam, of course, but as a specially created character whom he christened Alfred Wallace. My guess is that Adam had more than a little to do with the sudden resignations of several of his predecessors in the job, but it remains a guess—Wallace, quite reasonably, is close-mouthed on the subject. My guess is also that he's been around Los Angeles far longer than the amnesic trail to Las Vegas indicated. Maybe it's been years—eh, Wallace?"

Wallace raised his brows quizzically.

"In any event, he managed finally to land the job and to fool Roger Priam absolutely. Priam went to his death completely unaware that Wallace was *actually* Adam rather than the spurious substitute for Adam Priam thought he was palming off on the authorities. Priam never doubted for a moment that Adam's bones were still lying in the coral sand of that deserted West Indian island."

Ellery stared reflectively at Wallace, who was sipping his Scotch like a gentleman in his club. "I wonder what you really look like, Adam. The newspaper photos we dug up weren't much use . . . Of course, twenty-five years have made a big difference. But you wouldn't have trusted to that. Plastic work, almost certainly, and of the highest order; there isn't a sign of it. Maybe a little something to your vocal cords. And lots of practice with such

203

things as gait, tricks of speech, 'characteristic' gestures, and so on. It was probably all done years ago, so that you had plenty of time to obliterate all trace of—forgive me—of the old Adam. Priam never had a chance. Or Hill. And you had the virility Priam demanded in a secretary. You'd undoubtedly found out about that in your preliminary reconnaissance. A glimpse of Delia Priam, and you must have been absolutely delighted. Plum pudding to go with your roast beef."

Wallace smiled appreciatively.

"I don't know when—or how—Priam first let on that he wanted to be rid of Leander Hill. Maybe he never said so at all, in so many words. At least in the beginning. You were with him night and day, and you were studying him. You could hardly have remained blind to Priam's hatred. I think, Wallace," said Ellery, setting his feet on the coffee table, "yes, I think you got hold of Priam's proboscis very early with your magnetic grip, and steered it this way and that. It would be a technique that appealed to you, feeling your victim's desires and directing them, unsuspected, according to your own. Sensing that Priam wanted Hill dead, you led him around to becoming actively conscious of it. Then you let him chew on it. It took months, probably. But you had plenty of time, and you'd proved your patience.

"In the end, it became a passion with him.

"Of course, to do anything at all along that line he needed an accomplice. There couldn't be any question as to who the accomplice might be. It wouldn't surprise me if you dropped a few hints that you weren't altogether unfamiliar with violence . . . you had vague 'memories,' perhaps, that came and went conveniently through the curtain of your 'amnesia' . . . It was all very gradual, but one day you got there. It was out. And you were to do the 'legwork.' "

Wallace surveyed the flames dreamily. Keats, watching him, listening to Ellery, had the most childish sense that all this was happening elsewhere, to other people.

"Priam had plans of his own. They would be Priam-like plans, crude and explosive—a Molotov cocktail sort of thing. And you 'admired' them. But perhaps something a little less direct . . . ? In discussing the possibilities you may have suggested that there might be something in the common background of Priam and Hill that would give Priam—always Priam—a psychologically sound spring-board for a really clever plan. Eventually you got the story of Adam—of yourself—out of him. Because, of course, that's what you were after all along.

"After that, it was ridiculously easy. All you had to do was put ideas into Priam's head, so that they could come out of his mouth and, in doing so, convince him that they were original with him. In time you had the whole thing explicit. There was the plot that would give Priam the indestructible garment of innocence, Priam was convinced it was all his idea . . . and all the time it was the very plot you'd planned to use yourself. That must have been a great day, Wallace."

Ellery turned to Keats.

"From that point it was a mere matter of operations. He'd mastered the technique of cuckolding Priam, psychologically as well as maritally; at every stage he made Priam think Priam was directing events and that he, Wallace, was carrying them out; but at every stage it was Priam who was ordering exactly what Wallace wanted him to order.

"It was Wallace who dictated the note to Hill, with Priam doing the typing—just as you figured out, Keats. Wallace didn't call it dictation—he undoubtedly called it, humbly, 'suggestions.' And Priam typed away on a machine on which the *T* key was broken. Accident? There are no accidents where Wallace-Adam is concerned. He'd managed, somehow, and without Priam's knowledge, to break that key; and he managed to persuade Priam that there was no danger in using the typewriter that way, since a vital part of the plan was to see to it that Hill destroyed the note after he read it. Of course, what Wallace wanted was a record of that note *for us,* and if Hill hadn't secretly made a copy of it, you may be sure Wallace would have seen to it that a transcription was found—by me or by you or by someone like Laurel who would take it to us at once. In the end, the clue of the missing *T* would trap Priam through the new *T* on Priam's machine . . . just as Wallace planned."

The man beyond Keats permitted himself a slight smile. He was looking down at his glass, modestly.

"And when he realized what was at the back of Priam's mind," continued Ellery, "the plan to kill *him* . . . Wallace made use of that, too. He took advantage of events so that the biter would be bitten. When I told Wallace what I 'knew,' it coincided perfectly with his final move. The only trouble was—eh, Adam?—I knew a little too much."

Wallace raised his glass. Almost it was a salute. But

then he put it to his lips and it was hard to say if the gesture had meant anything at all.

KEATS STIRRED, shifting in the comfortable chair as if it were uncomfortable. There was a wagon track between his eyes, leaving his forehead full of ruts.

"I'm not going good tonight, Queen," he mumbled. "So far this all sounds to me like just theory. You say this man is Charles Adam. You put a lot of arguments together and it sounds great. Okay, so he's Charles Adam. But how could you have been sure? It's *possible* that he wasn't Charles Adam. That he was John Jones, or Stanley Brown, or Cyril St. Clair, or Patrick Silverstein. I say it's *possible*. Show me that it isn't."

Ellery laughed. "You're not getting me involved in a defense of what's been, not always admiringly, called the 'Queen method.' Fortunately, Keats, I *can* show you that it's *not* possible for this man to be anyone else *but* Charles Adam. Where did he tell us he got the name Alfred Wallace?"

"He said he picked it out of thin air when he got an amnesia attack and couldn't remember who he was." Keats glowered. "All of which was horse-radish."

"All of which was horse-radish," nodded Ellery, "except the fact that, whatever his name was, it certainly *wasn't* Alfred Wallace. He did pick that when he wanted an assumed name."

"So what? There's nothing unusual about the name Alfred Wallace."

"Wrong, Keats. There's something not only unusual and remarkable about the name Alfred Wallace, but unique.

"Alfred Wallace—Alfred Russel Wallace—was a contemporary of Charles Darwin's. Alfred Wallace was the naturalist who arrived at a formulation of the evolution theory almost simultaneously with Darwin, although independently. In fact, their respective announcements were first given to the world in the form of a joint essay read before the Linnaean Society in 1858, and published in the Society's *Journal* the same year. Darwin had drafted the outline of his 'Theory' in manuscript in 1842. Wallace, ill with fever in South America, came to the same conclusions and sent his findings to Darwin, which is how they came to be published simultaneously."

Ellery tapped his pipe against an ashtray. "And here we have a man up to his ears in the Hill-Priam case who carries the admittedly assumed name of Alfred Wallace. A case in which a naturalist named Charles Adam used the theory of evolution—fathered by Darwin and the nineteenth century Alfred Wallace—as the basis of a series of clues. Coincidence that the secretary of one of Adam's victims should select as his alias one of the two names associated with evolution? Out of the billions of possible name combinations? Just as Charles Adam founded his entire murder plan on his scientific knowledge, so he drew an alias out of his science's past. He would hardly have stooped to calling himself Darwin; the obviousness of that would have offended him. But the name Alfred Wallace is almost unknown to the general public. Perhaps the whole process was unconscious; it would be a delightful irony if this man, who prides himself on being the god of events, should be mortally tripped by his own unconscious mind."

KEATS GOT UP so suddenly that even Wallace was startled.

But the detective was paying no attention to Wallace. In the firelight his fair skin was a pebbled red as he scowled down at Ellery, who was regarding him inquiringly.

"So when you hired him as your secretary, Queen, you knew you were hiring Adam—a successful killer?"

"That's right, Keats."

"Why?"

Ellery waved his dead pipe. "Isn't it evident?"

"Not a bit. Why didn't you tell all this to me a long time ago?"

"You haven't thought it out, Lieutenant." Ellery stared into the fire, tapping his lips with the stem. "Not a word of this could have been brought out at the trial. Not a word of it constitutes legal evidence. None of it is proof as proof is construed in a court of law. Even if the story could have been spread before the court, on the record, in the absence of legal proof of any of its component parts it would certainly have resulted in a dismissal of a charge against Wallace, and it might even have so garbled things as to get Priam off too, or sentenced to a punishment that didn't fit his crime.

"I didn't want to chance Priam's squeezing out by reason of sheer complication and confusion, Keats. I preferred to let him get what was coming to him and try to deal with the gentleman in this chair later. And here he's been for a couple of months, Keats, under my eye and thumb, and I still haven't found the answer. Maybe you have a suggestion?"

"He's a damn murderer," grated Keats. "Granted he got a dirty deal twenty-five years ago . . . when he took the law into his own hands he became as bad as they were. And if that sounds like a Sunday school sermon, let it!"

"No, no, it's very true," said Ellery sadly. "There's no doubt about that at all, Lieutenant. He's a bad one. You know it, I know it, and he knows it. But he isn't talking, and what can you and I prove?"

"A rubber hose—"

"I don't believe would do it," said Ellery. "No, Keats, Wallace-Adam is a pretty special problem. Can we prove that he broke the T key on Priam's typewriter? Can we prove that he suggested the plan behind Priam's murder of Hill? Can we prove that he worked out the series of death threats against Priam . . . threats Priam boasted in court he'd sent to himself? Can we prove *anything* we know this fellow did or said or suggested or planned? A single thing, Keats?"

Wallace looked up at Lieutenant Keats of the Hollywood Division with respectful interest.

Keats glared back at him for fully three minutes.

Then the Hollywood detective reached for his hat, jammed it down over his ears, and stamped out.

The front door made a loud, derisive noise.

And Keats's car roared down the hill as if the devil were after it.

Ellery sighed. He began to refill his pipe.

"Damn you, Adam. What am I going to do with you?"

The man reached for another of Ellery's cigarets.

Smiling his calm, secretive, slightly annoying smile, he said, "You can call me Alfred."